SUNFLOWERS FOR SARITA

BOOK 4

CRYSTAL FALLS SERIES

DIANNE MILEY

This story is dedicated to mothers everywhere. You work tirelessly, willing to risk life and limb if need be, to protect, preserve, and provide for your children. The greatest, most important task anyone can do is to train up a child in the way he should go. May you always train your children in the ways of the Lord.

Thanks to God for my mother and my husband's mother who raised us both with Christian training. Their relentless dedication to our Lord Jesus Christ provided the example for my husband and me to raise our children in His ways with the help of God.

I pray that every reader seeks the Holy Spirit of God, not only for guidance in raising children, but for the comforts and peace of life-altering faith that enables us to be the very best that we can be - for our children, for ourselves, and for God's kingdom.

PRAISE FOR DIANNE MILEY

"*Sunflowers for Sarita* is a fast paced, high caliber romantic suspense. I couldn't stop reading!"
Mary Alice Monroe, NY Times bestselling author of Beach House Memories

"You have a real way with emotion and tension, and that kept me turning the pages."
Deidre Knight, The Knight Agency

"Your writing is fabulous and so much fun to read. You are a gifted storyteller."
Anne Seymour, Editor, The Wild Rose Press

FREE STORY when you SIGN UP for my newsletter at www.DianneMiley.com.

Sunflowers for Sarita
The Crystal Falls Series, Book 4

This is a work of fiction. Names, characters, places, and incidents are either the product of the author's imagination or are used fictitiously, and any resemblance to actual persons living or dead, is entirely coincidental.

COPYRIGHT 2013 by Dianne Miley
ISBN 9780990675334

Contact information: Dianne@diannemiley.com
Visit Author Dianne Miley at: www.diannemiley.com
Cover Design by Hannah Linder Designs
www.hannahlinderdesigns.com

Publishing History
Eden Press LLC First Edition, Electronic 2013, Print 2014
Second Edition 2023
Published in the United States of America

Dear Reader,

Thank you for reading Sarita's story. My goal as an author is to share a message that encourages you, the reader. I hope Sarita's experience resonates with life lessons of your own. Each one of us endures hardship and suffering in one form or another. Yet for those who trust in God, every trial brings us closer to Him resulting in greater understanding and stronger character. This brings peace and joy which nonbelievers cannot fathom.

Sarita leaves a lucrative but dishonorable profession to keep her baby and find a new career. She suffers financial difficulty, betrayal, and enormous loss. Meanwhile, Max Carter enjoys great financial wealth. Yet his money cannot repair his broken family or soothe the grief of losing a relationship with his son.

Only God can heal their brokenness. Through deep suffering and extreme trials, God draws them closer to Him. Once Sarita turns to God, she gains understanding and compassion that help her grow closer to God as well as Max. God brings peace, joy, and love.

As you face your personal trials, may you find comfort in our Lord Jesus Christ. My prayer is that every reader accepts Jesus as Savior and lives forever with Him in heaven.

If you have questions or would like to discuss salvation, please feel free to email me at dianne@diannemiley.com. I would be honored to guide you on this journey.

God Bless,
    Dianne Miley

"And we know that in all things God works for the good of those who love him, who have been called according to his purpose." Romans 8:28

BROKEN SUNFLOWERS

Hot August sunlight streamed through the display window of Willow Pond Interiors, but Sarita Santos stood frozen in the midday heat, chills running through her as the voice of the smalltown Ohio police chief reverberated from her cell phone.

"Ramone got parole. He was released this morning."

Icy fear prickled her scalp, surging through her with a sudden trickle of sweat down her back, all the way to the tips of her frigid toes.

"His attorney appealed to get him out early. I don't know how or why, but he won." Chief Hunter heaved a sigh. "We'll do all we can to protect you, Sarita. Stay away from Riverside and his old haunts."

Shivering, she dabbed perspiration from her brow. Her stomach pitched with the rush of heat and cold, nausea churning as if she'd just contracted the flu.

Ramone Valdez had murdered her best friend. When Sarita refused to abort his child, he tried to kill her too. Then she testified against him, and he swore revenge. After he went to prison, she'd moved to nearby Crystal Falls, cut all connections to her sordid past, and started a new life. But Riverside was only twenty-five miles away.

He'd track her down.

"Don't go near anyone connected to him," the chief warned.

Sarita sucked in a jagged breath. "What if he finds my mother? She watches Gracia." Scenes of horror flashed through her mind: Ramone busting through the door, yanking Gracia from her mother's arms, torturing her screaming child.

"Don't panic. Where does your mom live?"

"Here in Crystal Falls. In the apartment above the music shop." Her voice shook as bile burned her throat.

"Stay here in town. Your phone's unlisted, right? And your mother's?"

"Yes." Her voice cracked. "We only use cell phones."

"Good. Lie low for a while. Watch for anything suspicious and let us know. I'll ask the department in Riverside to keep an eye out for him. We'll do the same here."

"Thank you."

"I'll be checking in with you. Keep your daughter close and be safe."

Trembling, Sarita fumbled the phone into the pocket of her dress. Only then did she feel the bristles across the palm of her other hand. The woody stem of a sunflower crushed in her fist. Its fresh green scent filled her nostrils and oily sap covered her hand.

She dropped the broken flower as if it were razor wire.

Would Ramone hunt her down? Had prison deterred his promise of revenge, or hardened his heart even more?

She swallowed the acid taste and wiped her hand on a dust cloth. With a desperate prayer on her lips, she dialed her mother's number.

"Hello, mama?" she stammered.

"Sarita, what's wrong?"

"Mama, where's Gracia?"

"She's napping." An edge of irritation tainted her mother's voice as the opening music of her favorite soap opera played in the background.

"Will you check on her, please?"

"Why? What's wrong?"

"Quickly, Mama, please. Then lock all the windows and doors – especially the balcony over the back alley."

"But...?"

"Ramone's been released from prison."

"No - " Maria Santos gasped and the phone clamored as she dropped it. Rushed footsteps scuffled away and a door creaked shut. Muted sounds assured Sarita she was locking the windows. More rushed footsteps, the click of a deadbolt, and heavy breathing coursed through the phone line.

"She's safe." Her mother sounded more rattled than confident.

"Thank you, Mama. Please stay home and keep your eyes open. Don't let Gracia outside. The police will be watching the area."

"Okay." Maria heaved a breath. "Whew. It's hot in here already. Is it really necessary to lock the windows on the second floor?"

"I'm sorry, Mama. We can't take any chances. I wish you had air conditioning."

"Yeah. It's usually not this hot up here."

Northern Ohio summers rarely required more than an open window and a fan to circulate the breeze. A native Puerto Rican, her mother spent her youth in tropical heat without air conditioning. But she was older now, overweight, and acclimated to the cooler climate.

"We'll have to figure this out. Please just be careful, and I'll be there as soon as I can."

"Okay, honey. Try not to worry."

"I will. Thanks, Mama. Please pray."

Ramone would need more than a day to find her. After four years in the slammer, his first order of business would be booze and sex. He would likely return to Riverside and hole up with one of his drunken floosies.

While Sarita had worked her tail off to support them, he'd cheated plenty. Furious when she got pregnant, he could no longer rely on his star stripper to bring in the cash. He insisted on an abortion. When she refused, he orchestrated an 'accident' by cutting the brake lines on her car.

Injured and close to miscarriage, she got out of the hospital in time to testify against him. In prison by the time Gracia was born, he might not know that his child survived.

Sarita couldn't stop shaking. Even in smalltown Crystal Falls, her precious daughter could be in danger.

Her stomach roiled. She needed food but the last thing she wanted to do was eat. Sipping her chocolate espresso to settle her stomach, she resolved to keep busy. No customers wandered about for the moment.

As turmoil churned her mind, she struggled with an arrangement of sunflowers in the front window of the store. The warm sun, once welcome, now felt garish as she massaged her forehead to fend off a migraine. Taking deep breaths, she scanned the quaint main street of Willow Pond, checking pillared corners and brick alleys for any sign of Ramone.

A well-dressed man passed the window and caught her eye. After initial surprise, he grinned. Men often gawked at her looks without a care for the person inside. Much less what she was going through this minute.

As he opened the door, Sarita groaned inwardly. Drained and terrified, she just wanted to be left alone. She needed to focus on a way to hide from Ramone without leaving her job and everything she'd worked for.

The handsome man smiled as he approached her. "You look as sunny as those flowers."

"Thank you." She felt like a wreck after that phone call. She climbed from the display window, careful not to hike up her slim yellow dress. Ah - he must have meant her yellow dress and dark hair matched the sunflowers.

Wobbly on spiked heels, she righted herself on the slick tile floor.

He stuck out a hand and she braced herself for the onslaught of emotion his touch could bring. Handsome men still held power over her.

Like a gentleman, his firm handshake steadied her without letting on as she regained her balance. Too upset for his touch to cause the anticipated effect, she felt an odd comfort instead. She pulled back with cool grace and mentally shored up the talented interior designer she'd trained to be.

"Welcome to Willow Pond Interiors. I'm Sarita."

"Nice to meet you, Sarita. I'm Max Carter. I believe we've met before. I'm a friend of Chad and Vanessa James. Weren't you in their wedding?"

His sandy hair and trim frame looked familiar. She met his gaze. With a jolt of surprise, she remembered him. He'd caught her eye at the wedding two summers ago, and Vanessa hinted hard that he was interested. But after all Sarita had been through, she'd sworn off men.

She had her hands full raising a three-year-old and building a career. Now she had Ramone to worry about.

Besides, Max Carter, millionaire tycoon, lived a few notches above anyone who'd be interested in an ex-stripper with a toddler in tow.

"I'm surprised you remember." Her raw emotions precluded flattery.

"How could I forget?" Heat radiated from him in waves of spicy cologne and overheated male, threatening to melt her resolve like the chocolate stashed in her purse. *Lord, give me strength.*

"It was a beautiful wedding." She tried not to stammer,

determined to be professional and get to business. "It's nice to see you again. So how can I help you today?"

His expression registered disappointment, but he let the conversation shift.

"Vanessa recommended you to redecorate my great room. I have a large stone fireplace and cathedral ceilings. I'd like to make the big room feel more intimate." Seeming to regret his word choice, he cleared his throat and fortified his businesslike manner. "Cozy, that is." Avoiding eye contact, he glanced around the store.

"All right." She ignored the double meaning of his words. "We need to find your style. Let me show you around." Still shaken, she led him toward a grouping of sofas and chairs on teetering heels. She put on her professional face and fought an inclination to touch his arm for support. "Point out anything that strikes you, without concern whether it fits the room. I need to get a feel for your taste."

That was *all* she needed a feel for. His kindhearted gaze made her want to lean into him for a hug. How she needed one right now. But her weakness for affectionate comfort had betrayed her time and time again. Irresistible men had gotten her into this mess.

With this one, she'd have to be ultra careful to subdue her natural tendency toward physical contact. Any association with a client not only undermined professionalism, but it could also prove detrimental to her priority of protecting her daughter.

At least his presence distracted her from that looming threat. Pushing Ramone from her mind, she strived to focus.

They wandered through the store, perusing various styles and woods and colors. Max stopped to rest his hand on the back of a bold-shaped couch in a banana color much like her dress.

"I like this." He studied the sofa, and then looked toward a chair upholstered in a mango print. "That's interesting." He eyed bamboo tables and lamps. "I like the whole grouping."

"Do you like a tropical style?" Having grown up in Puerto Rico, Sarita gravitated toward Caribbean colors and forms.

"It reminds me of the beach, of carefree vacations." His smile reflected fond memories.

"What if we mix it up a bit?" She tossed lime and turquoise throw pillows onto the couch and chair. "Too much?"

Without batting an eye, his face broke into a childlike grin. "It's wild, but I like it." He scrubbed the sandy stubble on his chin. "I don't know how it'd go with my stone fireplace, though." He pulled snapshots from the pocket of his creamy linen shirt.

Excited to decorate in the style she adored, Sarita took the photos. Careful not to graze his fingers, she noted his tanned arms and lack of a wedding band. She glanced at the photos.

"How do you feel about plants?" she asked.

"Love them. Gardening is my hobby."

"Perfect!" She brightened. "Garden rooms and bringing the outdoors inside is my specialty. We could create a tropical oasis in your living room."

"Sounds great." With hesitant enthusiasm, he added, "But what about the rustic fireplace?"

"I'm sure we could make it work."

He smiled over a pause. "Yes, I'm sure we could." His alluring tone implied much more than decorating.

Barely able to breathe, she handed back the pictures with shaking hands. She needed air, needed space from this man and his tantalizing scent. She'd settle for a chair with a large table between them.

"Let's sit down and formulate a plan." The words came from some autopilot in her brain.

Max glanced at his watch. "Can we discuss it over lunch? There's a wonderful little bistro on Main Street and I'd be honored to buy you lunch."

If only she could lie and say she'd already eaten. Given the frightening call from Chief Hunter, she had no appetite whatsoever. As her mind darted for an excuse, the elderly store owner ambled to her rescue.

"Mrs. Kentosh," Sarita said gratefully. "This is Max Carter. He's redecorating his great room."

Reaching arthritic fingers toward Max, Mrs. Kentosh shook his hand with more gusto than a woman her age had a right to.

"Sarita, dear," she said. "Why don't you show Max our gallery." With a wink, she nodded toward the private conference room.

Relief swept over Sarita as she continued toward the room. Her elderly boss seemed to read her mind.

"Actually," Max addressed Mrs. Kentosh, "I wondered if I might take Ms. Santos to lunch while we discuss her ideas. I'd be happy to see the gallery later."

"How sweet of you!" the older woman gushed. "After that disturbing phone call, dear Sarita could certainly use a nice lunch out with a handsome young man."

How did she know about the phone call? Practically deaf, she had to be telepathic.

Sarita stared at Mrs. Kentosh. Read this: I don't want to go.

Mrs. Kentosh clasped Sarita's hand in hers. "Go have a nice lunch. And take your time, honey."

Max grinned from ear to ear.

She had no way out now.

SARITA TOTTERED down Main Street breathing in the spicy scent of the handsome millionaire at her side. She had too much at stake to get distracted by a man right now. Determined to insulate her heart and stick to business, she acted casual, like this hunk of a client didn't set her heart pounding at the thought of his touch and her life hadn't turned upside down with one phone call.

Jittery from too much caffeine, she dropped her purse as they walked toward the bistro door. Her stomach clenched. Wishing for a hole to crawl into, she bent to retrieve it from the brick sidewalk. To her horror, her spiked heel wedged in the mortar. Panicked, she yanked her foot free and careened toward the bricks face first.

She squeezed her eyes shut against the humiliation and braced for the fall.

Warm hands gripped her waist. Tingles raced through her, and her eyes popped open as Max righted her. She caught his shoulders. Unable to look him in the eye, she stared at his broad chest and balanced on one yellow stiletto and one bare foot. His firm touch shot delicious shivers clear to her toes. Her palms grew clammy, and her hands jerked away.

With a gasp, she met his eyes, deep and soulful.

"Let me get that for you." Steadying her with one warm hand planted on her waist, he bent to pull her shoe from the bricks and delicately slipped it on her foot.

She felt like Cinderella.

He looped his arm in hers, releasing butterflies in her belly, and walked her into the bistro as if it were the most natural thing in the world for a clumsy stripper to hang on the arm of a gorgeous millionaire stud.

Of course, he didn't know she'd been a stripper - unless Chad James had blabbed. Her stomach roiled again.

Once seated, Max set down the menu unopened. "The chicken salad sandwich is fantastic," he raved.

He placed his order promptly and she ordered the same. What did it matter? She couldn't eat anyway.

As soon as the waitress left their drinks, Sarita knocked over her water. As she babbled apologies, Max sopped it up with his napkin, dabbing the icy droplets on her hand. His eyes settled on hers with caring concern.

"Something certainly has you upset. You're a nervous wreck. I hope it's not me." He raised an enticing eyebrow.

"I had too much coffee." Her forced laugh sounded fake even to her own ears. "Mrs. Kentosh brought me a double chocolate espresso."

"No wonder. She's a sweet lady." He paused, as if unsure whether to broach his next sentence. "I thought maybe it was the disturbing phone call she mentioned."

"The call was a shock." Sarita wanted to strangle that woman. She needed to think this over, to figure out what to do, to pray. Instead, she stared at the table, listening to each mesmerizing breath of this tempting man who would never love her for more than her body.

Why had God brought him into her life - especially now?

"I'm a good listener if you need to talk." The gentle thoughtfulness in his voice sucked her in.

She did need to talk but had to remain professional.

A wistful sigh escaped her lips. Too bad a taste of her reality would thwart any notions he might have of getting involved.

APPREHENSION WASHED over Max as Sarita drew a ragged breath. When they'd met at the wedding, Chad warned him she had a lot of baggage. Vanessa encouraged Max at first, but later assured him Sarita wasn't interested in dating.

Now two years later, when Vanessa recommended her as a designer, tight-lipped Chad issued a warning glance but didn't elaborate. Everyone had baggage including Max. He longed to know Sarita, but the devastation in her eyes made him fear what he might learn.

"The police chief called." Her quivering voice caught his attention.

Whoa. Did he really want to know? His imagination ran amuck, but she plowed on.

"The man who murdered my best friend was released from prison." Barely audible, the words brought stark pain to her expression. "I testified against him."

Although highly inappropriate in a business setting, he yearned to reach out and touch her, to comfort and calm her. Besides, he'd hoped to get away from business when he invited her to lunch. He might need to rethink that.

"I'm sorry you lost your friend." Regret roughened his voice. "That must have been horrible for you."

She sniffed, blinking away tears. "That's all over now." She straightened and lifted her trembling chin.

Visibly shaken, she didn't seem convinced it was over. The threat of revenge weighed heavy in her every breath.

His muscles tensed and his protective instincts kicked into overdrive. How dare that creep frighten her this way.

"But that's not why we're here." She squared her shoulders and pulled out a notebook. "So, tell me how you use your great room."

Taken aback by the abrupt about face, he gulped down a protest.

Averting his eyes, she clasped a pen in her shaking hand. Worry lines creased her forehead.

Swallowing righteous anger, he answered decorating questions until the waitress brought their lunch. Sarita set her notes aside and surveyed the food before her.

The smell of fresh-baked bread stimulated his waning hunger.

"You've love it," he assured her.

She bent her head and stared at the food. Was she praying?

No doubt, she needed to dredge up her appetite. She picked up her fork and poked at a chunk of chicken.

He felt her pain in the distraught hesitation.

As much as he feared getting involved, every protective instinct in him wanted to comfort her, and spare her any more hurt. How would she protect herself if that lunatic came after her? Palpable fear emanated from her, as if she had no one to turn to and nowhere to go.

She may not be the Christian woman he'd been seeking, but weren't Christians supposed to help the lost and the suffering? He'd never met anyone who seemed as lost and suffering as Sarita Santos.

MONDAY MORNING SARITA LOADED FABRICS, paint, sketches, bamboo flooring samples, and other supplies into her small SUV. A far cry from her expensive red sports car, the used Ford Escape cost little, carried her supplies, and blasted through winter.

Since moving to Crystal Falls, she'd learned the town bore the brunt of lake effect snow. When Canadian winds sucked up the moisture of Lake Erie and dumped it in the form of snow on their idyllic town, the SUV proved invaluable on unplowed country roads. More importantly, Ramone would never expect the stripper with the red sports car to drive anything that resembled a minivan.

She hadn't seen that over-tanned hide nor one greasy hair of his. Still, going to Riverside made her skin crawl. The ritzy south hills suburbs weren't exactly Ramone's territory, yet one of these aristocrats could practically spit from his pillared balcony and hit the scum at the low end of town, if not for the tall, clipped hedges and high stone walls that separated them.

She slid a heavy iron curtain rod beside her seat.

Chief Hunter had located Ramone back in his old territory, bartending at some sleezy joint on the north side of town and renting the upstairs apartment. Thank goodness she'd convinced Mama to get out of the city.

She never imagined her mother caring for her child, but Mama had joined AA meetings and become a different person than the neglectful mother of Sarita's teenage years.

Sarita swore to protect her own daughter. Since learning of Ramone's release, she began looking for jobs out of state. Although she hadn't found anything yet, her stomach grew queasy at the thought of leaving Mrs. Kentosh. But one sign of Ramone and she was gone.

RED CADILLAC

Nearing Max's address, she pushed those thoughts from her mind. The impressive contemporary mansion didn't disappoint her, nor did the extensive landscaping. Max's passion for gardening showed. She breathed in the smell of fresh cut grass and fragrant roses blooming in the dog days of August as she carried supplies up the slate sidewalk.

Tall white snapdragons shone with fresh drops of water and drifts of black-eyed susans reminded her of the sunflower she'd crushed the day they met. In the shade of Japanese maples near the house, leafy hostas thrived with spikes of tiny flowers. Flanking the front entry, enormous urns spilled over with white impatiens and trailing green ivy.

Arms loaded with paraphernalia, Sarita rang the bell.

The leaded glass door opened immediately. Max's bright smile quickly turned to embarrassed surprise.

"Oh my." He took sketchbooks and reams of fabric from her arms and led her inside. His tanned biceps strained against the short sleeves of a pale yellow polo. "You shouldn't have carried all this yourself."

She found his protective chivalry adorable.

"Don't worry, there's more." She couldn't help giving him a teasing smile. She appraised the spacious architecture with pleased approval. Yet the modern style, leather sectional, and enormous TV screamed bachelor.

Max followed her back to the car and insisted on carrying the bulk of what remained.

Once they'd piled everything onto the living room carpet, he held up the iron curtain rod. "This doesn't look very tropical."

"That's not for here." Sarita snatched it with a nervous laugh. "It stays in my car."

A shock of sandy hair fell over his blue eyes as he gave her a quizzical look.

"In lieu of a baseball bat?" She raised her eyebrows, questioning his understanding. Sometimes she needed to take matters into her own hands. These days, she trusted iron. She patted the purse on her hip, feeling the shape of a small handgun inside.

"You should be safe here." His forehead creased with worry. "It's not a bad neighborhood."

"No, no." She laughed it off and laid the curtain rod near the door with her purse, making sure the secured zipper hid her gun. Pocketing her cell phone, she explained it away. "Sometimes I have to drive through bad areas. You never know these days."

Max furrowed his brow without another word. Grateful he didn't question her fears, she could get used to this guy. He knew when to talk and when to keep quiet.

Taking a deep breath, she tried to set her mind on the task. With trembling hands, she unrolled a yard of mango-colored fabric with a tropical leaf design and held it in front of the massive stone fireplace.

Max took one corner of the fabric and nodded his approval.

"Looks good." He gazed at her with an expression full of caring concern and a hint of alluring hope.

"Glad you like it. Me too." She carried the fabric to the sofa and draped it. Following her lead, Max held his corner and moved fluidly as if he'd worked with her for years. She'd never had a client so accommodating. Most expected royal treatment and never lifted a finger to help.

"The color really pops," he said. "But the walls look so drab."

"How does this strike you?" She picked up a paint chip called Banana Mania and held it against the taupe wall.

His face burst into that gorgeous childlike grin.

"When do we start painting?" he asked.

"We?" Her jaw dropped. Did he expect to help, at the rate he was paying?

"You don't think I'm going to let you do the work all by yourself, do you? What kind of gentleman would I be?"

"Well, I usually hire painters, but I'm sure we could cut the rate if you wanted to tackle the painting. I'd be happy to help you."

"Let's do it. I'd enjoy a chance to work side by side with you." His smile spoke volumes. Playful, yet not in a seductive, let-me-get-in-your-pants kind of way. This man seemed to honestly want to get to know her. And he was willing to work hard and get dirty to do it.

Was Max Carter the man for her?

Why did she have to meet him *now*?

AFTER TWO WEEKS of painting and decorating, Max was impressed that Sarita did everything herself but install the bamboo floors and plumb the fountain.

Pleasantly surprised that she was willing to work on Saturday, he sensed her rushing to finish his house.

He suspected her nerves had to do with the man who killed

her friend. The ever-present iron curtain rod beside her driver's seat made him wonder if the guy lived in Riverside. Sections of the city teemed with lowlifes like that.

Regardless, he'd had plenty of interior designers over the years and never had one completed a room in less than two weeks. The woman didn't flinch from hard work. He had gotten to know her all right. Intrigued, he perceived much more to Sarita Santos than met the eye.

He watched in awe as she tossed mango-colored pillows onto the bold curves of the sofa, bringing the room together with matching chairs and ottomans flanking the fireplace. Then she tucked pieces of lime green and peacock blue pottery around the room as accents and stacked a collection of tropical-themed books on the coffee table beside a blooming bromeliad.

"Whaddya think?" she asked with a frisky tilt of her head.

"I love it." He dipped his hand under a flowing water fountain adjoining the stone fireplace. "I can't believe how you transformed the fireplace. The stone really looks like part of a waterfall."

"And you can still burn a fire." Sarita pointed out logs behind an array of candles set on the summer hearth. "Just move the palms back a bit so they don't get singed."

"Those palms create the tropical look." Max checked the soil in one of three enormous plants that softened the massive stone wall. Two bordered the fireplace behind the mango chairs, and one blended seamlessly with the stone fountain in the adjacent corner. The gardener in him loved the outdoorsy effect. "You really pulled it off."

"Oh, ye of little faith." Sarita flipped her hair as if offended.

After working with her for weeks, he knew better. He'd learned more about her than he bargained for, and red flags waved insistently. Besides the madman who had killed her friend, she hinted at a troubled past, a family far beyond dysfunctional, and underlying distrust that he feared included God as well as men.

This single mother with the older, budget vehicle in his driveway posed doubts he couldn't ignore: the ever-present gold digger question. His ex-wife had carved out his heart like filet mignon and milked him for all he was worth. If he fell for Sarita, would she do the same?

He should cut and run, but she enticed him. He forced himself not to stare at her soulful dark eyes, shiny soft hair, and long languid curves that begged to be touched.

Behind the intrigue, she was sweet, honest, and unassuming. She showed no sign of interest beyond businesslike friendliness. With the job completed, he feared never seeing her again.

Unable to resist the challenge of a sexy but tormented vixen, words erupted from his mouth before he fully realized what he was doing.

"How about some dinner to celebrate my new great room?"

She hesitated a moment, searching his eyes. Before she opened her mouth, her smile said yes.

SARITA RIFLED THROUGH HER CLOSET. She hadn't been out with a man since that cheating car salesman nearly two years ago. What a mistake. Since then, she'd insulated herself from men, fighting the strong temptation of their affection as she dedicated herself to raising her daughter and dove headlong into her new career.

But this time, her career depended on it. She enjoyed spending time with Max and looked forward to a fun evening to relax and unwind. Yet prolonging Gracia's daycare grated on her conscience.

Sarita missed her daughter. As she dialed the phone, she

looked out the window to her mother's apartment above the music shop across the square.

"No problem," her mother answered the tenuous request. "You take care of your client. Gracia's happy watching her favorite movie."

Guilt stabbed Sarita, although she heard her daughter's excited laughter through the phone.

"The prince just fit the shoe on Cinderella," her mother reported with a laugh.

"Ah." As they said goodbyes, Sarita's mind wandered to her own shoe and the handsome prince who'd slipped it on her foot when she tripped on the brick sidewalk. Their first encounter made her feel cherished and precious, as if he were courting a treasured lady rather than hiring a decorator - or worse, chasing some floozy.

That moment changed everything. No matter how she tried, she could never see Max Carter as 'just a client.'

She walked to the bedroom and checked her reflection in the full-length mirror, hoping Max didn't get the wrong idea. Leading him on wouldn't be right, and she didn't want to hurt him. She wore white capris and a silky yellow blouse, opting for white wedge sandals rather than the yellow stilettos. Not too casual, not too sexy, she deemed it perfect for dinner with a client.

A door closed downstairs. She listened for the chimes of Frosty's Ice Cream Parlor below but heard footsteps on the creaking stairs instead.

With the knock on her door, she hurried to open it, dismayed by her eagerness to greet the illustrious Max Carter.

"Good evening," he said with a teasing, formal flair. He wore pressed khakis and a button-down shirt.

She couldn't resist a coy smile. "Would you like to come in, or shall we go?"

"I'd love to meet your daughter, if you don't mind."

"She's still with my mother." His interest bowled her over. No man, least of all Gracia's father, had ever taken an interest in her child. "I figured it would be easier for her to stay there until I got back."

"Oh, I see. For some reason, I expected them to be here. Maybe because I had a nanny." He winced as if regretting the admission.

"How nice for you." Sarita strived to keep the envy from her voice. "A nanny sounds wonderful."

He nodded, staring at the floor as he gripped the back of his neck. "We might as well go then." He took a perfunctory glance at her apartment.

Sarita stepped aside to give him a full view. "I told you I like the tropics."

His gaze roamed her tiny living room, taking in banana walls, mango and lime and peacock blue fabrics, the sisal rug, and potted palms, down to the tiny fountain on a bamboo end table.

"It's like a miniature version of my great room." Again, he cringed at his own insensitivity. "Sorry, I didn't mean that like it sounded."

"Don't be sorry," she said with a pinprick of hurt. "You're wealthy, and I'm not." She shrugged and grabbed her purse, catching a stunned look on his face. "I *loved* designing your room. I can't tell you how many times I've had to pretend to like some *hideous* decorating scheme. In the client's taste, of course."

Max laughed. "You are so unpretentious. That's what I love about you."

Seeing the playfulness in his expression, she didn't know what to think. She didn't need a relationship right now —especially not with a client. Yet this man was everything she wanted – and then some. If she didn't have Ramone hanging over her head, Max Carter would be under serious consideration.

On the way to Devon's Restaurant in his sleek white Porsche, Sarita grew warm with Max's closeness. She fidgeted and cracked her window open. Across the way, a field of sunflowers glowed in the bright August sun.

"Those flowers remind me of the day we met at the store."

Her gaze snapped to meet his.

"You wore yellow then too." His tentative smile tipped one corner of his sumptuous mouth.

"I can't believe you remember that."

"How could I forget?" One eyebrow rose in temptation. His eyes sparkled in the sunshine. "I never put a yellow spiked shoe on a foot before."

Heat crept through her. Confused by her reaction, she wondered if she felt bashful or an irrefutable chemistry.

Both, she feared. His sentimentality took her by surprise. Was it genuine or a ploy? She'd pegged Max as attracted to her looks, like too many men. Trying to ignore his tug on her heart, she sat up straighter, knees touching in an effort to remain professional.

In her last profession, men proclaimed her unforgettable. She needed to squelch this charisma of hers before it became her undoing.

At the restaurant, Max opened doors for her and pulled out her chair. Then this perfect gentleman surprised her by ordering the most expensive thing on the menu - lobster tail at market price with two ala carte sides. Was this some kind of test?

She refused to bite. She wanted the special - tilapia with mango salsa and wild rice. He raised an eyebrow when she placed her low-priced order. The waiter left and she took a sip of water.

"I love what you've done with my house, Sarita," Max said with all sincerity. "I'd like you to carry the look throughout the kitchen and dining room."

"We'd love to." Including the company in her reply made it feel less personal. "I'd recommend toning down the colors a bit for the kitchen though. You have a contemporary look with the granite and stainless. Bringing in the wall colors, some art, and a few accessories should do it. And plants, of course. Would you like to carry the bamboo floors throughout?"

"Yes, I would. How should we decorate the dining room?"

"Let's go crazy. Huge palms in the corners, bolder shades, new fabric on the chairs. A wazoo floral arrangement for your table." She spread her arms to demonstrate an enormous centerpiece.

Excited about another tropical project, Sarita struggled with mixed emotions. She hoped to stay long enough to finish the project. But while she adored working with Max, how long could she withstand his temptation? And how badly would he hurt her if she gave in?

Men like Max Carter didn't settle down with ex-strippers and their illegitimate kids. They might sow their wild oats with exotic Latin women, but they married respectable upper-class socialites who produced Harvard-bound blondes.

She didn't have a marshmallow's chance at a campfire. She would do best to stick to business and ignore any attraction to Max Carter. Otherwise, she was toast.

⁂

Sarita said goodnight to Max with a chaste handshake at the door to her building. She'd succeeded in keeping dinner professional, yet the look in his eyes hinted he had something else in mind. As he climbed into his car, she breathed in the spicy smell of him lingering on the air.

Fear seeped into her bones. She needed emotional support, and the comfort of a man's touch. Yet she needed independent strength, and the freedom to run if she had to.

Her mind swirled in confusion as she drove to the opposite end of the square to pick up Gracia.

Irritated to find another car parked beside her mother's

beat up Chevy, she double-parked behind it in the narrow alley. The old red Cadillac in her usual spot looked oddly familiar. Her stomach churned with apprehension. Perspiration beaded on her forehead as she ascended the sweltering stairwell.

With glassy eyes and a giddy smile, her mother opened the door. The reek of alcohol bombarded Sarita.

"Hey! Look who's here," Maria slurred. She flung the door to bounce off the wall and fell against the doorjamb. "It's a f...f... family reunion."

Sarita's stomach flip-flopped like a fish without water. Her brother Pedro sat at the table pouring a glass of rum. Skinny as a rail, he wore a silk shirt unbuttoned low to reveal his hairless chest. His slicked back hair and pencil thin mustache reminded her of his mentor - Ramone.

Frantic, she scanned the room for Gracia. Sarita sighed with relief to see her sleeping on the couch.

"Lookin' good, sis." Ogling her up and down, Pedro sashayed over and gave her a most un-brotherly hug.

She pulled away. Feeling dirty, she fought the urge to brush herself off.

"Have you seen Ramone?" she blurted.

"No!" he yelled. "I ain't seen him since he went to jail." The clipped words didn't ring true. "What kind of question is that for a brother you ain't seen in years?"

"Sorry." Angry he'd gotten her mother drunk, especially with Gracia there, she had trouble summoning brotherly love.

After months at AA, how could her mother let this happen? She'd finally gotten rid of that horrid husband who'd been her drinking buddy, and now she whooped it up with her prodigal son.

"Heard he was out of prison." Pedro kicked at a piece of lint on the carpet. His fidgeting made her suspicious.

"He swore revenge," Sarita said. "If you see him, don't tell him where I am. Please, Pedro. Don't tell him about Gracia or where Mama lives."

"Sheesh, calm down." Avoiding eye contact, he pitched his voice as if insulted. "I'm not gonna throw you to the sharks."

"Like when you introduced me to him?"

"Come on, sis." He looked at her then, challenge in his narrowed eyes. "You made a lot of money working for Ramone."

"Money's not the most important thing in life."

"Now, now." Maria stumbled to the table and sloshed rum into a glass. "Have a drink." She held out the glass to Sarita.

"No thanks, Mama." Disgust cut her to the core.

"Whatever." Pedro rolled his eyes. "You weren't complaining back then." He looked toward Gracia with an indifferent shrug. "But you got a kid now."

"That's right. And Ramone wanted her aborted. No one wants to watch a pregnant stripper. He killed Layla because she got pregnant, and he tried to kill me."

Maria slumped into a chair, drinking the rum she'd poured for Sarita.

Sarita wanted to rip the glass from Mama's hand, to slap some sense into her and slap Pedro across the face.

"Ramone is a murdering madman," she seethed. "Just remember that, *brother*. I don't want him to know Gracia exists. Comprende?"

"Si." He tossed the blasé word with a detached shake of his head.

Amazing how easily they lapsed into Spanish, even still.

"Bien, that's settled." Maria's dark eyes glazed over. Her chubby cheeks melded into the roll of fat that settled around her neck from her forty-pound weight gain since she quit drinking. She waved toward the mismatched chairs across the table. Flesh hanging from her arms swayed like wings. "Come on, have a drink."

Fury assaulted Sarita. She should have known better than to trust this woman with her daughter.

"I gotta get home." She draped Gracia over her shoulder. Her daughter barely stirred.

Sarita had such high hopes for her mother. They'd started a new relationship, and Gracia just lit up around her Abuela. If she weren't sound asleep, she'd be whining to stay. Thank goodness she'd slept through this debacle.

"How dare you bring Mama booze." She glowered at Pedro.

"She's a big girl. I didn't twist her arm." He capped the bottle and carried it by the neck.

Sarita never could trust him. He didn't keep his mouth shut about her whereabouts in high school, and she felt certain he wouldn't keep this big secret from his buddy Ramone.

"Sorry, Mama." Sarita kissed her mother's cheek, furious yet feeling like a deserter.

Maria's expression fell, a picture of sadness framed with salt and pepper curls. She turned to her son. "Pedro?"

"I gotta go too." He glared at his sister and slunk out on her heels.

Sarita wouldn't come back to this apartment. She'd see her mother elsewhere and try to get her back on the wagon. But somehow, she had to find another sitter before Monday.

Head pounding and arms shaking, she buckled Gracia into her car seat as Pedro climbed into his red Cadillac. Nausea rose in her throat as she drove the opposite direction of her apartment. Appalled that she couldn't trust her own brother, she didn't dare go home. The Caddy followed her out of town toward Springfield.

Miles dragged on with Pedro on her tail. What should she do? She could pull into Walmart, but what if he waited for her to leave? She'd never find him in the massive parking lot. She had to keep him in sight. He lived off this route, last she knew. Maybe he'd go home.

She passed his old street that skirted town, but he stayed behind her. The road veered toward Riverside, exactly where she wanted to avoid. She turned to check on Gracia. Her baby was fast asleep in her car seat.

Then the headlights behind her disappeared.

Her blood ran cold. Where was he?

FUNKY GLASSES & A PISTOL

F rantic, Sarita checked her car's side mirrors, and turned to look over her shoulder. A lighted sign advertised some seedy bar on the outskirts of Springfield.

She swerved into a side street and made a U-turn. Backtracking, she crawled past the bar. Headlights snapped off on an old red Cadillac and the dome light blinked on. Pedro stepped out of the light and into the dark parking lot. Sarita cruised by with her gaze glued to the rear view mirror the whole way home.

She shut off the engine and muttered a begrudging prayer before stepping from the car. God had delivered her - this time. But why had He allowed this situation in the first place?

Anger with God left a bitter taste in her mouth as she carried her child to bed. She tried to move beyond her treacherous past. Yet danger and wretchedness followed her.

SUNDAY AFTER CHURCH, Sarita stopped Chief Hunter on the sidewalk. Acting cheerful with Gracia at her side, she asked, "Have you seen Ramone around town?"

"No ma'am. I've been keeping an eye on the square and the alleys. My deputy drives through Willow Pond now and then during your working hours and I'm checking with my buddy in Riverside every chance I get."

"What's the word?" She casually swung Gracia's hand.

"Far as we can tell, Ramone's still bartending. Doesn't look like he has wheels yet. Walks down to the bar, up the street to the store. But there's an old Cadillac hanging around, giving him a ride now and then."

"Is it red?" Panic seeped into her voice. She knew Pedro was lying. Sarita tensed and Gracia tried to pull from her tightened grasp. She loosened her grip and softened her voice. "Sorry honey."

"Yeah, it's red." The chief scratched his head. "You know who it is?"

"My brother, Pedro." Sarita glanced down at Gracia, whose gaze followed a bug on the sidewalk. "They're friends."

"Oh." Hunter blinked.

"Pedro knows where my mom lives and who comes and goes." She directed her eyes at Gracia. Fighting to stay calm, Sarita whispered, "He was there last night."

The chief grasped her shoulder. "I'm sorry, Sarita. We had a call last night, south of town. A domestic, so I needed backup." Agitated, he adjusted his hat. "Turned out to be a waste of time."

South of town - the opposite direction from Pedro. A waste of time. She couldn't help but wonder if Ramone had set it up. Her frenzied mind ricocheted to various orchestrated scenarios.

Frowning, Hunter shook his head. "I'm sorry. There's just the two of us and we can't be everywhere."

"I understand." Yet people with friends in low places seemed to be everywhere all the time.

"Don't get paranoid, but I'd strongly recommend different arrangements." He shot a pointed look at Gracia.

"I'm already on it." She spotted her friend Vanessa walking out of church and smiled at her.

"We'll be on the lookout for that Caddy." Hunter hitched up his pants over a bulging gut. "Meanwhile, watch yourself honey." The concern in his eyes held fatherly affection.

She thanked him and scanned the dwindling crowd for Vanessa. Her friend was already climbing into her husband's massive truck. No matter, Sarita would call her after the James family enjoyed their Sunday dinner.

LATER THAT EVENING, Sarita knocked at the door of the colonial on Rose Hill Drive. The door burst open to Vanessa's smiling face. She bounded out with a huge hug for Sarita, and then whooshed Gracia up into her arms and tickled her belly.

"Nessa!" Gracia spouted between giggles.

From the great room, Chad waved an indifferent greeting.

"He's watching the race." Vanessa rolled her eyes. "Let's sit on the porch. It's so nice out."

They sat in rockers on the front porch while Gracia chased a butterfly into the yard.

"So, what's new, girlfriend?" Sarita asked. "How's married life treatin' ya?"

"It's wonderful! Sorry, Chad's not usually so rude."

"That's okay." Sarita shrugged. "He just doesn't like me."

"Of course, he likes you!"

Sarita raised an eyebrow.

"Okay, he's concerned about you and Max. Nothing personal."

"'Course not. But why would Chad care if I'm working with Max? Is he afraid I'll hussy up his house or something?"

"You're something else." Vanessa laughed, shaking her head. "In case you hadn't noticed, Max has the hots for you."

Sarita sighed. "I've been fighting off men since I was twelve, but all they care about is this." She motioned her hands down her body.

"It's more than that, Sarita." Vanessa searched her eyes. "He really cares about you. But Chad's afraid you'll think what you think and not take him seriously. He doesn't want to see his friend hurt again. That's all."

Again? Sarita sat back and let it sink in. "Max doesn't know what he's getting into. Have you heard Ramone's out of prison?"

"Oh, Sarita." Vanessa's porcelain skin grew even paler. Arms over her belly, she eyed Gracia. "What will you do?"

Sarita sighed. "I'm not sure. I left Riverside, abandoned my old friends and old life, did everything short of leaving the state and changing my name to disappear into the background. I bought an SUV for Pete's sake!" She twisted the silky dark hair draped over her shoulder. "I even considered cutting my hair."

"Don't do that!" Vanessa's eyes bulged as she touched her own platinum lengths. "Please don't cut your beautiful hair."

"I don't want to. It's the essence of who I am, and I've changed so much already."

"Good. Don't." Vanessa's certainty buoyed her.

"You don't think I'm too vain?"

"No." Vanessa shook her head. "I spent years uncomfortable with my looks, my life, everything about myself. If your hair makes you feel good about yourself, keep it. Don't let your self-esteem slip away."

"I almost did, after Gracia was born." Sarita frowned. "I had stretch marks, a paunch, and bags under my eyes. Even after losing the baby fat, my vanity needed some vestige of my past. Beneath the business clothes and baby blankets, the car seat and the SUV - my hair reminded me I was an attractive woman. I'll tell you - motherhood stripped all sexiness from my life."

Vanessa stilled. Her arms crossed over her belly. "Don't tell me that."

Sarita watched her friend. Her mouth curled up in a mischievous grin. "You have a secret you're bursting to tell?"

"No one knows yet," Vanessa whispered. "Just me and Chad."

Sarita embraced her friend. "Congratulations! I'm so happy for you."

"Yeah, Chad's over thirty and he's been anxious to start a family." Her face twisted. "Now what little sexiness I've finally found can be stripped from my life too."

"Oh no. You don't let that happen." Sarita motioned to the window. "That man in there, seduce him every chance you get. Take the baby next door to Abuela's if you have to. Keep your hair and take care of yourself and make time to feel sexy."

Vanessa looked at the floor, a deep blush rising to her hairline. Sarita couldn't help but smile.

"Your sister used to blush like that too."

"Layla? Nothing embarrassed her," Vanessa scoffed.

"Not once she came out of her shell." Sarita flipped a hand. "Of course, strippers come out a little too much," she added with a laugh. "But she was really bashful at first. It took a long time for her to feel comfortable in her skin."

"I never knew that."

"You two weren't as different as you think." Sadness washed over Sarita. "I miss her so much."

"Me too." Vanessa blinked away tears.

Loss and sadness hardened Sarita's resolve. She knew she should be trusting God to take care of her, but it didn't feel like He was doing anything. She needed to take matters into her own hands.

"Ramone's taken so much from me - my innocence, my

brothers, and my best friend. I won't let him take my daughter too."

"He won't risk going back to prison, will he?"

"I hope not. But just in case, I'm looking for jobs out of state. I hate leaving Crystal Falls, but I'll do what I have to. Including changing my name and cutting my hair."

"Pin it up and wear a wig."

Sarita twisted her hair into a bun and looked down her nose as if reading through bifocals.

"Excellent!"

"Good. But here's the urgent thing - I need a sitter for Gracia. Tomorrow."

"What happened to your mom?" Concern filled Vanessa's voice.

"Ramone might find her." Sarita wrung her hands, unable to admit Maria was drinking again. She hoped it was temporary. "It kills me to take Gracia from her, but I can't take any chances."

"I'm so sorry."

"Do you know anyone reliable?"

Vanessa brightened. "Julia!" Her hands flew up to either side of her face. "She retired from the tearoom, and she's been *begging* to babysit when we have kids. She never had children of her own. And she'd probably even come to your house." Vanessa scrunched her nose. "Her apartment has a lot of knick knacks and stuff."

"Do you think she can handle a three-year-old all day?"

"It's got to be easier than dealing with impatient customers, cranky old ladies, and that erratic tea kettle."

Sarita screwed up her face skeptically and searched her friend's eyes.

Vanessa's mouth dropped. "I don't have a clue what I'm in for, do I?"

Sarita shook her head. Her face widened with a grin. "No, ya don't. But you'll find out, just like the rest of us."

MAX SPOTTED Sarita's fuchsia blouse through the window of Willow Pond Interiors before he entered. Her black skirt covered too much of those gorgeous long legs, even as she leaned over to toss a purple pillow on a chair. The girl loved color.

He watched her a moment while she didn't know he was there. Even with her hair pinned up and some funky new glasses, she looked striking. Yet what drew him resonated much more than beauty. Something gentle, genuine, and vulnerable in her stirred him. He yearned to know her - to fill that empty longing in her eyes. He had a feeling she could fulfill his longings too - and be the soul mate of his heart.

Yet no one - least of all Sarita - would believe his motivation - not when she looked like *that*. He suspected she felt men were only interested in her body. Was that her reason for the librarian look?

Her distrust fueled his own doubts - would she love *him* for who he was - or for his bank account? He needed to know.

With apprehension, he strode through the door.

Sarita spotted him and whipped off the funky glasses, catching a tendril of hair and yanking it from her bun. She winced and thrust the glasses behind her back. "Hello Max."

"Hello." He couldn't help but smile. "That had to hurt."

She cocked her head. The loose hair draped seductively over her shoulder. "What had to hurt?"

"Catching your hair on those glasses you're trying to hide." He flashed an unstoppable grin. "Afraid I'll see your bookworm side?"

Her shoulders sagged. "Oh, forget it." She held up the multi-colored half-glasses for his inspection.

DIANNE MILEY

"Wow. Where's the gold chain around your neck? And aren't you a little young for reading glasses?"

"Yes, I am." She stood straighter. "I... I'm trying to look professional."

He didn't believe it for a minute. She was hiding from something, and he feared it had to do with that killer.

"Seems more incognito to me. So might I suggest less vibrant colors?" he teased.

She looked down at her fuchsia blouse and huffed a deflated breath. "I guess I'm not a neutral kind of gal."

"Nope, can't say there's anything 'neutral' about you." He meant it jokingly, but her eyes searched his with a penetrating look that moved his very soul.

She jerked her eyes away, breaking the trance.

"Are you ready to choose finishes for your kitchen and dining room?"

"Sure." He choked on the word and cleared his throat in an effort to ease the pinch around his heart. He couldn't let himself be suckered in by another pretty face. His ex-wife once had the same innocent-looking eyes. Dollar signs flashed behind them.

Sarita led him to a desk in the center of the store. Following, he noticed dark curls at the nape of her stately neck, squared shoulders held firm with impeccable posture, and a slim waist above shapely swaying hips.

He forced himself to look at his feet as they followed spiked black heels with a purposeful stride. Even there, her long legs tempted his eyes. He focused ahead on French doors to the conference room where she headed.

At the table, her long, slender fingers fanned a spray of paint chips. Manicured fuchsia nails picked out shades of mango and banana. He caught her eyes and electric magnetism charged between them. An inaudible gasp escaped her throat.

That gasp told him she felt it too. He was falling hard for

Sarita Santos. How could he learn her true character before it was too late?

Friday afternoon, Max admired Sarita supervising meticulous painters, burly flooring installers, and prissy upholsterers like a seasoned pro. To save time, they opted for professional painters this time. Max hated having his kitchen torn apart.

While the tradesmen worked, Sarita designed custom art for his dining room with pressed palm leaves framed in light bamboo with persimmon mats.

He didn't want the week to end, couldn't bear to face the weekend without her.

Near quitting time, he approached her. "Got a busy Labor Day weekend planned?"

"Not too bad." She brushed loose threads from a newly upholstered dining chair. "Vanessa and I are going to breakfast on Saturday, then shopping and errands. Sunday church and we're meeting my mom at the park on Labor Day. That's about it."

Max looped her arm and pulled her away from the fray of workers. "How about dinner tonight?"

She looked into his eyes. "I'm sorry, Max. I can't."

"Come on, you gotta eat." He nodded toward the scaffolding and paint cans in his kitchen. "I'm going out anyway." He wagged his eyebrows at her. "Didn't you have a good time last week?"

Her grin gave her away. "Yes, I did. I'd love to go, but I have a new sitter and I can't ask her to stay that late."

"A new sitter - how's that working out?"

"Wonderfully. Gracia is like the granddaughter Julia never

had. But she's an older woman and I don't think she can handle more than eight hours of chasing a three-year-old."

"Bring Gracia along! I love kids."

Clearly stunned, her eyes widened. "She isn't used to men."

His heart sang at her admission. He'd think this beautiful woman would have men hanging around non-stop.

"I'm not sure how she'll react," she balked.

"You need to find out sometime, don't you think?"

"Yeah, but with a client?" Her mouth dipped into a frown.

He understood professional ethics. From her point of view, he posed a risk to her job. Yet her classifying him that way stung more than he cared to acknowledge.

"I'd like you to consider me a friend."

She studied him as longing and caution conflicted in her expression. "Okay," she finally gave in. "But we'll have to go early. Gracia's ready for dinner when I pick her up, and she's in bed by eight-thirty."

"Okay." He remembered those precious first months with his son Luke - how his and his wife's schedules rotated around the baby. Then Deira up and left, stealing his child away, and demanding more money than he'd spent to support the three of them.

He'd battled for joint custody, but Deira insisted on dragging Luke into court. Max couldn't bear his young son's anguish. Better to settle for two weeks in the summer than force Luke to witness his mother's hostility. Maybe if she had her way, Deira would be less likely to turn his son against him.

"Someplace casual would be good." Sarita interrupted his thoughts. "I don't think they have booster seats at Devon's."

"Uh, probably not." He laughed, glad to clear his mind.

She glanced at the clock. "Oh my, it's going on five o'clock already? I gotta pick up Gracia and freshen up. Can you meet me at six?"

"I'll be at your door at six o'clock sharp." A bad feeling niggled at his brain. Was it fear she'd prove to be like Deira after all, or fear he'd lose his heart to her daughter before finding out?

AT TEN TO SIX, Max parked beside Sarita's SUV in the alley behind her apartment. The warm September sun glinted off the opening door of a black minivan parked deep in the alley. A blonde man getting out stopped awkwardly when Max approached the door to Sarita's stairway. He ducked into the back door of Frosty's Ice Cream Parlour directly below her apartment. The van door read 'Plumbers, Inc.' He was apparently as confused as uncreative.

Sarita answered the door wearing jeans and a white tank top. Her hair wrapped in a loose bun at the base of her neck.

"Will I blend in?"

"You look good in neutrals." He smiled with approval. "Honey, you look good in anything." He refused to tell her, but there was no hiding her gorgeous body in painted-on jeans and a tight tank top. She wouldn't 'blend in' even if she dressed like a bag lady.

"Thank you." She smiled uncertainly.

He'd let her unfounded worries run their course until she realized how paranoid she'd been.

"Gracia – are you ready?" she called.

"Yes, mama." A miniature version of Sarita appeared in the hallway. Beneath the dark curls, a red sundress fluttered when she walked. Her left shoe was untied, reminding of him of teaching Luke to tie his own shoes during those two weeks in June.

"Gracia, this is Mr. Carter." Sarita motioned to him. "Mr. Carter, my daughter Gracia."

"Hello, Gracia. I'm glad to meet you." He stuck out his hand to shake hers.

"Hi, Mr. Carter." Dipping her chin and batting her eyes, she shook his hand like a shy damsel in some historical drama.

"Are you hungry?" he asked as he bent to tie her shoe.

"Yes." She giggled with a bashful smile.

"Where would you like to eat?" On bended knee, Max remained her at her level.

Gracia looked to her mother as if for permission to speak.

"What's your favorite, Graz?" Sarita asked.

"The place with the smiley face cookies," she said.

"Cookies are always good." Max laughed. Little Gracia was her mother's daughter - gorgeous and charming. He'd never met a three-year-old with such an infectious personality. He adored her already.

As they descended the stairs, Sarita held her daughter's hand. In the parking lot, she said, "I'd better drive. Gracia still needs her car seat."

The chauvinist in him bristled at riding with his date. Besides, he loved driving the Porsche, and he didn't want to look emasculated in front of that weird plumber sitting in his van with a clipboard sprawled across the steering wheel.

"I don't mind driving." He wasn't sure how to insist without offending her. "It's no problem."

"I wanna ride in the white car!" Gracia beamed as she touched his fender with reverent fingertips.

"You sure you don't mind?" Sarita scrunched her face.

"Not at all," Max assured her. "Let's grab your stuff."

With Gracia buckled into the car seat, they settled in front. Sarita fished lip gloss from her purse and Max spotted a pistol tucked beside her silky makeup bag. The gun was small as a Derringer and just as deadly.

He'd laughed off the funky glasses and new hairstyle, but a gun?

SARITA JUGGLED the items in her purse to hide her tiny pistol, worried Max had seen it. She applied lip gloss and then quickly zipped her purse and tucked it between her feet, careful to keep it touching her and away from Gracia at all times.

"Smiley cookies, smiley cookies," Gracia chanted, swaying back and forth in her car seat. "Thank you, Max!"

"That's Mr. Carter!" Sarita said with a hint of agitation.

"But Mama, you call him Max."

So went the evening, with her mischievous little devil charming the Italian loafers off Max Carter.

After dinner, Max took them to the park on Crystal Falls square and gave Gracia unlimited quarters to buy food for the swans. Hugging her purse close to her body, Sarita kept her eyes peeled for anyone suspicious.

Once bored with the swans, Gracia ran around the park and over the stone footbridge until she'd worn herself out. Even Max looked a little frayed around the edges, despite his unstoppable grin. So tired she could barely stand, Gracia tumbled to the ground. Max scooped her up before she could cry.

"We'd better go before she gets cranky," Sarita warned.

"Mama knows best." Max winked and lifted Gracia onto his shoulders.

Sarita's heart fluttered at the fatherly way he treated her daughter. She'd never expected this natural tendency in a polished bachelor. How refreshing to meet a man who liked children.

As they approached the alley behind her apartment, Sarita spotted the black van that had parked beside Frosty's Ice Cream Parlour just after she got home from work.

A sense of unease crept through her.

"Frosty's must be having problems for the plumber to be here so late." Max shrugged it off and parked behind her SUV.

Angst prickled Sarita as goosebumps crawled up her arms. Disregarding her apprehension, she reminded herself how old the pipes were and how slowly her drains ran. She pulled out her keys, leaving her purse tucked safely on the floor as she removed Gracia from the car seat. She hugged her child protectively with a nervous eye on the ominous van as she unlocked her car.

Max fumbled to remove the car seat and reinstall it in her SUV as she offered instruction. Then he hit the remote lock button on his keys - a nice feature she no longer owned - and walked her upstairs and into her apartment.

"Read me a story." Gracia pulled Max to the bookshelf.

"Okay." Max winked at Sarita as he sat down.

"Sorry," Sarita mouthed, embarrassed at her daughter's presumption. "Bath first, Gracia." She looked to Max. "I'll read to her later if you'd rather get home."

Gracia let out a high-pitched whine.

"Get your bath like a good girl and then I'll read to you, Gracia." Max gave her a dramatic wink.

Placated, the child ran to the tub. After a bubble bath, two drawn-out stories, and a bear hug for Max, Gracia was finally tucked into bed.

"She was out before she hit the pillow." Sarita plopped down on the sofa beside Max.

"Typical woman. She runs 'til she drops." He smoothed a strand of hair from Sarita's face. "How do you do it?"

His touch, and the concern in his voice, stirred her emotions. She looked away with a shrug. "I do what I have to."

"A mother's work is never done, is it?" He glanced at the books scattered on the floor.

"No." She leaned toward the books.

Max caught her arm and pulled her back.

"Relax." He searched her face.

Mesmerized by the depth of compassion in his blue eyes, she sucked in a breath. Unable to withstand his scrutiny, she broke eye contact. Her focus dropped to his mouth.

His full lips twitched. His tongue slipped out to moisten them. She swallowed--hard--yet couldn't look away. He drew close and she leaned in.

Fingertips touched her cheek as his lips sizzled against hers. She nuzzled his hot mouth, drawn in by the passion that simmered between them since the day they'd met.

He curled a hand around her neck, pressing for more. She couldn't get enough of this gorgeous, delicious man.

But she couldn't have him.

With heart-wrenching determination, she broke the kiss.

She couldn't look him in the eye. She straightened her clothes, but he grasped her hand.

Her eyes shot up to lock with his.

"Is something wrong?" The desire heating his gaze cooled to a subtle burn.

She willed the yearning away, but it wouldn't go. She should turn her back and leave town, but she wouldn't forget him. Hopelessly lost in his gaze, she offered the best excuse she could think of in her vulnerable condition.

"You're a client."

A slow smile lit his face. "We can remedy that."

"No," she blurted.

"Then are you sure that's the problem?"

"No." Her voice came out a whisper.

"I'll wait until you're ready then." He stroked her hair and touched her heart.

When he stood to leave, a chill settled over her.

She couldn't tell him, but Max Carter was better off not getting involved with her. Once he realized her troubles, he'd be history. A man of his caliber wouldn't saddle himself with a woman who couldn't escape her turbulent past.

With a warm kiss on her cheek, he left.

She watched out the front window as his car backed out of the alley. Two tiny red taillights disappeared into the dark at the edge of town.

The lights and noise at Frosty's had gone out for the night. After nine, the town rolled up the sidewalks. Only the dim glow of streetlights lit Crystal Falls now - other than the oddly lit interior of Myrtle Winthrop's dress shop across the square.

Was Myrtle working late on a Friday night? Did the old gossip see Max here with her? If so, she'd undoubtedly spread hurtful rumors about them, as she was known to do.

Sarita could do nothing to muzzle that evil woman. She had to live her life. Let Myrtle Winthrop say what she would.

Forcing herself to put it out of her mind, she put Gracia's books on the shelf and grabbed her keys from the coffee table. She looked around for her purse and groaned.

She'd left it in Max's car.

How had she let herself get so distracted? She'd pulled out her keys to put Gracia's car seat in her SUV, and that plumber's van made her edgy. She should have remembered to grab her gun.

She couldn't even call Max. Her phone was in her purse.

A glance out the back window proved his white Porsche was gone. She'd seen his taillights, but somehow hoped they weren't his. Yet the black minivan remained. How odd. Surely, he should have packed up by now.

With a shiver, she locked the deadbolt. Tomorrow she'd borrow the neighbor's phone. She couldn't wake Gracia now. She threw on her pajamas and turned on Spanish television.

Comfy on the couch five minutes later, a knock on the door startled her. Max must have found her purse.

She unlocked the deadbolt and threw open the door.

Wearing sunglasses and a hat pulled low over his face, the plumber hid behind his clipboard.

Unexplainable fear niggled her. Chills ran up her spine. She couldn't see his face, only the edges of his blonde hair.

"They're having plumbing issues downstairs." His hoarse voice choked, "I need to check your pipes."

"Oh. But isn't Frosty's closed?" She blocked his entry and reached to close the door.

"Yeah, I'm on overtime," he choked out the words like a two-pack-a-day smoker. Somehow his voice rang phony.

"I see." The patch on his uniform shirt read 'Plumbers, Inc.' Yet everything about him creeped her out. Why was he wearing sunglasses at night? "I'd rather you came back in the morning."

Projecting his clipboard, he pressed forward. "It'll only take a minute."

She tried to stand her ground, but he plowed past her.

"You have to go." She pointed a shaky arm at the door. "Come back tomorrow." She grabbed his arm and pulled toward the door.

He yanked his arm free.

Panic slammed her. She crossed her arms in defiance, standing toe to toe with him as her knees quaked.

"Get out of my house." Her guttural command denied the terror consuming her.

"I don't think so." His cleared voice was oh-so-familiar. He closed the door and locked the deadbolt.

"NO." Sarita lunged toward him.

He lifted a hand to his face. She stopped dead when she spotted his gold bracelet.

He dragged his sunglasses down his nose.

His hard gaze shot to hers and Sarita gasped.

DUCT TAPE & HANDCUFFS

Every hair on her body stood on end as Sarita backed away. She didn't have her gun. She didn't have her phone.

Hugging herself, she stared at the stranger she once knew.

Prison hardened Ramone. His skin had turned leathery. His roguish brown eyes turned cold. His skin-and-bones frame appeared older than his thirty-five years.

"You sent me to that jail to rot," he seethed. "You won't get away with it, woman. You'll pay." He advanced on her.

Backing toward the hallway, she had to keep him away from Gracia.

Then it dawned on her - he'd seen Gracia getting in and out of the car. Did he recognize her as his daughter?

She froze in place as turmoil and fear boiled inside her.

His bleached mustache quivered as his lip curled. "You just got on with your life like I never existed." He shot an appraising look at her apartment. "Fancy digs. Even your friends got fancied up. Layla's snot-nosed little sister married into the James family," he snarled. "And her mother working at that prissy place!"

Sarita blinked. "You followed Vanessa and her mother?"

"If I hadn't followed her myself, I never would have believed it. Almost didn't recognize her coming out of the house all dolled up like that. Little Vanessa..." He whistled, lifting one bleached eyebrow. "She's done all right for herself. Marrying Chad James, running a business - who'd have thought? Layla must be rolling over in her grave."

"How dare you spy on her!"

"Well, it seems you left Riverside with no forwarding address - both you and your mother." He scowled. "Figured the Gallaghers were a long shot, but it didn't take nearly as long as I expected for you to show up with Layla's little sister."

"Stay away from Vanessa!" Protectiveness welled for her pregnant friend. Visions of Layla's mangled body, and the unborn child she'd lost in the car crash Ramone orchestrated had plagued Sarita for years.

"You don't tell *me* what to do." His scornful voice stirred her pain.

He'd tried to kill her too. Miraculously, she and Gracia survived. Sarita refused to give up on her struggling unborn baby to the detriment of her own health. And she'd do it again.

She'd die fighting to defend her daughter.

Squaring her shoulders, fists clenched at her sides, she leaned toward the menace.

"Get out!"

"Up for a fight, are you?" Feet planted, he raised a bleached eyebrow and smirked.

"You're not a fighter," She appraised him with disgust. You're a sleezeball." This creep would rape her before he'd beat her up.

"And you're any better?" His wicked laugh demeaned her.

"I don't torment the vulnerable." She raised her chin, knowing he'd hurt her by doing something evil to Gracia because she was small and defenseless. Once tired of his torturous revenge, he'd scheme some way to knock them off so he wouldn't get his hands dirty.

"Worried about your little girl?" he sneered.

Sarita charged toward him, ready to claw his eyes out. She summoned every survival instinct she'd learned as a stripper.

"Get out!" She got in his surprised face, close enough to smell the whiskey on his breath. "Get out of my house and don't ever show your face again."

He smiled wickedly.

Her rage reflected in his pupils.

"*My* money got you this place," he spat.

Her fist flew through the air.

It smacked his jaw with a thud.

He staggered.

She raised her other fist, but he grabbed her arms, twisting them in knots.

"You don't EVER hit me!" He cursed at her. His eyes flashed red as his breath burned hot across her face. Smoke and whiskey mingled in her nostrils.

He shoved her to the floor.

She scrambled to get up, but he pinned her.

"You remember your place, now?"

Nauseous terror assaulted her as he ground her face into the sisal rug.

"You're coming with me, you hear? We're going back to the strip club where you belong."

"No! Never!" Her words muffled against the rough flooring.

"Don't get no fool ideas." He twisted her hair in his fist. "I'm gettin' my life back. You're coming with me and putting that moneymaker back to work. Your mother can raise that kid."

"No!" Sarita's stomach clenched. Maria slipped and could be back to the bottle in no time. Her mother raising Gracia, going back to Ramone, stripping again - never!

They had to escape. She needed her gun, her phone - she needed Max. Her muscles tensed to make a run for it.

"Stay down!" Ramone's knees dug into her back, crushing her. He shoved her face to the floor and gripped her wrists. With the other hand, he pulled a roll of duct tape from his plumber's apron. Yanking a strip loose, he wrapped her wrists.

She squelched a scream for help. If Gracia awoke, she'd be thrust into this horror. Maybe he'd just leave her behind. He never wanted her anyway. Vanessa would find her in the morning when she showed up for breakfast. Gracia would be cared for and safe.

Would Gracia remember her mother if Ramone killed her? Would she be raised by her alcoholic grandmother and end up like Sarita had been before God turned her life around? Her gaze shifted to the hallway as a sob clogged her throat.

"I thought you had a miscarriage," Ramone thundered.

"I almost did, thanks to you." She glared at him.

"So, I have a kid." Hatred oozed from his words. "I told you to get that abortion."

"Gracia is *my* child. Not yours."

"Gracia. Nice name," he scoffed. "Just like your grandmother."

Horrified, Sarita shuddered. What other details did he recall? He knew her too well. She would never find safe refuge without changing her identity and gutting her life.

"Don't you dare hurt her," she seethed. She'd wait until he let down his guard and then make her move. This monster wasn't ruining her daughter's life.

"Shut up." Ramone tore another strip of duct tape and slapped it across her mouth.

Fine. He thought he had the upper hand. But God was on her side. Rallying bravery, she waited for her chance. And prayed.

Ramone grabbed her taped wrists and wrenched her to her feet. Pain seared through her back where his knees had dug. Her legs buckled.

"Get up!" Cursing, he jerked her upright.

She gasped, sucking in tape. Tasting plastic, her lips and tongue stuck in the glue.

A cry rang from Gracia's room. No!

Ramone twisted her arms behind her back and yanked her toward the hall.

"NO!" The bellow came from deep inside Sarita, barely muffled by the duct tape. She kicked and thrashed, fighting him to get free, anything to keep him away from her daughter.

He muscled her to the ground, pinning her.

Not this time. She threw back her head, butting him in the face. With the sound of crushing teeth, he growled in pain. Hot liquid drenched her hair. She smelled blood as he writhed on top of her.

With a jolt of adrenalin, she leapt from beneath him as a crash shook the building.

The door blew from its hinges. In an explosion of splintering wood, Max burst through. He aimed her pistol, looking for a target.

Gracia's screams pierced the night.

"Don't move." Gun trained on the trembling, bleeding Ramone, Max looked to her. His fierce anger melted to compassion.

Relief poured through her. She ran to him, burrowed into his side. One arm embraced her, pulled her into his warm safety. His other arm held the gun zeroed on her enemy.

"Ain't that sweet?" Ramone taunted.

Max scowled at him with contempt. He reached for the duct tape across Sarita's mouth and ripped it free.

With the stinging release, she wheezed, panting for breath.

"What did he do to you? Are you alright?" Max touched the blood in her hair.

"That's his blood," she said. "I'm all right. Thank God you're here."

"There's a price for my blood," Ramone warned.

Wailing echoed from the hall.

"Your daughter - " Max's face paled.

"He never touched her." Sarita turned to show him her taped hands. "Hurry. Let me get her."

Max pulled a pen knife from his pocket and carefully sliced the tape with one hand while aiming the gun at Ramone.

"You'll pay for this," Ramone retaliated. "You'll both pay." His hardened eyes narrowed. The raspy words came from some wicked source within him.

"You're going back to jail," Max seethed, a nerve jumping in his jaw. "The cops are on their way." Then he peeled the cut tape from her throbbing wrists with gentle care.

The depth of Max's sensitivity and concern surprised her. He risked his life for her. Yet he remained calm and cool despite Ramone's muttering threats.

The stark difference in these men sent shockwaves through her emotions.

Ramone shot a knowing look at Sarita as she ran for the hall. Somehow, he would use Max against her. She recognized the evil plotting in his eyes.

❋

SARITA ROCKED HER PRECIOUS BABY, hidden away in the bedroom when Chief Hunter arrived. Bad enough Gracia heard the violent invasion of her home, the sobbing child didn't need to see her criminal father. Sarita shivered. She dared not give him a close-up view of his daughter.

Gracia frantically sucked her thumb. Sarita cupped one hand over her child's tiny ear and pressed the other over her pounding heart. Her breaking voice sang lullabies to muffle the altercation in the other room.

Yet she heard Ramone's grunt with the click of handcuffs.

"You'll be sorry you ever crossed me, Sarita," he bellowed.

"You're going back where you belong. I'll get rid of that screaming kid."

"Shut up, Valdez," Chief Hunter ordered.

Sarita sucked in a breath and pressed tight over Gracia's ears. Her bulging eyes searched her mother's face and her thumb sat idle in her trembling mouth.

Hatred surged through Sarita. All he'd done - murdering her best friend, causing her brother's death, demanding she get an abortion and trying to kill her when she refused - none of it infuriated her more than seeing sheer terror on her child's face.

"I'll file a restraining order," the chief promised. With scuffling and shouts, they banged out the splintered doorway.

Swallowing hard, Sarita put on a happy face for her child. She cradled Gracia's head to her chest, swaying and soothing her. "The police took the bad man away, honey. He won't hurt you."

Max appeared in the doorway. His solemn expression twisted with the realization Gracia had heard the threat. He hurried to the rocker. Bending, he wrapped his arms around them both and held them in his protection for a long time.

Eventually calmed, Gracia began to squirm. She looked into her mother's face and touched the nasty rug burn on her cheek.

Sarita flinched. "Mommy has a boo-boo."

Gracia gently kissed it.

"Do you have some ointment?" Max asked.

Sarita nodded toward the hall. "In the bathroom cabinet."

Max hurried off. He returned with ointment and gingerly dabbed the sore spot.

"All better!" Gracia stuck her thumb back in her mouth and cuddled on her mama's lap.

Breathing a sigh of relief, Sarita looked into Max's face. His caring gaze comforted her, yet they shared a look knowing the situation was far from 'all better'.

STANDING GUARD IN THE DOORWAY, Max watched in awe as Sarita rocked her child back to sleep. The care of a loving mother always touched his soul. He'd lost both his parents at such a tender age, but Aunt Ruby bridged the grief to fill that gaping hole in his heart. Uncle Harley treated him as his own son. Max remembered with profound gratitude the love and sacrifice of his aunt and uncle who became his parents. Yet he blocked specific memories of those horrible early days.

He couldn't bear to see another child suffer like he had. He'd never forget the sheer terror on Aunt Ruby's face when she told him his parents died. The hollow emptiness he'd felt during childhood went back to that day. Other kids had mommies and daddies. Max had an aunt and uncle. He'd grown up with as much love as any, if not more. Yet even now he yearned for his parents, wondering how they might have influenced his life.

Sarita carried her precious child to bed, and Max vowed to protect them both, no matter the cost.

Clearly traumatized, she stood hesitantly over the bed. Max held her hand as they left the room, stopping dead when they entered the living room. Splintered wood covered the sisal rug and a shattered, gaping hole led to the hall.

"I need to fix that." Before she could argue, he removed the door pins and took down the remains of busted wood which he deposited in the hall. "Do you have a tape measure?"

"Of course." Sarita pulled a small toolbox from the coat closet. Max found a tape measure and screwdriver, along with a cordless drill and all manner of tools an interior designer would need.

On a hunch, he measured her bedroom door. Fortunately, it was the same size as the broken one. While Sarita vacuumed, he replaced the apartment door in quick order and even screwed on the deadbolt.

"Thank you." She hugged him with trembling arms as if she were clinging to a life preserver.

He stroked her hair. Exhausted, he led her to the sofa and cradled her across his lap.

"Why did you come back?" she asked.

"You left your purse in my car." He marveled at God's timing. What would have happened if he hadn't come back?

"Oh, that's right!" She lifted her face to his with gratitude. "Divine intervention?"

"Yeah, I think so."

Her gaze bore into his. He sensed her mind pondering the same questions as his. What did it all mean? Was there some unforeseen future for them?

"You don't want to get involved in this." She shook her head sadly. "I can't let you risk your life on my account."

"Listen, I'm glad I was here." He cupped her chin and held her gaze. "God knows what He's doing."

"But you don't understand." She stared at her fidgeting hands. "You don't know Ramone like I do."

After a pause, he asked, "Do you want to tell me about it?"

"It's a long story." Her voice quavered.

"I've got all night," he prompted.

"Yeah, me too. And it's bound to be a sleepless one." She looked him in the eye. "I don't talk about it much. Do you really want to hear it?"

"Sometimes it's good to get it all out. And it would help me understand." He gave her arm a reassuring squeeze.

She looked at him as if he were crazy to care. Yet something in her eyes begged someone to care, someone to love her, someone to protect and cherish her.

"I was only thirteen when we came to America," she began. "I grew up in Puerto Rico. My parents wanted a better life for us, but it didn't turn out that way. My older brothers got into trouble and my father drank himself to death."

He held her hand, imagining how painful her homelife must have been. How difficult to move to a foreign country at that turbulent age, and then watch your family fall apart.

"After Papa died, Mama started drinking. Then I had to support myself. My brother Pedro worked with Ramone, recruiting young girls as strippers. He recruited me."

Max winced.

She drew a heavy breath and watched his reaction.

"Chad mentioned that." He held her vulnerable gaze, squeezed her fingers as a show of understanding. "I'm sorry you had to resort to that. It must have been traumatic."

She shrugged with a frown, looking away. "I was scared, but at the beginning Ramone treated me like a princess. He sucks you in, gets you addicted to the money and the power over men, and then he takes it all away."

"What do you mean? He stops paying you?"

"Little by little. He starts giving you presents instead of cash. Stolen jewelry and furs, stuff like that. Says you don't need the money because he provides food and shelter. And clothing, what little we wore."

"So, you're trapped." Anger coursed through him at the abuse she'd endured.

"Exactly. My friend Layla couldn't take it. She'd fallen in love with my brother Jake; he bartended there. Desperate for him to leave his wife, and knowing Ramone wouldn't want a pregnant stripper, she stopped taking the pill. She got pregnant, but it backfired. Jake refused to leave his wife."

She paused, wringing her hands. Max held them still, willing her to continue. He knew this tragic story. Word got around in small towns. But he yearned to hear her side.

"Ramone heard them fighting and found out she was pregnant. Livid with both of them, he cut the brake lines on

Layla's car and tried to frame Jake for her death." She wiped a tear with trembling fingers. "Layla was my best friend. Jake was my brother. I lost them both."

"I'm so sorry." Max hated to see her cry. He wrapped her in his arms, stroking her silky hair. "I knew Layla was Vanessa's sister, but I had no idea she was your friend. And I didn't realize Jake was your brother. I'm so sorry."

"Thank you." Sarita squeezed her eyes shut against the grief. "We were so stupid," she said with regret. "Layla and I had no idea what Ramone was capable of. We both saw pregnancy as the only way out. By the time he killed Layla, I was already pregnant too. What was I thinking? Ramone would turn sentimental and become some family man?"

Feeling her hurt, Max didn't dare answer.

"He prized the money I brought in more than he cared about me - or his child. After Layla and Jake, he'd lost a star stripper and his best bartender. My pregnancy only intensified his crazed rage."

She leaned into the corner of the sofa and wrapped a protective arm over her belly. Anguish filled her face, as if Ramone stood there threatening her even now.

"He demanded I get an abortion, but I couldn't do that. He went ballistic. With no regard for the threat of prison, no respect whatsoever for my life or the baby, he staged another 'accident' to get rid of us."

Max's blood boiled at the audacity of Ramone Valdez. Pure selfish evil, the demon tried to murder his own child.

"That time he got caught. When I testified against him, he swore revenge. Now he's determined to get it." She clenched her teeth. Short bursts of breath flared her nostrils as tears pooled in her eyes.

Max gently guided her head to rest on his shoulder. Her tears soaked his shirt as he held her. He recognized that pain, that need to protect your child and the helpless frustration with circumstances beyond your control.

Now he understood her need for a pistol. Thank God she'd had the foresight to carry it, but it wasn't enough to protect her. Ramone was locked up for now, but Chief Hunter couldn't hold him long.

"You shouldn't get involved in this mess." She sniffled. "You have a good life. Don't ruin it by wasting your time on me."

"You are not a waste of time." His heartfelt words surprised them both. She stared up at him for an awkward moment. Then he touched her face. "I care about you, Sarita. That fool never deserved you. Or Gracia. And I won't stand by and let him terrorize you."

Her head jerked back a bit and she blinked, speechless. Seeming to gather her wits, she got up and walked to the kitchen. She looked out the window into the dark alley below.

"I appreciate that, but there's nothing you can do." Her tone implied she didn't believe his sincerity.

"Don't be so sure about that." He'd meant every word, and he would prove it.

"Thanks." She turned to him. "For everything. Thank you for a nice dinner and for spending time with Gracia. Most of all, thank you for risking your neck to rescue me."

The words resonated with her need to end the discussion and get some sleep. She looked dead on her feet.

He hated to leave her unprotected, but at this stage of their relationship, he'd spook her by offering to spend the night.

Anxious to see her as soon as possible, to ensure her safety, he stood and asked, "Can I take the two of you to breakfast in the morning?"

"I'd love to, but I have plans with Vanessa tomorrow." With a frown, she lifted a shaking hand to tuck her hair behind one ear.

"Sunday then?" He stepped toward her.

"You don't give up, do you?" She smiled.

"Not when it counts." He took her hand. "I want to see you again. I need to make sure you're all right." His heart melted at the sorrow and horror he saw in her eyes.

"I need to worship Sunday morning."

Overwhelmed with caring respect for her, he couldn't argue with the reverence in her voice.

"I need to thank God for protecting us - and bringing you."

Hope kindled that he'd found more than he expected in this special lady.

"May I escort you?" He prayed he wasn't pushing too hard.

A beaming smile lit her face, almost erasing the terror.

SUNDAY MORNING, bright September sunlight assailed Max after two sleepless nights. He dragged himself from bed, dressed in a shirt and tie, and drove to Sarita's.

Saturday night he'd driven by her house at midnight, unable to go to bed until he saw her car parked there. Tempted to make sure her door was locked, he knew Sarita would never trust him if she'd caught him sneaking around like some lunatic stalker. He hoped Myrtle Winthrop hadn't seen him driving by.

Sarita needed help and protection. The police could only do so much. He grimaced at the memory of her beautiful face contorted with horror as she'd cowered with her quaking child.

Unable to deny his growing feelings for her, Max couldn't stand by and see this precious woman and child harmed by that sadistic killer. Hope stirred at her insistence on worshipping this morning. Could she be the soulmate he'd been seeking?

LETTER TO VEGAS

He parked beside her SUV and bounded up the steps to her apartment. He knocked on the makeshift door right on time.

Sarita appeared in a sleeveless purple dress that clung in all the right places. Yet nothing was right about the haunted fear in her eyes. Their dark circles proved she hadn't slept in two nights either.

"Mornin' handsome." Too kind, her words soothed his weary heart.

"Mornin' gorgeous." He shot her a flirty grin, and then stifled a yawn.

It was contagious.

She blinked hard, eyes watering, and gave in to a huge yawn. They both burst out laughing.

"Better to laugh than cry." She kissed him on the cheek. "I was up half the night worrying how to protect my daughter from that monster," she admitted. "Looks like you were too." She touched his shadowed face. "Thank you again, for coming to my rescue."

"My pleasure." He covered her hand with his.

"God will get us through this," she said with surprising

confidence. Her eyes searched his, making him wonder if he was included in 'us.' He had the feeling she wondered the same thing.

THE WORSHIP SERVICE was the first Max had attended since his son's baptism over four years ago. The sermon stirred him, yet guilt stabbed his soul. He'd broken every promise to bring up his son in the Lord's instruction. Rather than standing as the manly leader of his family, he'd given in to his ex-wife's lack of cooperation. Now too late, Luke was unavailable to him.

He pushed it from his mind as he led Sarita to shake the pastor's hand on their way out. They shuffled through a throng of worshippers toward the door.

As soon as they stepped into the bright sunshine, Sarita scooped up Gracia like a lioness shielding her cub in an open field. Her eyes searched the landscape as if hungry hyenas could pop out of nowhere.

Max wrapped a protective arm around her and led them to the car. Sorrow filled his heart. He couldn't bear to see her endure the pain he had. Losing her child would break her. She'd been through too much already.

After a cautious, yet delicious lunch at the Parkside Café, they returned to the apartment for Gracia's afternoon nap.

"Would you like to sit on the balcony?" Sarita handed Max a glass of lemonade.

"Sure. We need to talk." He followed her outside to the sliver of porch overlooking the town square. Her antique metal lawn chairs, painted sunny yellow, swayed with a rocking motion as they sat. He stretched his legs out to rest on the iron railing between potted palms and bright pink hibiscus.

He noticed her talent for creating a cozy, garden-like

atmosphere from a narrow concrete slab. Fresh black paint covered the old metal railing and pots of flowering vines entwined it. She'd done well to cultivate the tropical plants in their northern climate. He could imagine the gardens she could create in a sunny locale with a longer growing season.

That's when an idea struck.

Taking a long sip of lemonade, he waited for a group of laughing teenagers to walk past and into Frosty's Ice Cream Parlour below. Across the square, Myrtle Winthrop swept the sidewalk in front of her store. The old gossip might spot him here with Sarita, but there was no way she could hear them. Let her tongue wag. He could do nothing to stop her.

"Sarita, I know a way to protect you," he said at last.

"Max, you've done more than enough." She crossed her arms, chin close to her chest as she looked at him. "It's not your responsibility to protect me. I don't expect your help." A glimmer of hope sparkled in her eyes, betraying her words and guarded expression.

She said she didn't *expect* his help - not that she didn't want it. He swallowed hard.

"I care about you too much not to help. I understand how it feels to worry about your child."

"You have a child?" Her eyes bulged with astonishment.

"Yes." The word choked him, yet he felt the need to explain. "I was married once, but not very long. My ex-wife has full custody of my son, thanks to her skills at lying and her penchant for California." Disgust seized him, strangling further explanation.

A million emotions crossed Sarita's expression. Pain covered them all.

"How old is he?"

"Four." Max didn't want to go there but had to give her something. "His name is Luke, and I can't see him without his mother dragging him through court to spite me." He gritted his teeth against bitterness wielding its ugly head.

"I'm so sorry - "

"Thank you." He cut her off, unable to bear the onslaught of emotions that discussion would bring. "So, I want to help you protect Gracia."

She shook her head. "It's too dangerous, Max. Ramone is a murderer. He never wanted Gracia. He wants to hurt *me*."

Taking Gracia would hurt her more than anything else. He knew the wrath of a spurned lover but didn't have the heart to enlighten her.

"I can't let you risk your life for me. You have a child of your own to consider." She sat ramrod straight, chin high.

"That's the point. I don't want you to go through what I have. I care about you, Sarita. I want to help you."

Narrowing her eyes, she looked perplexed. Her searching gaze sparked with hope as she waited for an explanation. She needed his help. But he knew she couldn't bring herself to accept it.

"I need to do this for *me*," he assured her. "To make restitution. I can't change the situation with my son. Lord knows I've tried. But if I can help spare you that pain, maybe in some small way, it would lessen my own."

Her body relaxed a bit. Tension ebbed from her as visible relief spread across her face.

"Are you sure?"

"Honey, I've got nothing to lose and everything to gain." He took her hand and she shuddered with emotion.

She blinked hard against welling tears. "You have no idea what you're getting into." She shook her head. "You have everything to lose."

At that moment, Myrtle spotted them and waved. Cringing inside, he lifted his fingers to her and shored up his resolve. "If I lose you, if you lose Gracia, nothing else matters."

"How can you say that?" Incredulous questions filled her face, her voice. "You have your life, your business, your *reputation*."

That word came out on a high pitch - a notable sore point. She glanced down at Myrtle.

The woman leaned on her broom, keeping a watchful eye as she chatted with passersby.

"You have family and friends. You have a chance someday with your son." Sarita swallowed. "And a lot of women out there deserve you more than I ever could."

Her low opinion of herself hit him like a sucker punch. It broke his heart how her past marred her self-esteem.

"I haven't found any." He faced her. "Not a one makes me feel like you do."

She sucked in a breath. How he longed to erase the stark fear in her eyes.

"Sarita." He squeezed her hand. "We don't know each other that well. But there's something about you - I can't explain it. Call it intuition, call it crazy, but I can't ignore what my gut's telling me. If I don't help you, I'll never forgive myself."

SARITA COULDN'T BELIEVE what she was hearing, but years of dealing with shameless men earned her the ability to distinguish wily lures from sincerity. Her analysis on Max pushed authentic past every barometer she knew.

"There's a place in South Carolina where I could take you and Gracia until we figure out what to do. You'd be safe there."

South Carolina sounded wonderful. Far enough away, yet not too far. And warm. After growing up in Puerto Rico, she'd never gotten used to the cold Ohio weather. She drew a heavy sigh. Tempted to run to her homeland, she knew Ramone would expect that. She had no connections in South Carolina - nothing Ramone could trace to track her down.

"Whaddya say?" Max urged.

She stared into his deep blue eyes, seeing nothing but honor and respect. Yet she couldn't bring herself to trust him with her sensual nature. She couldn't resist a handsome man's touch. In her vast experience with the male psyche, her hot-blooded Latin lust always led her astray.

Yet he seemed so different from the kind of men she'd always known. She feared trusting herself not to fall head over heels - leading to certain devastation. She'd either scare him off or blow it later. She had no idea how to sustain a lasting and healthy commitment. Her longest relationship was with Ramone. Bile rose to her throat.

"Are you okay?" Concern registered on Max's face.

She shook her head. "Ramone will expect me to run home to Puerto Rico. He'll torture my grandmother for information." Wringing her hands, she continued. "Even if I don't go there, he'll hound her."

"We can bring her to South Carolina with us."

Max's quick answer held little consolation.

"She won't leave home. I've already tried. She's afraid to fly and doesn't speak English. She came for my father's funeral and swore she'd never fly again."

"Then we need to convince Ramone you're not in Puerto Rico and your grandmother doesn't know where you are." He tapped a finger on his chin. Then his eyes lit up. "Write her a letter. Tell her you've gone out of town and will be out of touch for a while. Explain there's no phone service where you are. Then call and warn her Ramone may show up. Tell her to keep the letter as proof that she doesn't know where you are. That'll throw him off. He'll believe you're somewhere else."

Surprised at his ability to think on his feet, she realized how he was so successful. Running the performance shop for NASCAR clients as well as operating a profitable race team of his own made him strategic and decisive.

As much as running tempted her, she worried over the impact on Gracia, her job, her mother, even her apartment, for heaven's sake. This guy had a multi-million-dollar business at stake yet acted at a moment's notice.

He snapped his fingers. "I have a buddy in Nevada. I'll overnight the letter and ask him to mail it to your grandmother from there." Max smiled at his ingenious idea. "We can send one to your mom too. Tell her if anyone's looking for you, you headed to Vegas."

The idea had merit. Where better for a stripper to start over than Vegas? Yet Sarita had a bad feeling. Would a postmarked letter be enough to fool Ramone?

"A guy like Ramone could make a killing in Vegas. Maybe he'll relocate out there, hoping to find you eventually." Max caught her expression and his face fell. "Don't you think it's a good idea?"

"Yes, it's brilliant. Sending Ramone on a wild goose chase would be the perfect solution." She pasted on a smile and wrapped her arms around herself. "I just hope it works."

"ARE WE THERE YET?" Gracia whined from the back seat of Max's Escalade as they crossed the South Carolina line among the Labor Day traffic.

"Just a little longer, honey." Sarita shot her a reassuring smile, swallowing fear and uneasiness.

After a midnight rendezvous to hide her car in Max's race shop, they'd been on their way. They moved her plants to his dining room where the housekeeper would water them. He thought of everything - from emptying the fridge to pulling the blinds and putting a 'For Rent' sign in the front window of her apartment with no phone number. She called her landlord, the mayor, explaining as little as possible and assuring him the rent would be paid during her absence.

What was she doing headed to Charleston, South Carolina with a virtual stranger? Despite what seemed honorable intentions, she didn't know Max well enough to take a road trip with him, let alone trust him with her daughter's well being. God only knew how long he'd extend his hospitality, and what it would cost her in the end.

"We'll have lunch at the beach." Max's cheerful voice soothed her child.

"The beach!" Gracia clapped her hands, bouncing in her car seat. She'd never been to the ocean, but during the summer, Sarita often took her to the beach along Lake Erie.

Sarita couldn't wait to see the ocean again, to feel the warm breezes and sunshine that were so fleeting in the north. She relaxed in the soft leather seat, gratitude and a small measure of serenity washing over her as she eyed her rescuer.

Gracia shied from men, but she loved Max. Despite efforts to connect her daughter with the honorable James men, she realized with shame that the absence of a father left her daughter uncomfortable with the foreign gender.

Then Max came along like the father Gracia never had - like the friend and partner Sarita never had.

Closing her eyes against images of happy family life, a companion, and a partner who truly loved her, she pushed that from her mind. She refused to think beyond today, to even hope for anything more than a safe haven for a little while.

Max was just a nice guy helping someone in need. Unable to bear his handsome silhouette, she looked out the side window and squinted in the morning sun, noticing the vibrant green leaves. Mornings in Ohio grew chilly as autumn settled in. Golds, oranges, and reds had not shown in the trees yet, but many leaves withered and blew to the ground.

Thank heaven they'd scooted out long before dawn. Gracia

slept the first half of the twelve-hour drive. Now with stored-up energy and sunshine enticing her, the child squirmed in her seat. Max popped a Disney movie into the DVD player. They had three hours to go.

ON THE NORTH side of Charleston, in an area that was a far cry from hiss wealthy neighborhood, Max pulled off the freeway and headed toward a grocery store. He could have stopped at any fast-food drive through, but a picnic wasn't the same without real food. Besides, Gracia might get a kick out of the grocery store named unlike anything up north.

"Wanna grab some picnic food at the Piggly Wiggly?" he asked with a smirk.

Gracia's raucous laughter didn't disappoint. Even her angst-ridden mother broke into a genuine smile.

"What does a pig say?" Sarita asked.

"Oink, oink!" Gracia spurted between giggles.

"Let's see if we can scare up some lunch," Max teased as he grabbed a cart from the parking lot and swooshed Gracia into the seat. "Off to The Pig!"

Giddy with excitement, Gracia acted as if it were some grand adventure as they entered the store. "Off to The Pig!" she hailed from her perch in the cart. Much to the delight of passersby, she scrunched her nose with a silly "Oink, oink!"

Max hunted down a rotisserie chicken, southern-style potato salad, and a jug of sweet tea. Sarita added fresh-cut fruit, a wedge of cheddar, and a loaf of multigrain bread.

"You can't have bread without butter," he insisted as he wheeled toward the dairy aisle. "And *everything* tastes better with honey butter." He tossed some into the cart and tweaked Gracia's nose. She lapsed into giggles.

On the way to his SUV, Max turned somber. He'd stolen them away to safety. Now to deal with the rest. As if the fear of some lunatic coming after Sarita and Gracia weren't enough, he worried over the whole issue of Sarita finding out what kind of wealth he had.

"We're almost there, honey." Sarita buckled Gracia into the car seat in the back of his Escalade. She smiled at him, and he tried to reciprocate despite his sudden dread.

Although the Escalade, the Porsche, and his house in Riverside were pretty good indications, those mere crumbs didn't compare to the towering, decadent icing on the cake.

Staying at the mansion by the sea might tip her off to the extent of his wealth. His business venture with NASCAR was nothing compared with his inheritance. Old money from his great grandfather's textile mills financed hotels spanning the coast from the Carolinas to Florida. He'd never live long enough to spend the immense fortune they provided.

Uncle Harley managed the hotel franchise for now, but at sixty-three, his days as CEO were numbered. Aunt Ruby already hinted that Max would need to shoulder that responsibility soon.

Sarita had no clue of his vast inheritance. Was he making a huge mistake tipping his hand before he knew her real intentions? Could he ever trust her with his heart if he couldn't be sure whether *her* heart was true?

His ex had loved him at one time - before she realized what she could get her hands on. Would Sarita spend twenty grand a month on an American Express card as Deira had?

Money tainted everything.

He pulled out of the shopping center and hesitantly headed toward the Isle of Palms. Gracia was in awe of the Ravenel Bridge that spanned the wide Cooper River for two and a half miles and led into upscale Mount Pleasant.

"Wow, this is nice." Sarita marveled at the manicured business district. Nestled among trees, rows of shops and restaurants emerged. "Even the medians and lampposts are landscaped with plants and flowers. And they've kept so many trees."

"Yeah, Charleston is protective of its trees."

Max drove a few miles up Highway 17 and pulled onto the Isle of Palms connector.

As they neared the bridge over the intercoastal waterway, sunlight danced across rippling blue waters and waving green grasses of the marsh. Sarita sucked in a breath.

"Max, this is beautiful."

"Wait 'til you see the ocean." He smiled at her.

At the apex of the bridge, the blue Atlantic appeared on the horizon.

"Oh, Max!" Sarita breathed.

"Water!" Gracia exclaimed from the back seat.

Max realized his good fortune to own a home in such a beautiful place. He lived a charmed life – loving his work with NASCAR and wanting for nothing - except true love.

Maybe he'd never find someone who knew him well enough to finish his sentences like Ruby did for Harley. He yearned for someone he could trust implicitly with not only money, but with his innermost feelings, his heart, and his soul. He wanted a relationship like his aunt and uncle had. From the time Ruby's father hired Harley, he'd never shown an ounce of greed. He worked hard to earn his place in the company, and in Ruby's heart.

Would Sarita prove that honorable?

Regardless, he had to help her. He couldn't stand by and do nothing when he had the wherewithal to protect her and her precious child. He'd lost at love before, but risking a child wasn't an option.

Watching Sarita from the corner of his eye, he drove onto Palm Boulevard, past beachfront mansions of enormous proportions. Her eyes widened as he turned between massive brick pillars set in lush landscaping onto the palm tree-lined drive.

She stared up the cascading stairs to the columned veranda of the three-story beach house welcoming them.

"Are we here?" Gracia squealed with delight.

Sarita faced him.

"Welcome to the beach." He feigned excitement.

Her confused expression proved she sensed his unease.

He took a fortifying breath, smelling the enticing scent of sea and sand mingled with fresh cut grass. He parked at the bottom of the stairway. On either side of the entrance, bright pink blossoms of potted hibiscus glistened with water droplets. The gardener had done his job.

"Max, is this yours?" Sarita gasped.

"Oh, no," he lied. "It belongs to my aunt and uncle," he explained away as if they were some distant relatives. The deed held Harley's name, but only because his uncle could secure a multi-million-dollar loan easier than he could. Max made the payments, and as sole heir, it would remain his house whether they changed the deed or not.

"Wow." Sarita stared up at the house in awe. "A mansion on the beach. I never imagined a place like this."

"It's an investment." He downplayed the opulence. He should have known better than to bring her here. Revealing his family's wealth hinted at his own.

Here we go.

EYES BULGING, Sarita took in their surroundings. She knew Max was well-off, but never dreamed of luxury like this.

While she marveled at each intricate detail, Gracia waltzed across the inlaid marble foyer, past the elaborate sweeping staircase, and into the enormous gourmet kitchen as if this were any old house.

Max opened a custom pearwood cabinet below the giant island. He pulled out a picnic basket and thumped it onto the granite counter. He seemed distracted and brooding.

Sarita's stomach clenched. He already regretted bringing them here. What should she do now?

"What's in there?" Gracia pointed to the basket. Sarita cringed as her child scrambled onto a carved wooden stool to peek inside.

"Picnic dishes," Max said with a mood-lightening smile as he pulled out colorful plastic plates.

Gracia stood on the leather-upholstered seat. With no regard for the marbled high-end granite, she touched one reverent finger to the plate painted with beach umbrellas and flip-flops.

"Pretty," she whispered, as if those plastic dishes were the most precious thing in the room.

Sarita burst out laughing at the irony and Max broke into an unstoppable grin as he piled food into the basket. He snipped fresh mint sprigs from a pot on the windowsill as their clean scent filled the room. Then he stepped out to the deck and plucked a lemon from a huge potted tree. The citrusy smell intensified as he sliced the lemon, making her mouth water.

"Off to the beach!" He resumed his cheerful attitude as he tossed Sarita a beach blanket. He whooshed Gracia onto his shoulders and traipsed off, swinging the picnic basket in one hand while keeping a firm hold on her giggling daughter with the other.

Beneath the warm September sun, sweet iced tea with fresh mint and a squeeze of lemon tasted like nectar of the gods. Gracia had charmed Max out of his odd mood. They ate with light-hearted abandon.

Sea breezes, rolling waves, and the calming ambience of the beach made the chicken taste juicier, the melon sweeter, and the potato salad more flavorful than any she recalled. Satisfied and relaxed in body and soul, Sarita lifted her face to the sun.

Gracia chased sand pipers, splashing at the edge of the waves. Grateful for her ability to lighten a tense situation, Sarita kept one eye on her child and one on the reflective man beside her.

"So, what are you doing in Ohio when you can come to a place like this?" she asked.

His gaze jerked up. "Don't you like Crystal Falls?"

Taken aback, she stammered, "I love Crystal Falls. But this..." She gazed at the ocean view. In the foreground, Gracia giggled, playing in the sand. Taking it in anew, she still couldn't believe she was sitting here, couldn't imagine staying in a mansion on the beach. Yet this unassuming man had access to it all.

"It is beautiful." He leaned back on his elbows behind her, away from her scrutiny.

She'd have to contort her neck or reposition herself to make eye contact. She felt no inclination to do either.

Something kept him in Ohio - or something kept him away from here. Uncertain which, she wouldn't press.

"My son is in Ohio." Pain choked his voice, but he covered it with a chuckle. "And Aunt Ruby is here."

"Ah, your son. That explains it." Keeping an eye on Gracia, she leaned back for a face-to-face.

His irresistible grin provoked questions she couldn't stop.

"Did you grow up there? What brought you to Ohio in the first place? What about your parents? Do you get down here often?"

"Whoa - that's a lot of questions."

"Sorry." She dipped her chin. "But I'd be hitting this beach every chance I got. I can't imagine staying away from all this."

His smile fell away and a nerve ticked in his jaw.

What did she say wrong?

BAD LIAR

S arita hoped she hadn't pushed too far with her questions.

"First of all, my wife grew up in Ohio," Max said. "Ex-wife. Secondly, my parents passed away."

"Oh - " Before she could absorb all that, he continued.

"And third, I can't afford all this. It belongs to my aunt and uncle, remember?"

Yeah, she got that it belonged to his aunt and uncle. But the part about he couldn't afford it just didn't ring true. Something about his adamant defensiveness made her think he had a lot more money than he let on.

As if sensing her disbelief, he added, "It's been mortgaged to the hilt for renovations." He took a long sip of tea and didn't look her in the eye.

On the one hand, being a bad liar meant he didn't have much experience at it. On the other hand, he was still lying. Ramone had been smooth. She could never tell if he was lying, so she never believed a word he said.

She couldn't tolerate dishonesty. Up until now, she'd trusted Max. Otherwise she wouldn't have taken this journey with him. How could she have been so foolish? What else had he lied about that she hadn't caught on to? And if his aunt and uncle owned the mansion, where were they?

Playing along, she tossed her hair casually. "Nice place to retire. So, your aunt and uncle live here?"

"Oh no, they live in town."

Downtown? she wondered. In college, she'd studied the architecture in Charleston's prestigious historic district. Real estate ran in the millions South of Broad where ocean breezes cooled opulent piazzas and blue bloods inherited eighth generation mansions.

Based on the beach house, she doubted they rented a loft.

"The family shares the beach house. We're lucky to get it to ourselves this time." He laid it on thick and she wasn't buying it. But why would he lie? Was he a farce or did he think she was a gold digger? Either choice boiled her blood.

"And for the record, my aunt and uncle aren't retired. Harley runs a business and Ruby runs him ragged." His smirk lightened the mood and Sarita wanted to believe that much was true.

"I get down here as much as I can, but Aunt Ruby can be a control freak. I need my independence. That's why I joined the Navy. Then I went to college on the GI bill." He ran that home, as if he couldn't afford college without government assistance.

She could see him in the military but didn't buy the poor schlep bit. And she didn't get the connection between a controlling aunt and his joining the Navy.

"Where'd you go to college?" she asked.

"In Boston." His gaze evaded her.

Wasn't Harvard in Boston?

"That's where I met my ex." His fingers picked at a loose thread on the blanket.

"She dragged you to Ohio."

"Kicking and screaming." His laugh seemed genuine. "After four years in Boston, the cold and snow had gotten old. Yearning for home, I wanted to head south. No such luck."

"I'm surprised she didn't want to live here." Sarita looked out over the water to the horizon where blue met blue. Gracia stood marveling at the gulls above her. "What a beautiful place to raise a family."

Despite being irked at him, she immediately wished she hadn't brought up that cruel reminder of his son.

"I didn't live here - " seeming to catch himself, he started over. "We lived in Charlotte then. My aunt and uncle moved here later for Harley's, uh, business." The pause seemed as if he'd said more than he intended.

"What kind of business does he have?" Skeptical that she'd get a straight answer, she listened for deception.

"He works in the hotel industry." He didn't elaborate.

His vague evasion beat a lie. She wouldn't press. Harley's business didn't matter. Max's dishonesty mattered - and his reason for it.

She hated being misjudged. She'd made her share of mistakes, but never stooped to gold digging. Despite disreputable career choices, she'd worked hard for every penny, one way or the other.

Facing his affluence, she wondered if Max had done the same. So, he didn't grow up here. That didn't mean he spent summers picking fruit like she did. From age eleven, she'd worked all summer to earn money for school clothes and books. Rich kids went to camp or spent summers at the beach. Did he?

"You grew up in Charlotte?"

"Yeah." He nodded. "Hence my interest in stock car racing." He sat forward and brushed off his hands as if finished with this conversation.

"I see." Parts of his story rang true. Yet she couldn't bear his hesitance to look her in the eye. Saddened to lose trust in him, she so wanted him to be different.

MAX READ the distrust in Sarita's eyes. He couldn't carry on this façade any longer yet regretted ending the conversation on a sour note. Without a word, she rose and joined Gracia at the edge of the waves.

He had always been a bad liar. That was his undoing with Deira, and he didn't want to make the same mistakes twice.

When he'd tried the 'dose of your own medicine' by lying to his ex, she'd beat him at that game right down to taking full custody of Luke.

He shuddered. How could he hide his true wealth from Sarita without outright lying? The luxurious beach house spoke for itself. At least she didn't know Ruby and Harley raised him. He'd keep that detail to himself.

Galled at the need to hide who he was, he wondered why he'd ever brought her here. Couldn't he have found some out-of-the-way motel to hole up in? Or run off to Nevada and stayed with his buddy? Or a dozen other scenarios.

No, because some part of him wanted to impress her, to win her over with the very wealth he strived to hide. He wanted her to know the real Max Carter. He wanted to introduce her to Ruby and Harley, to seek their approval of Sarita as much as he dreaded Ruby's pressure to remarry.

Frustrated, he stood and ran his hands through his hair. Hadn't the Navy taught him anything about discipline? Hadn't he learned from his mistakes with Deira?

He'd joined the Navy to prove he could be his own man without depending on his uncle's money. Then he strove to raise his status by attending Harvard where gold-digging girls sought rich husbands. If only he'd known.

Seeking his own identity without Harley Wheeler's influence, he'd wanted no favors, no special treatment. To feel worthy, he needed to make his own way like everyone else. He hated being some spoiled rich kid whose every whim was met and handed to him with a couple hundreds on the side. As if he couldn't do it on his own.

He succeeded for a while. But when he started his own business, the banks turned down some no-name sailor from out of state. Regardless of his degree, the Ohio bank that held his mortgage didn't see quitting his steady job in finance for some upstart racing venture as a stable investment. He caved at the lure of easy money from Uncle Harley. That's when Deira had caught the whiff of hard cash.

Could Sarita be like her?

At the edge of the waves, she kicked seafoam with her laughing daughter. Deira never played with Luke that way. The sand would mess up her pedicure, and she couldn't bear getting near some disgusting sea creature. Martinis by the pool were more her style. He remembered the day they met.

Beside a pile of textbooks, Deira had sat pouting on a park bench. She stared at the broken strap on her designer handbag. He found her adorable. Now he realized how blind he was to the real woman he'd married.

Would his only son grow up to be like her? Did Max's genes have any chance of influencing his son? What a shame if Deira's convoluted values overpowered the faith and morals Max hoped to pass on to his only child.

Startled laughter broke his thoughts. A crashing wave knocked Gracia to the sand and soaked the hem of Sarita's shorts. His heart warmed at their good-natured fun. No, she seemed nothing like Deira. Sarita faced real danger and he felt compelled to protect her.

Yet she was human. With a child to support, would she be lured by money? He needed assurance she loved *him* before she fell in love with his fortune. Max renewed his determination to win her love.

He hated lying. Better to be evasive. He yearned to ask Harley's advice but remained cautious to introduce Sarita and hesitant to let Ruby get wise ideas about grandchildren where precocious Gracia was concerned.

Yet soon the day would come to see the aunt and uncle who raised him. Ruby would quickly grow attached to Gracia. He didn't want to get her hopes up. Should he present Sarita or go alone? Either way, he couldn't come to Charleston without visiting his family.

SAND AND SEA INVIGORATED SARITA. Bone-weary and stressed after traveling all night and half the day, she understood Max's irritability. She didn't drive, but she hadn't slept either. Yet the sunshine and salty air brought clarity as she waded the waves with her daughter.

Gracia should be safe here. That priority had driven them to leave in such haste she hadn't digested the details. Saintly Mrs. Kentosh had promised to hold her job, telling her to take her time to resolve things.

Her mother and grandmother would show Ramone the letters from Nevada. She told neither of them where she was headed so there'd be no chance of a slip-up.

The phone in her pocket vibrated. Sudden fear slammed her chest. She fumbled for the off button as Vanessa's name and number popped up. She'd asked Mama not to call so she couldn't be traced but hadn't notified her friend.

When would she be able to explain? How long before she could go home? Relocating to Willow Pond would be closer to work, but was it far enough away? Even if Ramone left town to hunt her down, he'd have his goons watching for her. Would she have to leave the new life she'd just begun - to start all over again somewhere else?

With her daughter at her feet, she stared into the ocean. Its rhythm calmed her as waves stole the sand beneath her. Contradictions - like life itself. And the man behind her.

She sensed Max watching her but refused to turn around. Let him stew a while. He ought to know why she walked away. She was falling hard for him but had zero tolerance for dishonesty. Unable to endure another relationship based on lies, she had trusted him with her story, trusted him to protect her, and trusted him with her daughter's life. Yet now she couldn't trust him to tell her the *truth*.

Why start this relationship anyway if she had to move far away?

Water rushed around her feet, confiscating the sand until she stood in two shifting holes. Gracia splashed with glee, jumping in the waves at her side.

Without a sound, the air around her became electrically charged as she felt Max's presence.

"Hey."

She stiffened at his voice. His nearness brought goosebumps to her flesh and butterflies fluttering in her belly. How could he do that to her after the scores of men she'd dated? Stunned at her reaction, she couldn't recall the last time a man had that effect on her.

With the tiniest turn of her head, she offered a half-smile of acknowledgement. He draped an arm over her shoulders, melting her reservations. Knowing she had to stand her ground on truth, she craved physical affection - her ultimate weakness - and had no strength to resist him.

She leaned into him, unwilling to sacrifice the warmth of his embrace.

Later she'd ask why he lied. Right now, she needed his comfort.

"You doing okay?" His whispered breath on her ear sent tingles racing through her.

Drawing closer, she wrapped her arms around him.

"I am now."

He chuckled, stroking her hair with magic fingers. His hot lips kissed her forehead and left a warm remembrance. Emotion stirred her as she reveled in his touch. She could fall hard for this man.

"Mommy, look!" Her child held up a pink shell.

"Pretty!" Sarita masked her worries. Releasing Max, she turned full attention to her precious daughter. Bending, she took the shell. "Let's clean off the sand." She rinsed it in the waves and examined it.

"Pretty!" Gracia mimicked her mama.

"You should keep this one, honey." Sarita's heart warmed as Gracia's eyes widened with wonder and amazement.

"I can keep it?"

"Of course. You can keep as many shells as you like."

Her child's face lit up as if proclaimed princess of the beach kingdom. She scampered off to stash her shell on the blanket. Then she scoured the beach for more.

"She's a delight." Max smiled, resuming his embrace as soon as Sarita stood.

"I have to protect her." Voice shaking, Sarita fought a sudden urge to cry.

He held her tight for a long moment as Gracia collected an armload of shells. "I've been thinking," he began. "We have some loose ends to tie up in Crystal Falls."

Sarita nodded. "I know. Ramone saw your protectiveness. He might suspect you're hiding me."

"He won't find your car at the shop. Brett hid it in a back room. Even if the door's open it's not visible."

Brett Mitchell worked for Max. Like her friend Vanessa, he'd married into the James family, founders of Crystal Falls. Son of the town mechanic, Brett was entangled in the fabric of that smalltown life like Opey in Mayberry.

He and his family were good people. Yet hearing his name brought the stark reminder that he'd found Jake's dead body. Her closest brother had been her only ally when their family ran amuck. Like her best friend Layla, he'd been killed.

Rattled by the memory, she tried to shake it off.

"Do you think Ramone's watching your apartment?" Max asked.

She nodded. "And my mom's - and your house. He's one persistent Pitbull. With his mind set on vengeance, he'll get it, no matter the consequences." She shuddered.

Max tightened his arms around her.

As much as she'd miss all she had in Crystal Falls, risking Gracia was far worse. She glanced at her daughter playing on the beach. Adrift, she stared out at the ocean.

"I'm not sure I'll *ever* be safe returning to Crystal Falls."

Max didn't say a word, but she felt his gaze heavy upon her. He drew her close and she burrowed into his heat. They watched her child scurrying in the sand without a care in the world.

"Hey man!"

Sarita jumped as a male voice boomed behind them.

BREAKING TIES

Sarita's head whipped around to see a huge man coming toward them. Every protective instinct in her went on alert. She scanned the beach for Gracia, ten feet away, and hurried toward her.

"Hey!" Max turned and strode toward the big black man and his female companion. "Ty, Lavonna, how are ya?"

Sarita's defenses eased as Max apparently knew this couple. She shot them an uncertain smile. Gracia peeked around her legs, seeming anxious to meet new people but looking up for mama's approval first. Good girl.

"Good to see you, man." Ty greeted Max with a manly hug.

"Good to see *you*!" Max thumped his muscular friend on the back and then bent to embrace the dainty, smiling woman. "Looking fine as always, Lavonna."

"Thank you, Max." She beamed, smoothing masses of windswept corkscrew curls from her face. Her gaze darted to Sarita, and then Gracia. "Hello." Hand outstretched, she stepped toward them. Ty joined her with a broad smile.

"Hi." Sarita held Gracia's hand for reassurance and moved toward the welcoming couple.

Max put his arm around her and made the introductions. He looked to Sarita. "Ty and Lavonna live next door." He nodded to the right. "Ty and I were in the Navy together. He's an Isle of Palms policeman and Lavonna manages a hotel here on the island."

Before she could stop herself, Sarita shot a surprised look at the massive beach house with four balconies and an infinity pool. She wondered how a police officer and hotel manager could afford all that.

"We're caretakers for the house while the owners make their grand living in New York City." Lavonna caught Sarita's eye with a bewitching smirk. "They're here about two months of the year and the rest of the time we have the house to ourselves."

"Awesome." Sarita could live with a gig like that.

Lavonna bent to Gracia's level. "How old are you?"

Acting shy, Gracia leaned into her mother and held up three fingers.

"Wow. Three years old and so pretty already. You look just like your mommy." Lavonna smiled up at Sarita.

Gracia beamed.

"Thank you." Sarita liked this woman already. It'd be nice to have a friend nearby.

"How long will you be in town?" Ty asked Max.

The million-dollar question.

"I'm not sure." Max looked to Sarita with a question in his eyes.

She nodded the go-ahead. Max apparently trusted these folks. The advantages of an informed cop next door, watching out for her, far outweighed her hesitant misgivings.

"We need some time to fortify things back home," he continued, then glanced down at Gracia. "There's a possible abductor on the loose."

Sarita appreciated the code language clear to everyone but Gracia.

Horror struck Lavonna's features. She watched Gracia like a protective mother hen. Ty's expression hardened with the look of a seasoned cop determined to seek justice. Serve and protect and all those noble notions had him squaring his shoulders and puffing out his chest like a rooster ready for a fight.

Sarita felt a measure of comfort in his reaction, but Gracia looked up with alarm. Their expressions slipped back to beach friendly.

"So, you needed a little vacation, did you?" Beneath Ty's casual voice, his responsiveness to danger simmered under the surface.

"Yep." Max tousled Gracia's hair. "Thought I'd show these ladies some fun at the beach."

"We got chicken at Piggly Wiggly." Gracia giggled.

"Oh, did you?" Lavonna reached out to stroke her hair and smiled at Sarita. "She's adorable." Beneath the admiration, longing settled in her eyes, along with compassion and fear.

Sarita read the telepathic message and returned one of her own. *Yeah, if I lost her, my life would be over.*

Max and Ty stepped aside and wandered off in private conversation. Good - give the cop the details because no place felt safe with Ramone on the hunt. Nevada might delay him, but he'd return from that wild goose chase more tenacious and vengeful than ever. How long would she have to hide? Would she and Gracia have to live on the run? What was she going to do?

"Wanna see my shells?" Gracia's wide doe eyes looked up at Lavonna. She'd taken to the woman like a long-lost friend.

"Oh, yes!" The two skipped off toward the blanket.

Lavonna's enthusiasm warmed Sarita's heart. She could use a friend right now. She couldn't call Vanessa, and how she missed Layla. She'd understood Sarita like the sister she never had. Their childhoods were so similar, their reactions identical.

Stripping somehow gave them power over the men who'd abused them. It showed Sarita's older brothers, and Layla's father, that they didn't have exclusive rights. Earning money for the innocence that had been stolen validated them somehow, proved their worth in some twisted, sick way.

No one understood that better than Layla. Her sister Vanessa knew the abuse but found saner ways to cope with the stigma. Good friend that she was, Vanessa couldn't replace Layla. And neither could this kind woman.

"Thank you so much for showing me your shells." Lavonna bent down on the blanket.

"Look at this one." Gracia gingerly picked up the biggest shell to show her new friend.

Sarita never felt more alone. She would never forgive Ramone for causing her friend's death, and her brother's. Jake was her only brother who didn't abuse her. He'd been her solace when slimy Pedro and jailbird Gilberto had seen her as fair game.

Then along came Ramone. Sarita had been the favorite in his harem. Yet he'd taken everything from her.

The fact that he still wanted to hurt her, to take away her child, burned a rage in her belly that wouldn't go away. Four years in prison wasn't long enough.

Seeing Gracia take to Lavonna, Sarita had to wonder - how would she respond to Ramone? What would he do to her innocent, trusting child? Would he torment her, or just kill her like he'd wanted done in the first place?

She shuddered, the horror fresh in her heart. Tears stung her eyes. She swiped at them, pushing the terrifying thoughts away. She couldn't let that happen. She had to remain strong and protect her precious daughter by whatever means necessary.

"Is that your favorite, Gracia?" She hastened toward her daughter. She needed to get her emotions under control. For Gracia's sake, she had to pretend all was well.

AFTER LYING low for a couple days, Max felt confident of Sarita and Gracia's safety. They'd fallen into a comfortable routine. Lazy mornings around the breakfast table were followed by a stretch on the beach. When the sun soared to scorching heights, they retreated for sweet iced tea, lunch on the shaded patio, and a cooling dip in the pool.

While Gracia took her afternoon nap, Max checked in with Brett and handled business. Sarita busied herself straightening the house or doing laundry. Then she'd wander outside to the garden, plucking spent blooms from the flowers, and pulling weeds and stray leaves from the beds.

He didn't discourage her with news the gardener arrived once a week. She seemed to need that connection to nature before she'd relax on the balcony with a book from his library.

Overlooking the vast gardens surrounding a natural stone pool with the ocean view beyond, she'd languish for hours reading about southern gardening or native plants. Being a member of Charleston's Garden Society, he cultivated an extensive collection of plants and books about them.

Today Sarita headed back to the kitchen with an old cookbook in her hand.

From his study nearby, he watched her as he talked to Brett on the phone. Sarita scrounged the cupboards and pulled out ingredients. His heart warmed at her domestic side. Smiling into the phone, he thanked Brett for taking care of business. Somewhat concerned to be out of touch from his business, he logged onto his computer to do some work.

Soon a heavenly cinnamon aroma tantalized him into the kitchen. He padded across the hard wood floor, came up behind Sarita and wrapped his arms around her.

"Hi." She let out a blissful sigh. Her eyes drifted shut as she leaned back and melted against him.

"Something smells wonderful. Whatcha baking?" he whispered into her long, soft hair.

She didn't move from his embrace or even open her eyes. "Snickerdoodles."

His heart leapt. "My favorites. How did you know?"

A smile lit her face as she looked up at him. She lifted a seductive eyebrow and let him wonder at her mind-reading abilities for several moments.

With a sly smile, she admitted, "That's where the book fell open and smudges covered the dogeared page."

He chuckled, low and warm against her hair. He could imagine living with this woman, and loving her, for a very long time.

His phone buzzed. He wanted to ignore it, but it could be Brett. With a groan, he read the caller ID. Dread slammed him like sucker punch.

Max attempted a reassuring smile as he pulled away from Sarita but failed miserably. His gut warned him the phone call wasn't good news.

"Hello Chief," he said with an eye on her.

She stiffened, hugging herself as she fell back against the counter. She watched him like a rabbit ready to run. If only he could protect her from the fear.

"We had to release Ramone." Regret filled the chief's voice. "He posted bail."

"I see." Max had less time than anticipated. He had to cover her trail. Now.

After a pause, the chief continued. "We have an informant watching him. Ramone drove past Sarita's apartment but never even slowed down. He headed to an old haunt, holed up with some stripper. I'm hoping he'll abandon his vendetta. But we'll keep an eye on him."

Max didn't put much faith in that. He thanked Chief Hunter and tucked the phone into his pocket. He faced the fragile woman in his kitchen.

"Ramone is out on bail."

She sucked in a ragged breath and collapsed on a stool. Head in her hands, she said, "I knew it wouldn't be long."

"I'm sorry, honey. He drove past your apartment but didn't stop. Maybe he'll give it up."

"He won't give up," she said with certainty as her body trembled. She glanced up the stairs toward her sleeping child. Her wide eyes brightened with tears.

Max took her in his arms. Squashing his emotions, he didn't have time for anger, worry, or even fear. He had to take action to protect Sarita and Gracia.

"We're going to keep her safe."

A plan began forming in his mind.

With no time for drama, he took her hand and led her to a cushy sofa facing a wall of windows that looked over the ocean. Max pulled her close to his side.

"Ramone saw us together," he began.

"I know," she fretted. "I'm not sure he's going to believe I went to Nevada. What if he figures it out and finds me here?"

"My uncle's last name's Wheeler and Ramone would have to do quite a bit of digging to link me here. I doubt he's that clever, but we can't take any chances."

"He's smarter than you think, and meaner."

Max searched her glistening eyes, afraid his plan would frighten or hurt her. He took her hand and spoke gently.

"I've been thinking, if Ramone thought we broke up, he wouldn't look toward me anymore. I could go to your apartment and pretend you left me." He waited for her response.

"That's a good idea." Her hands were shaking. "But I don't know if I can do it. What if - "

"You don't have to do anything. You and Gracia will stay here where you're safe." He kissed her forehead. "I'll go to your apartment as if I'm looking for you, but I'll be watching for Ramone or one of his lurking thugs. Does anyone else have a key to your apartment?"

"No. I didn't trust anyone." She looked into his eyes. "Not until I met you."

He didn't see that coming. Touched, he stroked her hair and kissed her cheek. She needed more comfort than that, so much more, and he longed to give it to her. But not now - Ramone was loose.

And she trusted *him*. He couldn't mess this up. He regretted the lies but admitting them now would only make her question him. He needed her complete trust to protect her from Ramone. To earn that trust, he had to tell her everything starting now. He'd come clean on the rest later.

"When I find your apartment empty, I'll get upset, question the neighbors, make a scene. Then I'll go to your mom's and question her. That should convince anyone watching that you left me high and dry." He winked.

"Okay." Despite his attempt to lighten the situation, Sarita looked vulnerable and lost. "But what am I supposed to do while you're gone? I don't even have a car."

"Stay here and lay low." He caught her gaze. "We'll stock up on groceries and such. There's a jeep in the garage in case of emergency, but let's not take any chances of being spotted."

She nodded. Like a beached shellfish, she hid in a magnificent shell laid right in plain sight if one knew where to look.

"I'll ask the mayor if anyone's called about your apartment," Max rambled on as she reeled from that last decision. "Just in case the missing phone number didn't work. He could tell folks the place isn't ready yet, which of course, it's not."

Her gut clenched. She'd waited almost a year for an available apartment on the town square. With painstaking care, she'd decorated with tropical style, scouring for bargains, and staying within her tight budget. The place suited her, comforted her, oozed her personality. She loved that apartment.

Yet she'd give it all up to keep Gracia safe. Nothing meant as much as Gracia - not her career, her church, her friends, even her new relationship with her mom.

She faced the reality of starting over - again. Anxiety and sorrow overwhelmed her. Tears coursed down her cheeks.

Max wrapped his arms around her and held her close.

MAX HATED MAKING A PUBLIC SPECTACLE. But he'd head to Crystal Falls and do what he had to do. To complete the rouse, he'd put on a sad face and go visit his old girlfriend. Sarita came up with that idea, the icing the cake. The flighty hairdresser did Myrtle's hair twice a week. News would spread fast.

"That ought to convince Ramone you're done with me," Sarita said with certainty.

And make him look like a womanizing jerk. He hated even *pretending* to be like that. Who else would notice - clients, business associates, friends? He'd regretted dating Tiffany from the moment he realized the woman had no loyalty and not a brain in her head. Her appearance stroked his ego, the same way it did for every other man she flirted with.

"Your old girlfriend should convince him." Fresh hope filled Sarita's voice. "Ramone will believe it because he'd act the same way."

Max cringed as he nodded in agreement. The possible ramifications ranked far less crucial than risking Gracia's life. He gritted his teeth and pushed it from his mind.

First, he needed to fortify Gracia and Sarita here. Ty and Lavonna worked long hours and Sarita wouldn't always be able to reach them. Not every situation justified calling the police. She needed someone who'd drop everything to help her, or hide her, if she felt the need.

Aunt Ruby would be willing and able. Anyone else might be at risk taking on the danger of Sarita's situation, but Aunt Ruby carried a fearless quality, along with unshakable faith, that seemed to ward off enemies. Partnered with strong and sensible Uncle Harley, she could protect Sarita as well as any cop in Charleston. She knew this town like the terrain of her back garden and was connected like kudzu to the roadside trees.

No one messed with Aunt Ruby. Even the Charleston bluebloods respected her, despite her out-of-state upbringing.

Max still hadn't contacted her and felt guilty over that. He contemplated visiting without Sarita, but that seemed dishonest at best, rude and conniving at worst.

Visiting with an ulterior motive was no better, but they needed to meet, and he'd run out of time.

"I need to introduce you to Aunt Ruby and Uncle Harley. Ruby's free during the day and always answers her phone." He paused. "She's quite the Charleston socialite, as you'll soon find out." He winked at Sarita.

She offered a pale smile.

"If you need anything at all, Aunt Ruby will be here for you - and I mean in seconds flat. That's how she is." He strove to reassure her, but a whirl of emotions crossed her expression. Okay, he might as well prepare her. She'd be seeing for herself soon enough. "Ruby and Harley might appear hoity-toity, living south of Broad and all that, but they'd give you the shirt off their back and that's the truth."

Sarita nodded solemnly.

"We'll visit them once Gracia wakes up. Then I'll head out and arrive in Crystal Falls by morning."

WHILE MAX SPOKE to his aunt on the phone, Sarita's stomach quivered with nerves. She was thankful he explained the situation so she wouldn't have to, yet her emotions swirled. Fear for her daughter's safety, and her own wellbeing, combined with emerging feelings for Max that would be best left buried. She hesitated to trust him yet felt an overwhelming inclination to do just that.

Furious, bitter resentment toward Ramone gnawed at her core. Grieving over the loss of her comfortable home, her long-worked-for career, and her beloved friends, she feared losing the closeness she'd found with her mother. Hurt and angry at the sting of Pedro's betrayal, she missed Jake, Layla, and her Abuela more than ever. Now meet-the-relatives jitters added to the volatile mix.

Max chatted with his aunt, promising to bring a 'friend' with him, as well as a 'little surprise'. Hinting about Gracia, he winked at Sarita.

"Sure, we'd love to come for dinner." He shot her an encouraging smile.

Dinner with his family - in a house south of Broad - with his socialite aunt and businessman uncle. Since his parents passed away, this carried the significance of meeting his parents. Like the beginning of a real relationship.

She'd been with dozens of men. Not one had ever introduced her to his parents.

An unquenchable longing for family washed over her. Since moving to America when she was thirteen, she'd missed her beloved grandmother in Puerto Rico and her parents had never been the same. They came for prosperity yet found nothing but grief and difficulty.

Her father began slow suicide by the bottle. After his death, her mother took up where he left off. Her older brothers fell into lives of crime, all but Jake who married into the James family. But his drinking and cheating drove Rachel to divorce. Then he was killed.

Sarita's looks had been her downfall. Her brother Pedro hooked her up with Ramone and she'd worked her way up the stripper food chain to be number one.

She shuddered, pushing it from her mind. She needed a different kind of family. She'd loved her friend Layla, but even their relationship was tainted by competition and jealousy. Then Layla got pregnant, and Ramone killed her.

No, the kind of family she longed for celebrated birth, and life, and built each other up rather than trampling one another for top position.

"You alright?" Max took her hand, held it warm in his as he set down his phone.

All she could do was shrug. "I don't want you to leave." She burrowed into his shoulder, needing his protection and comfort. Nervous and unsure about meeting his relatives, she felt vulnerable. "I don't know anyone here, and I don't know my way around. I'm dependent on strangers. I might as well be in a foreign country."

"Ah, but it's a beautiful one. And they speak English here."

"True." She pulled back to look into his eyes. "You've taken us in, shared this gorgeous house with us, fed us, protected us, and now you're traveling another 750 miles to fool my enemy and make sure we're safe." She shook her head. "I'm sorry. I shouldn't be whining."

He stroked her hair, giving the comfort she craved.

"Shhh," he whispered in her ear. "You're not whining."

"I'm scared." Her voice cracked, and so did her heart like it was breaking in two.

"That's understandable." He kissed her forehead. "I'll be back in a few days."

She wanted him to be back forever, with her. Longing filled

her. They'd never talked about forever. They shared one real kiss before this nightmare began. She'd fought the passion, afraid to trust him. But his genuine concern, his respect despite all he knew about her, won her over. She searched his eyes, not quite ready to trust him fully, yet tempted to take that chance. Would he hurt her like all the others? She tensed with fearful anticipation.

"And please don't worry about my old girlfriend."

His old girlfriend?

SCARLETT O'HARA

Was his old girlfriend a threat? That thought never crossed Sarita's mind. Should it have?

"She's a tramp and I'm not interested," Max said.

She stiffened, blinking hard. How many times had *she* been called that? He knew her background - so much for respect. All along she knew Max was too good for her. He might take her in as a charity case, even get cozy on the couch, but she had no place in his future. She didn't belong here, and she never would.

She'd been a fool to believe otherwise. Quick tears threatened to spill. She jumped up and ran to the window. Staring out at the ocean, she hugged herself and fought back the tears.

"Sarita, I... I didn't mean that like it sounded. I... my hairdresser..." Regret filled his voice. He couldn't take back the hurtful words. "Sarita, I'm sorry. You're nothing like her."

No, but she used to be.

MAX WANTED to kick himself into next week. Why on earth had he made a statement like that? He'd gotten too comfortable with her and forgotten where she'd been. It didn't even matter to him. She'd moved past it. With his history, he wasn't one to judge.

That look in her eyes did him in. Behind the uncertainty and fear, he saw a longing that matched his own. Neither was ready to take a step toward commitment, but despite her reserved hesitation, he sensed her falling for him as hard as he'd fallen for her.

His efforts to reassure her of his disinterest in Tiffany backfired. So, he shut up before he made it worse.

MAX DROVE along Murray Boulevard overlooking Charleston Harbor and heard Sarita's breath catch. Her eyes widened at the gorgeous view. He parked on the street. The Wheeler mansion stood tall above them in all its splendor. Massive white columns supported triple piazzas. Palmetto palm trees, symbolic of South Carolina, flanked the antebellum plantation-style house.

Max stole a glance at Sarita. Striking as always, she wore a designer sundress appropriate for dinner South of Broad. Although the high emotions had subsided, a subtle distance stood between them.

"The beach house and this too?" Her face glowed with an odd combination of childlike wonder, amazement, and reverence.

He pressed his lips into a hard line and nodded. Uncertainty buffeted him as he measured her reaction.

"I can't believe you left all this."

He shrugged. "Like I told you, I had to make my own way." He unbuckled his seatbelt. "It's always here when I come back."

She stared at him for a moment, and then gazed up at the beautiful house.

He faced the child in back. Thumb in her mouth, she sat staring at the two of them, seeming to assess their relationship like some wise old sage.

"Gracia, are you hungry?" he asked.

She nodded hard. Popping her thumb out of her mouth, she freed herself from the booster seat.

Sarita took her daughter's hand as they passed through the ornate iron gates. Taking in her surroundings like a tourist at the garden show, her eyes lingered on the clipped boxwood, late-blooming crape myrtles, budding camellias, and sweet-smelling roses.

She climbed the wide stone steps with reverence, seeming mesmerized by the detailed Corinthian columns, leaded glass doors, and huge plaster urns filled with red hibiscus and trailing vines.

"It's so beautiful, so historic," she said. "I feel like I'm in an old movie."

"Gone with the wind," he quipped, as lush ferns hanging between the columns swayed in the ocean breeze.

"Rhett has come to rescue me," she said with a smile.

Would she reject him like Scarlett?

Before he could ponder that, the double doors burst open and red-headed Ruby was upon them.

"Oh!" She lit up like Hollywood lights. "You must be Max's 'friend.'"

Her emphasis hinted at that persistent push for marriage. Max loved this woman, but her constant pressure forged his steel will to refuse divulging anything more than his desire to protect a 'friend.'

Sarita looked awestruck, like a debut actress attending the Oscars for the first time.

"Aunt Ruby, this is Sarita Santos. Sarita, my Aunt Ruby." The two shook hands. "And this is her daughter Gracia."

Ruby smoothed her skirt and bent down to the child.

"You must be my little surprise!" She placed her hands on Gracia's cheeks. Seeming unable to stop herself, she drew the girl in for a hug and planted a big smooch on her forehead. "You are just adorable!" she squealed with sheer delight.

Gracia basked in the affection. She reached up to pat Ruby's red curls. When they bounced back into place, she giggled. Tugging a curl, she let it spring back.

"Gracia, stop that!" Sarita pulled her child's hand from Ruby's hair.

"Oh my," Ruby's face glowed with delight. "It's been ages since a child graced my doorstep, let alone mussed my hair!"

It didn't take a seasoned director to pick up the tinge of sadness in those words. Max knew Ruby understood the situation with Luke. In this case, Ruby exerted no guilt or pressure, only empathy and compassion for the loss they both felt.

She turned to Sarita and took her hand. "Please, come in, dear and make yourself at home. Meet my husband, Harley."

Patient Uncle Harley waited at the foot of the stairs. The strong, silent type, he always stood on the sidelines at home. No one would guess the power and influence he wielded in business.

Max studied him with fresh eyes, imagining how Sarita saw him. Big and brawny, he wore a golf shirt and pressed khakis. The illusion of casual couldn't belie his businesslike demeanor nor hide the muscle beneath those stretched sleeves. He smelled of expensive cologne and looked like he'd just come from the barber. His course dark hair grayed at the temples.

"Pleased to meet you," he said with welcoming hospitality as he greeted Sarita with a hearty handshake. His distinguished face shone with kind eyes.

"So nice to meet you," Sarita responded warmly. "You have a beautiful home." Her gaze drifted to the staircase behind him.

"This is fabulous," she gushed. "I feel like Scarlett O'Hara will make her grand entrance any moment."

"Who's Scarlett Hair-a?" Gracia piped up.

Max pointed to Ruby with her bright red hair as they erupted in laughter. She bent down and tweaked Gracia's nose.

"Oh, my heavens," she exuded. "You're so adorable I can't stand it!" She scooped the child up in her arms and whooshed into the kitchen.

Sarita looked at him with fascination and amusement as they proceeded to the heart of the home behind Ruby.

"How would you like to supervise getting dinner on the table just like Max used to?" Ruby plopped Gracia in the middle of the marble island and the child giggled with glee. "He wasn't much older than you when he moved in with us."

Max cringed as his aunt continued.

"He was so sad after his parents died. He just clung to me. So, I'd lift him up in the air and plop him on the counter beside me while I cooked."

Sarita slipped a discreet look at Max. Her expression held a fragile combination of empathy and compassion, but the tilt of her chin hinted at disdain for his deceit.

He held his breath when she turned to Ruby.

"Did that make little Max feel better?" Her demeanor revealed nothing but sympathy.

"Oh, yes, he needed to be close. Tyke missed his parents something awful. So did we. My sister and her husband, Harley and I, our lives entwined like jasmine on a trellis. Suddenly half of us were cut off at the root. That car accident left a hole in our family that only heaven can fill." She shuddered, and then recovered with a smile.

"But thank the Lord Max stayed with us that night while his parents celebrated their anniversary. I was his favorite babysitter, you know." She beamed for a moment, and then shook her head. "Never expected I'd have the honor of raising him."

Sarita offered a sympathetic smile as if she'd known all along. Ruby couldn't have guessed that he'd regarded them as mere relatives.

Despite the urge to hide his face in shame, Max appreciated Sarita's regard for his aunt's feelings. Ruby would have been devastated if she knew he'd disowned her. Why had he never considered the women would talk?

He didn't know women at all.

"Sarita, dear, please come sit and tell me all about yourself." Ruby pulled out a padded leather bar stool and moved behind the island to prepare salads.

Sarita sat on the edge of the seat, a steadying hand on Gracia's knee.

"Well, I'm a single mom, as you can guess. I recently finished college, and I work as an interior designer."

"Ooooh, I just love interior design." Ruby leaned forward with intense interest. "Charleston overflows with such arts as well as people who appreciate them."

"Charleston was mentioned often in our textbooks." Sarita glanced around with approval. "Your home epitomizes our study of architectural design - both inside and out. The décor exemplifies its beautiful bones."

"Why thank you, dear. We do love it."

Max and Harley watched this exchange from the living room. Harley raised an eyebrow.

"They're taking to one another like biscuits and gravy," he commented.

"Yeah, I see." Max expected Ruby to adore Gracia but hadn't been so sure how she'd take to the sexy single mom. Ruby's fervor had him fidgeting in his four-hundred-dollar shoes. The red-haired wonder sent danger signs flashing through his head. Not only did he have to worry about Sarita going after his money, now he had to worry about Ruby going after Sarita.

She wanted him married with children. As wanna-be executive producer of his life, she seemed to find this gorgeous, exotic, talented interior designer fit that role to the proverbial T. She might regret her enthusiasm if she knew Sarita's past. Then again, she never batted an eyelash at the single mom thing.

Ruby firmly believed in forgiveness and second chances. She'd had her share in some past life Max heard about but couldn't even imagine. Her response to Sarita Santos terrified him.

"Ruby's really taking to the girls," Harley commented.

"Yeah, I noticed that twinkle in her eyes," Max admitted with dread.

"She won't give up on this one any time soon," Harley warned.

"Whatever. Tonight, I have more important things to worry about. I have to convince that ex-con we're not together before he gets wise."

"Come and eat," Ruby called before Harley could respond.

The quintessential hostess, Ruby served dinner as a casual affair. Gracious and bubbly, she put Sarita and Gracia at ease while serving her signature shrimp and grits. As always, the biscuits were fluffy and flaky, the vegetables fresh and flavorful, and the Southern peach pie melted in your mouth.

"This is delicious!" Sarita aahed over the entrée. "The shrimp is so plump and fresh. Nothing like the frozen kind back home."

"I only use local shrimp, of course," Ruby asserted.

"I've never eaten grits before. They're so creamy and good. They aren't gritty at all!" Sarita sounded surprised.

"Is that what you've heard up north?" Ruby asked with a mock scowl. "Only that horrid *instant* kind are gritty. Unless you don't cook 'em right." She raised her chin with a flourish and spooned a second helping on her plate.

Gracia laughed at her silly charade.

"Now eat up." Ruby waved her spoon toward the mountains of food. "Whatever you don't eat is going with you to Max's house."

Max's skin prickled with awareness at reference to *his* house. He glanced at Sarita and caught the daggers subdued in her smiling eyes.

"When are you heading north, son?" Harley asked in his reserved manner, as gracious as his wife.

Max dabbed his mouth with the linen napkin.

"Right after dinner. I'm packed and ready to go. If I drive all night, I can get a fresh start in the morning."

"Some fresh start," Ruby interjected. "You'll be falling asleep at the wheel and feel like a zombie the rest of the day."

"Why don't you fly?" Harley asked.

"I don't want any way of tracking my comings and goings. I'm staying under the radar."

Ruby rose an eyebrow in warning and wagged her finger. "You'd best get some sleep tonight and get your fresh start for driving. You'll feel better after a good night's rest. And at least you'll arrive safely." She laid down the law as if that was that.

Max frowned. Her bossiness grated on him.

"Ruby has some sixth sense about these things," Harley added in his calming voice. "You dare not ignore her or you'll likely regret it."

"Been there, done that." Max's resigned admission satisfied Ruby although he had no intention of meeting her demands.

HURT BY MAX'S DECEPTION, Sarita wanted to slam him for lying to her. Insinuating his rich aunt and uncle were just relatives was one thing, the outright lie about owning the beach house was another. What else had he lied about? How far did this go?

She silently fumed throughout dinner and knew Max sensed it. For all his hurry to head out, he picked at his dessert and smiled her way, apparently waiting for her to simmer down.

Fine. She wouldn't make a scene.

Yet once outside, the smiles ceased. Cool and distant, she marched to the car and buckled Gracia into her car seat. Thumb in her mouth, Gracia began nodding off. Max loaded Tupperware dishes of food into the trunk without a word.

Pouting in the front seat, she fought back tears. Her heart wrenched at his bald-faced lie. How dare he give her some brooding cold shoulder when he should be apologizing. Sure, he'd been taken advantage of, hurt in the past, but he didn't have to take it out on her. The least he could do was explain himself...

Whoa. The least he could do?

Despite his lies, he'd gone way out of his way to protect her and Gracia. After driving here in the middle of the night, housing and feeding them for days, he was leaving them in the protection of his home and family while he made another twelve-hour drive to cover their tracks.

In the privacy of his car, the air hung thick between them. He'd done more than anyone could expect to protect them. Now she realized his deception protected *himself*.

Although hurt at his lack of trust in her, she couldn't blame him. With more than enough grief and guilt on her shoulders, she couldn't bear him going away on a sour note. Glancing over at his handsome profile, she remembered what *he'd* been through, and her heart softened.

"I'm sorry about your parents." Her peace offering held genuine empathy. "How old were you when they died?"

"Four." His jaw clenched. Fighting raw emotion, his cool demeanor crumbled.

Gracia would be four in a few months. Barely older than her, he'd suffered that devastating loss.

"Do you remember them?" she murmured.

"Not much. Bits and pieces, little things." He quieted again, seeming hesitant to open up.

She yearned to bridge this distance, to relate to him and diffuse the conflict between them.

"Like what?"

He glanced at her sideways. Then he heaved a pent-up breath.

"It's weird. My most vivid memory is my mom catching me playing on the stairs. I'd just begun walking, and she was afraid I'd get hurt on the hardwood staircase. But I really wanted to climb those steps. I had a grand time sneaking up about three stairs. I can still remember hearing her high heels click across the marble. Her scolding was gentle, but she barricaded the staircase. It must have been some big deal at the time for me to remember that, of all things."

As much as she wanted to relate to him, Max's story was lost on Sarita. Hardwood staircases and marble floors did not grace middle class homes. Those two points reiterated his wealth, now from birth. Like a slap in the face, the reminder of his deception rekindled her resentment.

She pictured a doting mother, but high heels didn't portray a full-time mom. "What did your parents do for a living?"

"They ran a textile mill in North Carolina where I grew up." He heaved another breath, seeming relieved to open up. "Mom and Aunt Ruby inherited it from my grandfather." He seemed resigned to the fact that she was attuned to his fortune, realizing there was no sense trying to hide it any longer. "When Grandpa retired, my dad was promoted to CEO. He hired his friend Harley as the Chief Financial Officer. The rest, as they say, is history."

"Tight-knit family." Keeping a light tone, she bit back the envy that threatened to strangle her.

"Yeah. Losing my parents was hard on Ruby. And me."

"It's good you had each other." She strove to be

compassionate, but couldn't forget all that money didn't hurt, either. "Do you have any brothers or sisters?"

"No. I guess my mom had trouble getting pregnant." He paused. "Aunt Ruby never could carry a baby. They were sisters."

"You're an only child twice then."

"I guess you could say that." His wary tone warned her of shaky ground. She wanted to show empathy but could only think of the loving relationship Max shared with his aunt and uncle, and the double inheritance that made life so much easier.

The rest of the way, they dwelled on their own thoughts. At the beach house, Max unloaded the food but left his bags packed in the trunk. After getting her and Gracia settled in, he turned toward her.

"I guess I'm off now." He touched her cheek.

"I thought you were going to get some sleep," Sarita said.

"Don't start mimicking Ruby, okay?" Defensive, he dropped his hand and eyed her.

"Sorry." She wrapped her arms around him, desperate to regain closeness before he left. But he'd deceived Ruby too. Distrust niggled at her, even as she enjoyed his warm comfort.

"I'm sorry if you misunderstood." He worked his jaw as if wanting to say more but realizing the futility of excuses.

She needed to confront him about dishonesty but couldn't bear a confrontation as he was leaving.

"Ruby's overbearing," he concluded. "I go along so she'll lay off, but I refuse to let her order me around." He kissed Sarita's hair, sending tingles throughout her scalp. "I'm not twelve anymore."

CHASING SANDPIPERS

Max wasn't twenty anymore either. Thirty wasn't old, but after a long day, the 750-mile trip took its toll. By three A.M., he struggled to keep his eyes open. The Escalade's tires nudged the shoulder, jerking him alert. He resigned to finding a hotel.

Too bad he found himself in the middle of nowhere, somewhere in the foothills of West Virginia. Or had he crossed into southern Ohio? So close and yet so far.

A rest area sign loomed ahead. He could either crash in the car or crash the car. After losing his parents in a car accident, he wouldn't take the chance of that happening to his son. Max clung to hope that someday Luke would know his father.

He pulled into the rest area and parked. Adjusting the seat as far back as possible, he shifted to his side. He struggled to find a comfortable position with brake pedals under his feet, a steering wheel at his hip, and no soft pillow or blanket. He should move to the passenger side, or the back seat. But he was too tired to budge.

He might as well have slept at home in his nice cozy bed and left in the morning.

Aunt Ruby was right. Again. Would he ever listen? Not as long as she kept pushing. Her domineering made him resist. He couldn't help himself.

Another good thing about Sarita - she never told him what to do. She respected his intelligence and deferred to his judgment. Other than his deception, she presumed he knew best.

He toed off his shoes and banged his hip on the steering wheel. Yeah, he knew best all right.

MAX DROVE into Crystal Falls at lunchtime, starved and exhausted. He headed around the square toward Sarita's apartment. As he passed cars parked on the opposite side of the square, he slapped himself alert and scrutinized the scene.

Bull's eye. He recognized the red Cadillac Sarita had mentioned parked a block away. But no one sat in the car. On a hunch, Max figured Ramone hung out at Frosty's. The café and ice cream parlour below Sarita's apartment would be the perfect lookout point where he could blend into the crowd.

He parked on the street and headed into Frosty's. At the door, the wafting smell of burgers and fries made his mouth water. This place had the best cheeseburgers in Bloomfield County. Whether he spotted Ramone or not, he wasn't leaving without filling his belly.

Scanning the tiny café, he saw booths filled with laughing teenagers, a family with twins, and several tables with young professionals on their lunch break. He watched with yearning as a handsome couple in a corner booth stared into one another's eyes. He forced himself to look away. Ramone was nowhere in sight, but his gaze settled on a lone Latino sitting by the window.

The guy resembled Sarita. Could it be her brother Pedro? He

faced the alley driveway where Sarita usually parked. He'd see anyone coming in or out. Did he camp out here all day?

Max sat opposite him at the next table. He'd have clear vision of the guy without even looking up from his plate.

By stroke of luck, the older waitress who owned the place headed toward him in her strawberry ice cream-colored uniform. She'd have the scoop.

"What can I get for ya, honey?" Cracking her gum just like an old episode of *Flo* at her diner, she was a slice of Americana right here in Crystal Falls. Posed with her pad, she pulled a pencil from behind her ear.

"Double cheeseburger and fries, all the way."

"Milkshake with that?" she asked.

"Oh no." He patted his flat belly. Starved as he was, a milkshake would overdo it. "Just a Coke," he replied. He could go for sweet tea, but it wasn't common up north.

"Coming right up." The woman scribbled 'DFC' on her pad and turned to go.

"I was wondering," he blurted before she rushed off. "Have you seen the woman who lives upstairs?"

The waitress stopped in her tracks. She tucked the pencil behind her ear and frowned.

"I've been looking for her," Max said. Out the corner of his eye, Max caught the Latino looking up from his coffee.

"The dark-haired cutie with the little girl?" The waitress didn't wait for an answer. "She used to come in and out like clockwork. Off to work before nine, home by five-thirty, unloading groceries Saturday morning, and dressed for church on Sunday. But I haven't seen hide nor hair of her for nigh to a week now."

"Just great." Max pounded a fist on the table, acting out the best worried face he could muster.

"Has it been over a week?" She rubbed temple. "I'm not sure, but one morning I came in at six for the breakfast crowd and her car was already gone. Sorry, but I haven't seen it since."

"Have you heard anything? Noises upstairs, anyone coming around looking for her?"

"Are you her boyfriend?" She narrowed her eyes. "Haven't I seen you around?"

Max nodded, letting sadness seep into his face. He glimpsed the Latino staring into his coffee. All ears, his body leaned forward. Beneath a shock of greasy hair, he stole a look in their direction.

"Yeah, but we had a falling out." Max didn't broadcast it but spoke loud enough for the Latino to hear every word.

"I'm sorry to hear that." The waitress stilled with intense interest.

"Her old boyfriend came around." Max shook his head. "Bad news, as you can imagine. She said she was splitting town and we argued. I told her she could stay with me if she was afraid of him, but she'd have none of it. Said she was going to Nevada, of all places." He pounded a fist on the table. "Man, I never thought she'd go through with it."

The waitress got a frightened look. Turning away from the Latino, she whispered, "Be careful. You may not be the only one looking for her."

Max got quiet, laid the sorrow on thick. "I thought we had something going, you know?" He flashed puppy dog eyes at her. "I can't believe she just took off. Like she's gonna hide out west. I hope she doesn't end up in Vegas, ya know?"

Fear and a hint of bad memories flashed across the woman's face. "She probably has a good reason for leaving." She stuffed the pad into her apron as if to conclude this conversation. "That burger'll be up shortly." With a pat on his hand, she headed for the kitchen.

Max kept a discreet eye on the Latino. He finished his coffee. Then he stood with a smug expression. Tossing a five on the table, he waltzed out.

The guy headed across the square to the red Cadillac. Max

could follow him, but he'd accomplished his goal. Chief Hunter already knew the red Caddy and where Ramone holed up. He was keeping an eye on them. Besides, Max couldn't chance this guy suspecting anything.

And here comes that burger. He didn't eat greasy food often, and he was going to enjoy it. As soon as the waitress left with a smile, he snatched a fry and dipped it into the little cup of ketchup. Salty, greasy, potato skin heaven.

Biting into the sesame seed bun, he let the flavors mingle on his tongue - juicy beef, melted cheese, ripe tomato, crisp lettuce, tangy pickles and just the right combination of ketchup and mayo.

After the best tasting burger he'd ever had, it was time to call on the chief.

The Town Hall basement housed police headquarters. Hunter bent over a pile of paperwork when Max rapped on the open door frame. A large cardboard container lay open at the edge of his desk.

"Max, good to see you!" The chief stood to shake Max's hand. "Have a seat." He motioned to a chair and tossed the container with remnants of ketchup, grease, and bits of fries.

"I'm sorry to interrupt your lunch." Max hesitated at the chair.

"No, no." The big guy patted his bulging gut. "I've had my fill. Frosty's burger and fries - best in town. Time to get back to work."

Did the hefty man get the double too? Talk about a guilt trip.

"What brings you in?" His voice took on a hint of worry as he sat. "Is Sarita all right?"

Max settled into the chair. "Yeah, she's safe." He spoke in a low voice. "I came back to throw Ramone off her trail - to make it look like we're not together anymore."

"Good plan. How do you figure on doing that?"

"Well, I spotted the red Cadillac and found a Latino hanging out at Frosty's. Had some lunch and asked the waitress if she'd seen Sarita. Gave her a sob story that she left me for Nevada."

The chief leaned forward to say something when his cell phone rang. Flustered, he grabbed the vibrating gadget on his desk and checked the number. "Excuse me a minute." He punched a button and barked, "Yeah?"

His eyebrows shot up as he listened. "No kidding." Taking on a satisfied expression, he leaned back in his chair. "Max is here right now. I'll let him know."

Max's heart pounded with anticipation as the chief shut off the phone.

"Seems your buddy Ramone just checked out of his old girlfriend's with packed bags. Headed west on Route 90. Deputy followed him to the county line. Looks like your little ploy worked."

"Just now?" Max checked his watch. "Sarita's brother must have called Ramone as soon as he left Frosty's."

"No doubt." The chief leaned back with a smile.

"Maybe Ramone took the bait," Max said with uncertainty. It seemed too easy.

Route 90 west also led to the airport, or to Interstate 77 which headed south straight into the Carolinas. He kept his thoughts to himself, unwilling to name Sarita's location out loud, even in the police department. Max thanked the chief and headed out to see Sarita's mom. He needed to know if she'd seen Ramone.

Maria Santos answered the door with a drink in her hand. Not a good sign. It might be five o'clock somewhere, but it was barely after lunch in Crystal Falls.

Max had never met the woman, but Sarita briefed him on

what to expect. They shared some features, but this woman sported bags under her eyes, an unhealthy pallor, and a hundred extra pounds.

"Hello. Mrs. Santos?"

She looked Max up and down as a grin spread over her face. "How can I help ya, honey?"

"My name is Max Carter." He stuck out a hand to shake her hot, sweaty one. "I'm dating your daughter, Sarita."

Her face lit up. "That girl always finds the good-looking men." She took in his expensive haircut and Ralph Lauren polo, and then glanced up at the Escalade parked out front. "Looks like she hit the jackpot this time."

Cringing, Max managed a smile. "Thank you, ma'am."

She opened the door wide. "Well don't just stand there on the stoop. Come on in." Waving a hand, she led him into the dreary apartment.

A dog-eared *Good Housekeeping* magazine sprawled open on the well-worn sofa. Several half-empty glasses and an overflowing ashtray littered the coffee table. A rotating fan did nothing to squelch the stale reek of cigarettes and suffocating heat.

"Sorry, it's warm in here," she said. "Let's go outside." She led him to a tiny balcony with ancient metal chairs. Their peeling paint fluttered in the welcome breeze.

"Would you like a drink?" she offered.

"No thank you. I won't take much of your time."

"Why not? I've got all day." She plopped into a metal chair as it screeched under her weight.

He chose the cleanest chair and resisted a rude impulse to brush it off before he sat. How did Sarita turn out to be who she was when raised like this?

"Now that Sarita and Gracia are gone, I've got nothing but time on my hands." She swilled her drink.

"She really left?" He let sorrow pour over his face as his body drooped in the chair. "Do you know where she went?"

"She mailed me a letter from Nevada." Mrs. Santos shook her head. "Don't know why she'd go there."

He feigned a defeated sigh as relief surged through him. "Do you think she'll come back?"

"I don't know." She scrunched her pudgy face and looked him in the eye. "You sure you don't know where she is?" She pointed an accusing finger.

"No, ma'am." He squirmed under her scrutiny. He was such a bad liar. "She said her old boyfriend was hunting her down."

Her dark eyes bulged with terror and her olive skin turned ashen.

"He's a bad character." Her hands shook as she steadied the glass on her wide knee.

"Did he come here looking for Sarita?"

She nodded hard. Her jowls swayed and salt and pepper curls bounced around her head.

"He was real mean, honey. After I showed him the letter from Nevada, he said he oughta kill me, but Sarita wouldn't even care. That cut to the quick." She swirled the ice in her glass and took a gulp of what looked like ginger ale and smelled like rum.

"He said he needed the kid to hurt Sarita." Her glass sloshed as she set it down and leaned toward him with alcoholic breath. "He's after Gracia."

"Sarita will take care of her little girl." The confident words didn't match his gathering doubts or tense muscles.

"I didn't think that creep would follow her all the way out west. But I wish I hadn't told him where she was. He's out to get Gracia and he's one mean gringo."

"He's headed for Nevada?"

She nodded. "Sarita told me to tell him she left town, to show him the letter so he would leave me alone. He looked skeptical but he studied the postmark over and over." Her voice cracked. "He memorized the name of the town. I just know it."

Frowning, Max swallowed his revulsion. He leaned forward with compassion and placed his hand over hers.

"Try not to worry. Sarita's smart. She'll protect her daughter."

Worry seemed to drain from Maria like the sweat beading on her glass. If only Max felt so relieved. 'Skeptical' was not the reaction he'd wanted from Ramone. Panic seeped into his bones.

He'd left Sarita and Gracia alone and Ramone was on the loose, headed who knows where. Max debated whether to head straight back to Charleston then and there. But if he didn't get a decent night's sleep he'd nod off at the wheel. That wouldn't help anyone. And he needed to check on his business while he was in town. He had every confidence Brett would hold down the fort, yet there were issues to attend to - finances, bill paying, checking the mail.

He'd take care of business, see Tiffany, get some sleep, and be on the road before dawn.

Discounting his doubts as irrational, he reminded himself Ramone had no way of finding Sarita on the Isle of Palms. If he didn't head to Nevada, he'd likely look for her in Puerto Rico as she expected. The more Max thought about it, leaving the U.S. mainland would be the perfect choice for a man like Ramone.

SARITA CLOSED her phone after talking to Max. Surprised how much she missed him, she moped around the beach house, straightening up while Gracia napped. Despite good news that Ramone left town, she couldn't return to Crystal Falls. Pedro was watching and Ramone would be back, meaner than ever.

Homesick and lonely, she didn't know if she'd ever be able to return to the town she loved.

Hugging herself, wishing Max were there to hug her instead, she paced. Her bare feet felt the grittiness of sand on the hardwood floors. With nervous energy, she pulled out a broom and swept. The absent-minded task made her smile. She'd loved the beach as a child in Puerto Rico. How wonderful it would be for Gracia to grow up near the beach too.

Broom in hand, she stopped at the expanse of windows overlooking the ocean. The high afternoon sun sparkled across the water. Beautiful as it was, it didn't compare to the clear turquoise depths of the Caribbean.

She not only missed the water, but the vibrant colors of her homeland, the culture, the laid-back attitude, and the people. She missed her grandmother most of all. Her photo hung in Sarita's apartment like a shrine. She pictured Graciana Santos, whom she'd named Gracia after, hanging wash outside the tiny yellow cottage where she raised eight kids. The surrounding palm trees bent in the ocean breeze, offering peeks at the Caribbean Sea.

Puerto Rico would have been the perfect escape - if she hadn't blabbed how much she missed it to Ramone. Every frigid winter day, she'd griped about the cold, wishing for the balmy weather of her youth. He'd expect her to run there.

Besides, she had no money to get to Puerto Rico, and how would she find an interior design job in that poverty-stricken country? She'd worked too hard to abandon her dream career.

Maybe she should settle in South Carolina. If she found a job, she could get her own place. Charleston enjoyed a subtropical climate, beaches and palm trees, a quaintness similar to Crystal Falls and deep layers of history. For a designer, the architecture and artsy society rivaled any city in America. For a specialist in garden rooms, the long growing season and garden-oriented culture put her skills in high demand.

By week's end, the city had grown on her as she fell in love with Charleston - and with Max. He had family here. Would he stay if she did?

Could there be a happy-ever-after for them?

※

MAX SPENT the afternoon at Carter Racing catching up, then left his business in the capable hands of his administrative assistant and his good friend Brett. Too tired to push himself any longer, he resigned to getting a good night's sleep and driving back to Charleston early.

First, see Tiffany.

Thinking of Ramone's threat, Max mustered his most downtrodden face as he opened the salon door. Only two chairs had clients. One was Myrtle Winthrop. Her smile curled up like The Grinch Who Stole Christmas.

"Hey, Tiff." He nodded apologetically at Myrtle. "Can I get a trim?"

"Sure, Max." The vivacious blonde sauntered toward him, leaving Myrtle in smelly curlers to watch and listen. Tiff pointed to a chair.

Max sat, hating what he was about to do.

"You're early for a trim." Tiffany ran her long nails through the hair at his nape, sending chills through him. Her touch used to ignite him. Now he felt nothing but distaste for her fake nails, fake breasts, and fake concern.

"Guess I just wanted to see you." He offered a desperate smile, cringing at his own deception. He needed to manipulate the very rumor mill he detested.

She stood back and twirled a lock of her bleach-blond hair, raising one impossibly perfect brow. "'Bout time you came to your senses." Striking a seductive pose, she placed one hand on her rounded hip. "What happened to the brunette you were seeing?"

"Sarita?" He scrunched his face. "She left for Nevada. Running from some old boyfriend. Who needs that mess?" He looked up at her with lonely hope.

"Interesting." Tiffany shot a look at Myrtle. She whipped out a black cape and covered him, rubbing her hands along his neck as she fastened it. Her fingers raked through his hair, caressing his scalp. Jutting her chest, she rattled on about the good times they had.

His muscles tensed as he remembered her dragging him to look at Jaguars and her blatant hints about a huge diamond sale. Blocking out her jabber, he listened in on Myrtle's conversation with the woman beside her.

"He didn't even spend the night," she whispered. "As soon as they left the balcony, he was out the door."

Was Myrtle Winthrop actually telling the truth? Or was she talking about someone else?

After the unnecessary haircut and a generous tip for Tiffany, Max headed home to the south hills of Riverside. His house looked lived in, just the way he liked it. Yet the windows sparkled, and the bamboo floors shone from his housekeeper's visit earlier that week. The plants, both his and Sarita's, grew healthy and green. The décor made him long for Sarita.

He dialed her number.

"Max!" She sounded excited to hear from him. Wind and waves roared in the background.

"Hey there. You're at the beach, aren't you?"

"Of course. Sunset on the beach." Her voice rang with merriment. "That's the routine."

"It sounds windy," he noted.

"Yeah, it's spitting rain. We're all alone out here."

Sudden, fierce longings overwhelmed him. He yearned to be

alone on that beach with Sarita, to see that smile, kiss those lips, and wrap his arms around her.

A wave of happy memories made him miss her as if he'd been gone for months. The surprising part was that he longed for Charleston almost as much as he longed for her. Their happiest moments happened there. They'd gotten to know each other, and at the beach house he'd fallen in love with her.

That realization struck him like a wallop.

"I miss you," she whispered.

"I miss you more," he admitted like some lovesick goof.

"When are you coming back?" Her voice filled with longing, accentuating his.

"Tomorrow." Excitement thrilled him at the thought of seeing her again. He'd only been gone a day.

"Good! It's not the same without you. Gracia keeps asking when you're coming home."

"How's she doing?" He smiled at the thought of that little cutie playing in the sand.

"Just making sandcastles. She's - " Sarita drew in a sharp breath. "She was right here. Where is she?" Her voice rose with alarm. "Oh! Oh no!" Her breath came fast. Wind whistled over the phone as it jostled with her running. "She's chasing sand pipers. Gracia!" she called out. "No! Gracia, come back!" With breathless desperation Sarita's terrified voice huffed into the phone. "She's almost to the pier!" She gasped.

Max's heart plummeted. With the whoosh of air and a thud, her phone hit the beach. A whisper of sand swept by with the pound of footsteps receding in the distance.

Then a far-off wail punctuated the air waves.

"Nnnooooooo!" Beginning low, the guttural groan intensified to a high-pitched scream.

CLOUDS COVERED THE MOON

"Sarita! Sarita, are you alright?" Max yelled into the phone. Her muffled wails faded into the distance. Then nothing.

His blood froze. His heart stopped as he waited ten, twenty, thirty seconds. A full minute passed, then two, three. He heard nothing but the ocean, waves rushing in. The calming rhythm threatened to drive him mad with its roar against the far away silence. So far away, too far for him to do anything but listen with horror and regret.

Unable to bear it, he ended the call. Hitting speed dial for his friend Ty, he got voicemail. Max growled a desperate message. Then he dialed 911 and gave what little information he knew to the impatient operator and hung up in frustration.

Gracia. His mind reeled with the possibilities. She could have wandered into the ocean. Sarita might be able to save her.

But his gut told him otherwise.

Ramone. The scumbag did his homework. Max thought he could hide his wealth, but he underestimated Ramone. The monster found her.

STINGING rain pelted the deserted seashore beneath a dark, angry sky.

Sheer terror knifed through Sarita as she raced across the expanse of beach. "Noooooooo!"

Panicked, she tripped, her feet mired in the sand. As she struggled to catch her running daughter, the distance between them grew.

Too close to the water, her child ducked into the shadows of the pier. A dark figure appeared. Gracia screamed, turning to run.

Sarita's heart stopped.

The man snatched up Gracia and ran from the beach.

Sarita shrieked. "Stop him! Someone stop him! He has my baby!" She bolted - gasping, reaching, wailing. Not a soul heard her but the monster who stole her child.

Arms outstretched toward her mother over the man's shoulder, Gracia howled as her horrified face disappeared behind a building.

Adrenalin propelled Sarita to the path, toward the sound of her daughter's cries. She sailed between the buildings and reached pavement in time to see a small black car peel away.

Her head whirled in search of help. She patted her clothes for her phone. It was gone. She'd dropped it on the beach.

A tall stranger stepped from a restaurant, pointing a remote toward a blinking SUV.

Sarita lunged for him. "Follow that car!" she screamed, arms flailing like a crazy woman.

The man's eyes bugged out. He looked toward the road and then back to her. "What car?" He stepped backward, dropping his keys into his pocket as he put distance and his large vehicle between them.

Her head spun. The car was gone. "Gracia! My baby!" she wailed in desperation, arms outstretched toward the empty road. She turned toward the baffled man. "Call 911!" she ordered. "He... he took... my... my baby!"

The energy surge drained from her as she dissolved into a bawling heap. Staring into the sky, she begged, "Why God? Why did you let him take my baby?"

WHEN MAX'S PHONE RANG, he almost dropped it on the floor snatching it from his pocket. He fumbled for the answer button with breathless anticipation. "Sarita?"

The male caller chuckled. "No, Max. It's Chief Hunter. Missing her already, huh?"

Max gulped. Hunter didn't know the half of it. "What's up, Chief?" he asked with a brusque manner.

Hunter cleared his throat, getting to business as if chastised. "We did a little research on Ramone. I talked to the stripper he was staying with. She was happy to help. The creep left her high and dry. He slept with her, ate her food, and drank her booze. Once he had his fill, he ignored her and used her Internet all day. Then he got a phone call around lunch time and took off like a bat outta hell. Stole her car and every cent she had."

A sick tension pervaded Max. Every muscle in his body contracted with fear. Ramone knew Max was here and Sarita was unprotected.

"That stripper was so ticked," the chief continued. "She let us check her computer to track his searches."

Hunter paused. "He googled you, Max. Found your background records, where you lived and went to school, married and divorced, where your son lives. Then he zoned in on your aunt and uncle who had custody of you as a child. It appears they have money?"

Max's head throbbed. Coming here had shifted the focus on him, not taken it away. How could he have been so stupid? How could he have left her all alone?

Hunter's voice took on a sense of urgency. "I don't know where Sarita's hiding, but if it's in South Carolina, get her out of there *now*. Ramone booked a flight that landed at the Charleston airport a couple hours ago. He mapped your uncle's residences on Murray Boulevard and the Isle of Palms."

Intense fear and rage erupted in Max. His fists bunched.

"Thanks, Chief." He pushed the off button and hurled the phone against the wall.

HOURS LATER, Sarita curled into a ball of agony on the sofa. In shock, she ignored the detectives commiserating by the door before letting themselves out with a few staid words. Ty manned a wired phone in the front room, giving Sarita privacy and space.

Uncle Harley whispered a solemn, "Take care of yourself," and headed home.

Aunt Ruby stayed, sitting close. She lit a tropical-scented candle that lent fragrance and light to the empty, lifeless room.

Gracia was gone.

Cried out, Sarita had no tears left. Like a zombie, she stared out at the dark sea as her world crumbled around her. She'd let her precious daughter be snatched away. She turned to answer the phone and Gracia wandered off, unaware of the danger. Then in a flash, he took her.

She shuddered. What kind of mother was she? Far worse than her own mother's alcoholic neglect, she'd let her baby be *kidnapped* while she was distracted by a *man*. She wanted to weep but no tears came. Her body stilled in stunned silence.

Clouds covered the moon. Waves crashed against the shore as a gathering storm whipped up the sea. Palm fronds battered the house, but nothing could batter Sarita worse than the vision of her daughter screaming in the arms of that madman. The scene ran through her mind over and over, torturing her.

Aunt Ruby's hand patted her knee.

"Stop blaming yourself. Children wander off, that's what they do. You couldn't have known that... that *man* was out there."

Anguish suffocated Sarita inside the calm cocoon where she hid.

"But I did know." She ground out, like a chick pecking its way out of an egg. Her shell cracked. Light streamed in, air rushed her lungs, and she fought her way out of the shell. She pounded her knees, kicking and bellowing, "I knew he was out there, threatening to hurt Gracia. That's why we came here." Her face contorted with pain. "What have I done? Oh Lord, what's he doing to her?" she wailed to her Father in heaven.

"No, no, you can't think that way." Ruby's long arms wrapped around her quaking body. "The Lord is watching over her. He'll protect your child and bring her back to you. You have to believe that. We'll do everything in our power to get her back. We'll put that criminal in jail where he belongs."

Sarita shook her head. "What did I ever see in him? I let a monster father my child."

"Shush now." Ruby smoothed her hair. The soothing sensation calmed Sarita a bit. "You stop thinking that way. Blaming yourself doesn't help. We have to figure out where he'd take her, and you know the man. Be grateful for that. Start thinking where he'd go, what he knows, how he thinks."

Like a mother hen, Ruby stretched her wings over Sarita. She smelled of gardenias and cinnamon. Sarita snuggled close and let herself be comforted as her thoughts drifted to Ramone's mind, that wicked, evil place.

She cringed with the memory as the stench of whiskey and cigarette smoke came back to her. Once again, she was eighteen, standing on that stage.

Desperation had prevailed over humiliation. Feeling dirty, she peeled off her clothes for Ramone only. Her fingers fumbled with every button as her heart hammered.

"Dance," he ordered.

Needing approval and acceptance as much as she needed to survive on the streets, she swallowed the agonizing shame. Dead inside, she reached for that cold chrome pole.

Ramone had leered with a greasy smirk of possession and lust.

Shriveling, her insides flinched as she pushed the memory away. She knew him all right. Ramone owned and controlled. Anyone who defied him became his prey. He stalked and tortured, watched his victims swing in the wind and enjoyed every second of it.

Was that the answer?

She jerked back.

Ruby startled. "What is it?"

"He's close," she declared with certainty. "He wants to see me suffer. Wherever he's hiding, it's nearby."

WITH NO FLIGHTS available until the next day, the drive from Crystal Falls to Charleston took twelve hours even for a man on a mission. Max burst into the dim, silent house in the wee hours of morning. Sarita stared out the dark window as Ruby stroked her hair.

"Sarita," he said with desperate yearning.

She leapt from the sofa and ran to him. They held one another like lovers long separated. It felt so good to be with her, to have her in his arms. Yet grief twisted around him like a leaden mass of barbed wire, heavy and penetrating, strangling him with painful jabs that tore at his very being.

For a long time, neither spoke. They took what little solace they could from one another. He breathed in the scent of her herbal shampoo and reveled in her clinging warmth.

Then he sensed movement. Aunt Ruby wandered into the kitchen. In a moment, she returned with a tray of steaming tea and fragrant, hot cinnamon rolls. She left it on the coffee table and slipped out the door.

The woman was a saint, and oh-so-perceptive.

Sarita loosened her embrace. "Ruby's wonderful."

"Yeah, I know." Guilt washed over him for ever needing to get away from her. How many horrid emotions could pile on him in one day? He needed that calming tea.

He led Sarita to the sofa. They didn't speak. No words could quell the pain. They sat and he put a mug to her lips. She drank. They fortified themselves with tea and a bite to eat, then they fell asleep in each other's arms.

TALKING CAME IN THE MORNING.

The house phone shrilled at six a.m. The Isle of Palms chief of police wanted to question Max.

Sitting at the police station without coffee, let alone breakfast,

Max swallowed the toothpaste taste in his mouth as he talked and talked.

They covered how he'd met Sarita, his brief dealings with Ramone, his encounter with the Latino at the café in Crystal Falls, and the events leading to the kidnapping.

But did the cops need to know every aspect of his relationship with Sarita, his entire background, details about his son and ex-wife, his business, his aunt and uncle, his upbringing for Pete's sake?

Did the man know everything in his brain yet?

Unlike Chief Hunter in Crystal Falls, this smalltown cop sat straight and trim, polished and strictly by-the-book. Max studied his tanned face, all serious and eager to crack the biggest case of his young career.

"Do you have any coffee?" Max needed a break, and he needed caffeine.

Chief Sullivan's hard mask evaporated into a smile.

"Sure. I'm sorry, where's my southern hospitality?" He stood and walked to the door. "Cream and sugar?"

Max turned to the lanky yet muscular man, built like a surfer. As a matter of fact, Max recalled that face and build carrying a bright blue board across the beach.

The hint of recognition flickered as though Max saw him for the first time. Due to sheer exhaustion and the lack of caffeine, he'd been in a fog for the last hour.

Sullivan stood waiting for his answer.

"Just black, thank you."

As soon as the chief left the room, Max thought of Gracia.

Was she sheltered from the rain? Was she cold and hungry? Had she cried all night, screaming with nightmares each time she dozed off like her mama had?

The chief returned with coffee. Max fought back those thoughts, focusing on the mug. Deep blue and inscribed 'Isle of Palms', it sported the palm tree and moon insignia representing

South Carolina's state flag. The coffee smelled of freshly ground beans and went down smooth.

"Are we about done here?" Max gathered his bearings. "I think you know everything there is to know about me."

"Not quite." Sullivan squirmed in his chair. "You own a sizable business. Your aunt and uncle are quite wealthy." He leaned forward intently. "What's your financial situation?"

Max set the coffee aside. "That's none of your business."

Sullivan raised an eyebrow. "Let me put it this way, how much is Sarita worth to you? How much - "

"You've got a lot of nerve, buddy." Didn't surfer cop think Max could attract a beautiful woman on his own merits? Rage mounted inside him. He hurtled to his feet, towering over the unflinching chief, fists clenched at his sides. "Who do you think you are? You're supposed to be finding Gracia, not analyzing my relationships."

"Calm down, Max." Sullivan half-raised his hands in surrender. "Have a seat and I'll explain. This isn't about your relationship. But I have a feeling it *is* about your money."

Max stood glowering.

"Please sit down and let me finish."

Max stared him down for a moment. Then he perched at the edge of his seat, ready to jump down the man's throat.

"From Ramone's perspective, would you pay a ransom?" Sullivan tightened his jaw. "How much is the little girl worth? I mean in dollars."

Max's heart stopped.

Once Ramone found the connection to Uncle Harley, it hadn't been that tough. Max hadn't expected him to look that hard, hadn't expected he'd be a target at all. He'd worried about Sarita hurting him because of his money. It turned out his money hurt her.

"She's worth every cent I have," he admitted.

Taken aback, Sullivan commented, "But you've only known her a month?"

"I know what she's going through." Max had lost his child to a custody battle. Sarita lost hers to a kidnapper. He could only imagine her devastation and fear.

Sullivan nodded. With a grim expression, he discussed tapping phones and police surveillance.

"We'll find this perpetrator," Sullivan assured Max as he dismissed him.

The month with Sarita felt as if he'd known her forever. He'd met his match. Was she his soul mate?

Would she even want to be with him after this was over? Or would she resent the sight of him and his money and the pain it caused her and Gracia?

Would Gracia even survive?

Anguish filled him as he wandered through the day. Ty kept vigil near the phone with wires and recording devices at the ready. Sarita huddled on the sofa with a blank stare. Max tried to comfort her, to feed her, but nothing worked.

He retreated to the balcony. Wind whipped his hair as he looked out at the stormy sea. Some fool in a small fishing boat sat among the choppy waves with a fishing pole. The idiot risked his life as if a fish would find his bait in rough waters. Max's gut churned with disgust. He didn't need the authorities diverted to some overturned amateur boater when they needed to be looking for Gracia.

DAY DRAGGED INTO NIGHT. At last, the phone rang.

Sarita's stomach clenched as she jumped from the sofa.

"It's the chief," Ty said as he checked caller ID. He snatched up the phone. "Evening, chief. We're on speaker phone. What's the news?"

She hunched over the phone as Max came up behind her with a comforting hug. Chief Sullivan's voice boomed across the wires.

"They found the stolen black Honda with Ohio plates abandoned at the airport in Mount Pleasant," he reported.

Her heart dropped to the soles of her feet. Gone. Gracia was gone. Her body stiffened. She stood leaden, unable to move or speak.

"A worker saw a child fitting Gracia's description walking around the airport."

"Was she alright? Did she look hurt?" Max asked.

Sarita's brain struggled for words, but she remained frozen.

"The child appeared groggy, but she may have been drugged to keep her quiet."

"D... dr... drugged?" Sarita choked out. Tears blurred her vision as she searched Ty's face. Hugging herself, she twisted her shirt in her fingers.

Max's arm held her shoulders, squeezing tight.

"Did she look *drugged* or *injured*?" Ty asked. "Give it to us straight."

"Groggy. No visible blood or bruises. That's all I know. He could have given her something as harmless as Benadryl."

Her knees turned to jelly. Her twisting fingers wrenched a hole through her shirt.

"Look, folks, don't panic," the chief's voice resonated from the phone. "I promise we're doing all we can. Ty cut the speaker."

"Yes sir," Ty responded with military respect. He listened to the phone intently and ended the call with police formalities.

Sarita's head throbbed. With a moaning wail, sobs poured from her. Her legs buckled. Max caught her and sat her in a chair. On his knees beside her, he smoothed her hair.

"I know you're scared, honey." Max whispered in her ear. "But we have to stay calm. We need to think clearly."

"That's right." Ty bent down and looked her in the eye. "We need your help to find Gracia."

"O...k... kay." The raspy whisper caught in her throat.

"Good." Ty swallowed hard. He squeezed her knee and his eyes locked with hers.

Stomach clenched, she braced herself.

"Listen, a charter left for Bermuda shortly after the kidnapping." His gaze flickered to Max and then back to her. "We suspect he's fled the country."

"Noooo." Her body went limp as a dish rag. Pain seared her gut like she'd been punched in the stomach. She'd been so certain he'd stay close.

"We don't have jurisdiction in Bermuda, but there's no guarantee he'll stay there. We're investigating, but our resources are limited." Ty laid a hand on his friend's shoulder.

"I'll hire a private detective," Max croaked.

"That would help," Ty said, "but they're expensive."

Sarita didn't want him spending more money. He had helped so much already. Yet she couldn't bring herself to stop him from doing all he could to find Gracia. Conflict twisted her insides. She had no way to pay him back.

Except her body. She'd vowed not to do that anymore, but she'd do anything to find Gracia.

Not that he'd expect her to. Max was 110% hot-blooded male, but he showed her far too much respect to accept sexual favors as repayment.

Oh Lord, I don't know how I'll ever repay him, but whatever it takes, please help us find Gracia.

"Don't worry about the cost." Max's jaw set with renewed determination. Anger flamed in his eyes. "But where'd this moron Ramone come up with cash to charter a plane?" he asked. "He just got out of prison."

"You'd be surprised at the stash some prisoners have on the outside," Ty said. "Criminals find a way to get their hands on money."

Just like he got his hands on Gracia. Sarita squeezed her eyes shut against the horrible nightmare, but it played through her mind again. Her precious daughter screaming, reaching for her, calling her name, yet for all her desperate struggle, her thrashing feet had mired in the sand.

Tearing at her hair, Sarita heard male voices trying to calm her, but they couldn't drown out the sound of her daughter's screams.

Nausea surged and bile exploded from her, covering Max and Ty and the hardwood floor.

HEADLINES

The long, sleepless night dragged on.

Max rocked Sarita in his arms but couldn't calm her. Years of intense military training, followed by a degree from Harvard Business School qualified him to handle any challenge. Yet nothing prepared him to face Sarita's debilitating grief.

He couldn't bear it, yet nothing he could do would stop the devastating assault.

Ty slept on the sofa near the phone, recorder at the ready. At least he got some sleep.

Early in the morning, the phone rang.

Ty scrambled up, headphones on in a flash, alert as a soldier awakened by gunfire. He motioned for Max to answer.

"Nevada, my eye," were Ramone's first words. "Do you think I'm an idiot?"

"Where's Gracia?" Max demanded.

"Let me talk to her!" Sarita yelled into the phone.

"She ain't here." Ramone's tone was dry and amused. "You know I don't like kids. Couldn't stand the sniveling and whining all day. Typical woman - always wanting what they can't have."

Sarita gasped. Max's muscles tensed at his callous tone.

"Where is she? If you hurt her - "

"I'm not stupid." Ramone cut off Max's threat. "She's being taken care of. I can't get ransom for a dead kid."

"Don't touch that child," Max warned.

"Whatcha gonna do, hotshot? Throw a bag of money at me?" Ramone chortled a bitter, wicked laugh. "Tell ya what. Do that first and she won't get hurt. Make it an even million, I'm not greedy. Meet me at the abandoned dock off Seafood Road. Monday at midnight. No cops or the girl dies."

"Where's Seafood - "

The phone clicked off before the trace could locate him.

Max turned to Sarita. Her pallid face wrenched his heart. Tears streamed down her cheeks. He held her to him, soaking her tears with his shirt. She clung to him with desperation, pawing at his shoulders.

"Is my baby alive?"

Max had to think. "He said she wasn't there, but I think I heard weeping in the background."

"We'll play it over for you, Sarita," Ty offered.

As the seasoned cop rewound the recorder, Sarita bent with her ear over the machine. Clutching herself in a frantic hug, her painful anticipation made Max's heart ache.

Faint sniffling sounds emanated from the phone. Sarita's eyes lit with a hint of relief from the debilitating fear.

"Where's Seafood Road?" Sudden panic overcame him. "How can I meet him when I don't even know where it is? And how am I supposed to come up with a million dollars by Monday night?"

"Awendaw - north up the coast," Ty answered with confidence. "Pretty desolate area, wiped out by Hurricane Hugo back when."

Max's jaw loosened a bit with his friend's reassuring voice. Ty was the best in the business.

The tape replayed. Sarita bent close to listen. A sniffle sounded in the background, then a sob.

"I hear her!" Sarita's eyes sparked. "My poor baby. She's alive!" She clung to Max. "Please bring her back to me," she begged Ty.

"We'll do everything we can, Miss," Ty assured her. "My team knows this shoreline like their own backyard. If she's out there, we'll find her."

※

SARITA FLED to pace the third-floor balcony, alone with her thoughts as the sun set over the island. The sky turned lavender and pink with streaks of bright orange. Boats dotted the water, from a cruise ship heading for the open sea to a small boat close to shore with a fishing pole. The fisherman adjusted his hat and a glint of gold flashed on his wrist.

She shuddered with the reminder of Ramone's flashy jewelry. How many dollars had he ripped from her G-string to pay for his gold habit?

The French doors opened behind her. Max neared to rest his hands on her shoulders. How she needed to forget.

Leaning into him, the mango sun warmed her face and Max's heat warmed her back. Yet nothing could warm her heart.

Tired of futile words, neither of them spoke. He lifted her hair and massaged her neck. Her head fell forward as he kneaded some of the tension away. His heavenly touch seeped into her bones, calming her.

Then he reached for her hand and led her to the glider.

Sarita leaned back into the cushions as he settled beside her. His thigh rubbed hers and his arm draped over her weary but soothed shoulders.

Grateful for his comfort, she cuddled close. Her thoughts poured forth.

"I don't think he's in Bermuda," she confided.

He stared out at the sea for a moment. "Where do you think Ramone is?"

"I really thought he'd stay close by. But he has family in the Dominican Republic. It's a quick flight from Bermuda." Her gaze drifted south, past Sullivan's Island and into the Atlantic. Was her baby out there? Was she alright? "He couldn't be bothered with a child. Maybe he dumped her on his mother." Sarita cringed.

"Will she take good care of her?"

"I don't know her." Anguish washed over her. "But the woman raised Ramone and he's downright evil."

"There must be some good in him, somewhere, or you wouldn't have been with him." Max squeezed her shoulders. "Besides, he's Gracia's father, and there isn't an evil bone in her body."

She looked into his eyes. "You always know how to make me feel better. How do you do that?"

Smiling, he kissed her nose. "I try to make the best of the circumstances."

"Things don't always turn out for the best."

"Assume the best, prepare for the worst." His jaw tightened. "If you're equipped to handle worst case scenario, and don't paralyze yourself with worry, then you can deal with the situation with a clear head."

She nodded, letting his encouragement wash over her as she drank in his love. His brows creased with concern, but his eyes held only admiration and longing. Was all that for her? And Gracia?

He touched her face with the lightest stroke across her cheek. He made her feel cherished, beautiful, and loved.

His eyes, so filled with affection, searched hers. Did he read her same emotions? How she loved this man!

Leaning forward, he gazed down at her lips. They twitched with yearning. Kiss me! Oh yes, kiss me, make me forget everything.

She met his lips with hers, let her eyes drift shut, let the sensation take her away. He wrapped his warm arms around her and ravaged her mouth. He felt so good, so right. She belonged with him. She loved Max Carter and felt certain he loved her.

He shifted, pulling them to their feet, pressing her to his hot, hard body. She wanted him, needed him, but guilt snaked into her mind.

Her baby was gone. How could she be gratifying her own desires when she needed to find Gracia?

He broke off the kiss, leaving her panting as his lips trailed down her neck. She melted in his arms as he held her. His passion and vitality fortified her.

She needed this. Yes, she needed to find her baby. But right now, she needed Max's strength and comfort. Right now, she needed to forget.

*

KIDNAPPING AT IOP

Max stared at the headline as he stood on the front porch wearing nothing but pajama pants. Absently scratching his bare chest, he threw the paper onto a teakwood table without reading another word. He needed coffee, strong and black.

Turning away from the sunlit gardens, he padded into the kitchen. He'd heard Sarita up and down the stairs into the wee hours of the morning and dared not wake her. He quietly started the coffee. Unable to sleep himself, he felt lousy.

That stupid headline didn't help. Who could have told the press?

Maybe a beachcomber had heard Sarita screaming after the fact. Someone from the restaurant or any beachfront resident might not have been bothered to help but couldn't keep their beady eyes away from the windows. Someone from the police station might have reported the story as well.

Thank goodness the reporters hadn't called the house - yet.

He poured a mug of steaming brew before the pot filled. He might as well see what they had to say and get it over with.

His insides knotted. Surely Ramone knew what the papers said by now.

Max slipped outside and settled into a cushy chair behind climbing jasmine that screened him from the gardener watering roses below.

He stared at the shocking words.

Three-year-old daughter of an Ohio stripper was kidnapped yesterday from the Isle of Palms beach. Graciana Santos was snatched from the beach while chasing sand pipers. Her mother, Sarita Santos, identified the kidnapper as Ramone Valdez, the child's estranged father.

Recently released from prison, Valdez allegedly violated parole when he left the state of Ohio. He served time for the attempted murder of Ms. Santos and her then unborn child. At the time, Valdez employed Santos at his gentlemen's club in northern Ohio.

Valdez swore revenge for Santos' testimony that landed him in prison for the last four years. The police department of Crystal Falls, Ohio filed a restraining order against Valdez in August after he assaulted Ms. Santos in her home.

After witnessing the assault, businessman Max Carter, owner of Carter Racing in Riverside, Ohio, stole away with Santos and her child to his beach front property on the Isle of Palms, bringing crime to this quiet community. Continued on page 2.

Max read and re-read the last sentence. He couldn't believe his eyes. They actually blamed *him* for bringing crime here. No matter that the newspaper editor played golf with Uncle Harley. Sensationalism sold papers and they'd done it up good.

He'd considered calling 'America's Most Wanted' for help finding Gracia. Now he wondered what getting the story on the news and the resulting publicity would entail. How would it affect Sarita? Would they find Gracia, or would notoriety drive Ramone deeper into hiding, making it even more difficult to find her?

He'd already left the country. Would he do something drastic - kill Gracia and dump her in the ocean? Or would he disguise himself, so he'd never be recognized?

Max sipped his coffee. It went down hot, burning his constricted throat. Lord God, what should he do? Why was this happening?

His world spun out of control. Sarita would be crushed under public scrutiny. Ty advised avoiding the media, as he'd seen innocent people become demonized by the press. The police did not suspect Sarita and Max. Why create a frenzied media who questioned that?

Ty suggested posting flyers would be more valuable, more likely to draw out true witnesses. Mass television and newspaper exposure often attracted fringe lunatics seeking attention. Max sought to prevent that nightmare.

Tempted to wad up the paper and burn it in the fireplace, he couldn't stop reading. He had to know what was reported. Carter Racing would need damage control after this fiasco.

The story continued on page two. After exposing every seedy tidbit from Sarita's past, including her alcoholic Puerto Rican parents, they moved on to Max.

The story reeked of Myrtle Winthrop, concluding with details of his son Luke's custody arrangement, insinuating Max was a bad father. The assessment drove a knife into his heart.

The picture painted two bad parents who allowed an innocent child to be kidnapped. Never mind the murdering monster that did the deed.

Rage curled in his gut. He snatched the paper from his lap and wrenched it in half. Grabbing up the pieces, he ripped them into a shredded pile.

Curse words rose to his throat. He washed them down with a shot of strong coffee.

He had a child to find and a million dollars to pull out of thin air. Now he had to protect Sarita from prying eyes and whispering lips that could further damage her fragile mental state. How could people be so cruel?

Bits of newspaper fluttered onto the lawn. He couldn't let Sarita see the paper. With a curt nod to the bewildered gardener, he stomped onto the grass to pick up the pieces and stuffed the whole mess in the trash can.

Swallowing the fury that consumed him, he went inside, away from curious stares. Pacing the kitchen, he clenched his fists, needing to pound something and imagining Ramone's face in striking distance.

His heart raced and his taut muscles threatened to snap. If he didn't busy his hands, he'd explode.

He gathered ingredients to make breakfast. Food would calm his nerves and his sweet girl would need fortification to face the day.

THE SMELLS of sizzling bacon and wafting cinnamon coaxed Sarita awake. Hmmm...wonderful. She enjoyed a languid stretch. Max made breakfast and Gracia loved bacon.

Realization slapped her in the face. How could she have forgotten - even for a split second - that Gracia was gone?

The gravity of the situation weighed her down before she could lift her legs from bed. She buried her head in the pillow, hiding beneath the down comforter.

Reggae music drifted up the stairs, floating on the scents of breakfast. She didn't want to eat. She didn't want to face another dreadful day.

Yesterday she ate nothing. Max tried so hard to feed her. He insisted on nutrition to maintain her health. Gracia needed her to be strong. Now the persistent man enticed her rumbling stomach with cinnamon and bacon.

The sun shone through the open slats of the plantation shutters, creating patterns of light across the hard wood floor, the white bedding, and her tanned arms.

She kicked off the blankets, letting warm sea breezes wash over her skin. The rhythm of the waves lulled her back toward sleep.

The happy music inched up a notch, as if Max wanted to wake her. Breakfast must be ready. Somehow the man always made her smile, despite the dire circumstances.

Sarita rose from bed with less resistance than she expected. After a quick freshening up, she threw on shorts and a camisole. The happy music put a spring in her step as she headed downstairs toward the delicious aroma, anxious to see Max.

She gasped when she saw him.

Bare-chested, his tanned torso angled to a trim waist and low-riding plaid pajamas. He looked up from a fragrant griddle of French toast.

"Mornin' sunshine." His smiling eyes caught hers. Bluer than blue, they held a sadness behind the pleasure to see her.

"Mornin' handsome," she replied with her best southern accent.

Lost in each other's gazes, they moved toward one another as if magnets pulled them together. Once close enough to touch, they stood inches apart, staring at one another with sleepy smiles until the force became too powerful to resist.

Max pulled her close. His heat penetrated her very soul. His hands ran up and down her back, his hair nuzzled her jaw, and his hot mouth kissed her neck.

Heaven. If only life were so perfect. Her pulse raced with her emotions - yearning, desire, and love, all tainted by guilt. Her insides cringed.

The gravity of the situation snapped her out of the trance.

Max stilled, lips on her collarbone. He kissed her there, pulling back as he did so. Hands cradling her neck, he looked into her eyes with compassion - and love?

"How can I enjoy this when..." Sarita choked. "When my daughter is missing?"

"We'll find her." His determined gaze fortified her. He kissed her forehead. "Breakfast is ready," he said with a smile.

Swirls of cinnamon and butter oozed into the crevices of thick French bread dripping with pure maple syrup. She took a bite. Her tastebuds danced a tango as her eyes drifted shut with sheer delight. Real maple tasted so much better than the cheap stuff she bought.

Hungrier than she imagined, she polished off Max's mouth-watering creation and reached for a crisp slice of bacon.

His phone buzzed.

"Brett, my man," Max greeted his friend's call.

As he listened, his smile faded, and then turned to a frown. His uh-huhs and hm-hmms told her nothing, but lines formed across his forehead as he raked his hands through his hair.

She pushed away her plate and listened for clues. The bread formed a lump in her stomach. Did whatever happened in Crystal Falls have anything to do with Gracia? What rumors had Myrtle spread this time?

"I agree." Max looked at Sarita. "That would be best for the business, but I can't. Sarita needs me here and I refuse to leave her." The intensity in his eyes took her breath away. "I can't explain, but my being here is pivotal in finding Gracia. When this is over, you'll understand."

As his hand clasped over hers, she gulped down guilt too overwhelming to deal with.

"I'll do what I can from here. I hate to dump this on you, Brett, but you have to handle damage control on that end. I know you're up to it. I trust you. Go with your gut dealing with Bo. You know him better than I do."

More uh-huhs and hm-hmms. "I understand. I know you're doing two jobs. I'm sorry, Brett. Please don't bail on me now."

Sarita held her breath as he hung up the phone.

"Business issues," he said with a furrowed brow. He leaned across the table to kiss her cheek. "Don't worry about it. We have a full plate here." He looked down at her untouched bacon. "Speaking of which, let's finish our breakfast."

No longer hungry, she couldn't eat another bite. Dying to know what happened, she couldn't bear to hear it. She feared vicious rumors she couldn't stop.

"If you need to go, I understand." Her voice quaked. She couldn't imagine dealing with this alone but couldn't take the blame on her conscience. "You have a business to take care of."

The passion in his eyes felt palpable as they locked with hers. "What I need to do is find Gracia. I'm not gonna blow our best chance for the sake of *business*." His jaw clenched. "Money comes and money goes. Business can't compete with the importance of people in my life. *You* are my priority. You and Gracia."

As if he couldn't withstand the intensity of that admission, he looked away and released her hand. "I'm not leaving, and that's that."

MILLION DOLLAR BABY

Sarita stared at his fidgeting hands as Max picked up his fork. What just happened here? Was he turning his back on his business to stay with her? He seemed as dedicated to finding Gracia as if she were his own child. Did he really say she was his priority? She *and Gracia*? Did he mean that?

Glimpses of commitment, life-long love, and marriage flitted at the edges of her mind. She pushed those images away. True love was too much to hope for a poor girl from Puerto Rico, a stripper, an unwed mother with a missing daughter.

She couldn't survive another heartbreak. Romance happened in movies and books, not in real life. True love would never find Sarita Santos.

Sunday threatened to drag on in agony. But after breakfast, Ruby and Harley showed up in their Sunday best.

"You two need to get out of this house for a while," Ruby

insisted. "And you could sure use some prayers. Now run off and get dressed for church."

Sarita watched with amusement as Max did as he was told, without argument. They arrived at St. Michael's Episcopal fifteen minutes early. The picturesque white steeple highlighted a clear azure sky. Sunlight beamed down, too cheerful for Sarita's somber mood.

The sermon couldn't penetrate her thoughts. Immersed in constant prayer, she heard none of the words, yet God's presence poured over her.

Max also seemed slightly more at ease.

Bless her heart, Ruby knew how much they needed that. After the noon service, she insisted they come to her home on the harbor for a stroll along the water, through White Point Gardens, and up and down the pretty streets South of Broad.

Antebellum mansions nestled among magnolia trees and live oaks dripping with Spanish moss. Window boxes overflowed with vinca and geraniums, pinks and purple salvia, ivy, and impatiens. Handwrought iron gates offered peeks at secret gardens filled with fragrant gardenias, budding camellias, and the pink blush of blooming sweetgrass. Hedges of azalea lined cobblestone driveways and jasmine climbed arbors.

Sarita reveled in the quaint beauty and enjoyed Ruby's chatty history of Charleston. Most of all, she appreciated the illusion of normal life for a while.

After the invigorating walk, she and Ruby settled in the sunroom. Max and Harley retreated to the adjoining den where they discussed financial options to come up with the ransom. Harley whispered something about the newspaper. When she looked their way, Max gave her a wink and pulled his uncle out to the piazza.

Curiosity rose, but before she could ask, Ruby jumped up, commanding her attention.

"Here." Ruby pulled a book from her shelves and handed it to

Sarita. The cover exploded with colorful flowers and read 'Charleston Gardens'. "Some of the gardens we saw are featured in here." She opened the book across Sarita's lap and thumbed through the pages.

Sarita appreciated Ruby's warm hospitality. Yet no matter how welcome the distraction of beautiful gardens, her stomach knotted with nerves.

MONDAY STRETCHED on with pervasive dread. While Max was on the phone or at the bank liquidating funds from every conceivable source, Sarita could do nothing.

After making her car payment and paying rent for her unused apartment, she wrote a check that drained her checking account - one hundred and seventy-five dollars. She only had that much because she hadn't bought groceries or paid a sitter.

The idea of not needing a sitter created a lump in her throat. Unable to swallow, let alone speak, she approached Max's desk and handed him the check.

Words eluded him as well. His eyes met hers with solemn gratitude, as if that tiny amount would really make a difference. She fully expected him to toss it back, telling her not to worry about it. Instead, he took her check and tucked it into the zippered bank envelope with the growing funds. That silent moment of respect meant more than she could express.

She laid her head on his shoulder, choking back tears. Swiveling from the desk, he pulled her onto his lap. For a few precious moments, he held her and kissed her hair.

Resenting the urgency of their deadline, she dragged herself from his embrace so he could continue the desperate hunt for money. As she stood to go, he held her fingertips. His searching eyes resonated the yearning to comfort and be comforted, and the sorrow that it had to wait.

She squeezed his fingers and released them. Their gazes held a moment before she turned to go.

As she walked away, he heaved a sigh and picked up the phone again.

Soon Ty called and Max hurried to meet with the police. Sarita grabbed her purse.

"No, Sarita," he insisted. "Stay here and pray."

Devastating fear brought fresh tears.

"Hey." Max smoothed the tears away. "You know how volatile this situation is. One mistake and we blow it. If I weren't a SEAL, and if Ty didn't vouch for me, they'd never allow my involvement."

She squeezed her eyes shut against the pain. "I'm glad you'll be there for Gracia."

"I know you want to be there, but it's too dangerous. Pray," Max begged her, "that's the best thing you can do."

He walked out. She collapsed to her knees, bent over the sofa. Tears coursed down her cheeks.

"Please, God, bring Gracia home safely. Please protect her. Don't let him hurt her. Please bring her home to me."

She spent the afternoon on her knees, her cries growing in desperation. At last, her tears dried up. She'd begged the same words, over and over, and had no words left. She left Gracia's life in God's hands, and a small measure of peace settled over her.

Around eight o'clock, Max called.

"How's it going?" She twisted her hair, waiting for the news.

"We're ready," he assured her. "At the last minute, I managed to gather up the rest of the money, and the cops have a foolproof plan."

"Foolproof?" she asked with reluctant hope.

"We have plans and back-up plans to rescue Gracia and put

Valdez back in prison where he belongs. As long as he brings her, it should go off without a hitch."

Her fragile hope deflated, and a cold knot twisted in her stomach. "What if he doesn't bring her?"

Visions of her precious daughter lying bloody and dead penetrated her troubled mind. No, she shook her head, squeezing her eyes closed against her greatest fear. Ramone was evil, but surely his own sweet child would get under his skin. God would protect her. Sarita had to believe that.

God will protect her. She practiced the mantra in her mind.

Max's voice came through gentle and sure. "If that creep doesn't bring Gracia, then we either capture him and torment him 'til he gives up her location, or we tail him until we find her."

She didn't dare think it, yet the words escaped her. "What if he gets away?"

"Not an option." His voice cracked. The false confidence identified the wrench in their foolproof plan.

DRESSED IN BLACK, Max arrived at the designated rendezvous point on Seafood Road. The shoreline and flat landscape made it impossible to bring vehicles anywhere near the dock, but divers hid along the shore and cops lined the distant tree line. The satchel of money weighed heavy on his shoulder. He dared not lose it without rescuing Sarita's daughter.

Gracia's face flitted through his mind, smiling, giggling. He remembered her sitting in the grocery cart at Piggly Wiggly, oinking at little old ladies and burly men alike. Even a hoodlum-looking dude with a case of cheap beer had given in to a half-smile.

That hoodlum's face turned to Ramone's as images of blood and young death flooded his mind.

No! He refused to consider it. Losing Gracia couldn't happen. Tragedy often brought people closer to God, but Sarita had suffered too much already. She'd been down that path. God wouldn't destroy her fragile faith by taking her precious child. Max had to believe that, or he'd never get through this.

Systematically, he gathered the visions and emotions and tucked them away. Fear, terror, and sentimentality had no place here. Today he was a warrior. Courage and faith became his arsenal - the strength of God his armor.

He needed it. The dim light of a small boat bobbed in the approaching waves. The silhouette of a man appeared in the moonlight. Behind him, a smaller silhouette sat stock still.

His heart lurched. Blood pounded through his temples.

"Stick to the plan." Ty's words whispered through his invisible earpiece. "You can do this."

Max stared across the water, willing his mind to play it cool, calculated. He rehearsed the plan in his mind.

Take control of the situation. Demand to get the girl before giving up the money. Once Gracia is safe, set the bag on the ground between us. Let him come after it. He wants that money as much as I want Gracia.

He reminded himself of the chief's words, trying to believe them. *Ramone's got more to lose than you do. She ain't even your kid.* That struck a sour note. She wasn't his child, yet his protectiveness felt as strong as for Luke. He forced himself to move on with the chief's mantra.

Ramone's freedom and his very life are at stake. Play on his desperation. Get him out there alone so we have a clear shot at him.

The approaching boat hit the dock, hard. Gracia's head jerked back and forth. She must have gotten whiplash, yet she didn't make a sound. At least none he heard above the wind and the waves.

Wobbling to his feet, Ramone climbed out of the boat with the finesse of a buffalo in quicksand. He yanked the rope to tie off but let the boat drift away from the dock. It banged into the pilings with each wave. He was no Navy SEAL, or amateur boater for that matter. Like that idiot fishing in the storm.

A light bulb blinked on - same type of boat, same stupidity. He'd been watching the beach house right under their noses.

Fresh anger surged through Max. He tamped it down as Ramone headed up the dock.

Think clearly - here and now.

He left Gracia in the drifting boat. Max worried for her safety. She still didn't move. She must be drugged and tied down. His heart leapt, but he swallowed the emotions. Not now. Get her out of there and she'll be safe.

Max stood at the edge of the dock. Ramone approached him, stopping halfway.

"You alone?" Ramone sneered.

"You see anyone else?" Max motioned to the dark, deserted surroundings at this forlorn dock tucked into the bay.

"Don't mean you ain't got the cops hiding out there."

"Get the girl," Max demanded.

"Show me the money." Ramone pulled a flashlight from his pocket and flicked it on. The light illuminated his surly face and inappropriate attire. Unprepared for a confrontation, the guy wore shorts with no shirt and flip flops. He wouldn't run far in those. How stupid could he get?

He aimed the light at the bag of money. Blinded, Max set the bag on the old wooden dock and unzipped it. He pulled it open to reveal the cash.

Ramone took several steps forward to peer into the bag.

"Hold it right there." Max held up a hand. "You're not seeing one dollar until I get the girl." He zipped up the bag and yanked it close to his feet.

Ramone shone the flashlight into the dark water at the edges of the dock. Then he scanned the surrounding shoreline, squinting into the darkness.

Max prayed he wouldn't detect the fox-holed officers hiding in the bushes, nor the blacked-out SUVs behind camouflaged screening with guns and flood lights at the ready. The coastguard had an undercover vessel a hundred yards out, disguised as a fishing boat anchored for the night.

"No cops," Ramone snarled.

"You made that clear." Max was a bad liar, so why blow it? "I'm sticking to the plan." Whose plan he didn't say.

"You got cops hiding and the girl dies." Ramone pulled a pistol from his baggy shorts and aimed it at the boat.

Max's breath caught. "I got it," he choked out. "Give me Gracia and you get the money. No need for violence."

"You just remember I got this gun, pretty boy." Ramone waved it around as he headed up the dock.

When he jumped into the boat, Gracia's head jolted but she didn't make a sound. He must have taped her mouth, Max realized with dread. The poor child would be traumatized for life.

Ramone's hand jerked out to steady her head. Then he stood blocking Max's view of her as he ripped at ropes. Once loose, her small body keened over. Ramone shoved her upright until he got the ropes free. Then he slung her over his shoulder like a sack of potatoes.

Something wasn't right. Gracia had too much fight in her to flop around like a rag doll. And the rough way he handled her, like she was some object not a human being. She was his daughter!

Max's gut wrenched. She had to be drugged.

Or was she dead?

No. He wouldn't bring a corpse. If he'd killed her, he would have dumped her in the sea, and he'd never get his money.

She had to be drugged.

As Ramone approached, Gracia's limp body flounced on his shoulder. Her dark hair blew in the wind, hiding her face. The sorrow in Max's chest competed with his rage. She looked much thinner than she'd been a few days ago. Her little denim shorts and tiny pink shirt hung on her body. If Max didn't recognize her clothes, he'd wonder if it were Gracia. This lifeless child didn't resemble her at all.

Again, he pushed away the fear she was dead.

Max hefted the duffel and walked toward Ramone. They stared each other down like the duel it was. Gazes locked, they eased closer until Max could see the whites of his eyes. Ramone stopped a mere five feet away. Even in the dim moonlight, the sight of Gracia's limp, emaciated body shocked Max.

Ramone eased her from his shoulder and held her in his arms.

Max slid the duffel to the ground in front of him. Every sense on alert, he made a grab for Gracia.

Ramone jerked away. In a sudden, shocking maneuver, he heaved the tiny child into the air. Arms and legs flailing, Gracia plunged into the sea.

Max dove in after her. His Navy SEAL training kicked in and he twirled up, knowing a thirty-pound body wouldn't sink as fast as his. Searching the black depths, he detected a light spot. He sliced through the water like a missile zoned in on its target. She sank headfirst, arms and legs bent at odd angles floated from her torso.

Nothing felt right.

Gunfire pierced the air above him.

Max seized the lifeless body. The head jerked up and painted black eyes peered at him. A dummy!

He sailed for the surface. "Don't kill him! It's not Gracia!" Max waved his arms for attention. Bullets whizzed by. They couldn't hear him. He ducked for cover.

On the other side of the dock, a motor roared to life. Max leapt beneath the surface, swimming flat-out for the boat. Soon inches from the propeller, he fought to match its speed but couldn't keep up. He needed air, but kept swimming, reaching, praying for a break. Let the engine falter, God, help me make a jump for it. His lungs screamed for air.

Then the boat launched out of reach. Caught in the churning wake, Max's air-starved throat gulped down sea water as he struggled to the surface. Bobbing in the waves, he vomited the salty brine and gasped for air.

Red, white, and blue lights slashed through the dark like the Fourth of July on acid. To his left, the lights of a coast guard boat blinked while its engines sputtered and coughed, refusing to start.

"Catch him, you idiots!" The scream chafed his raw throat, only to be lost in the wind.

As footsteps pounded the dock and spotlights shone into the water around him, the small white boat disappeared into the ocean's blackness. Even its roar muted into wind and waves.

Just out of reach, the image burned into his brain. The green Evinrude, the prop begging to mangle him, the chipped white fiberglass with faded black numbers: SC4266CH.

SARITA WAITED into the wee hours of the night, antsy to call Max but afraid to disrupt an urgent situation. Why wasn't he calling her? What was happening?

Where was her baby?

Headlights appeared in the driveway below. Heart racing, she ran to the front door and threw it open. Max climbed the steps, alone.

"Where's Gracia?" she croaked.

His sad face filled with disappointment. He clasped her hands and drew close.

"He didn't bring her, honey, but we'll find her."

"He didn't bring her? You don't know where she is? But that was the deal!"

"He brought a dummy." Max embraced her as she dissolved into tears.

"A dummy?" Sarita couldn't wrap her mind around what he was telling her. "Ramone brought a dummy? Where's Gracia? Where's my baby?" Her voice rose to a chilling pitch.

He pulled back to look at her. His hands cupped her face. The sadness and concern in his eyes tore at her heart. He loved Gracia too. She saw it in his eyes.

And he loved her.

"We can trace the boat. Once bullets starting flying, Ramone dropped the money scrambling for the boat. He'll be back. We'll catch him and we'll find Gracia." His soft whisper held steely determination.

They didn't have Ramone and they didn't find Gracia. They were right back where they started. She searched Max's eyes for any sign of hope.

A study in contrast, his moist eyes and furrowed brows belied the set jaw, flaring nostrils, and gritted teeth. She believed him. He'd do everything humanly possible. And by the grace of God, if Gracia was alive, Max would find her.

If Gracia was alive.

Why would Ramone bring a dummy if Gracia was alive? It was a bad omen. She knew it, Max knew it, and the cops knew it, no matter what they'd tell her.

Nausea clenched her gut, rose to her throat. She ran for the bathroom, wishing she hadn't eaten.

LATER THAT AFTERNOON, Max grew impatient as Ty followed a school bus, stop after infuriating stop, into the little seaside town of McClellanville. They'd traced the boat as a rental from Ray's Marina. North up the coast between Charleston and Georgetown, the community had grown out of the shrimping industry.

Max read the map as Ty turned onto little side streets along the coast, behind that blasted bus all the way. They couldn't find Ray's Marina and it didn't help trying to look around an enormous yellow wall with blinking red lights.

Finally, the bus pulled to the side of the road. The bus driver must have gotten nervous with a police car on her tail.

As they passed, the fifty-something woman stuck her head out the window. "Can I help you officers?"

Ty stopped.

"We're looking for Ray's Marina," Max said.

Her freckled face lit up. "That's my husband's shop." She pointed north. Opening her mouth, then closing it again, her face dropped as fast as her arm. "Is he in trouble?"

"No, no," Ty said. "We're looking for a boat he rented."

"Oh!" She pointed again, giving hasty directions to turn here and bear right there and wind up at the marina.

"Sure, thanks," Max said with little assurance at all.

SPAGHETTIOS & FROOT LOOPS

An hour later, Max puzzled over the map. They had scoured the coastline north of McClellanville but couldn't find Ray's Marina. Ty wheeled the car into an abandoned gravel drive and snatched the map in frustration.

"Where are we?" he asked.

"Here." Max pointed to a faint line along the coast. "I think."

"I know this area. I can't understand where it could be." Ty rubbed his forehead, staring out at the trees.

An older green Buick pulled in behind them.

"What now?" Ty threw down the map with a huff and climbed out of the car.

A curly-haired woman hopped out of the car and rushed toward him. On instinct, Ty's right hand went to his pistol. His left tensed, at the ready.

The woman looked familiar - the bus driver!

"You fellas lost?" she asked.

"We followed your directions, ma'am," Ty answered with respect. "But we can't find that marina for life of us."

"Follow me." The agile woman turned on her heel and jumped

back in the car. She took care backing out, and then zipped up the road.

Ty stayed on her tail through the forest around twists and turns, following rutted gravel paths that didn't begin to look like roads. Then the woods opened to an ocean vista.

The morning sun sparkled on a calm azure sea. Beneath a cloudless blue sky, a bright green strip of marsh grass teemed with egrets and gulls. A fish leapt from the water, seized by the beak of a pelican that dove in from nowhere.

A creek cut through the marsh to the right. On its shallow banks, fiddler crabs scurried over pluff mud singing their clicking songs.

To the left lay a small marina. Kayaks and johnboats, fishing vessels, party pontoons, and sailboats lined the docked inlet beside a white cinder block building with hurricane shutters and a ridged steel roof. Painted blue letters across the front read *Ray's Marina*.

Max chuckled. Obscure didn't begin to describe it. "If the bus driver hadn't shown up, we'd never have found this place."

"No joke." Ty parked in the gravel lot. He got out of the car scratching his head.

The lady bus driver approached with her hand outstretched. "Nice to meet you officers. I'm Anne."

A screen door banged on the building and a tall, lanky man appeared. His weathered brow furrowed at the sight of them.

"There's Ray now." Anne stepped toward the rugged sailor and grabbed his arm. "These officers are looking for a boat you rented."

"They are?" Worry settled in his deep blue eyes.

"I can't figure out how the guy found this place," Ty remarked. "I've lived here all my life and I couldn't find it. Good thing your wife showed up."

"You from McClellanville?" Ray scowled at Ty's Isle of Palms badge.

"Charleston, actually." Ty reached out for a handshake.

"Humph. That explains it." Taking his good, sweet time, Ray shook his hand.

"I'm Ty Ravenel, IOP Police." Ty thumped Max's shoulder. "Max Carter, Navy SEAL."

"Ray was in the Navy." Anne smiled as her husband's face brightened a bit.

Ray shook Max's hand with gusto. "So whadda you fellas want?"

Ty explained, noting a young girl was kidnapped to appeal to Ray's compassion and sense of urgency.

When he'd finished, Ray furrowed his brow. "Which boat you talking about? Got lots of boats."

"Small fishing boat, SC4266CH." Ty showed him a photo of Ramone. "Rented by this guy, Ramone Valdez. He's just been released from prison on parole. Shouldn't have left Ohio."

"Ohio?" Ray grumbled under his breath. A curse word preceded "Yankees".

"I knew that boat was a bad omen," Anne chimed in. "Numbers add up to six-six-six."

Her fisherman husband waved a calloused hand. He shook his head and walked into the building.

Max shot a puzzled look at Ty. Unfazed, Ty followed. Max and Anne stepped in behind him.

Moving at the speed of a loggerhead turtle, Ray held the door for them. He meandered behind the well-worn counter and shuffled through a dog-eared accordion file.

"Nothing under Valdez." He flipped to the pocket marked 'S'. "I thought so. Pedro Santos. That's the name he used."

Max sucked in a breath. Sarita's brother.

"Gave some bogus address on IOP. Yeah, this dope can afford a beach house." Ray thumped the paperwork on the counter. "I got no grounds to discriminate but I questioned him anyway. Said he was living with a friend there." He shrugged.

The invoice read 53 Palm Boulevard - Max's address. Ramone sent them chasing their own tails. Oh, he was sly. But even a fox got caught when he stayed in the hen house too long.

Ramone would get caught all right. But would Gracia still be alive?

"How long did he rent the boat?" Ty asked.

"Three days. It's due back tomorrow." Ray shot a look at his wife. "I was worried about that guy who didn't know an engine propeller from a beanie cap." He turned to Ty. "Did he damage my boat?"

"Not that we could tell," Ty answered.

"He won't be back." Dread filled Max's prediction.

"Oh yes he will," Ty said with certainty. "He'll need fuel. And I'll hit every boat fueling station within 50 miles and tell them that boat's a missing rental. We'll post wanted flyers with his picture - everywhere but here. No one in these parts takes kindly to a boat thief, least of all an ex-con kidnapper."

"Got that right," Ray agreed. He wrapped an arm around Anne's shoulders. Smiling for the first time since they arrived, his tone hinted at vigilantism. "We'll help spread the word."

Devastated though she was, Sarita felt grateful for something she could do. Wednesday morning, she hopped in the car with Max for a ride to Aunt Ruby's.

The coast guard was searching for the boat. While Max and Ty and the IOP and McClellanville police departments hatched a new plan, Sarita and Aunt Ruby would blanket the area with flyers showing photos and descriptions of Gracia, Ramone, and the infamous boat. If they showed up at a fuel station, marina, store, or restaurant anywhere along the coast, someone would recognize them.

Distress gave way to angry determination. She would find her daughter and send that villain back to prison where he belonged. If he hurt her...

No. She refused to let those thoughts cloud her mind. God promised to protect His children.

Max laid a hand on her knee as he pulled to the side of Murray Boulevard. Across the street, the harbor lay calm and peaceful beneath the clear blue sky, a reassurance that God was in control. A light breeze fluttered Sarita's hair as she stepped toward the hand-wrought iron gate.

At the top of the driveway, Aunt Ruby bent over the trunk of her little red BMW convertible. Sarita couldn't help but smile. This might even be fun.

The gate creaked when Max opened it. Ruby turned on her heel with feisty protectiveness like a Doberman wearing red curls. Seeing them, she laid a hand on her chest with relief. She snatched a stack of flyers from the trunk and pranced toward them.

"Good, you're early." She kissed them each on the cheek and handed them flyers. "What do you think?"

Sarita's stomach flipped. Below the bold word, MISSING, was her precious daughter's photo next to that monster's. As if seeing her child on a milk carton, she couldn't grapple with the turmoil of horror, rage, and fear churning inside her.

Feeling faint, she clutched Max's arm and shoved the flyer back at Ruby.

Instantly, Ruby's demeanor changed from determined crusader to concerned mama. "Honey, you don't have to do this." She led Sarita to a nearby garden bench. "Why don't you stay here? You can sit on the piazza sipping lemonade and watch the boats out in the harbor. I have some nice chicken salad for lunch."

An orange tabby appeared from behind a hydrangea and rubbed Sarita's legs, looking up at her with emerald eyes.

"Emmy will keep you company." Max chimed in. "And we'll be back before supper."

Sarita was tempted. Yet she stood in defiance, careful not to falter.

"I appreciate everything you all are doing, but Gracia is *my* daughter. I got her into this mess, and I need to help find her and bring her home."

"Don't even go there, missy," Ruby shook a finger at her. "This is *not* your fault."

Max's eyebrows shot up so fast, Sarita almost laughed. But Ruby's note of confidence buoyed her.

"Maybe so, maybe not." She planted her hands on her hips, hoping to appear stubborn without fainting. "But I'm going and that's that."

ARMED WITH A THOUSAND FLYERS, a staple gun, a long list of marinas, and the GPS in Ruby's little red convertible, they headed north up Highway 17. They had the top down, their hair pinned up, and two chilled bottles of water sweating in the cup holders.

Starting as far north as Georgetown, they worked their way down the coast. They'd concentrate on McClellanville, heading inland to blanket the area, then back down the coast all the way to Charleston. Every business owner they met posted the flyer with Gracia's photo - and Ramone's. That creep wouldn't get off the boat without seeing his face plastered on docks, light poles, and every tackable surface along the shore.

That would work once. Then he'd be smart enough to

disguise himself. They had to catch him that first time. They needed a tip.

By noon they'd covered McClellanville and northern Awendaw, skipping Ray's Marina on purpose. Ruby pulled into a little seafood restaurant along Highway 17.

"Hungry?" she asked.

Sarita shrugged. "A little, I guess."

"The she-crab soup is delicious here." Ruby hopped out of the car without raising the convertible top.

Sarita couldn't believe she'd ever been to this hole-in-the-wall so far from Charleston. Nor could she fathom leaving this expensive car parked outside with the top down.

The dark walls of the tiny restaurant sported mounted fish and photos of smiling men with their big catch, whether a huge swordfish or a boatload of shrimp. Smells of fresh seafood and boiling grease filled the air.

They walked across the worn wooden floor and sat at a wobbly table with a red-checked oilcloth and a candleholder of lumpy red glass straight out of the 1970s.

"Afternoon, y'all." A young waitress in a denim skirt and orange tank top meandered over with two menus.

They both ordered the she-crab soup. Sarita enjoyed the unique flavor and gobbled it up along with crunchy sweet hushpuppies.

Ruby smiled her approval. As they waited for the bill, she pulled a flyer from her tote bag.

Gracia's face on that poster haunted Sarita. Would her daughter have lunch today? Where was she? What had Ramone done to her? What was she doing right now?

She blocked the frightening possibilities that bombarded her mind. No. He couldn't hurt his daughter that way. He wanted revenge on *her*, not Gracia. Ramone had no reason to hurt his child, and every reason to keep her alive so he could collect his stinking ransom.

"You alright?" Ruby turned the flyer facedown.

Brought back to the moment, Sarita looked into the caring eyes of this woman who'd befriended her.

"Yeah, I'm okay." Encouraged, she smiled with gratitude. "Thank you - for everything."

"Don't mention it." Ruby squeezed her hand. "We'll find her. Someone's going to recognize that creep, and Max is gonna nail him."

Sarita hoped to heaven she was right.

"You just keep praying, honey. God's listening. He's protecting little Gracia. You can bet your sweet bippy, He is."

Sarita couldn't help but smile at the phrases that came out of this woman's mouth.

When the waitress returned, Ruby handed her the flyer.

"May we post this outside? My friend's daughter was kidnapped by this hooligan."

Horror struck the young woman's face. Her hand flew to her chest. "How awful! I can't even imagine!" She peered at the photo. "Whoa! I saw that guy!"

"Where?" Sarita's pulse stuttered.

"At the store across the street." She pointed, her voice rising with excitement. "He caught my attention because he acted suspicious, didn't seem to be from around here. He came alone but bought a lot of food. SpaghettiOs and Froot Loops and animal crackers. Weird, he sure didn't seem the type to have a kid." The waitress shifted on her feet. "Not that adults don't eat those things, but from the looks of him, I'd expect chips, beer, and a pack of smokes."

"When?" Sarita's heart leapt. "When was he here?"

"Last night, right after work, about nine-fifteen."

"She's alive!" Sarita grabbed Ruby's arms across the table.

Ruby face lit up. "And thank the Lord, he's feeding her."

AFTER COMPLETING their mission with renewed hope, Sarita stared at a flyer on the way home. Gracia was alive! She touched the photo, longing to stroke her daughter's hair and kiss her chubby cheeks. She looked forward to reading her stories and tucking her into bed at night. How she'd missed that simple ritual, that special bond they shared at bedtime.

Revenge drove Ramone to steal her daughter, but he hadn't killed her. He even bought her animal crackers.

Sweet Gracia had gotten through that calloused heart. Did he regret wanting to abort her?

Sarita examined the photo. Gracia had Ramone's long, thin nose, his straight eyebrows and strong jawline. She sucked in a breath. Thankfully his *looks* weren't bad, just his behavior.

Gracia shared her mother's smile, eyes, and personality. Sarita would teach her daughter right from wrong and eradicate that vicious cycle of sin.

As Ruby turned onto East Bay Street, she glanced in the rearview mirror. "Max is right behind us."

Sarita turned and waved. His face lit up with a smile. A tiny thrill ran through her. She couldn't wait to share her news face to face. His grin made her wonder if he had good news too.

Ruby knew the shortcuts around rush hour and Max stayed on her tail all the way to the house. On Max's heels, Harley arrived home from the office.

Sarita jumped from the car and ran toward the men.

"She's alive!" Jitters jumped through her like she'd drunk three pots of coffee spiked with Red Bull.

"Did you see her?" Max asked in a rush.

"No, but we met a waitress who recognized Ramone. He bought SpaghettiOs and Froot Loops."

"Your flyers are working." Max beamed.

Harley's face turned downright skeptical. He seemed to brace himself for a blow.

Sarita turned to the man she loved. "She's alive, Max! He bought animal crackers too. Ramone wouldn't eat that stuff. He's feeding Gracia!"

Max hugged her tight for a long moment. Ruby pulled Harley into the kitchen. Sarita couldn't make out her whispered scolding, but heard Harley's distinct mutter, "She needs to be prepared."

No matter. She reveled in Max's embrace, and the truth she knew. Gracia was alive, she felt it in her bones. They would find her.

Max pulled back to face her with sparkling eyes. "Ramone showed up at Ray's Marina."

"What happened?" Sarita felt a smile spread over her face and all through her. They'd catch him and bring Gracia home.

"Ray called 911 and the coast guard chased him down. But he had a good lead and slipped over a sandbar where the bigger boat couldn't navigate. By the time they maneuvered around it, he was gone."

"They lost him?" Her heart plummeted.

"We know where he is." His face beamed. "On a hunch, Ray invited Ty and me on a little fishing expedition off the coast of a remote island. There's an abandoned fishing shack where his father took him as a kid. We spotted Ray's boat tied up behind some grass off an inlet."

Sarita's eyes bugged out and her heart raced. Ruby squealed from the kitchen doorway. Despite his doubts, Harley grinned.

"Why didn't you get her?" Sarita wanted to jump in a boat and head out to that island this minute.

Max gripped her arms, stared into her eyes. "We can't go unprepared. The coast guard and the police devised a plan. After dark, we're going in with a plan and plenty of back up."

Her heart hammered. "*You're* going? But you could get hurt."

"I'm a Navy SEAL. I have the training, and most importantly, Gracia knows me. It's tough for a stranger in a wetsuit to nab a young child without scaring the daylights out of her. Gracia's reaction could sabotage the whole operation. Her relationship with me is our ace in the hole. We met with local authorities, and they agreed to work with me."

He checked his watch. "We're meeting in 45 minutes to go over the final plan and prepare. I have to gather my gear."

Sarita caught his arm and pulled him to the privacy of the piazza. Without a word, she nestled into his arms.

He held her, closer than any man she'd ever known.

"Gracia's coming home," he promised.

DARKNESS SETTLED OVER THE SEA. Max and a team of Navy SEALs, coast guardsmen, and police boarded the small rescue boat. With lights out and the engines at half throttle, they headed for the tiny island where Ramone held Gracia captive.

Trolling almost silently, the coastguard captain maneuvered at the inlet to block the rental boat's escape. Two SEALs hid beneath the dock perched at the edge of the water. The rest of the team made shore and followed a path to the fishing shack. Max and a recognizance guy crept toward the cabin wearing night-vision goggles.

They peeked into darkened windows of the one-room shack. Four cots lined the walls. One had an adult-sized person sprawled on it. The other three appeared empty.

Max peered closer, his heart pounding. Where was Gracia?

His gaze darted across the littered floor - duffel bags, clothes, and beer cans. A cooler sat in the corner - too small to hold a child. The place had no appliances and no bathroom. One last frantic look found nowhere for Gracia to hide.

He pushed away from the building, the greenish glow of night vision scanning the landscape for any sign of Gracia.

There! A tiny outhouse stood at the tree line.

His gut wrenched at what he might find.

Pushing it from his mind, he made eye contact with the recon guy, motioned to the outhouse, and crept toward it. He sensed the careful watch of team members hiding in the tropical brush.

As he approached, Ty stepped from behind a tree. Gun at the ready, he aimed for the door as Max eased it open.

Nothing. Save gagging stench and buzzing flies, the outhouse stood empty.

They'd lost her again. Tearing at his hair, Max gulped down air to quell the rising nausea of devastation. He turned to Ty for any sign of hope.

Behind goggles and gear, his friend's disappointment showed. Then he nodded toward the cabin, ambushed by cops. One big cop kicked in the door. In a flash, five men crashed inside. Cursing and barked police demands reverberated from the ensuing scuffle.

Moments later, two more of McClellanville's finest dragged a kicking, handcuffed male out the door.

Max stepped forward for a closer look. The skinny guy wore dark, short-cropped curls and a goatee. Not Ramone, it was the guy from Frosty's.

"I didn't do nothing!" the irate man screeched. "You got the wrong dude. I've been framed!"

So where were Ramone and Gracia?

M.I.A

"Let me get this straight." Sarita sank onto the sofa and rubbed her temples. "You found my brother, but not Gracia or Ramone."

She'd spent hours staring out at the black sea, praying, expecting Max to come beaming through the door with her sleeping child in his arms. Instead, he appeared empty-handed, bedraggled, and looking like something that crawled out of the marsh.

Was this how God answered prayers? Did she need a God like that? She gritted her teeth.

"Your brother says Ramone invited him and his girlfriend on a fishing trip. He stuck them there watching Gracia."

Sarita cringed. Pedro was mean and Carlene hated kids. Stomach churning, she swallowed bile.

"Where's my baby?" Her voice squeaked out on a sob. "What has he done with her?"

Max knelt beside the sofa, dripping on the rug, and caressed her arm. "She's alive and well. Pedro said Ramone called her his 'little insurance policy'. He made sure Pedro's girlfriend took care of her."

Max didn't know Carlene. What horrors had Gracia been through? How much would she endure? She may be alive but couldn't be well.

Sarita squeezed her eyes shut.

"We're gonna find her and bring her home," Max assured her.

That's all Sarita wanted, all she thought about. But Gracia would be scarred for life.

"Does Pedro know where Ramone went?" She dreaded the answer, any answer.

Max shook his head with sadness. "He said he was taking her someplace safe."

"Didn't the coastguard follow him? Didn't they have him under surveillance? You said the boat was there at the island."

"Right after he lost the coastguard, Ramone showed up in a rush and grabbed Gracia. He had Pedro drop them off at the Cadillac and return to the island with the boat. Ramone took Gracia and Carlene with him and left Pedro holding the bag."

"El stupido," she muttered under her breath.

Max nodded in agreement. "By the time Ray spotted his boat, Ramone was already gone."

"Where do you think he is?" She watched his reaction for any sign of hope.

His face screwed up in agony. "I have no idea. We confiscated the boat, but he's got the Cadillac."

Sarita choked on a sob.

He squeezed her hand. "I'm sorry, honey. We're doing all we can." Searching her eyes, he promised, "We're going to find Gracia. Ramone wants the ransom, or he wouldn't have taken her with him. We'll hear from him again soon."

She nodded, unable to speak as tears streamed down her cheeks. Gracia was out there, somewhere, with that murderer.

A CRACK of thunder startled Max awake. He bolted upright in bed as the lightning flash lit up his bedroom. Too groggy to get up, he adjusted the pillows and lay back down. Dog-tired, he'd fallen into a fitful sleep. How long would he lie awake now, tormented by this living nightmare? Through the balcony's French doors, he watched a storm gather over the sea.

Between rumbles of thunder, the phone rang.

His gut clenched. No one called at this hour except for a dire emergency. He feared the worst. Was Gracia dead?

He answered with an uncertain tone filled with dread.

"Enjoying the light show?" Ramone's voice carried amused sarcasm.

"Where's Gracia?" Max demanded.

"With me, of course. Tell you what, let's trade. I know you have the money. No need to bring your little cop groupies. Just you and me. I get the money; you get the girl. Four-thirty under the Isle of Palms pier."

The line went dead. Max shot a look at the clock. Four-twenty! He leapt out of bed and threw on some clothes. Then he snatched up the phone and dialed Ty's number. Thank God his friend lived next door. Ramone didn't count on that.

Ty picked up on the second ring. "Max? Did Ramone call?"

"We've got ten minutes to meet him at the pier."

"I'll be there."

"Four-thirty sharp. How do you want to work this?"

"Same plan. I'll worry about my end. You get Gracia."

"It's a go." Max hung up, grabbed the satchel of cash, and stalked down the hall. Thank God, he'd kept it handy, expecting such an emergency.

"Max?"

He stopped dead at Sarita's frightened voice.

"It's on, honey." He turned and met her in a hug at her bedroom door. "I gotta get your girl." He kissed her forehead and hit the stairs running.

Rain pelted his back as Max shot down the wooden boardwalk that led to the beach. Racing over wet sand, he reached the pier in record time. Lightning silhouetted a tall figure leaning against one of the huge wooden supports beneath the pier. Waves rocked a small raft tied to a water bound pylon.

What kind of lunatic took a raft out in a storm like this? He couldn't rent another boat, so he'd bought a raft.

Hair at the back of Max's neck stood on end as he ran. Was Gracia in that boat? Where was she? His job was to rescue her. Ty would nab Ramone.

Max went into Navy SEAL mode. Why hadn't he worn his wet suit? Ramone made sure he had no time to think.

Work with what you've got, that was his mantra. He had on a t-shirt, khaki shorts, and running shoes. At least they'd grip on the wet sand.

He drew close enough to see the evil smirk on Ramone's face. The man held up a hand to stop him.

"Close enough. Got the money?"

Max lifted the bag. "Where's Gracia?"

Ramone nodded to the boat.

"Get her or you won't see a dime."

"Let's go, Navy boy." He chuckled as lightning split the sky. "Nice night for a swim."

Fists clenched, Max headed for the boat.

Where was Ty? His peripheral vision yielded no clues.

Ramone treaded water and Max followed, keeping the duffel over his head. They reached the boat chest deep in the waves.

"She's under there." Ramone motioned to a lump beneath a wet blanket.

The dark hole felt like a trap. On alert, he heaved the duffel to his shoulder and inched forward.

Ramone grabbed for the money, shoving Max's face in the water.

Max held tight to the bag and jerked up his head.

Equal in height, Max was stronger, but Ramone was wiry and agile. He slipped a foot behind Max's ankle and knocked him down in the waves.

Struggling to regain his footing, Max kept hold of the duffel. Ramone held his head under water. Clawing for the money, he kicked, kneed, and elbowed Max.

Enough. Max maneuvered a foot between them. In one smooth motion, he planted his shoe on Ramone's gut and pushed off with all his might.

Ramone sailed into the air, flailing, and screaming. With a giant splash, he landed ten feet away.

Max dove in after him and Ty appeared from nowhere. The two manhandled Ramone onto the beach in time to see the red taillights of an old Cadillac flying toward the main road.

His elation dissolved into knowing defeat. Gracia must be in the getaway car.

Ty slapped dripping cuffs on Ramone and secured him to a pylon. Then he ran for a spot beneath the dock. He snatched up his radio and called in an APB on the Cadillac.

Then Ty pulled the wet duffel from his shoulder and looked him over. "You alright?"

Max had saved the cash, but his job was to save Gracia.

His heart sank to the soles of his soaked feet. How would he explain this miserable failure to Sarita?

"WHERE'S GRACIA?" Sarita dropped into a glider on the balcony and stared out at the lavender dawn.

"She's still missing." Max's voice wrenched.

She put a hand over her mouth and muffled a sob. Her world tilted off its axis and she felt like it would never be righted.

"I'm so sorry, honey." His warm hand rubbed her thigh. "Pedro said his girlfriend has Gracia."

Her stomach pitched. Not that woman.

"The cops nabbed Pedro in the getaway car, but Gracia wasn't with him. The island shack was abandoned."

"I thought they already arrested Pedro."

"They couldn't hold him. There was no proof he'd done anything but be at the wrong place at the wrong time."

"EVEN AFTER RAMONE FRAMED HIM, my own brother betrayed me. How could he hurt me like this?"

"For money." Max wrapped his arm over her shoulders. "He assured us Gracia is fine. His girlfriend is taking care of her."

Sarita winced. "Carlene is the last person on earth I'd trust with my child. She scheduled her fourth abortion between a con job and a drug deal."

Sarita remembered the agony she went through when Ramone insisted that she abort Gracia. No human being with an ounce of empathy could do that and not feel horrendous guilt - to kill the innocent life right inside you - your own baby.

Despite her fear of Ramone and the temptation to do what seemed easier at the time, even then she'd known she'd regret it. Now she was grateful that she'd been strong enough to say no. Even if she never saw Gracia again, the joy of the last three years had been worth every sacrifice.

She dabbed at fresh tears.

Carlene's heart of stone held no empathy. And now she had Gracia.

"Maybe she'll regret all that after being with Gracia," said ever-hopeful Max.

"You don't know Carlene." Sarita's comment silenced him. He had the perception to see that his encouragement wasn't working. He left her to her thoughts while staying close in case she cared to share them.

Not yet. She rested her weary head on his shoulder. He snuggled close and held her. How different he was than any man she'd ever met. He loved Gracia when her own father didn't.

Sarita had hoped Ramone would change, that once she announced her pregnancy, he'd be excited to have a child.

She couldn't have been more wrong. He'd flown into a rage, insisting she get an abortion. Frightened, she agreed, to keep his angry fists at bay.

But she couldn't do it. The child was hers too.

She kept her baby and got rid of Ramone. He'd been retaliating ever since, but she didn't regret it for one moment.

Motherhood might have softened Carlene. But she hated kids. Where had that witch taken her daughter and what had she done to her? A horrifying image accosted Sarita of Gracia locked in a closet with her mouth taped.

Serious doubt settled into her bones. Finding Carlene with Gracia put the woman at risk. Without the child as evidence, they had nothing on her.

Sarita's insides convulsed with sick realization.

Carlene would save her own skin by getting rid of Gracia, once and for all. The vast ocean provided a perfect escape.

"God help me," she whimpered, holding her belly to keep the nausea down.

"She's all right." Max pulled her close and stroked her hair. "I feel it in my bones. We're going to find her."

"That's *not* what I feel." She choked out.

"Don't be afraid. God is with Gracia, and He'll give you

strength too." He kissed the top of her head. "Fear is exactly what the enemy wants."

"How can I not be afraid?" Her raspy voice squeaked.

"Trust God," he replied with sincerity and true concern. Yet his answer sounded pat to her agonizing heart.

"God lets bad things happen." Her heart hardened to a stone. "If He wanted to protect Gracia, why did he let her get kidnapped?"

"I don't know. We may never know." He took her chin in his hand. "But I know this: God is with you whatever happens. And Gracia is Carlene's ticket to a million bucks." He lifted an eyebrow. "Ramone and Pedro are in jail, so she doesn't have to share it. Don't tell me she's gonna throw that money overboard."

How did he know she envisioned Gracia being thrown overboard?

Sarita stared into his face, so perceptive, so loving. His eyes reflected streaks of brightening yellow across the sky.

"Look at the sunrise." He pointed out a fiery sliver popping onto the horizon. "The dawn of a new day," he said with hopeful anticipation.

THE NEW DAY brought no revelations. Neither did the next day, or the day after that. Days dragged into a week, with no word from Carlene.

Max paced the balcony outside Ty's home office. An ocean breeze ruffled his hair as his flip flops slapped on the weathered wood.

His friend appeared with two glasses of sweet tea.

"What do we do now?" Max pleaded, still pacing.

"We're doing all we can," Ty said with a sigh. "My guys are

investigating all possible leads. We personally notified every police department from Crystal Falls to Key West. The coast guard and Navy are on alert. We have flyers posted everywhere. As a last resort, we called America's Most Wanted. They booked us next month."

"Next month!" Max rounded on his friend.

"Hey man, relax." Ty motioned to a chair, but Max ignored it. "You blowing a gasket isn't gonna help."

"What *is* gonna help?" Exasperated, Max stalked toward the railing, clenching his fists.

Ty set down the sweet tea on a table between two chairs. He caught up to Max and grabbed his arm. Max whirled around, ready to deck somebody. Ty planted a big hand on his shoulder and looked him hard in the eye.

"Patience. That would help. Taking it out on me ain't helping. I'm doing all I can." Ty's firm voice softened. "I'm your friend. And if those fists of yours come around my head that could be the end of that."

Max's muscles tensed. Adrenalin pumped so hard he was ready to take a swing at Ty.

He let out a breath, pent up too long, and flexed his hands. A shiver started at his scalp, running through him to the tips of his toes. His body quivered like a dog shaking off mud.

"Got that out of your system?" his friend teased.

"Yeah. I'm sorry, man." Max felt like dirt. After all Ty had done, the last thing he deserved was the brunt of Max's anger.

"Hey brother, I understand what you're going through." Ty slapped him on the back. "This business is stinking frustrating, but that ain't nothing compared to losing one of your own."

Losing her? Max's eyes shot up in alarm.

"We're gonna find her," Ty backpedaled. "Chief's leaning hard on Pedro. Getting all the information he can on Carlene. And Pedro's more than willing to throw her under the bus for his own freedom."

"Nice guy." Max snorted. "What's he know?"

"Sit down and we'll talk." Ty moved to a chair and sat.

Feeling chastised, Max followed. The cushions comforted his sore body. He hadn't even realized how his muscles ached from all that tension. He took a drink of cold, sweet tea and downed the whole glass.

"That cool you off?" Ty said with a grin.

"Maybe." Max wouldn't giving him too much.

"Want another one?"

"Later. What do you know about Carlene?"

"Born and raised in Miami. Parents were low-level crooks - dad was a bookie and mom had a penchant for shoplifting. Divorced when she was 14. Carlene roamed the streets and ran into Pedro, fresh off the boat from Puerto Rico. They hit it off, but his family was headed for Ohio. Carlene stowed away in their camper to go with him."

"What a love story." Max's voice dripped sarcasm.

"Oh yeah. Pedro's father kicked her out on her butt. She headed to the nearest strip club to find a job. That's where she met Ramone. She wasn't pretty enough to dance, but good enough to be a topless waitress."

"Nice."

"Yeah. She dragged Pedro in to be Ramone's right-hand man and the rest is history."

"Hmm. Does she still have connections in Miami? Family?"

"Her dad passed away and her mom's in jail. She has a sister and two brothers, but they haven't heard from her in years."

"Do you think she'd go back there?"

"Yeah, Miami's my bet. Pedro said they talked about going back to Florida. She's halfway there, but she does have connections in Ohio. We're investigating those leads too." Looking thoughtful, Ty took a long sip of iced tea.

"She's got to be desperate. Pedro sold her up the river."

"True." Ty set down his glass and looked out at the sea. "Her phone's out of service. She's lying low."

"What about Gracia? What does he think she'll do with her?"

Ty sucked in a breath and blew it out. Agony contorted his face. "Pedro said she hates kids, hated Gracia's sniffling for her mother."

Max tensed, felt his fists bunch again.

Ty shot a look at his hands.

Max squirmed under the scrutiny. Flexing his fingers, he took deep breaths of warm sea air. His pulse began to slow as he fought the urge to pace the length of the balcony again. He gripped the arms of the chair.

"Pedro doesn't see her trying to get a ransom," Ty continued. "Carlene would rather sneak behind your back and rob you blind." He paused, frowning with disapproval. "He thinks she'll dump Gracia somewhere and steal the money."

"Dump her where?" Max's heart clogged his throat.

"Maybe with Pedro's mom - Sarita's mom. Carlene begged Pedro to let her take Gracia to her grandmother's while he stole the money out from under Ramone."

"*My* money?"

"Yeah. She wanted to break into your house. But Pedro was afraid of Ramone. Plus, Sarita was always at the house."

"Sarita would have nailed him for sure. And Maria would have Gracia." What a shame it didn't go down that way.

"Yeah." Ty swallowed hard. "But Carlene must have changed her plan. Before we lost the track on her phone, she was headed south. We're hoping she'll take Gracia to her sister. But desperate people make irrational moves, so we're alert to anything. Any word from your P.I.?"

"No. The guy's one step behind y'all. I'm ready to fire him. What we need is her picture on America's Most Wanted," Max conceded, now desperate enough to risk the devastating publicity. "We need it now," he fumed.

As the dark sky turned tangerine over a steel blue sea, Sarita sat on the balcony willing the phone to ring. All night she'd waited, prayed, thinking of her daughter's fitful sleep. Did she wake to nightmares in some sleazy motel? In the back seat of a stolen car? Where was that horrid woman taking her?

Sarita stared into her cold cup of tea, swirled it around and let it slosh over the rim. Standing, she tossed it out over the balcony and watched the stream of amber liquid sparkle in the speck of sunlight gathering at the horizon. As tea splashed to the grassy sand below, she banged her empty cup onto the weathered wood railing.

Dawn had broken and Gracia would be awaking. Would she be afraid to open her eyes? What would she be wearing or eating for breakfast?

Sarita stared out at the sea. Sunrise cast a mango glow over the water. The half sun grew round as it light the sky with beams of lemon and orange. Angry at its beauty, she couldn't enjoy the view. She couldn't eat, couldn't sleep, couldn't think.

A burst of anger released her soul after a long night of staring into the darkness with catatonic numbness.

She snatched the mug and hurled it. Sailing through the air, it landed on the beach with a soft thud. It didn't even break.

Fury whipped through her at warp speed. Sarita kicked the railing, yanked at her hair, and let out a blood-curdling scream.

Grabbing a chair, she hefted it into the air and thrust it over the balcony. Falling fast, it hit the ground hard and smashed into pieces.

Sick satisfaction swept through her. She turned to grab another chair but stopped dead. Max appeared with a stern look of disapproval.

BUBBLE GUM & CHEERWINE

C hapter 15- Bubble Gum & Cheerwine

"What's gotten into you, Sarita?" Max stared hard at her.

She felt like a rebel teen being scolded by her father. Max's condemnation stung, far more than she cared to admit.

Was she gonna pay for that chair? That's what her father would have asked. And he would've seen that she did too. She'd worked hard for her father's approval - all for naught.

She met Max's hard stare. She tried to read his eyes, his expression, his voice. Did he think she'd gone mad? Did he resent bringing her here, creating all these problems, costing him money in lost business, groceries, and now chairs? Did he wish he'd never stepped into Willow Pond Interiors and met this complicated crazy woman?

All her anger deflated on a breath. Unable to stand the intensity of his gaze, she turned to the railing, staring down at the broken chair.

Her life crumbled to shambles. She'd lost her daughter, her

home, and her career. As if anything could be worse than all that, she realized in an angry, frightening revelation that she'd lost her faith.

She had wasted her time praying all night, praying for days, weeks, and years for Gracia's protection and safety.

Feeling Max's proximity behind her, she sucked in a breath.

His touch on her arm made her flinch as if he'd scorched her with a burning cigarette.

His hand flew back.

"Sarita - " His voice filled with horror and confusion. "Are you alright?"

Fresh rage flooded her veins. She whirled on him.

"No, I'm not all right! I'll pay for the stupid chair. I don't know how or when, since I lost my job and I'm down to my last four dollars, but I'll repay you."

"I don't want your money. I don't care about the chair."

She sensed pity in his voice but couldn't look at his face.

"We'll find Gracia, honey." He raised his hands as if he wanted to hug her, but when she didn't respond, he dropped them. "Everything will be all right. God is on our side."

"God?" At that moment she snapped, clear and final. "God took her away from me. He let her be captured by the one man on this earth who hated her before she was ever born."

"God didn't do that." Max shook his head.

"He allowed it! What good is a God like that? I've prayed my heart out, Max. I've prayed over Gracia since the day she was born. And where has it gotten me? She's gone. The one person who ever meant anything to me is gone."

His face registered genuine hurt but her anger could not be contained.

"God doesn't care about me."

"That's not true. God cares, and I care."

"Don't you dare preach to me." Her muscles tensed and she wanted to seize something, or someone, and beat the living pulp out of it. "You don't know what I've been through." She shot a judgmental look at his palatial home. Her eyes narrowed and her jaw clenched. Her shoulders rose, her chest inflated, and her fists bunched.

Max took a step back.

"I'm not the enemy," he murmured. "And you don't know what *I've* been through." With great sorrow in his eyes, he hung his head and walked away.

Sarita knew he'd been through some stuff. But how bad could it be? Money made everything easier. Plus, he had a supportive family. She turned to the ocean, looking out at the million-dollar view. How could he even insinuate he understood her problems? She fumed, wanting to bust another expensive chair to smithereens.

MAX KEPT HIS DISTANCE. Once Sarita calmed down, she'd realize how foolish and uncaring she'd been. Until then, he avoided her. Swallowing his hurt, he reminded himself what she was going through. Recalling those days after losing custody of Luke, he'd treated Tiffany, his staff, Aunt Ruby, and Uncle Harley with the undeserved brunt of his frustrated rage. Much to his shame, he'd even lashed out at the housekeeper to the point of her tears. Once he realized what he'd done, he apologized. Sarita would too.

He understood her fears and her behavior. Sharing those fears, her accusations sting all the more.

Pushing those feelings aside, he had work to do. First order of business was checking in with Ty for any progress.

"Carlene was sighted at a pawn shop near Ft. Lauderdale last night, and outside Miami this morning at a convenience store," Ty reported. "The flyers are working, but the cops can't find her."

Max called the private detective he'd hired. The phone rang six times and went to voice mail. Max left an urgent message and did some internet research on Carlene's family in Miami.

The detective called back at noon.

"I was up all night driving." The PI yawned, stumbling over his words like he had a hangover. "She's in Ft. Lauderdale."

"Who's on the phone?" a female voice whined. "Come back to bed," she purred.

The phone muffled. "Be right back." Then unmuffled he said, "Carlene pawned some jewelry."

"Yeah, yesterday. She was in Miami this morning." Max gritted his teeth against righteous anger. "By now, who knows where? You're two steps behind the cops. Aren't you checking in with them?"

The guy stammered an incoherent excuse.

"You're fired. Send me the bill." Max slammed down the phone.

The former cop turned detective, an old friend of Ty's, had fallen on hard times since his recent divorce. Yet he seemed more interested in chasing skirts than criminals. Max might as well look himself.

Every sighting of Carlene had been made by someone who'd seen the flyers blanketed across the south by local police. Hitting small towns for food but avoiding cities, she made her way to Miami.

Suspecting she hid out with a relative, Ty had contacted the local authorities and would keep Max apprised of any news.

Days dragged into the weekend with no word. Carlene seemed to have fallen off the map.

SATURDAY MORNING, Max tied his shoes for a run on the beach. Sarita walked into the kitchen. He rose from the bench by the door.

"Would you like to run with me?" He asked with a glimmer of hope.

She whirled to face him, hands on hips. "Run with you? You've been running every morning this week and never bothered to ask me. I assumed you were running away from me."

Stunned, he struggled for a congenial response. "Uh, I thought you needed your space, some time to, uh..."

"To what? Come to my senses? Accept my fate?"

"Cool off?" He raised an eyebrow, hoping to charm her.

"Oh, so now I'm a hothead." Her eyes bulged with rage. Her arms cut through the air. "On top of being a crazy, irrational, unemployed mooch."

Backing toward the door, Max had no idea how to defuse her.

Nostrils practically breathing fire, she stomped toward him, ready for another round. He wasn't about to give her any ammunition.

Without a word, he walked out the door. Behind him, he heard her bellowing and slamming things around the kitchen. A cold ball of fear knotted in his gut. He couldn't live like this. He'd been worried about catatonic. Her surly rage was worse.

AFTER HIS RUN, Max found the house eerily quiet. Nothing appeared damaged in the kitchen. He spotted Sarita on the balcony, pacing like a caged tiger. He scooted away for a quick shower, and then hunkered down at his computer.

When Ruby called to invite them to dinner, he hoped she'd be able to help. Sarita would likely behave there, and Ruby always knew what to do. Why hadn't he called her sooner?

⁂

AUNT RUBY MET them on the piazza with a subdued smile.

Max stepped into his aunt's open arms. Ruby always made him feel better.

Uncle Harley met Sarita with a hug, but she stiffened in his embrace. Max feared it would hurt his uncle's feelings, but Harley gave her a sympathetic pat on the back. Ruby received the same cool reception and responded with similar understanding.

They empathized with Sarita's hell. Max did too, but it wasn't so easy living with her.

In the marble foyer, he noticed a gorgeous new painting.

"Hey, you guys bought the latest landscape by Patricia Madison Lusk."

"You guys?" Aunt Ruby's eyes bugged out. "You've been living up north too long, boy! When I hear people born and raised in the south say, 'you guys', it makes me cringe. To hear my own boy talk like that sets my blood boiling!"

"Ah, come off it, Roob." Max used the ridiculous nickname when she got on her high horse as his way of bringing her down a peg.

"Don't be calling me Roob!" She gave him a loving shove. "Too much northern influence down here and you know it. It's a darn shame our very culture has been diluted."

"This country's always been a melting pot," Harley interjected. "'Bout time the south realized that."

"Hooey." Ruby waved a hand at him and turned to her new artwork. "Y'all enjoy that painting of the lowcountry now."

At her teasing, a sense of calm swept over him. Everything would be all right.

"It's fabulous, isn't it?" He shot a smiling look at Sarita. She stared at the expensive art with disdain. Max recognized her judgment. Paintings by the native Charleston artist cost well over a grand. This huge one had to fetch two or three.

"Yeah, fabulous." Sarcasm dripped from her voice. Sarita crossed her arms over her chest with a frown.

"Barbecue's ready," Ruby announced as if she hadn't even noticed Sarita's rudeness. "Just need to take the cornbread out of the oven." She skipped off to the kitchen.

Maybe coming here was a mistake. Max didn't know what else to do. He left Sarita standing there with her disapproval and headed into the parlour with his uncle.

She meandered into the kitchen with Ruby.

During dinner, she ate with a pasted-on smile and even complimented Ruby's cooking. All manners and politeness, her demeanor felt like the eye of the storm. Any moment, she could unleash hell's fury.

"Sarita's a good cook, too." He caught her eye and smiled. Despite her cold stare, he continued. "She scrounged through my kitchen, found a cookbook, and made some delicious meals. Snickerdoodles too."

"Don't patronize me." Her glare warned of darkness and danger.

Why had that set her off?

"It was a compliment." He touched her hand, hoping to restore some semblance of cordiality.

She snatched her hand away.

"Sarita, I know what you're going through, but - "

"Don't even pretend you understand." The swirling winds of her hurricane unleashed a torrent. "You haven't lost your child, your home, your career, everything you ever cared about."

Max winced. He didn't even make the list of what she cared about. Neither had God.

"Actually, honey, he did lose everything," Ruby interjected. "Twice in fact."

"Twice?" Her question held more quarrel than concern.

"Let's not even go there." Max had no intention of playing this game of who'd been through how much.

Ruby raised an eyebrow at him but then faced Sarita and continued to say her peace. "I'm glad you asked. It will help you understand. At four years old, Max lost his parents to a drunk driver. Thank God he was here with Harley and me. But he lost his family, his home, everything he'd ever known. His sufferings might not be the same as yours, honey, but he understands loss."

Sarita crossed her arms and frowned. Uncle Harley laid a calming hand on Ruby's arm in warning. She ignored it.

"Losing everything the second time," Ruby continued, "Max had a promising career in the Navy, but his ex-wife's theatrics forced him to give it up. She divorced him anyway, and now he can't even see his son without causing more heartbreak than any child deserves."

Sarita's face contorted. Her breath came in huffs. She surged to her feet, slashing an arm over Ruby's perfect table to point an angry finger in Max's face. "At least you know where your son is!" She jabbed that finger to her chest. "My child was kidnapped!"

Harley stared speechless and wide-eyed Ruby leaned back in her chair.

"You're right." Max forced himself calm. "But faith will bring you through. God is with Gracia, and with you," he promised from experience.

"You expect me to trust *God*?" she railed. "Where was God when that monster stole my child? Or when he tried to force me into an abortion? Or when I had to support myself and no one would hire a fifteen-year-old but the local strip club? Where was

God when my daddy died, and my mama was always drunk, and my brothers raped me?"

Ruby clasped a hand over her mouth and Harley blinked hard, jaw set. Horrified as he was, Max held his ground.

"Right there beside you," he answered. "God made sure you grew up into a beautiful woman, despite the horrible circumstances. He gave you the strength to get out of that situation, get an education, and make a better life for you and your daughter. Your newfound faith and Gracia were the good that came out of it all."

Sarita thrust her hands on her hips. "So that makes it all right? Why couldn't Gracia have a nice, normal father?"

What about me? Max wanted to say. But it was no use.

"You can't possibly understand," she accused. "You have Ruby and Harley. And money makes everything easier."

Ah, she admitted it - the class divide they couldn't cross. She didn't think he suffered because he had money.

He swallowed welling anger. She'd become so distraught, he feared she'd have a nervous breakdown. He steadied his voice before speaking.

"All the money in the world didn't save my parents, didn't create a loving marriage, and didn't grant custody of my son," he said quietly. "Money doesn't bring love or happiness, Sarita. On the contrary, it causes more problems than it solves. Deidre and Ramone's greed are case in point. Money can't bring Gracia back. Don't you see that?"

She would never understand him. She didn't even want to. His money had come between them, as it always did.

"If it weren't for supporting Luke and the hope of giving him an education and financial security, I'd give it all to charity."

Her face registered surprise but held its raw fury. Staring him down, she narrowed her eyes in challenge.

"You have that hope because your child's not dead." The words struck him like lightning. She whirled from the table and rushed outside, the winds of a storm that couldn't be contained.

Standing at the railing with the backdrop of the sea, she faced the wind as her hair swirled around her head like Medusa.

Once enthralled with her beauty, Max saw nothing but anger and ugly attitude.

He'd thought they had something, whether or not they found Gracia. While doing everything in his power to find her beloved little girl, he'd protected Sarita, taken her into his home, his family, and his heart. He was falling in love with her, and thought she felt the same. He'd even considered sharing his life with her.

Now that seemed impossible.

Max stood and turned to his aunt. "I can't do this anymore. I care about her, but I can't live with her. Can she stay here, or should I book a hotel?"

"You leave her here. She needs some mothering." Ruby wrapped him in a hug and Harley joined in an uncharacteristic group hug. Their warm arms surrounded Max, but his heart hardened to a block of ice in his chest.

"She's just upset, son." Deep sadness shadowed Harley's face. "She'll come around."

Max nodded with no conviction. Sheer exhaustion had beaten him down. After weeks of puzzling over Ramone's next move day and night, trying to outwit him, and coping with Sarita's mood swings from catatonic to surly, he couldn't take any more. Drained physically, mentally, and emotionally, the super-human strength of his Navy SEAL days had depleted. Devastation crashed over him in waves.

Unwilling to risk another confrontation by passing Sarita, he headed for the kitchen door. On the counter, Aunt Ruby's old-fashioned peach cobbler sat untouched. The smell of his favorite dessert, glistening and warm from the oven, turned his stomach.

He slipped out the door and down the drive. As he rounded the corner of the house, he felt Sarita's stare from the balcony above. Marching toward the car, he hoped she wouldn't call him. He'd had enough, but if she came running in apology, he might give in.

The vibe he felt, as her eyes burned a hole into his back, conveyed no regret. He wasn't her enemy, but he sure felt like she was his. His sixth sense registered boiling, bitter resentment.

Sorry my son's not dead, he muttered under his breath. He refused to believe her daughter was dead, either. Hurt and angry as he was, he'd continue the search for Gracia.

But his search for love was over.

JAW CLENCHED, Sarita stared after Max. Too enraged to reach out to him, deep, debilitating envy wrapped cords around her heart.

His car disappeared around the bend.

And then the fear set in.

Sudden realization struck her full force. She wanted to stop him, to apologize, to chase down his car. But she froze in place, knowing it was too late.

He was right. She didn't know what he'd been through.

But she knew enough.

She hadn't thought much about him losing his parents. He was so young, and he had a wealthy aunt and uncle who loved him and cared for him.

But that didn't make the loss any less devastating. Her parents had always been distant, preoccupied with their own problems. Yet she never got over the blow of losing her father. How much worse if they'd been close? To lose two loving parents in one fell swoop must have been unbearable for a young boy.

He never got over it either, but thank God, Ruby and Harley

helped get him through it. He grew up to be a fine man. And then his heart was broken again.

She never considered the full ramifications of his divorce. Divorce was so common, and he was so wealthy, it seemed like an ordinary occurrence - so different than her circumstances. She hadn't known he'd lost a career and had to start over. After that witch dragged him away from home and family, she landed an additional kick in the teeth by manipulating his career as well. Then she left him anyway.

His circumstances weren't like hers, but just as traumatic. He'd lost his child to an evil ex too. Permanent damage was done, years were lost. His son wasn't dead, but who knew if he'd ever see him again? Adding insult to injury, his ex made fatherhood a court battle, a horror in his son's life.

How could he bear the relentless assault?

At least Ramone was sent off to prison. Max had no such break. That evil woman exacted revenge every day of his life with full cooperation of the legal system.

Sarita shuddered at the heartbreaking pain that must have wrought. What a miracle he showed an interest in women at all.

Just like she'd been afraid to love another man.

Indeed, Max understood better than anyone. That's why he'd done so much to help her. That strong, resilient man had suffered loss. He'd grieved, he'd pulled himself up by his bootstraps, and he'd been victimized too. He'd been through hell and back.

He understood.

He'd asked nothing of her but civility. And she blew it. Now she was homeless, jobless, childless! She lost everything, including the faith that had gotten her through. Now she'd lost the one man who understood. The one man who cared.

The one man she ever loved.

What had she done?

OVER THE NEXT WEEK, Max's heart hardened with each passing day. He'd do the right thing. He'd find Gracia and make sure she and Sarita were safe. Then he'd go back to his business and never look back.

He pulled two icy bottles of Cheerwine soda from the refrigerator and headed for Ty's backyard where he spent most of his time these days. He couldn't bear hanging out at home with memories of Sarita floating around like a taunting ghost.

He found Ty painting an Adirondack chair a bright apple green. Dots of multi-colored paint freckled his chocolatey skin.

"Hey man, take a break." Max handed him a drink and took a refreshing sip of his own. The sweet cherry cola tingled across his tastebuds.

"Thank you, bro." Ty took the bottle and wiped its cold condensation across his perspiring forehead. "No breaks for me, though." He glanced at his watch. "Lavonna wants these chairs painted and my shift starts in two hours." He twisted the lid off the bottle and took a deep drink.

"Ah." Max assessed the four chairs sitting on newspaper spread over the patio. An aqua blue one gleamed with wet paint. A lemon yellow one looked half dry in the sun. Ty had a few strokes of green on his current project, and a fourth chair stood by in obvious need of color.

"You got another brush?"

"Ready and waiting for ya." Ty pointed out a small can of paint with a fresh brush resting on top. A clean stir stick and a screwdriver sat beside it. "Where ya been all morning?"

"On the phone with Brett, wrapping up some business." Max shook his head as he wedged the screwdriver under the paint can lid. "Some of us have to work for a living, ya know."

189

"Oh, is that it?" Ty raised an eyebrow and laughed at their old joke.

Max's friend lucked out with a sweet deal as caretaker of the beach house, although he and Lavonna still worked their butts off to maintain a decent standard of living.

Ty grew up poor as dirt and joined the military to afford an education. Max joined to prove he could make it on his own without his uncle's money.

Max opened the paint. "Bubble gum pink?" He grimaced at Ty.

"Yep, saved that one for you. It's not my color." He modeled his paint-spattered hands. "Figured you better get used to it, hanging out with a woman like you've been."

Max scowled and threw down the screwdriver.

"Ouch. Sore subject?" Ty sounded apologetic. "Where is Sarita anyway? I haven't seen her around."

"Staying with Aunt Ruby. She's been impossible to live with."

"Sorry to hear that, man." Ty focused on his brush strokes. "Von and I thought maybe she was the one."

"Yeah, me too," Max admitted. "But tragedy either brings out the best or the worst in people. Sarita's shown her true colors."

"That's a darn shame. She can be a sweetie, from what I've seen. And a looker too." Ty whistled long and low.

"Yep." Max stirred the paint. "But she's turned away from God and that's not a pretty sight."

"Not cool. But she'll come around. Once we find her girl..."

"No." Max shook his head. "She's failed the ultimate test. I can't go through that pain again."

"So, you're gonna cut and run?"

"You gotta know when to hold 'em and know when to fold 'em." Max's attempt at humor fell flat.

"What about the girl?" Ty asked.

"I'm with you for the long haul. We'll find Gracia. I don't give up, you know that."

The look in his friend's eyes spoke volumes, but he didn't say a word.

Max persisted in the search, in business, in reaching his life's goals. Although no quitter, he gave up on love. It hurt too much.

They painted in silence, knowing one another's thoughts and respectful to keep them private.

With meticulous brush strokes, Max covered the chair in gleaming bubble gum pink. With the last flick of the brush, he set it on the paint can and gulped down his cherry-flavored drink.

A blast of reggae music startled him. He choked on the soda, spitting reddish-brown liquid on the fresh pink paint.

Ty sputtered a laugh and grabbed his ringing phone.

"Lieutenant Ravenel." His voice took on the seriousness of his position.

Max found a paper towel and dabbed Cheerwine from the bubblegum paint. How ridiculous was that? A good second coat should correct the damage.

"In Miami," Ty was saying. "Her hometown, just as we suspected." After some humphs and yeahs, a no or two, he hung up.

NOT FEELING THE LOVE

Max's heart thumped with anticipation.

"They found Carlene," Ty said with bated breath. "But not Gracia. I'm sorry, man."

The climbing height of emotion screeched to a halt as Max rode the roller coaster barreling to the bottom. He searched his friend's eyes, pulse pounding, waiting for details.

"Carlene was arrested in Miami for attempting to steal a car." Ty stifled a smirk. "Grand theft auto is a little out of her league. She's a two-bit thief but riding the bus is below her."

"What happened to her car?"

"It turned up at an impound lot. After avoiding big cities with her zigzag across the south, she left it at a charter dock in Miami central."

"She chartered a boat? Where?"

"We don't know." Ty huffed a sigh. "It's a huge operation. They have daily charters up and down Florida, along the Gulf coast, all over the Caribbean and Mexico, even South America. She could have gone anywhere."

"And dropped off Gracia."

Ty sucked his lips into his mouth and nodded. "Trouble is, in a lot of those places a little Latin orphan is so commonplace, no one will ever notice. She could go unreported for years, living on the streets, and begging for food like hundreds of others."

"No." Max pounded his fist on the chair, smooshing wet pink paint. He jerked away, not caring about the paint dripping from his hand. "Can't the cops get it out of her? Where'd she take Gracia?"

"She denies ever seeing Gracia, even knowing of her existence. She claims she hasn't seen Pedro in weeks, so she left him and went home to Miami."

"That's such a crock - "

"Wait, there's more. They searched her purse, and she had photos of your house, the time schedules of you and your neighbors, including me and Lavonna."

Max's mouth dropped open. "She was serious about robbing me?"

"She claims Pedro planted that stuff on her. That he's trying to pin the blame on her for kidnapping some girl she never heard of. Yet she hasn't seen him for weeks..." he concluded with sarcasm.

"Her word against his."

"Yeah, but Pedro swore she'd planned that all along. Burglary is more her style. Take the dough when no one's looking and disappear. No dealing with the kid, the cops, or some high-risk meet. As a bonus, she can use the girl for future extortion. *'Give me cash or I'll hurt the girl.'* She could milk that cow indefinitely."

"Oh no, she won't." Max clenched his fists, every muscle in his body tense. "I'll find Gracia if I have to track Carlene's steps myself. If I have to search every island in the Caribbean!"

"Now just hold your horses." Ty grasped his arm and looked him straight in the eye. "Don't go off half-cocked and blow this thing out of the water. Let us do our jobs."

"Fine." Max yanked his arm away. "But if you guys don't come up with something soon, I'll go down there and wrangle it out of her myself."

Ty caught his eye and repeated himself. "Let us do our jobs."

Max stared him down, but Ty's level gaze had an unwelcome calming effect. After a few moments, the fury subsided.

"Hey, man, you're my friend." Ty put an arm over his shoulders.

As his warmth and confidence seeped in, Max's breathing evened out and his heart stopped racing.

"I've trusted you with more information than I'm allowed to share." Ty caught his eye with a look of concern. "Don't go acting stupid. I could lose my job, and we could lose Gracia forever."

Max nodded, knowing the cops were professionals doing everything they could. In an impossible situation, they'd made great strides. Yet it needed to happen faster. The chances of finding Gracia alive grew slimmer with every passing hour. But they had leads, and they had Carlene. She knew where Gracia was. Somehow, they'd squeeze it out of her.

Cops had protocol and proven methods, just like the Navy.

"No nonsense, okay?" Ty pleaded.

"No nonsense," Max agreed, looking into his friend's eyes.

"So do you want to share the news, or do I have the honors?"

"Ugh. I gotta tell Sarita." Max dreaded facing her, let alone with bittersweet news.

"Someone's gotta do it." Ty was matter of fact.

"Aunt Ruby will have my hide if I don't tell her myself."

"I figured as much." Annoying amusement crept into Ty's voice.

With a heavy sigh, Max turned toward his car.

"Hey, thanks for the help, man." Ty shot a smirk at the pink chair. Smudged brown spots streamed rivers through the wet paint. A large fist print textured one armrest.

"Sorry." Max picked up a rag and wiped off his hand. "Hey, any time you need someone to come over and create extra work for ya, give me a call, man."

"Will do. Same here." Ty grinned with a look that said, 'I owe you.'

That day would come, but right now Max faced a different kind of music.

With news like this, a phone call was a coward's way out. If he continued this search for Gracia - and his heart told him that he couldn't give up on her - he'd have to face Sarita sooner or later. He might as well get it over with.

He went inside and washed the pink paint off his hands. He changed into casual business clothes. He had business to take care of. This wasn't a social visit.

Shoring up his resolve, he drove to Murray Boulevard with his jaw set and a cold stone wall around his heart. He'd been hurt enough in this lifetime. He grew angry with himself for letting it happen again.

Chad James was right. He should have kept his distance from Sarita Santos. Dating a woman with a past like hers flirted with danger. Life brought enough trouble without hunting it down.

SARITA STOOD ON THE PIAZZA, looking out over the harbor when her cell phone rang. Max finally called! She fumbled the phone out of her pocket and almost dropped it over the railing. She jabbed the answer button.

"Hello?"

"Sarita?" It was some elderly woman, not Max. Devastated, she wanted to toss the phone into the garden.

"This is Mrs. Kentosh."

"Oh! Mrs. Kentosh - hello!"

"How are you doing?" Her boss's voice sounded tentative.

"Not so good, I'm afraid." She should explain, but she couldn't bear to discuss it. Hadn't the woman read the newspapers?

"I'm sorry to hear that." The lady waited for an explanation. When none came, she cleared her throat. "Well, I was wondering when you were coming back to work?"

"I don't know." It was all she could muster.

"Oh. Um, honey, I can't wait forever. I need help here."

"Then hire someone else, Mrs. K." The reply stumbled out without real thought. "I'm sorry, but I can't come back now." She gritted her teeth. She wasn't leaving until she found Gracia.

The woman mumbled apologies, bemoaning her situation. The words didn't penetrate as Sarita inserted 'uh-huhs' at her pauses and 'I understand' when it seemed appropriate.

At last, she said goodbye. Sarita shoved the phone deep into her pocket. How would she ever find a job she loved so much? How would she ever adapt to working again in her fragile mental state?

Days had dragged on with not a word from Max. Now that he'd abandoned her, how long would Ruby take her in? What was she going to do? Here she was, in all this opulence, and she didn't know how she'd support herself.

Below her, vacationing families took in the sights of the harbor and beautiful architecture of downtown Charleston. Joggers ran by in shorts and sneakers, sweat pouring from their bodies in the eighty-five-degree weather of October first. An elderly, overdressed lady walked a yippy dog with a rhinestone-studded collar. A bicyclist zipped around leashes and strollers.

Closer to the water, a black man with a pickup truck pulled out fishing gear and set up his poles over the stone wall. A sailboat floated by with its colorful sails billowing in the breeze.

All those people enjoyed themselves in the middle of a weekday. Didn't anyone have to work?

Life went on around her, yet Sarita had lost all zest for life.

Off in the distance, a container ship passed on its way to Italy or China or some far off port. Could she stow away in the belly of a boat, riding to some unknown city where she could live out her life pretending none of this ever happened?

"You look like you're a million miles away." Ruby stood behind her holding two chilled goblets with mint sprigs on the rim. "Mint juleps," she announced in a too-cheerful voice. "Nothing cooler on a hot day."

Sarita took the glass and looked into the woman's soulful eyes. "I was wondering where that ship is headed."

Ruby set down her glass and perched in the chair beside her. "Don't be getting no fool ideas, now, ya hear?"

Sarita just looked at her. Was she a mind reader?

After a long stare down, Ruby relaxed in the chair. Tired of standing, Sarita sat beside her and picked up the icy drink.

"I have a sixth sense about these things. Women's intuition grows stronger with life experience - old age. You'll see one day."

"I don't want to live that long. Life hurts."

Ruby sighed. "That it does. And love hurts too, or else you wouldn't be so upset over Gracia. And Max."

Sarita shot her a warning look. *Don't even go there.*

Ruby ignored it.

"Everything will work out. Max will find little Gracia, and he'll find room in his heart for you, too." Ruby patted her knee with affection.

"Yeah, right. Everything's coming up roses, and I need to stop and smell them."

"Gracia's alive, honey. I just know it."

"Well, I don't."

"Give it time. You'll find your way. All that busyness in a young person's life gets in the way. Once you be still and listen to God, He'll show you what's what and give you strength and peace of mind."

Strength and peace of mind? She had to drag herself out of bed in the morning after nightmares kept her tossing all night.

Needing a drink for this sermon, she took a sip of the sugared concoction. The cool mint soothed, but Ruby left out the alcohol.

"Don't you like the julep?" Ruby sounded offended. "I only serve 'em virgin, you know."

"It's refreshing." She couldn't quite muster a smile.

"Then why the frown?"

Sarita shook her head with exasperation.

"You don't give up, girl, you hear? God's protecting Gracia this very minute. And don't give up on Max, either. He's been hurt more than you know. But I see the look in his eyes when you're around. He loves you."

"I'm not feeling the love."

"Well, get ready, because here he comes with his tail between his legs," Ruby gloated.

Sarita gripped the arms of her chair as Max's Escalade pulled up to the curb.

He stepped out and stood tall, closing the door with his chest out and shoulders back. His stiff, brisk walk reminded her of his military training.

A tiny urge wanted to run to him and apologize, wrap her arms around him and kiss his neck. But his demeanor warned against it. Rather than having his tail between his legs, he looked more like he'd come to read her the riot act.

Even Ruby sat planted in her chair, knuckles white against the curved arms and holding her breath.

Looking up to the piazza, he acknowledged them with a curt nod. He took the steps with military precision and stopped to face them in his buttoned-down shirt and pressed khakis.

"Afternoon, ladies." The clipped greeting sank any hopes of reconciliation.

Terror flooded Sarita's mind. Was he leaving? Going home to resume his business? He had a life to live. Had he given up on her and given up on finding Gracia? Dread paralyzed her. She held her breath, unable to speak.

"Good afternoon, Max." Ruby's stern response warned him to be nice.

"I have news." He flexed his fingers as if releasing pent-up tension. "Carlene was arrested in Miami. She's in police custody."

Sarita's hope raced to a peak of exhilaration.

He looked toward her but didn't meet her eyes. "They didn't find Gracia."

As if falling off a cliff, she grabbed for a lifeline.

"Does she know where Gracia is?"

Max shook his head. "Probably, but she denies it."

Shock waves racked her mind and body.

"Why?" Ruby puzzled. "Ramone and Pedro are already in jail. She's not protecting them, and she never asked for a ransom, so why won't she give us Gracia?"

"She never liked me." Sarita found the words, but emotion clogged inside her.

"She's protecting herself." Max's matter-of-fact tone matched Sarita's lack of emotion. "If she knows where Gracia is, she admits being an accessory to kidnapping."

As he explained the dreaded details, and the police plan of attack, her stomach knotted tighter and tighter, and her insides threatened to cave in on themselves.

"What about the witness protection program?" Ruby asked. "Can't they cut her a deal?"

"They already have Ramone and Pedro in custody with plenty of evidence. They don't need her testimony."

"Oh, come on!" Ruby slapped the arms of her chair with exasperation. "There's got to be a way."

"We're working on it." Max ground his teeth and stared at the wall.

"We?" Sarita sensed a glimmer of hope. "You're staying to help find Gracia?"

He caught her eyes at last, with a dark, hard stare.

"Yes. I don't give up when the going gets tough."

She studied his face, weighing her words.

"So, you haven't given up on me?"

His jaw tightened. "Sarita, I'll do everything I can to find Gracia. But don't pretend you care about me. It's obvious I mean nothing to you."

"That's not true." She loved Max. Despite her devastation, she had to speak now or risk losing him forever. She found her bearings and stood. "We need to talk."

His eyes grew harder and darker. "There's nothing to talk about." Turning on his heel, he marched down the steps and threw open the gate. Without a second glance, he climbed into his fancy SUV and zoomed off.

Stunned, Sarita sank into the chair, her heart dropping as fast as her bottom. She stared at the gate banging in the wind, the empty parking space on the street.

"Sarita, I'm so sorry." Ruby patted her knee. "If there's anything I can do..."

"Sure, so much for woman's intuition."

DAY LAPSED INTO NIGHT, night into day. Sarita hid beneath the blankets as the sun peeking through the blinds, climbing high. With no reason to get out of bed, sleep was the only escape from her horrid reality.

Why go through the motions of living, all the while feeling dead inside? Her precious daughter could be hurt and hungry on some street corner in Miami or lying at the bottom of the ocean.

Sarita couldn't face either horrifying possibility. She curled into a ball of aching agony. When sleep eluded her, death seemed the only exodus.

Yet she didn't have the gumption, or the energy, to do anything about it. If there was a God in heaven, why didn't He take her now? She'd rather die than endure this torture.

But there was no God. Any God she cared to believe in would never do this. The pain was too great to bear. The image of her daughter suffering hurt far worse than death. Sarita couldn't think about it, or she'd go insane. No, Gracia had to be in heaven, if such a place existed.

Grief paralyzed her body and hardened her heart to a stone. Tears that once racked her body and cleansed her soul would no longer come. She had no relief.

Yet the niggling, tiny possibility of Gracia being alive would not let her rest. If Gracia was found, hurt, and needing her mama, Sarita had to be ready. She had to be strong and prepare herself.

That hope dwindled with every passing day, with every persistent knock on the bedroom door.

She buried herself further beneath the covers.

"I'm coming in, Sarita," Aunt Ruby announced herself. "You can't hide in there all day."

The door creaked open.

"Humph."

Sarita imagined her standing in the doorway, hands on her hips. Footsteps padded closer, and she sensed Ruby's presence above her. A hand took hold of her shoulder and shook it.

"Time to face the world, sleepyhead. Breakfast is long over, but lunch is ready."

"Go away." Even as the words slipped out on a whisper, Sarita couldn't believe she'd had the nerve to utter them.

"Oh, no you don't, missy. This is my house, and I most certainly will not 'go away.'" Ruby yanked the blanket from Sarita's head.

She covered her head with her arms, wondering if Ruby would slap her mouth for such disrespect.

Ruby grasped her arms and pulled her to a sitting position.

"Okay, I'm up." Sarita squinted against the light of day.

"Not yet." Ruby pulled some more until her feet scrambled to the floor. Sarita adjusted her skimpy lingerie as Ruby dragged her to the dresser and opened a drawer. "Get yourself dressed and come down for lunch. It's on the table."

She whirled around and was gone with a whoosh of the door.

Sarita stared at the rumpled bed. She didn't dare crawl back in.

Dressed in shorts and a tank top, she descended the stairs and entered a kitchen so bright it hurt her eyes. Ruby had arranged the table with fresh flowers, colorful plates of chicken salad on dark raisin bread, dishes of mixed fruit, and cut-glass goblets of sweet tea.

"Good morning, Sarita!" Her sing song words defied the fact that it was one in the afternoon, and she'd just dragged her house guest from bed.

"Mornin', Aunt Ruby."

They sat across from one another. Ruby said grace and began to eat. The food looked delicious. Sarita hadn't eaten a bite since this time yesterday. She forked a small strawberry and popped it in her mouth. Sweet heaven.

"I know you're upset, Sarita. And believe you me, I know all about grief. I lost my sister - my best friend in the world, my parents, and three babies - miscarried. I didn't want to get out of bed either." For all her compassion, Ruby didn't waste time with small talk. Of course, they'd been there, done that, for days upon days. Although an understanding listener, and not a bad Christian counselor, she'd found a lost cause.

"I'm telling you, Gracia's alive and we're gonna find her. In the meantime, we need to make sure her mama's ready for her. That means healthy and eating, mentally stable, and showing your face among the living."

The woman's mission had Sarita's name all over it.

Sarita took a tiny bite of her sandwich as if to say, all right, I'm eating, and here's my face. But the mentally stable part eluded her.

With a look of satisfaction, Ruby ate a strawberry. She hummed hm-hmmm in the back of her throat.

The reprieve was short-lived.

"I called your mother this morning."

Sarita's gaze shot up to meet hers. "How's Mama?"

"Call and ask her yourself."

Reading between the lines, something was wrong.

"She hasn't heard from Carlene. No enlightened info on Carlene's family either. She had no clue Pedro was even in jail. Hasn't heard from either of them in weeks." She paused and swirled the ice in her tea.

"Or you. Your mama seemed really sad about that. I didn't dare mention my concerns about you. You need to call her. She bumbled around, and just didn't sound right."

The words dropped like a bomb. She was drunk before noon. Sarita's spirits plummeted worse than ever.

Ruby kept going, still on her mission.

"Since she couldn't help, I used my own devices. I have connections in this town. A friend of mine is a psychologist."

"Oh no." Sarita pushed away from the table and stood. "You can force me out of bed, this *is* your house, but you can't force me to see some shrink."

Ruby stood and bent over the small table, nose to nose with her. "I'm doing no such thing. I simply talked to the woman, so sit down and relax." She placed her hands on Sarita's shoulders and eased her into the chair. Then she settled across from her and sipped her sweet tea.

Sarita stared at the flowers on the table, focusing on one tiny yellow petal. Her head spun. Ruby consulted a shrink about her, and Mama was drinking again. Gracia was missing, and Max had abandoned her. Her hard-earned education and budding career had gone down the drain.

It all meant nothing - Gracia was gone!

"Honey, you've been traumatized, and it's not over. Your reactions are perfectly normal. But still, we can't allow this downward spiral to continue. It can drag you so far down you may not be able to come back up."

No kidding.

"My friend suggested getting you out of the house for a few hours a day. Back into the mainstream. She thinks what you need is a nice little job to take your mind off your troubles."

"A job?" A whole new fear gripped Sarita's heart. Was Ruby ready to throw her out? Was she tired of supporting a sniveling hopeless case?

SELF-PRESERVATION

Sarita set down her fork, unwilling to eat another bite of Ruby's food. How would she handle a new job? She could barely function.

"Thank you for what you've done for me, Ruby. It's more than anyone could expect." Pushing back from the table, the words on her tongue defied her growing panic. "I won't ask any more of you. I'll just..."

"You'll just sit tight and let me finish." Ruby grasped her hand, steadying her in place.

"I vowed to help you and that's what I intend to do. You need time to recover from this thing, but you also need something to take your mind off it. A purpose for living and a reason to get out of bed in the morning." She paused, letting that much sink in.

"There's a whole big world out there and it's a nicer place with Sarita Santos as a part of it." Ruby patted her hand with encouragement.

Sarita didn't see how she could do it. All she wanted to do was sleep and forget the world existed. She looked up at Ruby's sympathetic smile.

The mooching had to end. She needed an income.

Sitting a little straighter, she supposed she could give it a try. Heaven forbid that Ruby got fed up with her like Max had and tossed her out. Self-preservation kicked in, and she bolstered her courage. She had to find a job.

"Do you have any friends in interior design? Oh, ye of great connections." A joke? Had she really made a joke?

"Why that's the best part." Ruby grinned at her humor. "I know just the place for you. I called a friend of mine who owns a kitschy little gift shop in old Mount Pleasant. She's looking to branch out into textiles and design. She has a good eye, but no formal education. She needs someone to guide her. It's pretty low-key, no high pressure. She'd love to have you come in a few hours a day, maybe ten o'clock until two. Minimal hours, minimal pay - but it'd be a good place to start. It'll give you some perspective and a new focus."

"Perfect." Sarita's heart hammered. Perspective on what? Life without Gracia? Moving on felt sacrilegious. A new focus sounded like a betrayal - like her daughter didn't matter. Intense grief rocked her core.

A sob welled within her, lodging in her throat. Her eyes filled with tears, spilling before she could stop them. She covered her face with her hands. For days she'd been stoic, and now at the idea of a job she fell apart.

Ruby's arms wrapped around her. Sarita turned into her warm embrace and wept on her shoulder.

THE HEAT of summer dissipated with October's milder weather. Max worked at his computer reading the September income statement his bookkeeper had emailed. It reflected a sharp dip in sales. Brett and the crew excelled at their jobs but couldn't cover Max's responsibilities too.

He hadn't brought in a new client for months, nor had he pampered the tried-and-true ones. If he didn't get back to business soon the results could be disastrous. He needed some face time with the heavy hitters - Bo Hatley and the like.

Yet finding Gracia came first. He'd send Brett on the road if he had to, but then the shop would suffer. He prayed it didn't come to that.

God, please let Gracia be safe. And please help me find her - soon.

He stood to stretch, enjoying an ocean breeze through the open windows that encircled his second-floor office. The view beckoned, so he stepped onto the balcony. On the ground below, Ty and Lavonna hauled bags of groceries from their car.

"Hey there!" He waved to the neighbors.

"Hey," Ty called up. "Barbeque Saturday. You're on my team, bro." Every October Ty invited him to their annual backyard BBQ. The event of the season, Max looked forward to rousing games of beach volleyball with his buddies followed by a cool swim and Ty's fall-off-the-bone ribs.

"My friends are looking forward to meeting Sarita," Lavonna said as she carried an armload of bags into the house.

Max stiffened. He hadn't seen her since the day he announced Carlene's arrest. And he didn't want to see her. The past week he'd spent reliving her words: *So, you haven't given up on me?* Over and over, he saw her hope dashed by devastating agony. Hurt emanated from her in waves as he marched off, refusing to speak to her.

Summoning every ounce of fortitude, he had to walk away. He'd wanted to take her in his arms and ease her pain. He cared too much for his own good.

He reminded himself of her remarks about Ruby's painting, her utter shock at spending that much money on something to hang on a wall. Sure, Sarita was a decorator. But the cash flow of her clients in small town Ohio couldn't compare to the money in Old Charleston. South of Broad housed the elite and wealthy. Max's family fit right in.

Sarita did not. The class divide didn't matter to him. He'd enjoy giving her beautiful, expensive things and treating her like royalty. He'd love to keep the maid and gardener so Sarita could relax on the beach.

But he didn't want that *expected* of him. He couldn't tolerate another woman who looked to him for what she could *get* rather than looking to love him.

How he'd wanted Sarita to be the real deal. Now he doubted real love could ever happen for a man with his means.

He couldn't deny he loved her. She just didn't love him back. She suffered a different kind of loss - what he could provide.

Max couldn't live like that again. The pain was too great, the cost too high. Loneliness hurt far less. At least that's what he kept telling himself.

Building a wall around his heart, he stacked the bricks of bad memories and past hurts, and then fortified it with Sarita's worrisome attitude and questionable remarks. The wall suffocated his love for her, exactly as he wanted. Sure, it hurt now, but he'd be a whole lot better off in the future.

He needed a safe future - without Sarita Santos slicing his heart into little pieces. The sooner he found Gracia, the sooner the two of them could be on their way back to Crystal Falls and out of his life forever.

But a week had passed, and the Miami police hadn't gotten word one out of Carlene. Frustrated, Max returned to the computer. He clicked through the Delta website for a flight to Miami. He'd retrace Carlene's footsteps, talk to her sister, post flyers with Gracia's photo. And keep praying. Maybe by the grace of God, he'd find Gracia alive.

As he browsed flight times, his doorbell rang.

He didn't want to face Ty and explain Sarita. He debated not answering the door, but he'd been raised better than to be rude like that. He pushed back his chair and trudged downstairs.

Cross breezes blew through the first floor. Across the expansive rooms, Aunt Ruby stood at the screened door with a plate of snickerdoodles in her hand.

Worse than Ty, she even brought a bribe. Apprehension grew as Max took his good, sweet time getting to the door.

"Hey Roob." He pushed open the screen to let her in. His casual greeting warned that he would not succumb to her authority. A grown man, he didn't have to obey her every whim anymore. He was not running back to Sarita, nor was he going over there for dinner this weekend.

"Max." Her tone returned her own warning.

As a cocky teenager, he'd coined the nickname Roob and been severely grounded with the scolding, 'I am your elder and will be respected as such. You will call me Aunt Ruby or ma'am.'

She held out the plate for his inspection. "I brought cookies." She raised her chin with confidence.

"Thank you, ma'am. Come on in." He took the cookies and led her to the kitchen where he poured two glasses of sweet tea. They proceeded to the balcony and sat. He braced himself for the expected lecture.

"I suppose you think you know why I'm here," she began.

"Yes, ma'am, I suppose I do." He grabbed a cookie from the plate and took a big bite.

"Well, there are some things you don't know, young man."

Here it comes. He finished off the cookie and washed it down with sweet tea.

"As you well know, Sarita is a new Christian. Her faith has slipped to a dangerous level and it's your Christian duty to bolster her."

Max choked on his tea, almost spitting in her face. He'd

expected a guilt trip, but here was a different tack. He coughed and pounded his chest, forcing himself to swallow.

"My Christian duty?" he sputtered.

"Yes, sir, that's what I said." She raised her chin again, with that 'holier than thou' self-righteous attitude he despised. Ruby wasn't quite a saint, pride being her one flaw.

Well, that and the stubbornness that would kick in next. He'd hear what she had to say whether he wanted to or not. He might as well get it over with.

"What do you expect me to do about it?" His question didn't mean he was going to do it.

"Forgive her."

Ah, that. "Hmm. Okay. I can do that. But it doesn't mean I'm going to wear my heart on my sleeve."

She looked out at the water, offering a reprieve from her scrutiny. "If you don't trust her, you haven't forgiven her. You're still holding it against her."

As he didn't want to admit it, she had him there.

"What do you expect?" He glared at her, incredulous that she didn't understand. "You know what I've been through."

"Yes, I do. And you know what Sarita's been through." She let that sit for a moment before catching his eye. She watched his face as it sunk in. "You've been through hell and back, but Sarita is sitting in hell."

Man, he knew what that felt like. "True. At least I knew Deira took care of Luke. Sarita doesn't know if Gracia has food or shelter, if she's being tortured, if she's even alive. What parent can withstand that?"

Ruby nodded. "No matter how callous her behavior, under the circumstances, how can we judge her?"

"Yeah, and she doesn't even have a family who cares. Not that y'all haven't been kind and caring," he added quickly.

"But we're virtual strangers," Ruby agreed with understanding.

"Adding pain to her agony, I deserted her." His heart wrenched at her sorrow.

"She needs you, Max."

He took a deep breath.

"Her friends and family live 750 miles away. Her own brother got her into this mess, and her mama's a drunk. When I called Maria for information on Carlene, the poor woman could barely answer the phone."

"Sarita only speaks of her grandmother with longing affection," Max agreed. "And she lives in Puerto Rico." He couldn't imagine going through what he had without the support of his family and friends. Yet his ordeal paled in comparison to what Sarita had to endure.

He didn't wish that kind of pain on his worst enemy.

"God has a reason for everything, a purpose for pain and trials. God allows our suffering so we can understand others."

"And so, we can help Sarita."

For years he'd been praying, begging God for the right woman. If God sent Sarita, she had to be the one.

Her face flashed through his mind - the sheer devastation when he walked away. How could he?

Wanting to take her in his arms right then and ease her pain, he stood.

"Okay, let's go." He moved toward the French doors.

Ruby stepped across the balcony and grabbed his arm to stop him.

"She's not home."

"Where is she?" He shook off her grasp. Panic struck his heart. "Did she run off? What happened to her?"

"She's at work."

"Work?" He was incredulous. "You sent her off to work?"

Ruby's face fell, as if realizing how cruel that sounded. "Well, uh, Susan thought it would help. Get her mind off her troubles, get her out of the house."

"Susan? You mean that quack shrink of yours?"

"She's a psychologist and a friend of mine. I don't see her professionally."

"No, you just administer her advice to others that she doesn't even know."

"The principles are the same whether she knows you or not."

"Yeah, she really helped me."

"Well, maybe if you'd followed her advice..."

"Look, Aunt Ruby, don't even go there. I'm in no mood to rehash how I should have 'communicated' with Deira. That woman didn't know Deira. Communication was impossible."

"I know." Ruby sat back into her chair. "I was referring to going to your happy place. Remember?"

"Oh. Yeah, maybe I should have done that," he conceded.

"It helped when your parents died. We tried to recreate your happiest memories that didn't involve your parents. We had picnics on the piazza, I took you to the beach, Harley took you fishing. The process took time, but it worked."

"That might not be a bad idea for Sarita." He strained his brain for what made Sarita happy before Gracia was born. One place came to mind.

"She's easier to talk to than Deira, isn't she?"

"Yeah." His long sigh couldn't release the regret mounted inside him. "I get the communication thing, okay?" Max glared a look that said they'd finished that discussion.

Ruby backed off, leaning into her chair, and folding her arms over her belly. Not wanting to take out his frustrations on her, he turned to the railing and stared out at the sea.

Communication made all the difference. All Sarita wanted that day was to talk to him. But he'd refused. Just like Deira had done to him.

The hurt in Sarita's voice haunted him. He knew that hurt, felt it still. And he hated being the jerk that caused it. He'd wanted to whip around and take her in his arms. Since then, he struggled daily to forget that pain in her eyes.

But he couldn't - and didn't want to anymore. He wanted to take the hurt away. Even if it meant his own pain, he loved her too much not to take that risk.

Facing the wind and the waves, he kept his voice cautious.

"When can I see her?"

BONE tired at two in the afternoon, Sarita drove home from work. Well, home was a relative term. She no longer had a home. She no longer had anything of value, including her faith.

She once considered God her friend, but she'd given up talking to Him. Up in the lofty heavens, He apparently had better things to do than concern himself with rescuing a little Latin girl.

God didn't care and who needed a friend like that?

On the other hand, her friend Vanessa cared too much. Sarita longed to talk to her but refused to burden her pregnant friend with fears and worries. Vanessa didn't need to upset her fragile system and risk the child she carried. Besides, just like God, she was too far away.

Sarita needed a friend beside her. She relied on her ex-client's dutiful aunt, obligated to house the sniveling homeless girl. Pretty darned pathetic.

Driving across the Ravenel Bridge in Uncle Harley's old Mercedes, she swiped streaming tears, smoothing her hair from her face. Wind from the open windows whipped her hair around. At least the other drivers couldn't see her crying.

With surprise, she realized she didn't care if they did. At one time, Sarita had been so vain. She'd never have let strangers see her vulnerable or heaven forbid, with messy hair and tears ruining her makeup.

Now the tears came so fast and hard she had trouble seeing the road. Prayer used to help her but was now useless. She struggled to get through the four-hour workday without breaking down.

Today a woman came in with a dark-haired little girl and Sarita had to excuse herself to the restroom. Somehow, she managed to get it together, and then hid out in back until the woman left. Lily, her kind boss, took care of the customer and understood enough not to mention Sarita's disappearing act.

Sarita enjoyed working with Lily this past week. Getting out of the house helped, but as soon as she left the gift shop the water works began again.

They bottled up so much during those four hours that a dam burst on her way home from work. She couldn't keep driving over the bridge this way. She could cause an accident.

But how did she make it stop?

After exiting Route 17 on East Bay Street, she drove through the bustling midday traffic. At every crosswalk, scurrying businesspeople wove their way around flocks of lollygagging tourists. One silly woman stood in the middle of the road with her camera aimed at The Customs House while the light turned green. Her blushing husband pulled her out of the path of an oncoming tour bus.

At last Sarita passed Rainbow Row, where the bustling gave way to a view of the harbor, dotted here and there with sea-gazers. Around the bend at the tip of the peninsula, the shade of White Point Gardens beckoned on her right while the sea opened to the left.

Like a breath of fresh air, the gorgeous surroundings calmed her racing pulse. Then the gardens faded in the rearview mirror as she drove by the row of mansions facing the harbor. She looked for the three-story brick one with columns on the front and triple piazzas on the side.

Where it stood, four houses up, Max's Escalade parked out front.

Her heart leapt, and her pulse went into overdrive. Desperate to see him, she went crazy wondering why he was here.

Had there been a break in the case? Did they find Gracia?

She started to hyperventilate. *Oh, God, please...*

No. God isn't listening.

Maybe Max came to see her. Did she have a chance with him?

In her fragile mental state, she didn't dare get her hopes up. If they were dashed, she'd crash and fall to pieces. It could be bad news, but she couldn't go there either.

Taking a fortifying breath, she parked next to Ruby's red convertible and steeled herself to face him. Kicked into self-preservation mode, she prepared for the worst.

Gracia was dead and Max didn't love her.

HAPPY PLACE

Sarita's pounding heart froze to a block of ice in her chest. Chills ran down her back and her gut twisted into a huge knot. Her innards threatened to strangle her.

She stiffened as if her spine were a steel rod. She picked up her purse and climbed from the creaky car. Like a robot, she took the side stairs one by one, walked across the lower piazza, and opened the screen door.

Ruby looked up from her seat at the breakfast bar. An air of victory beamed from her smile.

Sarita's heart skipped a beat.

Max caught her eyes, searching her face. The span of hardwood floor and granite counter between them felt like a million miles. Despite his cautious vibe, his smile warmed.

She stood paralyzed in the doorway. They stared at one another, sizing up the feelings between them over what seemed an unsurmountable distance.

"Well, come on in." Ruby jumped from her stool and padded across the floor to pull her inside. "You're letting the bugs in."

The screen door banged behind her, punctuating the air like some old southern movie.

"Have a seat." Ruby led her to the counter and pulled out a leather-padded stool across from Max.

Their eyes locked, growing more intense as she drew close. Ruby scurried around the kitchen and placed a tall glass of lemonade in front of her.

"Thank you." Sarita's gaze never wavered from Max. In her peripheral vision, Aunt Ruby disappeared to the nether regions of the house.

"I miss you." His first words surprised her.

Reconciliation, then? No news about Gracia? She looked down, hope for her daughter withering inside her. Always just beneath the surface, tears welled again, and she had no power to stop them.

"I'm so sorry." Max reached across the counter and took her hand in both of his. "I'm sorry I hurt you, especially now. I have no excuse, and worst of all, I do understand your pain. I let my own issues affect my behavior, and I'm truly sorry." He squeezed her hand and caught her eyes again.

Regret lined his face, and she believed him. She knew he'd been through pain, indeed still experienced it. She respected and understood that. Yet it didn't compare to what she was dealing with. He knew that too. She saw it in his face, heard it in his voice.

"I'm sorry, there's no news about Gracia yet."

At the mention of her name, a sob choked Sarita. Tears gushed forth.

"Oh, honey." Max came around the counter and took her in his arms. His strong hands rubbed her back, and he pulled her into his heated embrace.

She melted beneath his touch. Head on his shoulder, she let the tears flow. Her body relaxed, her mind calmed, and her heart thawed. Jumbled emotions fused into one feeling: love for this awesome man.

Dare she hope he loved her too? He'd come back to her, apologized, and given her comfort beyond words.

After the tears subsided, soothing peace washed over her.

He must have sensed it.

Max pulled back to look at her face. Caring concern filled his features, and hope glimmered in his eyes.

"You okay?"

She nodded and allowed the faintest smile.

"Sarita."

Her breath caught at the loving way he said her name. The tiniest thrill shot through her, warming her heart.

He caressed her back. Her eyes fluttered closed with the delicious tingles. She let her head fall to his chest and breathed in the warm, spicy scent of him. Holding him close, she never wanted to let go.

With a kiss on the top of her head, he whispered, "I have an idea. Let's sit down and talk."

"Hmm." She held him tighter. He could tell her his idea, but she wasn't moving.

A soft chuckle murmured in his throat. He leaned forward and slipped an arm behind her knees. He lifted her from the stool.

Breezing through the kitchen in his arms felt like floating on a cloud, the most romantic experience she'd ever had.

He carried her to the sun porch and settled her in his lap on the double chaise with chintz upholstery exploding with pink cabbage roses. White wicker and ferns, a view of the fragrant rose garden and a tinkling fountain created a scene like a romance novel. And she was living it.

She giggled like a child on his lap. But Max didn't hold her like her daddy, that was for sure. They found a comfortable position in the big cushy chair, and she lay across his chest. He stroked her hair, and his heat warmed her as a light breeze cooled her skin. Delicious.

With sublime comfort, she fully relaxed for the first time in weeks. So tired, she drifted toward sweet sleep. He smoothed the hair from her face and tucked it behind her ear.

"Do you want to hear my idea?"

"Hut-uh." With the negative sound, she nuzzled into his chest. No, she wanted him to hold her there forever. She wanted to forget all her problems and float into heavenly dreamland in his arms. *Please don't ruin this, Max...*

But he started talking anyway.

"I can't believe I'm telling you this," Max began, "but when I was going through the divorce, Ruby's 'psychologist' friend suggested going to my 'happy place'."

"Hmm. Did it work?" She was too tired to argue the merits of Ruby's psychologist friend.

"No. I didn't go."

"Why not?" She nuzzled his chest, hiding her amusement.

He shrugged. "Male stubbornness? The belief that whatever that shrink had to say was baloney? Defiance at being patronized? Rebellion against Aunt Ruby treating me like a little boy incapable of handling my own emotions? The list goes on."

"I see." She smiled against him. "Do you think it would have worked?"

"In retrospect, yeah, I do."

"Where's your happy place?"

"At the beach house." He chuckled. "Reason number five-hundred-and-forty-three why I didn't leave Crystal Falls: dealing with Aunt Ruby when I couldn't even deal with my own life."

"I can understand that." She looked up at him. "Mine's the beach too. In Puerto Rico behind my grandmother's house."

"Your grandmother has beachfront property?"

"She's two streets in, but it's a short walk. We went to the beach every day when I was growing up."

"Were you and your grandmother close?"

"She was my rock. I miss her so much."

Max looked thoughtful.

"Abuela always knew what to say. She supported me no matter what. I could use her strength right now."

"How old were you when you came to America?"

"Thirteen."

He grimaced. "Tough age."

"Yeah, the worst possible time to leave your happy place!"

Max took her hand. "I'd say it's time to go back. I want to take you to Puerto Rico."

His soft words hit her like a mist of cool water on a hot day. She sprang up on her elbows.

"Seriously? Now?"

"You need your happy place. Now."

In his arms was a happy place.

"And you need your grandmother's support."

She nodded. He was right about that. "But what about Gracia?"

"That's the beauty of it. Miami's on the way. I'll search for Gracia while you visit your grandmother."

"No." She shook her head. "I'll help search for Gracia. I need to be with you, Max." She clung to him. "I can't go off to Puerto Rico while you look for her alone. I want to be there when you find her. She's *my* child. I need - "

"What you need is healing." Max cut her off with adamant resolve. "You need your grandmother. You need to be prepared when Gracia comes home."

When, not if. She blinked back tears.

"Right now, you're not prepared to deal with the situations we might run into, let alone the conditions we might find." He paused, looking into her eyes. "Gracia will be traumatized, and she'll need her mama to be ready to handle that." He laid it out - bare, raw, and in her face.

She sucked in a ragged breath. If Gracia came home tonight,

emotionally distraught, physically injured, and mentally disturbed, Sarita would fall apart.

Tears spilled over as she searched Max's face. His features set, but his eyes held compassion and understanding.

And love? She wasn't ready for that - if real love even existed.

She wiped her tears and sat up in the big chair. Scooting against the upholstered arm, she tented her knees over his lap. Physical contact made her dependent and weak; she needed to be strong. She placed her palms down on either side of her, arms taut and shoulders squared.

"You're right," she admitted. "I won't be able to handle it. Gracia deserves better. I have to restore my mental and emotional stability."

"So, you'll visit your grandmother?" His face relaxed into almost a smile.

"She'll help me heal."

Max's face beamed.

"I'll miss you, Max. Please don't be gone too long."

His touch on her cheek made her heart flutter. Hugs comforted, but gentle caresses awakened her desire. She swallowed hard, fighting the temptation to ravish him with kisses.

If she pulled away, he'd be hurt. He didn't understand her weakness for physical affection. She had to conquer it to be strong.

Steeling herself, she allowed his touch. Fighting the craving for more, she concentrated on Gracia.

"When my daughter comes home, I'll be ready." The declaration sought to convince herself more than Max.

When Gracia came home, not *if*. She had to believe that. She had to be strong to help her little girl.

"I'm praying for you both," Max said.

Sarita stiffened. "What does God care?" She couldn't keep the disgust from her voice.

His hand jerked back. "Of course, God cares."

"God doesn't care about me."

His face screwed up as if in pain.

"God allowed this horror, and now He's nowhere to be found. You and Ty, Ruby and Harley and the police are the ones helping me."

He looked into her eyes. "I've felt abandoned by God too. But He never really left me. I see that now, and one day you'll see it too."

TROUBLED by Sarita's attitude toward God, Max regretted getting cozy with her in the sunroom. Her hesitation at physical affection confirmed his suspicions that their relationship wasn't going to work.

During the flight to Miami, he renewed his determination to find Gracia and be on his way. More personable than she'd been in weeks, Sarita grew anxious to see her grandmother after many years. Yet she remained emotionally distant.

As the plane descended, she gazed out the window.

"There's Miami." She pointed out the coastline beneath the clouds.

"There's a five-hour layover in Miami before your flight leaves for Puerto Rico. I thought we could get some lunch, maybe do a little sightseeing," Max suggested. He hoped to bolster her good mood and keep it going as long as possible.

She'd be alone during the short jaunt to San Juan, but then her grandmother could pick up where he'd left off.

"I've been thinking." Sarita's tone made him apprehensive. "I want to talk to Carlene."

Panic struck his heart. "That's not a good idea." She was in no frame of mind to deal with Carlene.

"Why not?" She bristled. Not a good sign.

"Look, honey. From Ty's reports, the woman is uncooperative at best, downright nasty at worst. You don't need to deal with that. Please, let me handle it."

"But she knows me. We're not buddy-buddy or anything, but she's been with my brother a long time." On a roll, she kept going when he opened his mouth to stop her. "We have family connections. That's a much different dynamic than some stranger grilling her - or a cop who wants to throw her in jail. If she faced me, woman to woman, maybe she'd talk to me."

"I'm not so sure about that." She had a point, but he wasn't convinced Carlene carried the empathy gene.

"Max, I have to try. My daughter's in jeopardy!"

She headed for a total snit. He held up a hand to calm her, but she swiped it away.

"I have a chance to ask that woman where she left my daughter, and I'm going to. With or without you!"

"WHAT ARE *YOU* DOING HERE?"

Shocked at Carlene's appearance, Sarita bit her lip to keep her jaw from dropping. The woman had never been pretty, but years of hard living aged her much more than her thirty years. She fidgeted in wrinkled orange prison garb. A shaking hand pushed a strand of ratty hair toward a bunched ponytail, exposing the leathery creases of her scowl. With no makeup for camouflage, premature age spots mottled her complexion and blemishes sprouted over her jawline.

"Hello Carlene." Sarita struggled to be polite. "I'm sorry you're here."

"Bull!" the woman exploded, pointing a bony finger as if she'd launch through the glass. "You don't give a hoot about me."

True, Sarita regretted the circumstances, but not that she'd been caught. Carlene saw through her - straight to the point then. She squared her shoulders.

"Listen, I know we've never been close."

"No kidding." Narrowing her hooded eyes lengthened crow's feet across her temples. Deep lines surrounded her set mouth, pursed as if sucking a cigarette. "So whadda you want?"

"I want to know where Gracia is."

Carlene snorted. "You came down here to ask me about that brat of yours? I ain't seen her. Ask your boyfriend Ramone."

"He's in jail. Please, tell me where she is, and I'll help you get out of here."

She leaned back in her chair, needle-scarred arms crossed over her chest.

"She's three years old, Carlene. Can't you imagine how scared she must be?"

"I told you, I ain't seen her." Her dark eyes took on a hard stare that bore right through Sarita and pinned to the wall behind her.

Submitting to her non-existent compassion proved pointless. This woman had how many abortions? Sarita thought the accumulated guilt would play to her favor, but Max had called this one. This selfish waste of humanity wasn't giving up anything that would incriminate herself.

Sarita stood and stared back into those cold gray eyes.

"Fine. But you're condemning an innocent child, and you're condemning yourself."

She turned on her heel and stalked away.

"I ain't condemning no one!" Carlene screamed behind her. "I ain't seen that little brat!"

In the waiting room, Max caught her eyes with a combination of expectation and dread.

"How'd it go?" he asked.

"You were right, she won't admit anything."

"I'm sorry, honey." Max took her hand.

"You expected as much." Numb, she leaned into him.

"She's a cornered rat. I didn't want you to face that."

"There has to be another way." Sarita refused to let Carlene dissuade her. "What about her sister? Maybe she has Gracia, or another relative. I want to talk to her sister." Sarita walked toward the door with determination.

"Oh no." Max grasped her arm to slow her down. "Don't get all fired up, Sarita. You have a plane to catch."

She spun to face him.

"This is my fight, Max. It's about time I got fired up. And it feels good to be doing something, even if the first try didn't work. I need to do this, Max. I want to see her sister."

He looked into her eyes. "You're dealing with this better than I expected."

"I'm not as fragile as you think. I had a shock, that's all."

He searched her face. "You want to see Jolene, huh?"

She scrunched her face. "Who names their kids Carlene and Jolene?"

Max laughed. "Their mama, apparently."

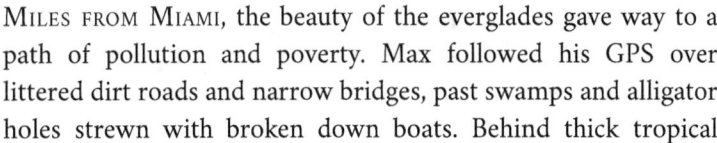

MILES FROM MIAMI, the beauty of the everglades gave way to a path of pollution and poverty. Max followed his GPS over littered dirt roads and narrow bridges, past swamps and alligator holes strewn with broken down boats. Behind thick tropical foliage, primitive shacks and ancient mobile homes dotted the landscape. Every one had a boat parked beside it.

The GPS squawked. The rusted mailbox to his left read six-three-three-six in faded red paint. He pulled into the end of the rutted drive, just off the road and stopped. He didn't want to bury the rental car in mud.

At the end of the long, winding path, a rounded, rusty trailer, circa 1950, sported a Confederate flag as a curtain. A massive mud-covered pickup with at least a two-foot lift kit towered over the tiny trailer. A beaten-up airboat sat idle in the mosquito-infested swamp.

He exchanged worried looks with Sarita, almost hoping Gracia *wasn't* here. Tension hung in the air-conditioned car as thick as the dragonflies swarming the windows.

"Here we are, white trash central," he joked to lighten the mood.

Sarita half-smiled. "Do you think Gracia is here?"

He squeezed her hand. "Let's find out."

When he opened the car door, hot, thick air buffeted him. Sweat sprouted from every pore on his body. Sarita met him at the front of the car.

Dragonflies dive-bombed them as he waved off mosquitoes the size of bumble bees. Hand-in-hand, they maneuvered up the potholed path strewn with puddles big enough to swallow a Volkswagen. As they picked their way past bubbling quicksand, his shoes buried to the laces in mud.

Sarita yelped. She wobbled on one foot. The other muddy foot had no shoe.

With a laugh, he pulled her flip-flop from the suction of mud. He remembered the day they'd met. Placing that spiked yellow heel on her foot gave him a view of her sexy legs that burned into his brain. To this day, that vision floated through his dreams.

"They won't stay on in this mud." She plunked her bare foot

into the sopping mess and steadied herself with a hand on his shoulder as she peeled the other flip-flop from her muddy foot.

A far cry from that spiked yellow heel, he held up her sandals to let the mud drip off.

Then Sarita gasped, cowering beneath him.

He dropped the shoes and covered her with his arms and body.

"What is it?" Panic filled his voice as his gaze searched the woods for signs of danger.

Face buried in his chest, she pointed behind him.

He whipped around, keeping his protective hold on her.

An alligator hung bleeding from a tree, twitching in the heat.

A measure of relief poured over him. He'd expected to find some redneck pointing a shotgun. Yet this was a fresh kill. Someone had to be home - and armed.

"It's okay," he soothed. "Gator hunting is common here."

Sarita shook beneath him. "It's still moving!"

"Just nerves. That gator's not going anywhere but the frypan."

"Eeeeeeeewww." She jerked away, hugging herself and hopping from foot to foot like an old cartoon of a housewife jumping on the sofa to get away from a mouse.

If not for the gravity of the situation, he'd burst out laughing at the look on her face.

"Don't people eat gator in Puerto Rico?"

"Not in *my* back yard!" she said with horror. "Why is it hanging in a tree?"

"The blood has to be drained before butchering."

"How do you know this?" Her voice rose to a creeped-out pitch.

"Chad's a hunter. But he strings up deer, not gators."

"Whatever." She kept her arms crossed over her stomach.

"Ready?" he asked.

"No, but let's go." She peeked at the trailer ahead.

He bent to retrieve her shoes, but they'd been sucked in deep.

"Forget it," she said. "I'll never wear them again anyway."

He wrapped an arm around her, thinking how vulnerable she was wearing no shoes, shorts, a tiny tank top, and her heart on her sleeve.

As they neared the trailer, a malnourished hound dog slowly stood. Lugging a heavy chain, it meandered toward them with a single moaning howl.

A man appeared from the woods, wearing a T-shirt with the sleeves torn off, ripped cut-offs, and a grimy hat. The dog cowered, covering its head with its paws. The redneck grabbed a shot gun leaning against a tree and kicked the whimpering dog.

Then he pointed the gun in their direction.

"Git off my property," he snarled.

GATOR BAIT

Max's heart clogged in his throat. Protective instincts kicked in, and he shoved Sarita behind him. His heart lurched at her quaking. Then he raised his hands into clear view. Sarita followed his lead. Smart girl.

He needed to get her out of here, but if they turned to run, the guy could shoot them down. Training told him he had a better chance of talking his way out of this.

"If Gracia is here," Sarita breathed, barely moving her lips. "We have to get her away from him."

Much as he hated to jeopardize Sarita's life, it was too late. He might as well get what they came for.

"We don't mean any harm, sir. We came to see Jolene."

"What you want with her?" His voice grew defensive.

They had the right place.

"We just want to talk to her. We know her sister."

"That no-good piece of trash," he muttered.

Talk about the pot calling the kettle black.

Sarita's raised hands quivered in his peripheral vision. She remained silent and kept his pace as he stepped forward with forced nonchalance, trying to strategize a plan.

The trailer door swung open. He grabbed Sarita, yanking her close behind him, and pulling her into a crouched position.

A tiny woman popped out the door with a red ponytail bobbing from the top of her head. She scowled at the man.

"Put that thing down!" she yelled. "And don't be bad-mouthing my sister!" She wagged a finger at him. "Ain't like you never done time."

The man cursed, waving her off. He continued to watch Max with narrowed eyes but lowered the gun.

"We spoke to Carlene." Max took Sarita's hand and pulled her to stand. With ease and caution, he closed the distance between them and the woman. "If we had some information, it might clear her." Doubtful, but the ploy worked.

"I'll do what I can to help." The woman wrung her hands and perched on the edge of a rotting redwood deck that served as a doorstep.

"Don't be telling them Yankees nothin'," the man warned.

"You shush!" She glowered at him. "She's *my* sister and I'll help her iffen I can."

He shook his head but backed off.

Max led Sarita to face the woman.

"Have a seat." She patted the crumbling redwood. "Would you like a snort?" She pointed to a jar of white lightning on the step.

"No, thank you," Max said.

Sarita shook her head.

"Don't be givin' 'em my liquor!" The man took a step forward.

"Southern hospitality, you know," she said. "He ain't got none." She glared at the man, and he glared right back.

At least he stayed put about fifty feet away. The gun remained pointed to the ground.

They faced a live grenade, and this lunatic had his hand on the trigger. The faster Max got this done, the better. If he made this guy feel good about himself, it might defuse the situation.

"You have a right kind woman, here, sir." Max directed his words to the man. "We won't take much of your time."

He gave Max a curt nod.

Max led Sarita to the edge of the deck and motioned for her to sit between him and Jolene figuring she'd be safest there. He didn't want to insult these folks by being standoffish. He sat beside Sarita with a protective arm around her trembling shoulders.

"You related to Pedro?" Jolene examined Sarita's face.

Max held his breath, unsure whether that was an advantage.

"He's my brother." Sarita's words came out shaky.

"Definite resemblance." Jolene nodded. "They've had their differences, that's for sure. But Carlene loves that scoundrel."

"The cops claim she ran off with a little girl." Max redirected the conversation. "Do you know anything about that?"

"Poor little thing." Jolene looked sad. "She missed her mama so." Her eyes widened at Sarita. "You her mama?"

"Yes, is she here?" Sarita looked ready to jump out of her skin.

Jolene shook her head.

"Carlene chartered a boat and took off with her. Came back without her and I ain't seen her since. She wouldn't tell me where she took her." Her eyes welled with tears.

Stark horror filled Sarita's face.

"I wanted to keep her, but he wouldn't let me." Jolene scowled at the man. "Ain't got no kids of my own." She looked down as her voice lowered to a whisper. "He's shooting blanks."

Max tensed with alarm, watching the guy with the gun from the corner of his eye. No visible reaction, but this situation could escalate in a heartbeat.

"I'm sorry to hear that, ma'am." He stood, taking Sarita's hand. They needed to get out of here. Now.

But one final question.

"Do you know which charter she used?"

"Bubba's - only one in town." Jolene pointed the opposite direction they'd come.

"Thank you, ma'am. We appreciate your help."

"Don't run off already." She looked disappointed to see them leave.

"You've been more than generous with your time, ma'am." He gave her a polite nod. He looked to the man and waved. "Thank you, sir."

Eyes still narrowed, hand on the gun, the guy didn't flinch.

Max turned to go, and Sarita stuck close beside him. The hair on the back of his neck stood on end at the thought of that guy behind his back. Was he googling Sarita, laughing under his breath at their hasty retreat, or planning his attack?

With a pasted-on smile, Max glanced over his shoulder.

The man hadn't moved.

He pulled Sarita along. Guilt stabbed him at rushing her through the mud with no shoes. Heaven forbid if they had to make a run for it.

Each yard felt like a hundred. They passed the hanging gator and the quicksand, every milestone a relief.

At last, they reached the car, and he opened the door for Sarita. She glanced at her mud-covered feet but hurried inside. Slamming her door, he looked back.

The man had disappeared. Jolene sat alone on the porch, looking forlorn.

Panic struck him full force. His gaze darted through the trees, but no sign of Shotgun Sam.

He ran to the driver's side and jumped in. Where were the keys? He patted his pockets. Yanking out the keys, he fumbled them into the ignition and cranked the starter.

Rrrrrr, rrrrrrrr, rrrrrrrr, rrrrrrrr. Nothing.

Sarita's knees were shaking.

God, please help me.

Rrrrrrr, rrrrrrrr, rrrrrrr, rrrrrr, vrooooommmmm!

Thank you, God!

He jammed the gearshift into reverse and hightailed it out of there as fast as he could. He didn't care if he looked 'yella'. All that mattered was getting Sarita out of there safe and sound.

Racing up the dirt road, the tires threw rooster tails of mud in their wake. Jarred by the washboard bumps, he hit a pothole that bounced him so hard his head struck the roof.

With a cry, Sarita grabbed the dash.

"Sorry." After checking the rearview mirror, he let off the gas and took a deep breath to slow his racing heart. Few times in his life had he been that scared. First when his parents died, then when Deira won custody of Luke, again when Gracia was kidnapped, and now when Sarita's life was threatened.

Never mind his own life. He'd faced death before. Confronting the enemy as a Navy SEAL had pumped his adrenalin and made him determined to win. The altercations with Ramone enraged him. But losing those he loved terrified him.

Several miles up the road, he pulled to the side and looked over at Sarita.

Hugging herself didn't quell the uncontrollable shaking. Her entire body trembled. She turned her tear-streaked face to him. Unbearable pain filled her eyes.

And greater fear than he had ever known. To lose a child...

He threw the car into park and reached across to wrap his arms around her. She grabbed onto him, clinging, sobbing on his shoulder.

Stroking her hair and rubbing her back, he didn't know how long they sat there with the car running but it was long enough for her to cry herself out.

She sniffled, raising her head.

"I'm sorry." She dabbed at his soaked shirt.

"Don't be." He smoothed the hair from her face and wiped her tears.

She reached in her purse for a tissue and blew her nose like an elephant with a head cold.

"Feel better?" he asked with half a smile.

"No." She shook her head in misery. "Gracia is dead." She said it with certainty. "Jolene admitted it - Carlene took off on a boat with her and came back without her. She d...du...m...ped my b...b...baby in the ocean."

"No." Adamant, he shook his head. "Carlene wouldn't dump Gracia from a chartered boat. She left her somewhere. The Bahamas or the Virgin Islands aren't that far. I'll find out where that charter runs and ask Bubba if he saw Gracia."

Distraught and inconsolable, Sarita heaved dry sobs.

"I might as well be dead, too," she wailed. "I have no reason to live."

Her words cut Max to the core.

"Let me be your reason, Sarita," he whispered. "I need you."

Face in her hands, she shook her head. "You don't need me, Max. All I've done is mess up your life."

"That's not true. I was miserable without you. I love you."

"No, you don't," she disagreed. "Men love my body but no one loves *me*."

Stunned, he realized the stark parallels in their distrust of the opposite sex.

"Sarita." He touched her face. "I love you for who you are. You are beautiful from the *inside* out."

"How can you say that?" Her face scrunched in agony. "I gave up my soul to men who used me as a plaything."

"Circumstances beyond your control made you desperate. You realized that mistake and moved past it. If you think your looks are all you have going for you, you're selling yourself short."

She gave him a sidelong glance. Uncertainty filled her searching eyes.

"We have something in common." He took a fortifying breath,

with a mental prayer that he wouldn't say this wrong. "For years, I've been afraid to trust women. Until you, I thought women only wanted my money." He paused, watching her reaction.

Her brows crinkled and tears sprang to her eyes. "I'm not like that."

"No, you're not. I'm sorry I ever doubted you. I got lost behind the businessman and the money and didn't think anyone cared who I am inside."

"I care." She caught his eyes. "I know exactly what you mean. Talk about lost. I'm tainted, but you've been kind and comforting."

"Sarita, I love you."

"Max, I love you too."

For a long time they held each other, grateful for this revelation and the understanding they shared. Max prayed Sarita's feelings of worthlessness would subside, that she'd be able to survive whatever happened. He shook off gathering doubts before she sensed them.

A soft dinging drew his attention to the dash.

A red light blinked the shape of a gas pump and the words *Low Fuel* glared back at him.

Holy moly - how long had they been sitting here with the engine running?

"We're out of gas!" Sarita began to hyperventilate.

"No, we're not. It's just low." He put the car in gear and began to drive. Angst crept through him as he wondered how far they were from the nearest gas station.

Where in God's green earth *were* they? He'd headed the direction Jolene said they'd find the charter - the opposite direction they'd come. He considered backtracking but hadn't seen a gas station for miles. And he didn't want to pass that trailer again.

He pulled out his cell phone to get GPS. No signal.

Full blown panic ripped through him. He shut off the AC to

conserve fuel. In five minutes, the cool wore off. Stifling heat forced him to roll down the windows.

"Where are we?" Sarita's voice wavered.

"The Everglades." He was in no mood to elaborate. And he didn't have a clue.

"You don't have to get snippy about it."

"Do we have a map?" he asked in a huff.

"No," she barked. Yet she proceeded to rifle through the glove compartment. She pulled out the rental agreement and the car's manual. She threw them back inside the dash and slammed the door.

Why hadn't he had the foresight to buy a stinking map? How stupid to assume the Everglades would have cell service.

Max drove on for miles in the suffocating heat. Wiping his forehead every three seconds, he watched the fuel gauge dip below empty and beyond. At last, they pulled onto a main road.

The car sputtered.

He jerked back and forth in the seat, as if his movement would push the car further. The engine choked out.

"No!"

Sarita began to cry again. Hadn't she run out of tears yet?

Exasperated, he realized she was right. He wouldn't be in this mess if it wasn't for her pretty little butt.

"Arrrrrgh!" he growled and pounded the steering wheel. The car rolled to a stop, and he threw it in park.

"What now?" she asked between sobs.

"I'm hoofing it," he said. "Wait here."

"Oh no! I'm not sitting here by myself." She opened the car door and stepped out with her mud-encrusted bare feet.

"Sarita, you can't walk like that."

"Watch me." She shut the door and proceeded up the road.

"Fine." He slammed out and caught up to her, catching her wince as gravel poked through the muck on her feet. Chunks of dried mud left a trail behind her.

It was almost funny, but he wasn't laughing.

They walked for miles without a word, as the mid-afternoon sun bore down in sweltering waves. After the tropical forest they'd just driven through, this road sizzled in the sun surrounded by a steaming swamp. Gators floated like logs on either side of them. He swatted a thousand mosquitoes and waved away dragonflies buzzing his head.

In his frustration and anger, he hadn't thought to offer Sarita his shoes. He looked down at her feet. Beneath the remaining layer of mud, her soles edged with little cuts.

He grabbed her arm to stop her.

"Sarita, look at your feet!"

"I feel them. I don't need to see them." Misery dripped from her voice.

"No, stop!" He forced her to sit at the edge of the road. He turned up her foot to find a mass of festered, red blisters. Some ripped open with jagged cuts, filling with bloody dirt.

"How are you even walking?"

She shrugged. "I'm getting used to the pain."

"Sarita, I'm so sorry." Massive guilt tore a hole in his heart. "I didn't even think to give you my shoes. Some southern gentleman I am. More like a self-centered jerk." He slapped himself on the head. "I feel like such a heel."

Sitting there in the gravel and sand, she looked at him. "Hardy har-har."

"What?" He searched her deadpan face.

"A heel? Are you making a joke, Mr. Carter?" Her eyes held the faintest twinkle.

A chuckle emerged from Sarita. Delirious, she leaned back and giggled, holding her stomach, and kicking her blistered feet.

Unable to take it, he erupted in guffaws. The horror of their situation slipped away.

But it didn't last.

Sarita tried on his shoes. Too big, they fell off her feet. He couldn't help her.

"You can't walk anymore, shoes or not," Max told her. "Not with those blisters."

"What now?" she asked.

"We'll just have to wait for someone to pass by and hope they're kind enough to give us a ride." He looked up and down the deserted road. "Or hope my phone picks up a blasted signal."

He shaded his phone, trying to read the screen in the glaring sunlight. The battery had gone dead.

He wanted to hurl it into the swamp but was too tired to lift his arm that far.

Sarita laid her head on his shoulder, defusing his anger.

"Guess we'd better start praying," Max said.

"Yeah, right. That'll work." Sarcasm filled her exhausted voice.

Too worn out to argue, he also felt abandoned by God at that point.

The sun beat down and zapped their energy. They succumbed, huddled at the side of the road, stranded, and parched. So tired, he lay down, just for a minute. Sarita curled up beside him like a trusting child, making him feel worse.

This vulnerable woman and her child needed his help. But nothing he had done to find Gracia worked, and now this.

He failed them.

UNCONTROLLABLE SHAKING ROCKED MAX. Pulled from bone-weary slumber, he groaned and rolled over. His face burned and his body ached everywhere. Even his scalp hurt.

The infernal shaking didn't stop.

"Hey, buddy, you alright?" A strange male voice asked.

Who was that? Where am I? Max pried his eyes open. They felt swollen and hurt like a bee sting. He struggled to focus. A weathered face looked down at him, full of concern beneath the shade of an old fishing hat.

His lips were glued together. Cracking them open elicited more pain. Max tried to speak but his tongue stuck to the roof of his mouth.

The old man produced a bottle of water and poured it into his mouth. Max lapped it up like a dog after a run through the desert. Then the flow stopped.

"We gotta save some for your lady here," the man said. "This is all I got."

Sarita! Max turned to find her sprawled at the edge of the road, red as a tomato and covered with bug bites. Her mouth and eyes swelled shut.

He grabbed her shoulders and shook her.

"Yeeeeow!" Her eyes popped open, and her fingers and toes stuck out like she'd suffered an electrical shock.

"Easy there, fella," the old man cried. "She's sunburnt as a baby at the beach." Then he quieted, bending low. Putting a finger to his lips, he pointed up the road a piece.

Not twenty feet away, an enormous gator sunned on the bank of the steaming swamp. It lifted its snout to sniff in their direction.

ANGELS AMONG US

Sarita groaned. Pain seared every inch of her skin.

"Shhhhh." Max patted his fingers on her mouth. Even his gentle touch hurt her scorched lips.

"Owwwwwwww." The roar growled from within her as she tried to get up. Max held her down. His touch hurt. What was he doing?

A strange hissing sound diverted her attention.

A huge alligator bared its teeth at them, hissing from deep in its throat. Paralyzed by fear, she wanted to run, but Max's grip on her shoulders kept her in place, his touch biting into her sunburned skin.

"Don't move," whispered an old man beside Max. Who was that guy? She stared at the gator, too petrified to move, to think, to do anything but watch and wait.

After an agonizing minute of frozen silence, the creature's mouth eased shut. It retreated, slipping into the swamp at the edge of the road.

Max released his hold on her, letting out a breath.

"Y'all gotta be careful out here," the man warned. He pointed to scratch marks at the edge of the road not a foot from Sarita's head. "Lucky I got here before dusk when the gators get hungry."

Sarita lifted to her elbows and winced in pain. She blinked at the old man, and then looked around at the destitute surroundings. Under the glaring sun, she had no shelter, no water, and no shoes. An ancient pickup truck parked nearby must belong to the old man.

In agony, she pried open her parched mouth, but words wouldn't come.

"Here ya go." Their rescuer put a bottle of water to her lips, and she guzzled it. He took the empty bottle away and she licked every drop from her cracked lips.

"W... what's g... going on?" she croaked.

The old man looked to Max. "That your Chevy back a piece?"

Max nodded. "Out of gas. Couldn't go any further."

The old man shook his head.

"I'm Chuck Morris. Not the actor, so don't get smart. That's Morris with an M." He stuck out his hand and Max shook it.

"Max Carter. This is Sarita Santos."

Chuck reached for Sarita's hand, but instead of shaking it, he helped her up.

"Come on Miss Sarita, let's get you out of here." He motioned to his pickup. "I got a can of gas in the back. Nearest station is twenty miles yonder." He pointed the direction they'd been walking.

Sarita's eyes widened at Max. She winced at the motion and noticed how burnt she was despite the pigment in her Latin skin. Itchy welts covered her arms and legs, but she dared not scratch.

She looked over Max. His eyes swelled to slits and his lips cracked with blisters. On his arms and legs, every blond hair stood out against his cherry red skin. Ouch.

Chuck held the underside of Sarita's arm as he led her toward the truck. She crept over the scorching asphalt, grimacing with each barefoot step. He opened the truck door and cool AC rushed out to greet her, as refreshing as the four ounces of water.

Thank you, God, for this kind man.

She climbed into the truck, inch by agonizing inch, scooting to the middle of the worn bench seat. Max stepped in behind her, careful not to let their burned skin touch.

Chuck made a U-turn and drove back to their rental car. They must have walked over five miles. After emptying his gas can into the tank, he gave Max directions to the gas station.

"Just follow me," he said. "I'm headed into town."

Max handed him cash for the gasoline.

"Keep yer money." Chuck held up a hand. "Done my good deed for the day. At my age, every one counts." He pointed to their arms and legs. "Get yourself some zinc oxide for that sunburn. It'll take out the sting. Drug store's next door to the gas station." The spry old man winked and hopped into his truck.

The inside of the car felt like an oven. The leather seat scalded her tender thighs. Max touched the steering wheel and yelped. He scrounged a tissue to buffer the burn and cranked the key with determination.

As soon as the engine sputtered to life, Max cranked the AC. He gave Chuck thumbs up and the old man led the way toward town.

Sarita laid her head back and moaned. Sprawled out, she minimized any contact with her scorching skin. A cluster of red welts on her thigh itched like crazy. She scraped her nails across them.

"Yow!" The scratch was worse than the maddening itch.

"Don't scratch," Max growled. His arms stuck out at weird angles as he tried to drive without aggravating his sunburn.

Fresh despair filled her. Could her misery be any worse? Every inch of her seared with pain and her blistered feet throbbed. She'd put Max through all this, and for what? Gracia could be at the bottom of the ocean.

Desperate for a hug, she wrapped her arms around herself but touching her own skin brought more pain than comfort. Why had she been rescued to face this debilitating reality?

"He should have left me to die," she whimpered. "I have nothing to live for."

＊

TOO WIPED out to deal with Sarita's grief, Max said a silent prayer. Fighting pain, he gripped the scorching steering wheel. Thankful when she let it drop, he watched her nod off as the car cooled. The drive to town was every bit of twenty-five miles from where they'd run out of gas. If not for Chuck, they'd have been gator bait.

As they approached the first red light, Mr. Morris with an M pointed out his window to the gas station. Max pulled in and Sarita's head popped up.

He turned to wave goodbye.

Only a beat-up Cadillac sat at the red light. Chuck's pickup wasn't at the gas station, or the drug store next door, or in the parking lot across the street. Like an angel sent from God, he rescued them and then disappeared.

"Where did he go?" Sarita bolted upright, pointing out the window. "He was right there," she choked out. "His truck vanished into thin air!"

"Maybe he was an angel." Max watched for her reaction.

Sarita frowned with disbelief. She settled back in the seat with exhaustion, but her eyes scanned the intersection.

Max shook his head. Conserving his voice, he needed water.

He left the car running, AC cranked, at the gas pump as he hurried inside. Whispering a silent prayer that it didn't burst into flames in this heat, he begged God to let Sarita recover - not just from the heat stroke, but from her lost faith, and whatever they found, or didn't find, regarding Gracia.

In search of water, he wandered through the store, unable to move quickly. Yet his mind raced.

No matter how Sarita's attitude toward God frightened him, or her unrelenting grief created a chasm he couldn't bridge, he couldn't guard his heart. He fell deeper in love with her every day. He had to help her through this.

Yet the devil on his shoulder blamed him. His money tempted Ramone to kidnap Gracia. For Sarita's sake, Max needed to drop her with her grandmother and get out of her life. She'd heal and recover, back in her happy place. Eventually she'd rebuild her life.

Max shook off the conflict in his head and grabbed four enormous bottles of water. At the checkout, he spotted a dark chocolate Dove bar. He'd learned it was Sarita's favorite treat, yet she seldom allowed herself to indulge. He grabbed one for each of them.

Carrying his booty to the car, he couldn't wait to guzzle that icy cold water. When he opened the car door, Sarita stirred. Her eyes pried open, and he handed her a bottle.

She sprang to life and ripped off the lid, slamming the water to her lips and gulping it down. Max did the same. After downing two giant bottles, they sat gasping with relief.

"Water never tasted so good," Sarita said with gratitude.

These words came from the woman who wanted him to leave her for dead. He pulled out the chocolate. Her eyes went wide, and she grabbed it from him like a starving child.

"My favorite!" She tore off the wrapper and bit in. As the chocolate hit her tongue, she leaned back in the seat and let it melt in her mouth. A look of sublime bliss lit her face. She had no death wish.

He'd expected her to gobble it down, but Sarita never failed to surprise him.

Max enjoyed the simple pleasure with her, careful to let the chocolate melt on his tongue as well. Sarita's way delighted beyond expression.

After filling the gas tank, Max headed to the drug store next door for zinc oxide and a Florida map. In the drug store parking lot, he and Sarita lathered one another with the cooling cream.

"The old man knew what he was talking about," Max noted.

"How nice of him to help us," Sarita said.

"Yeah, he was an angel." Max hinted again at his suspicion, hoping a refreshed Sarita would respond more favorably.

She ignored his comment, as if God had nothing to do with it. He planted the seed, but she wasn't ready to talk about it.

"I missed my flight." Regret lined her sunburned face.

Was she refuting that God took care of her?

"Will you get credit for the cost?" she asked.

"Don't worry about it." Grateful he could well afford the change fee, he understood the value of a hundred and fifty dollars to Sarita.

"Maybe I shouldn't go." She capped the zinc oxide. "I don't want to burden my grandmother. She's old and..."

"She'd be thrilled to see you. How many years has it been?"

"I haven't seen her since I was 18. She came for my father's funeral."

"Ten years is too long, don't you think? She won't be around forever. Take this chance, Sarita."

"I don't want her to see me like this. And I don't want you to pay my way." She looked out at the street and tears began to flow. "After all I'd accomplished in the last few years, it's come to this. What's the point? Maybe I should jump off the boat too."

"Sarita... stop." He dabbed her tears. "That's what family does for each other. They pick you up when you're down. I'm sure your grandmother will be grateful for the chance to help you."

"I wish you'd go with me."

"I know, sweetie. But I have to look for Gracia." If he didn't find her, or heaven forbid if she was dead, would Sarita ever recover?

Her sorrowful eyes looked up at him.

"Trials make us stronger," he whispered with as much conviction as he could muster. Knowing from experience, he reminded himself as much as her. He needed all the strength he could get at this point.

She frowned and climbed into the car.

As much as he cared for her, he wasn't sure they should pursue this relationship. Was he blaming the devil for his uncertainty or was God trying to tell him something? He'd prayed himself to sleep for nights on end, but God remained silent.

If Sarita turned from God, shouldn't he seek a soulmate who shared his faith? Maybe he should try to lead her back to God, yet his feelings precluded being just friends.

Besides, without his money, there'd be no ransom.

Was that the answer he'd been looking for? Maybe whoever had Gracia would give her up. With Sarita in Puerto Rico and Max getting on with his life, money would not be a motivation to hold Gracia. Surely Carlene's contact would grow tired of caring for her with no hope of remuneration. Meanwhile, Sarita would heal with her grandmother's spiritual guidance.

Had he finally figured out the right thing to do?

He got in the car and studied her.

"The trials are more than I can bear." Her defeated face convinced him more than ever. He couldn't reach her.

Today she might be enjoying chocolate, but if Gracia were dead, Sarita could slip into that dark hole and never return. He couldn't shake that vision.

If she killed herself over this, it'd be two lives lost. He'd carry their deaths on his head. Why had he kept her on the phone when she should have been watching her child at the beach?

He caused this and had to make it right. God help him because he sure couldn't do it alone.

PEERING THROUGH THE AIRPLANE WINDOW, Sarita watched the coast of Puerto Rico materialize beneath the clouds. Proud and prominent, the San Felipe Fort stood on a peninsula jutting from San Juan surrounded by the sparkling turquoise waters of the Caribbean Sea.

White sandy beaches gave way to the city, sprinkled with swaying coconut palms, colorful old buildings, and a new row of hotels she didn't recognize. With dismay, she spotted a cruise ship. Passengers poured out of its belly, overflowing the boardwalk and swarming shops and restaurants like ants at a picnic.

Tourists brought money to the island - along with traffic, trash, and twisted ideas that all Americans were rich. The tourists had inspired her parents to emigrate.

Born and raised here, she filled with nostalgia. A rush of belonging and a sense of home washed over her in waves. Should she return to her homeland?

Was this her destiny? *God, if you're listening, please show me what to do. Please help me find Gracia. Lead me to her.*

The strongest feeling swept through her. At once she knew coming to Puerto Rico was best for her. The last time she'd felt God speaking to her, she'd been convinced not to have an abortion. She shivered as chills ran up and down her spine.

"You okay?" Max asked. Sitting beside her on the plane, he agreed to accompany her to Puerto Rico with no hesitation at the cost. He quietly read a NASCAR magazine while she'd been lost in her own world. Now he studied her.

"I have a good feeling." She smiled at the concern on his sunburned face. "Thank you for bringing me here and coming with me." Gratitude overwhelmed her at the sacrifices he'd made for her. "You've done so much for me. How can I ever thank you?" Tears sprang to her eyes.

"Don't thank me," he insisted, as if he didn't want her owing him. "God is the one who brought you through this." Max let that sit with her for a few moments.

"You're right," she admitted. "Chuck Morris had to be sent by God. We walked for miles and never saw a soul. Only God knows how much longer before we were gator bait."

Max nodded with agreement.

"He came along in the nick of time," she continued, "and then he disappeared into the great beyond."

"Do you believe he was an angel?" Max asked.

"He just vanished. There's no other explanation, is there?"

"I don't think so."

She couldn't keep from smiling. "God certainly has a sense of humor. Chuck Morris with an M and that ancient truck."

She wanted to make light of the situation, but Max grew solemn.

"God will take care of you, Sarita. No matter what happens."

She looked into his eyes and read the unspoken words.

"If Gracia is dead, I have to live with that." Tears sprung to her eyes, but she kept going. "I don't know how I can face that, but I can't do it without God. I don't know if I can do it *with* God." An escape by suicide seemed the only way. Yet she knew it wasn't the answer.

"God sent an angel yesterday. And He has plenty more where Chuck came from. He will help you through it, one day at a time."

She didn't know how she'd manage. The welling tears spilled down her face.

"God has a purpose for your life. That's why He sent Chuck to rescue you."

She wiped her tears, recognizing that truth. How odd Max hadn't included his purpose in God's rescue.

"If Gracia is dead, I don't think I can go on. And if..." she couldn't say it. Shaking her head, she choked on the words.

"If we don't find her?" Max asked.

She nodded, squeezing her eyes against more tears. "I can't keep going like this..." her voice trailed off.

"No, you can't."

Her gaze shot up to his. Was he agreeing she should end her life?

"Not this way. But if you lean on God, he'll sustain you. You have to keep going, Sarita."

"Why? What do I have to live for?"

Pain seared his expression. She wanted to live for him, but he'd given up on her. Could she go on without Gracia?

"Live for hope. What if Gracia's found later and you're not there to care for her?"

Struck by the stark horror of Gracia being found only to learn her mother committed suicide, Sarita realized that could never be an option. Only a selfish failure took her own life, thwarting God's will and leaving loved ones to deal with the fallout.

"You're right. I never considered that," she admitted.

"Sarita, you are more valuable than you realize. Not just as a mother, but as a wonderful human being. You are caring and passionate, loyal, talented, and creative. Restore your joy and your hope. There's so much potential for your future. I hope you'll remember what you've meant to me, and to everyone who knows you. Whether or not Gracia survives, God has a purpose for your life. He will reveal it in time."

His gentle tone carried a matter-of-fact quality, a businesslike distance that pierced her to the core. Worse, his words regarded their relationship as over.

Yet his words rang true. She'd been through so much, yet after each trial, life improved exponentially. She'd been crushed when her father died and gone on a path of destruction. But God raised her from the pit of despair when he'd given her Gracia. Now she couldn't imagine going on without her child. But in time, life with Max could be fabulous.

God had brought this wonderful man into her life, and she was letting their relationship dissolve without a fight. Could she win back his love if she let go of the anger that tore them apart? Could she let God heal her pain? Was He preparing her for something better than she'd ever known?

She placed her sunburned hand over Max's, and he startled at her touch. His expression softened as he gazed down at her.

"Remember what you said about God protecting me throughout my life?" she asked. "Through painful circumstances, God made me stronger to prepare me for something better."

Speechless, he nodded. A glimmer of hope lit his eyes.

"Life with you would be something better." She swallowed a lump the size of Kansas. "I have to go on, God help me, and I don't want to lose you too." She choked out the words. "Whether or not we find Gracia, I want you beside me, Max. I hope you'll forgive me for the way I've treated you. Even when I turned from God, He provided you as my strength."

Max turned to face her. "Sarita, I forgive you. I want you beside me too, but..." His expression fell as a thousand unspoken words crossed his expression. "But I have to find Gracia." Guilt wracked his voice as he looked past her and out the window. A man on a mission, he'd given up his entire life for her. Yet his demeanor told her this time would be the last. They couldn't search the globe forever. At some point Max had to go back to work and she needed to reassemble her life. She couldn't imagine going on without Gracia, or without Max.

Suddenly, as if God had whispered in her ear, Sarita knew her child was alive, and they would find her soon.

"We're going to find her."

He tenderly kissed her sunburned forehead. "While you rest

and recover, I'll search Miami. First, I'll find Bubba's Charter and talk to the captain of that boat."

The pilot announced their arrival in San Juan and the stewardesses gave landing instructions. Sarita stared out the window at the coast of her beloved homeland.

"How far is your grandmother from the city?" Max asked.

Thinking of her grandmother, of seeing her again after all these years, filled her with bittersweet joy.

"See that bay to the east?" Sarita pointed. "I used to play on the beach near there. Her house is two streets in, beneath the grove of coconut palms."

A bubble of excitement surfaced for the first time in weeks. Abuela would be so surprised to see her. How much had she aged in over a decade? Sarita pictured her slicing mangoes in the kitchen or tending hibiscus in the yard.

"You look happier than I've seen you in weeks."

"I'm looking forward to seeing mi abuela." She kissed him lightly. "And I have you."

His painful-looking smile pulled his blistering skin. He disregarded the affirmation of their relationship, but Sarita was too excited to worry about it now. When the plane landed, she couldn't get out of the airport fast enough. Ignoring the pain of her blistered feet, she hustled in her cushy new sneakers. Max hailed a lively, Spanish-speaking driver in a wild, multi-colored taxi. Sarita gave him the address. She could barely understand his thick accent.

She'd been away too long.

Hillsides dotted with little houses rolled by past pineapple and sugar cane fields. Trucks loaded with cane headed for the Bacardi rum plant. Kapok and mahogany trees, coconut palms, poincianas, and wild orchids grew along the roadside against a backdrop of misty green mountains.

They skimmed past El Yunque rain forest where a flock of green parrots squawked in protest. As a young girl, Sarita had tattled on her brothers for taunting the birds. Abuela told the boys to leave those birds alone; they were protecting their young.

Abuela had done the same for her. While Papa labored in the cane fields and Mama worked at the fishery, Abuela made sure Sarita and her brothers were looked after and well fed. She spent her days cooking for her family and anyone else who graced her doorstep.

They pulled onto the street where Sarita grew up. The same rutted dirt road led to the same houses bordering the nature reserve. Abuela's little yellow casa nestled among palms, tree ferns, and blooming hibiscus.

Sarita was home.

"I'd like to meet your grandmother before my flight leaves for Miami," Max said as the cabbie helped him unload her luggage. "Please ask the driver to pick me up in two hours," he requested.

Sarita gave the instructions in rusty Spanish as Max handed the driver payment and a generous tip. The cabbie nodded with a heartfelt 'gracias', and his dark eyes widened at the amount. Like a spooked lizard, he darted off in his crazy car before Max changed his mind.

"She's home." Sarita pointed to Abuela's old bicycle sitting in its place beside the porch. Salt air wreaked havoc on the blue paint. Enormous baskets on the handlebars and sides were worn from use. "Abuela doesn't drive," she explained. "She's used that bike since I was little for grocery shopping and everything else."

"She must be one fit granny," Max said. Despite his lighthearted words, sorrow overshadowed him. His doubts remained.

Sarita pushed her worries aside and headed up the narrow dirt path lined with rocks and impatiens that led to the front door. Blue Caribbean butterflies flitted through the garden where bromeliads and orchids bloomed alongside ginger lily that perfumed the intoxicating ocean breeze.

Sarita recognized the breadfruit tree she'd helped plant as a child. Now twenty feet tall and laden with green fruit, the tree shaded the entire yard.

On the front porch, Abuela's 1950s metal chairs sat in a colorful row as they always had. Yet they sported pink, green, and blue paint instead of the orange, red, and yellow she remembered as a kid.

Everything changed, yet nothing had changed.

She knocked on the front door, knowing Abuela would scold her for not coming right in.

"Vamos en," Spanish words called from inside. "Estoy en la cocina."

What a joy to hear her voice!

"Come in. She's in the kitchen," Sarita translated for Max. "She doesn't speak English." She pushed open the screen door and he followed her inside.

Pausing a moment, she took in the familiar room.

Nothing had changed. Abuela had the same ancient green sofa, same antique bamboo tables, and the same pillows with tropical leaves she'd stitched herself.

Healthy potted palms stood in every corner, and a giant bouquet of pink hibiscus, fragrant orange jasmine, and palm fronds filled a jug on the coffee table.

"I see where you get your decorating sense," Max whispered.

Sarita beamed. "Yeah, I never realized that before."

Her grandmother had been the best influence on her life in terms of faith, encouragement, and support. Without her example, Sarita would have been a terrible mother. In fact, she might have gone through with the abortion if not for the basic morals and spiritual values she'd learned on her grandmother's knee.

"Juanita, get in here and help me," Abuela called in Spanish. "What are you knocking for?"

Sarita peeked around the corner into the kitchen. Abuela stood at the sink, peeling papayas. Same as always, she wore an old house dress, hummed a tune, and looked out the window as she worked.

"Abuela, it's me," Sarita said in Spanish.

Abuela's head spun around. She dropped the knife and a papaya slipped from her hand.

"Sarita!" She ran over and wrapped her in a long, hard hug. "It's been so long. I'm so glad to see you!"

Wincing from the sunburn, Sarita hugged Abuela tight.

"Who's Juanita?" she teased.

Abuela broke off the hug and waved a hand. "Some old biddy who comes over to gossip. Never mind her, let me look at you!" She placed two sticky hands on Sarita's red cheeks and looked into her eyes.

"Too much sun!" she exclaimed, clicking her tongue.

Sarita examined her grandmother's weathered face. Her dark eyes had grown cloudy. Age spots and wrinkles had multiplied from the Caribbean sun. Yet her face shone with wisdom - and knowing.

"Something's wrong," she announced. "I see sadness, hardship, and worry."

"Si," Sarita admitted. She looked to Max and then at the floor.

"Who's this?" Abuela asked with suspicion.

"Mi amigo bien, Max Carter. My good friend," she interpreted for Max's benefit. She grasped his hand, needing support.

"Where's your daughter?" Abuela asked.

Tears sprang to Sarita's eyes. "She's... missing."

Horror covered Abuela's face. "No..." She ran to the window and looked out. With curious relief, she led them to the sofa.

"Sit," she ordered. "Tell me what happened."

Sarita didn't want to talk about it or think about it. She came here to enjoy Abuela and ease the pain. But she also came to heal.

Her grandmother could only help if she knew what Sarita dealt with. As much as she didn't want to upset her, Abuela deserved the truth. Yet she dreaded wading through this horrible grief.

With a steadying breath, Sarita described Ramone's threats and Gracia's kidnapping. Her grandmother's face registered shock and then horror as tears ran down her cheeks for the great-grandchild she'd never met.

Sarita explained their search but left out Pedro's involvement. No sense upsetting Abuela with her grandson's illegal escapades - not to mention his horrendous betrayal.

"How terrible." Her grandmother's face contorted. "I get a child and you lose yours."

FRIENDS IN LOW PLACES

"**W**hat???" Her sixty-something grandmother had a child? "I'm caring for Pedro's daughter."

Sarita worked her mouth to form a million questions, but her tongue twisted in knots.

"Haven't seen that hoodlum in years and he didn't even stop to visit." A deep scowl lined Abuela's face. "He sent his girlfriend to drop her off."

Unable to process the information, Sarita froze. She stared at Max, but he didn't have a clue what her grandmother just said.

Abuela rattled on. "Melita won't speak. But I love her anyway. She reminds me of you as a child."

Sarita's heart leapt as she forced words to come.

"Where is she?" she cried in panic. "It's Gracia!"

Max gripped her arm, puzzlement on his face as he tried to decipher the conversation.

"No, she's Melita, *Pedro's* daughter." Abuela reiterated.

"Pedro doesn't have a daughter!"

The old woman blinked.

"Pedro's girlfriend took Gracia. Where is she?" Frantic, Sarita jumped from the sofa and raced from room to room.

"Playing in the yard!" Abuela pointed to the back door.

Sarita threw open the door and lapsed into slow-motion as the scene took her back in time. Beneath blooming hibiscus where the grass wouldn't grow, she saw a vision of her three-year-old self drawing pictures with a stick on the sandy ground.

"Gracia?" her tentative voice squeaked out as she willed her frozen feet to move.

The girl looked up with alarm. Her shadowed eyes widened, and her mouth dropped open. The stick fell from her hand.

"Poor child is traumatized," Abuela whispered. "I'm trying to teach her Spanish, but she won't speak. Barely even eats."

Sarita stepped forward cautiously.

"Gracia, it's me. Mama."

The child's thin, drawn face scrunched up, and tears spouted forth. She jumped to her feet and broke into a run calling, "Mama! Mama!"

Almost unbelieving, Sarita's heart hammered as her feet ran toward her daughter but seemed to take forever to reach her.

"Gracia!" Relief and joy poured through her as they met in the center of the yard. Sarita swept her up and spun with elation, squeezing her daughter's emaciated body so hard she could feel her bones. Gracia's arms around her neck choked the wind out of her. Sarita couldn't speak, couldn't breathe.

It was the greatest feeling in the world.

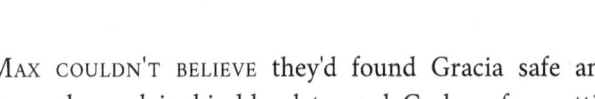

Max couldn't believe they'd found Gracia safe and sound. Anger burned in his blood toward Carlene for putting Sarita through needless pain, all for the sake of saving her own skin. The child shied away from everyone but her mother.

After a joyful afternoon reunion, the taxi driver returned.

Instead of heading to the airport, Max had everyone jump in the cab and took them to the finest restaurant in the area. Then they relaxed at Abuela's house before preparing for bed. Fast asleep, Gracia curled into a ball on her mama's lap.

"I still want to find Bubba's and question that boat captain," Max told Sarita. "If he identifies Carlene, we can make a case against her."

"I don't even care anymore." She nuzzled her sleeping daughter's hair.

Max touched her cheek.

"I understand. You stay here with your grandmother and Gracia. Visit as long as you like. But I have to see that Carlene is locked up permanently. Ramone and Pedro too. If these people get off, who's to say they won't pull something like this again?"

Sarita shuddered.

"Okay. Go to Miami." She searched his eyes. "But thank you for staying tonight - and for the wonderful celebration dinner. Thank God, you brought me here. What would I ever do without you?"

Guilt knotted his nerves. Without him, Sarita wouldn't have taken her eyes off Gracia on that beach. Ramone wouldn't have kidnapped her precious child with hopes of a million-dollar ransom.

Now she had her daughter back. If they returned to life on the Isle of Palms, his money would continue to be a threat. She'd be better off if he secured her enemies in jail and then got out of her life before they made parole. Pained to lose her, he feared his money would continue to be a threat and continue to come between them.

Besides, he'd been considering relocating back to Charleston. At this point, he needed his happy place too. Once again, he prayed for direction. Each time he said that prayer, his gut told him Charleston should be his home.

Sarita had no ties there and probably wouldn't want to stay in the place where her daughter was kidnapped.

She looked happier than he'd ever seen her. He loved her too much to mess that up. Maybe if he made a quiet exit, she'd stay in Puerto Rico. She'd be safer here. Bungling Pedro wouldn't dare show his face and even sly Ramone couldn't get blood from a rock.

SARITA REVELED in her daughter's care. Gracia had some issues to overcome, but each day she grew more comfortable and less fearful. She ate voraciously and began talking again. She had fun learning Spanish and grew excited to communicate with Abuela in the most basic ways.

When a neighbor stopped over, a dark Latin man like Ramone and Pedro, Gracia hid behind Sarita and trembled. Thank heaven Max was blond.

After a few days, Sarita felt Gracia was ready to get out of the house. She chose a time when most families were home having dinner and headed to the shore. As soon as the beach came into sight Gracia froze and began sobbing. Sarita kicked herself for not realizing it would be a problem. She held her daughter, soothing and telling her she was safe.

Then a speed boat roared past.

Gracia wailed with terror. Sarita gathered up her flailing, screaming daughter and took her home as fast as possible. She had her work cut out for her if she ever wanted to make sandcastles with her daughter again. Or sit on Max's balcony and look out at the ocean. Sheesh, every room in his house looked out at the ocean.

She'd been praying for direction about staying in Charleston.

Intuition pulled her that direction, but considering the kidnapping happened there, she didn't quite understand why it felt right. Gracia might never be comfortable living where she'd been kidnapped, and Sarita couldn't blame her.

But there was hope. Her bond with Gracia, always strong, had grown tenfold. The connection just clicked. As if reading one another's minds, at the same times they felt playful, sleepy, hungry, or cuddly, in total sync. They spent every moment of the day together and slept snuggled together at night.

Best of all, Abuela enjoyed the happy reunion with them.

Falling into an easy routine, they took long walks through the beautiful Puerto Rican countryside. Abuela showed Gracia the school Sarita went to, the tiny market where they shopped, and the little white church Abuela still attended. They visited family and friends Sarita hadn't seen in years. With the friendly interaction, Gracia's discomfort with strangers lessened somewhat, but she still trembled around men.

Sarita rose early in the mornings. While Abuela stayed inside with Gracia tucked into bed, she slipped away to her happy place - the beach. As much as she enjoyed time with her daughter and grandmother, she needed this quiet time alone. It became her mental therapy, her prayer time, her method of healing. She watched the sunrise and enjoyed a morning swim, reminding herself that Ramone was locked in jail and wouldn't be lurking on the beach or anywhere else.

Max would see to that.

After her swim, she called him daily. He was determined to protect her and Gracia from ever dealing with Ramone again. But his businesslike demeanor created an emotional distance and their closeness slipped away.

She'd prayed endlessly over their relationship. Now confident he loved her for herself, not her body, she felt certain God brought them together. Marriage lingered at the edge of her mind, but Max seemed to be pulling back.

On their sixth day apart, she became desperate. She spread a blanket on a secluded spot on the beach. With a lazy stretch, she dialed Max's number.

"Good morning," he answered.

"Hey baby, how ya doin'?" In her sexiest voice, she laid on the charm.

"I'm fine. I have something to ask you." He was all business, all the time anymore.

"Ask away," she whispered into the phone. "I'd do anything to bring you back to me."

From his uncomfortable chuckle, she could imagine him getting hot around the collar, pulling his shirt away from his neck and sucking in air.

"It's about Gracia."

His words felt like a cold slap. Everything was about Gracia. They'd found her. She slept safe in her bed. She was healing, and so was Sarita.

Motherhood always held first priority, but as a woman, she needed Max's attention, his affection, and most of all his love. They'd been on the brink of something real, something permanent, and he was letting it slip away. Ever since Miami, he'd been distant and cool to her. Why?

His coldness pierced her.

"Are you there?" he asked with alarm.

"Yes." The word came out sharp as an icicle.

"Uh, okay then," he stammered. "I, uh, finally reached the boat captain. He's one tough guy to pin down. Always off on a charter."

He proceeded to explain. Something about Carlene... a disguise... blah-blah-blah...

She blinked back tears, but they pushed forth anyway. Who even cared? She lay here, lonely and hurting, while the love of her life went on and on about technicalities and legal systems when she needed him to give her just an ounce of loving attention.

Why couldn't he have stayed with her, spent time with her, helped her recover from the unbelievable horror she'd been through? She sat on a tropical beach in paradise - all alone.

"They want Gracia to identify Carlene from a line up."

"What?" With a jerk, she raised up on her elbows.

"They need Gracia to identify Carlene."

"No!" she shouted. "She's just starting to recover from that trauma. I won't force her to face that woman again. I'm not putting my child through that." She sat ramrod straight, anger and resentment coursing through her. If Gracia was all-important to him, why would he even ask such a thing?

Max heaved a sigh. "Okay. I understand. What about a picture? Could she choose Carlene from a photo line up?"

Sarita gritted her teeth in silence.

"Here's the deal." Exasperation came through his voice loud and clear. "The boat captain didn't recognize Carlene. If Gracia doesn't identify her, she'll walk. If she walks, that gives Ramone and Pedro ammunition too." Brief pause.

"If Ramone gets parole, who knows what evil vengeance he has planned? Do you want that monster coming after you again? And Gracia?" His voice became determined and hard. "Do this now, Sarita, or run from him for the rest of your life."

The terror of that truth struck her heart. Every day in prison made Ramone more evil. He wouldn't give up; he wouldn't stop pursuing her. He'd have his revenge...

She couldn't let that happen.

In a rush of adrenalin, her brain formed a plan.

"Okay, here's *my* deal. I'll only go along with this if an officer comes to the house, where Gracia feels safe. A female officer, someone friendly who looks nothing like Carlene. The motherly type, in plain clothes. No badges or guns."

Max sighed. "I'll see what I can do."

"You do that." Sarita clicked off the phone and threw it in the sand.

Everything about this went against her grain. Gracia didn't need to deal with cops and lawyers. She needed to forget this whole thing happened, not relive it over and over.

Not only was his cool distance insulting and hurtful, but Max also had a dreadful idea of what was best for her and Gracia. She'd been a fool to let herself fall for him.

PHONES and wet sand didn't mix well. Even though she'd used an old toothbrush to clean the buttons on her phone, they stuck. After stewing all day and tossing and turning all night, Sarita tried to call Max the next morning with a begrudging attitude. She pressed the 286 of Max's phone number and got a string of sixes.

Six-six-six - what kind of bad omen was that? She shut the phone off and on, cleaned it again, tried everything to no avail. Her grandmother didn't have a phone. There had to be one in town somewhere, but she didn't want to talk to Max that much. Let *him* stew a while.

She peeled another layer of burnt skin from her feet, putting him out of her mind. Exfoliating sand and preserving salt water helped her blisters heal in record time.

Sunshine and clear turquoise waters took her away to their tropical paradise. Maybe she and Gracia should start a new life here with Abuela. She wondered if she could find a job in a gift shop or something. They only needed money for food and clothing. If she sold her car back in Ohio, she ought to have enough money to buy a bicycle, for heaven's sake.

Doubts crept in over her lost career, her student loans, what type of education Gracia would have, and her daughter's limited opportunities. Did it matter if they were safe and happy?

Could she be happy without Max?

And would they be safe if Ramone went free? She tried to pray, but her mind swirled with conflicting thoughts and fears all day long and into another sleepless night.

*

AROUND NOON THE NEXT DAY, Sarita looked up from her lunch and saw the crazy-colored cab pull up out front. Max slammed his way out. He blazed a path to the porch and banged on the door.

Sarita threw the screen open. "Sheesh, don't break the door down!"

"Why haven't you called me? Where's Gracia?" He scanned the room.

"Hi Max!" Gracia looked up from her lunch.

"Hi honey." His voice softened with obvious relief. Then he turned back to Sarita, mad as a screaming parrot again.

"My phone is broken." She crossed her arms over her chest, daring him to argue.

"Surely there's a phone somewhere on this island!"

Abuela walked in from the kitchen, one hand on her hip and a butcher knife poised in the other. With a stern look on her face, she jabbered something in Spanish that Sarita couldn't make out. Yet the message was clear.

Max took a step backward, waving his hands out in front of him. "Hola senora," he stuttered. "Mi sorry."

Abuela understood his pathetic translation and looked to Sarita.

"It's okay," Sarita assured her in Spanish. "He's upset that I haven't called. My phone is broken."

Abuela pointed the knife at him like a wagging finger of

shame, muttered more indecipherable Spanish and turned on her heel back to the kitchen.

Gracia's face filled with alarm.

"It's okay, honey." Sarita went to her and wrapped her in a hug. "Abuela's trying to protect us. She doesn't know Max."

"I'm sorry." Max raked a hand through his hair.

Gracia looked up at him wide-eyed.

He smoothed her hair and bent to her level. "Is it all right if I talk to your mom outside?"

Gracia backed away from him. She nodded and stuck her thumb in her mouth.

"We'll be back in a minute, okay?"

"Okay," she mumbled around her thumb.

Sarita led Max into the back yard where two ancient metal chairs, painted bright yellow, sat in the shade of a kapok tree. She waved to Gracia watching them out the window.

"I'm sorry," Max repeated. "I was crazy with worry. And a little cranky since I haven't slept in two days."

"Yeah, me either."

His gaze shot over at her. "What's wrong?"

"Oh nothing." She huffed a dramatic sigh and plopped down on the chair. "You just want me to throw my daughter to the sharks."

"They're not sharks, Sarita." He sat beside her. "They want to protect her."

"Does she look in danger to you?"

He watched Gracia for a moment. She nibbled on mangoes.

"Not today," he conceded.

Sarita almost felt victorious but sensed a warning coming.

"She didn't seem in danger chasing sand pipers at the beach either."

The brunt truth of his words dropped like a bomb. She felt an urge to grab her baby, run and hide. But that would frighten her.

"What did you find out in Miami?" Desperation filled her voice.

Max looked into her eyes with compassion.

"The police insist Gracia has to come there. That's where the crime took place," he explained. "They have no jurisdiction here. While Puerto Rico is an American commonwealth, taking her testimony here complicates the process. And they can't justify the expense of shipping manpower and equipment."

Sarita nodded. It all made sense, but she didn't like it.

"Vacation is over, I guess," she said.

"Will you go?" Encouragement filled his voice.

She searched his eyes. "Only if Gracia agrees to it."

AFTER A REFRESHING LUNCH of fruit and fish, Sarita and Max took Gracia into the back yard. They sat on a blanket, and he presented gifts - a rubber ball, a cuddly doll, and a bottle of bubbles. Gracia shied from Max, but when he blew bubbles, she chased them around the yard.

Sarita gradually introduced her questions.

"Did you have any toys while you were gone?"

"Nah. That lady gave me a pen and paper. She said I could draw pictures. No crayons, though." Gracia popped a big bubble and laughed.

"What did the lady do?" Sarita asked with bated breath. She wasn't sure she wanted to know.

"Drive and drive!" Gracia became animated. She scowled and pretended she steered a car. "She drove all day and all night. There were trees, trees, trees. The road was really bumpy and dirty." She scrunched her face and jumped up and down. "I bounced all over. The dirt made me cough and she said, 'Shut up!'"

Sarita cringed. How dare that woman treat her child that way. Then a horrific thought occurred to her.

"Where did you sleep at night?" She struggled to keep the horror from her voice.

"In the car." Gracia shrugged. "She went on the side of the road. I slept in front 'cause I'm smaller. It was really hot, and I got bug bites." She made a face and rubbed her arms as if shooing bugs away. Then she gave Max a shy look. She whispered to Sarita, "I had to go potty in the ditch. That was yucky."

Horrified, Sarita wondered how long Gracia had gone without a bath. They took back roads and slept in the car while Carlene avoided the cops. Sarita felt more confident with the decision they'd made to forego a media circus. While it could have given them leads, considering Carlene's methods *without* that exposure, her going even farther underground could have done more harm than good.

She shot a knowing look at Max. If she could read minds, she'd swear he thought the same thing.

Her head swirled with questions.

"Did you ever get a bath? What did you eat?"

Gracia shrugged. "I had a bath at her friend's house. They fed us, too. The rest of the time we ate stuff from the gas station."

"The gas station!" Sarita imagined her daughter eating cookies and chips for dinner. Wary, she asked, "What friends?"

Gracia whirled from the bubbles. She sat on the blanket, close to her mom. Her eyes widened as she launched into a story.

"They lived out in the woods. It was all wet and muddy with lots of skeeters."

"Skeeters?" Sarita rose her eyebrows.

"You know, Mama, muh-skee-tas. Skeeters!"

She'd picked up the lingo of those people?

Max had the gall to chuckle.

"They had a big hole full of alligators in the back yard." Gracia's eyes bulged like golf balls, and she scooted close to her mama's side. "The man throwed big rats in there. They were still alive! The gators ate 'em." Gracia shuddered beneath Sarita's embrace.

Sarita held her tight. "I'm so sorry you had to see that."

Gracia squirmed away to catch her mother's eyes. She put both hands on Sarita's cheeks and spoke solemnly. "That man laughed, Mama. But I was really scared."

Sarita pulled her child close again. "I'm so glad it's all over, sweetie." She kissed her hair.

For a few moments, they sat comforting one another, grateful to be together.

"Did you meet anyone else?" Max asked.

Sarita shook her head. She didn't want to hear any more, didn't want her daughter going through that all over again.

But Gracia jumped up, eager to share her horrid adventure.

"Yeah! The lady was nice. When I got scared, she picked me up. We walked through big puddles. Baby fish were swimming in there!" Gracia waved her hands with excitement as she spoke. "Then the water leaked out. She said, 'Tide's gone out.' But a little crab was still in the mud! He was clicking his claws at me." She demonstrated with great drama and giggled.

Carlene had a lot of friends in low places. Literally.

Gracia brightened. "I wanted to stay with her. She said she never had a little girl of her own." She made a face. "But the man was mad all the time and had a big gun. I was glad he stayed outside."

"So, you weren't there long?"

"One night." Gracia held up a finger. "The lady washed me up and fed me hotdogs. She told me a story about Goldilocks and tucked me in. The bed was soft. No bugs! But in the morning, I heard yelling. That man said, 'You ain't keeping her!'"

Sarita winced at the rejection Gracia must have felt. Yet she was relieved her daughter didn't spend more than one night under his roof. Who knew what he might have done to her?

"Then the mean lady took me away. She put on a big hat and sunglasses. We went on a boat."

"Tell us about the boat," Max encouraged.

"It was big and went creak, creak, creak. It went like this all the time." She stood and leaned this way and that with her arms out for balance. "I threw up. I didn't like that boat."

"I'm sorry to hear that," Max said.

Sarita gathered her daughter in her arms. "But that boat brought you to Abuela, didn't it?" she asked.

"Yes! Abuela gave me a cool bath 'cause I was so hot, and she fed me yummy chicken stuff. Better than gas station food!"

She looked at her mother with wide eyes.

"I was sick of cookies!"

They shared a good laugh. Sarita was relieved to know what had happened with Carlene. She was still afraid to know what had happened with Ramone.

"Why didn't you tell me all this before?" Sarita asked.

REVENGE

G racia shrugged. "You didn't want to talk about it."
Realization dawned. *Sarita* couldn't deal with what had happened. But Gracia couldn't just forget the huge ordeal. She *needed* to share her story with those closest to her, get it off her chest, and get *through* it, not over it.

Parts of her story seemed exciting to her, adventurous. Others terrified her, but she seemed eager to talk about it.

Her experience with Ramone would come out. But not today. Sarita couldn't take any more.

She shot a look at Max. His knowing expression did not hold a hint of judgment.

"Gracia, come here." She patted her lap. "I have something important to ask you."

Her child skipped over and cuddled on her lap.

"Do you remember what the mean lady looks like?"

"Of course, Mama. I was with her for days and days."

"Are you afraid of her?"

Gracia made a face. "No, I just don't like her."

"The police want to make sure she doesn't take another little girl."

"But she didn't take me." Gracia shuddered. "That man did."

Not today. Enough for now.

"That man's already in jail, honey."

"Is Carlene going to jail?"

It was the first time Gracia called her by name.

"She'll go to jail for a long time if you tell them she took you on the boat. Then she can't scare another little girl."

Gracia blinked hard. "Good. I didn't like that."

"If Carlene were in a group of people, would you be able to tell us which one is her?"

Gracia nodded.

"Are you okay with seeing her again?"

Gracia nodded again. "I don't want her to scare anyone else."

PEOPLE PACKED the streets of Miami. Gracia became nervous, shying behind Sarita, clinging whenever a male Latino got too close, which happened about every thirty seconds. Sarita's heart sank that her daughter feared her own people. Thanks to her no-good rotten father.

Sarita wished she'd had the sense back then to be with a good man like Max. None of this would have happened, and she would have married before having a child. Of course, then she wouldn't have Gracia.

Max always told her God works everything for the good of those who love Him. Gracia was alive and well and at her side with Max.

He opened the door to the Miami police department and led them past a throng of criminals and sobbing women.

"We're here to see Lieutenant Gonzalez," he told the Latino receptionist.

Sarita fit in here as if she were back in Puerto Rico. Surprised, she realized she *liked* standing out from the crowd. What a breakthrough after her tumultuous high school years. Her classmates called her every greasy name imaginable. She'd wished for blond hair and blue eyes.

Over the years, she'd restored pride in her heritage. She vowed to share that with Gracia and instill her daughter with self-esteem. God made everyone unique and loved them all.

"Good morning, Ms. Santos."

Sarita looked into the deep brown eyes of the handsome lieutenant and sucked in a breath. Despite their preparations, Gracia scurried behind her legs, trembling like a cornered rabbit.

Sarita bent to her daughter's level and took both of Gracia's hands in hers. "Honey, this is a policeman. And see, he looks like you and me and the people in Puerto Rico."

"Mama," Gracia said in a loud whisper, "he looks like the bad man who took me away."

Sarita shot a look to Lt. Gonzalez, seeking understanding. Max had warned him this could be an issue.

"He's not like that man, honey. Policeman Gonzalez is your friend."

Gracia searched her mother's eyes, and then gave the lieutenant a wary look.

He bent to her level but kept some distance.

"Hi Gracia." He spoke gently. "I have a little girl your age. I understand how you must feel."

Gracia sucked hard on her thumb, staring him down.

"My friends call me L.T. I'd like to be your friend."

She retreated further behind Sarita's legs.

"Tell you what," he said. "I have a teddy bear in my office. Would you like to come and see her?"

Gracia nodded, the thumb in her mouth moving in sync with her head.

With a broad smile, L.T. led them to his office. He gestured to a small sofa where they all sat together. Then he opened a closet and pulled out a big brown teddy bear with a bright pink bow. He set the bear on the sofa next to Gracia.

She touched the soft fur with one finger. Looking to her mama for approval, she held Sarita's loving gaze.

"That bear's been awful lonely here in the closet," L.T. said. "She doesn't even have a name. If you name her, she might want to go home with you."

Gracia shot a wide-eyed look at her mother.

Sarita smiled at her daughter, then at the kind policeman.

Seeming reassured, Gracia's thumb popped out of her mouth, and she pulled the bear into her lap.

L.T. leaned against his desk. "I'll let you think for a bit while I get ready. I'll see you in a few minutes, okay?"

All eyes settled on Gracia, but she focused on that bear. Brows furrowed in thought, she nodded as the lieutenant left with a smile.

Fingering the satiny pink bow, she whispered, "Rosa."

"Very good, honey." Sarita said.

"That's pink in Spanish," Gracia informed Max with an air of knowledge.

"Abuela taught you well." Max smoothed the child's hair, and she didn't pull away.

Gracia concentrated on the bear's face. "Can I name her Rosa?"

"That's a very pretty name," Max said.

"I like it," Sarita agreed.

"Rosa." Gracia made the bear dance on her lap.

Sarita's heart warmed. She wondered how Carlene could be so heartless toward this precious child. Then again, she didn't throw Gracia overboard. Could subconscious guilt have affected Carlene?

Only a heart of stone wouldn't feel sorrow over four abortions. Had those lost lives protected Gracia's?

Wow. She knew God brought everything together for good for those who love Him. But the notion that *any* good might come from those horrific circumstances was staggering. Yet those babies lived with God in heaven, not with that horrible woman.

She needed to stop questioning God. He knew everything didn't He?

If she believed that, she had to believe He knew the best for Gracia, and for her.

A small measure of peace washed over her. Everything would be all right.

They waited for nearly an hour. Gracia grew antsy while Sarita and Max wondered what was going on.

When L.T. returned, he appeared irritated and didn't even ask about the bear's name. Sarita found it odd, considering how thoughtful he'd been up until then.

"Okay, I think we're ready." His curt tone surprised her even more. Something was wrong.

Leaving Max to wait, Sarita and Gracia followed L.T. through corridors that twisted and turned into the belly of the building. He seated them in a dark room with a long table and several chairs lined up on one side. Across from the table a huge window lit from within. Lines marked the back wall with height measurements.

Like a scene from a movie, six women marched into the narrow room and stood in line against the wall. They wore prison garb, handcuffs, and angry, defeated scowls. All six had bleach-blond hair and a skinny, five-foot-six frame.

Sarita recognized Carlene and sucked in a breath. At the same time, Gracia's eyes bulged. She hugged the bear and clung to her mother's side.

"Gracia," L.T. whispered. His comforting demeanor returned. "Do you see the lady who took you on the boat?"

Gracia pointed to Carlene, her tiny finger shaking. "That one."

As the line up looked bored and impatient, Carlene became antsy and agitated. Then she erupted. Hurdling herself at the window, she pounded handcuffed fists on the thick glass.

"You got nothing on me, you hear!" Her muffled screams penetrated the 'sound-proof' window. "I had nothing to do with that little brat!"

Sarita's heart pounded. She pulled Gracia onto her lap, burying the child's face in her chest and covering her ears. Gracia whimpered, shaking, and grasping her mother. The bear fell to the floor.

Cops burst in. Two grabbed Carlene to restrain her and two shuffled the other startled women away. Carlene kicked and fought until the cops hit her with a TASER.

Stunned at the scene before her, Sarita clung to her daughter, hiding behind the table. Carlene contracted in pain as a seizure dropped her to the floor. A wet spot appeared on her orange pants and grew to cover her bottom.

Sarita shuddered at the horror of it. The room quieted.

Gracia stole a peek as Carlene's body went limp. Sucking hard on her thumb, she reached for the fallen bear.

Sarita grabbed the bear and then shielded her child's eyes and ears from that horrid woman.

A warm hand rested on her shoulder.

"I'm so sorry you had to witness that," L.T. said. "She's been uncooperative all morning. That's why you had to wait so long. I'm sorry for that too." He smoothed Gracia's hair. "Don't feel bad about what she said."

Gracia peeked up at him.

"A personal insult is likely toward someone you're acquainted with. It only convinces me you're telling the truth."

"How dare her," Sarita muttered.

"Let's get you out of here." L.T. pulled them from the room as police scuffled beyond the window.

In the hallway, they heard Carlene moaning in pain as they neared a door marked 'Authorized Personnel Only' in bold red letters. L.T. hurried them along, but the door burst open just as they reached it.

Two cops carried Carlene out by her arms and legs, bumping into the lieutenant. He tried to shove them back in the room, but their prisoner went into some sort of spasm. It took all three of them to contain her.

Sarita scooped Gracia into her arms and huddled against the wall.

"Is Carlene all right?" Gracia asked in high-pitched panic.

Carlene's head spun around. Her glazed eyes focused as she shook off the effects of the TASER.

"You!" she snarled. "How do you know my name?"

"Your sister called you Carlene." Gracia blinked wide eyes.

"I don't even know you." The woman narrowed her stare.

"You took me on a boat, and I threw up on you."

"You little brat!" Carlene scowled at Gracia. "That stench gagged me all the whole way to Puerto Rico." Struggling to get free, she moaned in agony as she twisted against restraints on her wrists and ankles.

The police kept her in a firm grip.

"We've heard enough." L.T. pushed the three of them back into the room. "Take her out the back!" He slammed the door and muttered under his breath. "Morons."

"Is Carlene going to jail?" Gracia's eyes bugged out.

"Yes, miss. She just confessed in front of three police officers. Again, I'm sorry you had to deal with that."

Catching Sarita's eye, his irritated voice filled with regret. "These days everybody's got their head up..." He cleared his throat, catching his language. "Up in the ozone."

Sarita nodded. In her arms, Gracia clung to her, gripping the bear by a paw.

"She won't be bothering you anymore." His gaze shifted to Gracia. "I promise you that."

Gracia nodded and wiggled to get down.

They met Max back in L.T.'s office.

"How'd it go?" Max stood to greet them.

"She incriminated herself," L.T. stated with confidence.

"She called me a brat," Gracia piped up. "That's what she always called me."

"You're *not* a brat." Max sat down to look into her eyes. Gracia climbed into his lap like it was the most natural thing in the world.

"Well, that's what she called me." She plunked Rosa into her lap and talked to the bear. "She said, 'If they did things *my* way, we wouldn't have to deal with that little brat, and we'd all be rich.'"

Puzzled, Max looked from Gracia to Sarita to L.T.

"Who are 'they'?" L.T. asked.

"Pedro and Ramone." Gracia said in a matter-of-fact tone, bouncing the bear with each name.

As the adults stared in shock, the flood gates burst open.

"She yelled at Pedro all the time. She said, 'Take the money and leave that little brat. Everybody's happy. But nooooo,'" Animated with the dramatization, Gracia shook her head at the bear and launched into an imitation of Carlene.

"Pedro's scared of Ramone, and Ramone has to get *revenge*." She quoted as if word-for-word. "'Landed themselves back in prison." She shook a finger at the bear. "If it wasn't for that brat, I wouldn't be running from the cops." She made a face. "Now what am I gonna do?"

Gracia brightened with an evil grin. "My sister always wanted a kid." She furrowed her brows. "Not me. Kids are messy. I hope Ramone rots in jail. All for stupid revenge!"

The adults stared in silence as Gracia grew quiet and smoothed Rosa's fur. Then they exchanged wide-eyed looks. Before anyone mustered a word, Gracia laid the bear across her lap and looked up at Sarita.

"Mama, what's *revenge?*"

ONE BIG HAPPY FAMILY

Getting all that off her chest seemed to help Gracia get past the bad experience. Sarita's watered-down explanation of revenge seemed to satisfy her child. For now.

Children recovered quickly. The short episode stood in contrast to Gracia's otherwise happy childhood. She already showed signs of getting on with her life.

Yet Sarita agonized over the issue that Ramone was Gracia's father. Someday, probably soon, she'd ask about him. How would she react to knowing that the monster who kidnapped her was her father? Knowledge like that could scar her for life.

Over a year ago, when Gracia first asked if she had a daddy, Sarita confessed he was in prison. Gracia had shaken it off as if it were no consequence. She was happy without him.

That would change once she went to school. Then she'd have friends with daddies who loved them and made their families complete. Gracia would feel the void.

But for now, she seemed gratified to play a part in keeping those bad people in jail so they couldn't hurt someone else. The fact that the worst of them was her father hadn't registered.

At last, the grueling day at the police department ended.

"How about some dinner?" Max pulled into a Caribbean restaurant. The atmosphere helped Sarita remember the enjoyable time with her grandmother.

The waitress gave Gracia crayons and paper to keep her occupied while they studied the menu offering jerk chicken, fried yucca, and coconut shrimp.

She rolled her eyes, searching the menu for some resemblance of her grandmother's cooking. At least the place played reggae music and got the tropical colors right. A huge palm plant stood in the corner and large windows let in the Miami sunlight streaked across Gracia's paper and crayons.

"What are you drawing?" Max asked.

"Our family," came the quick answer.

Terror struck Sarita's heart as she imagined a drawing of Ramone in handcuffs. Her gaze shot down to Gracia's artwork.

Four stick figures - two tall and two short - lined up across the paper. One of each had long hair and a skirt. The other two had no hair, no skirt. Smiles filled their circle heads. It looked like a normal family - a mommy and daddy, a boy and a girl.

But Gracia didn't have such a family.

Horrified, Sarita wondered if Gracia had figured out Ramone was her father. "Honey, who's this?" she pointed to the man.

"Max," the child stated with disbelief. "He's my daddy." Gracia's tone implied her mother should know that by now.

Sarita's mouth fell open. She looked to Max's astonished face and their eyes locked. Both speechless, a thousand unspoken words and feelings resonated between them.

Fear, uncertainty, vulnerability, and shock emanated from Max. Beneath it all, his eyes held a deep sorrow.

Max rested a hand on Gracia's shoulder but didn't say a word.

Sarita's breath caught. Her face heated as she felt her daughter's stare. But she couldn't take her eyes off Max.

Regret filled his features. Keeping one hand on Gracia's

shoulder, he touched Sarita's fingers with the other. Love shone in his eyes, his smile, his touch. Yet something held him back.

Overwhelmed with emotion, Sarita broke eye contact. Blinking back tears, she looked down at her child.

Gracia smiled, oblivious to their shock. Seeming satisfied with the little bomb she'd dropped, she pulled out a pink crayon to color her skirt in the drawing.

Too stunned to deal with these emotions in the middle of a restaurant, Sarita pushed a hundred questions to the back of her brain.

Yet one glared beyond ignoring.

"Who's the little boy?" Sarita pointed to the picture, hoping to heaven Gracia hadn't child-sized Ramone.

"My brother," she said, all innocence and grace.

"Do you want a little brother?" Sarita asked.

"Luke's not little. He's bigger than me!" Gracia looked at her mother as if she'd lost her marbles.

Sarita shot a look at Max. He appeared as bewildered as she felt. They'd never mentioned Luke.

"How do you know about Luke?" Max asked.

"I saw him in the picture on your fireplace. Aunt Ruby had his picture too - with you. She said he's your son." She picked up a purple crayon and colored intensely. "She said if y'all got married, he'd be my big brother."

Sarita and Max's gazes collided. Her shock mixed with his obvious annoyance.

"Ruby," he muttered under his breath.

"Don't you just love her?" Sarita asked. "She's got my daughter saying *y'all* and you and me getting married."

"Oh yeah. Love her." His sarcastic tone revealed his discomfort. "Busybody drove me crazy growing up."

"Ruby is not a busybody," Sarita reprimanded.

Max smiled. "Harley calls her that when she meddles in other people's business. Really gets her goat."

Gracia's head shot up. "She has a goat?"

They shared a nervous laugh, but sorrow filled Sarita's heart. Max didn't want to marry her. She couldn't blame him. Stripping tainted her in ways that a new career could never erase.

AFTER ANOTHER DAY of tying things up in Miami, at last they returned to the Isle of Palms. The noon day sun glinted on Aunt Ruby's red convertible sitting in the driveway at the beach house, along with several cars with Ohio plates.

As soon as Max parked, the welcome committee burst through the front door.

Ruby flew down the steps with open arms. Close behind followed the whole gang from Crystal Falls - Sarita's mother, Vanessa and Chad, Laura and Brett, Rachel and Elliot and all the kids, along with Mr. and Mrs. James. Then a sprawling bunch of balloons pushed through the doorway with Harley bringing up the rear. People spilled from the house until the porch overflowed onto the front lawn.

Sarita's heart overflowed with joy as Gracia lit up like the sun bursting onto the horizon. She ran into her grandmother's arms for a huge twirl-me-around hug.

"I love you, Abuela," Gracia squealed.

"Mi nieta," Maria gasped as joyous tears streamed down her cheeks. She squeezed the stuffing out of her granddaughter.

Sarita joined their tearful embrace, and then shared blissful greetings with Vanessa. Budding pregnancy bloomed on her slender frame, and her face glowed with joy.

"I've missed you so much," Sarita whispered in Vanessa's ear. "Thank you for coming."

"Missed me, huh?" Vanessa pulled back to look in her eyes. "Then why haven't you called me, or answered your phone?"

"Ah, my phone's a long story." Sarita cringed at the distance she'd allowed in their friendship. "And my head's been in a nasty place. You didn't need to hear that."

"Sarita, I'm your friend." Vanessa cradled her cheek.

The gesture brought fresh tears. Sarita hugged her hard, vowing not to let distance separate them again. She'd need her friendship more than ever to get over Max.

The James clan bustled in around them. Sarita's heart overflowed as each one hugged and kissed her, choking back tears as they whispered thanksgiving and praises to God.

One by one, they encircled Gracia who still clung to her grandmother. Maria released her and the child rushed to Ruby and Harley. Max took the balloons. His reserved uncle hugged Gracia with tears in his eyes. Ruby cupped her face and planted a lipstick kiss on her forehead.

"We're so glad you're all right!" Harley's voice came out hoarse and rough. Ruby stood with a hand on his shoulder, speechless for once as she dabbed her face with a tissue.

"Come on in," Ruby croaked, waving them all toward the steps.

The sparkling house smelled like fresh lemons and scented candles. October breezes flowed through the open windows. A framed photograph of Max, Sarita, and Gracia took center stage on the coffee table beside a sweetgrass basket holding Gracia's collection of shells.

Seeming undone by the onslaught of emotion, Ruby did what every self-respecting Southern mama did when her children came home. "Let's get you something to eat."

Talk about an understatement. The sideboard in the dining room was laden with mountains of Shem Creek shrimp, Carolina red rice, corn-on-the-cob, collards, cheesy tomato pie, sweet potato biscuits, and her famous peach cobbler.

The woman should run a bed and breakfast or something.

"Wow. I know about southern hospitality and all, but you've outdone yourself, Ruby," Mrs. James complimented.

Ever-enthusiastic Ruby blushed as emotion got to her. She blinked her moist eyes rapidly. Heaven forbid if Ms. Perfection let her mascara run.

The front doorbell rang.

"I'll get that." Harley hurried off and returned with Ty and Lavonne as Ruby composed herself.

Their friends greeted them with warm hugs. Lavonne shot a sympathetic look at Ruby who indeed had tiny trails of mascara near her eyes.

"Now let's eat," Harley covered for his wife, placing a protective hand on her shoulder. "Ruby slaved all day and we don't want it to get cold."

The table was set, like everything else, with flair. She'd pulled out colorful Fiesta ware - no china at the beach house - and arranged cheerful daisies for a centerpiece.

Harley pulled out a chair for Ruby, setting the example of a well-mannered Southern gentleman, and all the men followed suit.

When Max pulled out a chair for her mother, Maria teared up again. Her mother hadn't been treated with such respect in a very long time.

"Why are you crying?" Gracia asked. "Aren't you happy?"

"Oh, honey chile," Maria leaned forward and grasped her hand. "These are tears of joy! I never used to understand that, but the years are catching up with me. Now I get all emotional and cry like a little old lady at a wedding." She waved a hand and shook her head.

No chance of covering up with a child around.

"It's wonderful and sweet." Sarita hoped to ease her embarrassment.

Ruby nodded in agreement, leaning toward Maria with a hug. The unlikely pair found an unexpected bond.

Seated on the deck after the spectacular meal, Lavonne handed Sarita a beautiful seashell picture frame.

"We brought you a little something."

"Well, thank you."

The photo captured the three of them on the beach at sunset. Sarita's hair blew back in the breeze as she leaned into Max. He had one arm draped over her shoulders and held Gracia in the other. The child pointed toward the sun. Silhouetted against a tangerine and lilac sky, they stood grounded by the dark sea.

"Thank you." Sarita was breathless.

"When did you take this?" Max asked.

"The first night you were here," Lavonne answered. "I was sitting on the balcony, photographing the sunset like I do sometimes. The three of you just appeared in my lens, and you looked so content. Like you belonged here, together."

Sarita and Max looked at each other.

"I hope you're staying a while." Ty offered a knowing grin.

"Uh, yeah, for now I guess," Max sputtered. "We haven't thought that far ahead."

Harley chuckled. "Well, it looks like Gracia's made herself at home." He gestured toward Gracia, who waltzed from the kitchen biting into a ripe peach as juice dripped down her arm.

She couldn't seem to get enough to eat since they'd found her. In the last few days, she'd already gained weight and seemed to have grown an inch or two.

"She's adorable. I hope you'll stay," Lavonne pleaded. "It's nice to have a friend close by. I'd sure miss you if you go."

Sarita looked to her mother who offered an approving smile and wiped Gracia's arm. A quick glance around the table found approval from all, despite a hint of sadness in Vanessa's smile.

These people acted as if she and Max were a permanent item. Yet Sarita didn't know where they stood. They finally found

Gracia, and now Max seemed to be pulling away. His job was done.

Trials make you stronger. She remembered Max's words and cherished them. She hoped she never lived through a trial like this again. She'd thought it brought her and Max together, with more substance than ordinary life ever could have. They'd seen what each other were made of - in good times and bad. They learned what was important, deep down. She thought they had bonded, so what held him back?

As a bonus, this experience had brought her close to his wonderful, welcoming uncle, his adorable, meddling aunt, and his jewels of friends. She wondered how long it would have taken them to bond if they hadn't been through the fire together.

She watched Gracia, back to her old self, chatting with Uncle Harley like the grandfather she never had.

Could she start a new life here? Did she want that? Would Max be a part of it? She wondered what God's plan was for her. Surprising herself, she realized that was the most important question of all.

BY SUNSET, exhaustion overtook Sarita. Excited chatter with her guests dwindled to yawning conversation on the balcony. The week's events had taken their toll.

"You need some rest." Max took her hand as he recognized her weariness.

She smiled at his concern. "No, no, I'm fine. I haven't seen my friends in weeks."

"We'll be here tomorrow." Vanessa stood with one hand on her back as the slight bulge of her belly protruded forward.

Sarita stood with her friend. She opened the sliding screen to find Chad snapping a dishtowel at Brett's rear end while he placed a platter on a high shelf.

"What's going on in here?" Vanessa asked in mock disgust as they entered the spotless kitchen. Laura and Rachel peeked in from the living room.

"Never you mind," Chad retorted in a mock female voice. He jutted his chest and placed a hand on his hip. "A man's work is just never done."

"Oh, don't give me that," Brett ripped the towel from his hand and zapped his friend's belly.

"Hey!" Chad rubbed the spot as Elliot snuck behind him and zinged a wet towel to his backside. "Yow! What the...?"

"Payback time!" Elliot shouted while Chad squirmed away.

"Listen, you hooligans," Vanessa teased. "Take the horseplay outside."

"No, have a good time," Sarita insisted.

"There's a volleyball net out on the beach if you're interested, and plenty of equipment in the garage - frisbees, boogie boards, and the like." Max said. "Make yourselves at home, and we'll see you in the morning."

The guys gave them hugs and promised to simmer down. Vanessa, Laura, and Rachel vowed to keep their liberated husbands at their word as they hugged Sarita. Ruby and Harley took Mr. and Mrs. James home to their quieter house, but Maria wanted to stay with Gracia. The tired toddler sucked her thumb while everyone gave her goodnight kisses. Then she went upstairs with her grandmother.

Sarita and Max retreated to the third-floor balcony.

"Finally, a moment alone." Max grew serious. "We need to talk."

"You bet we do." She struggled to keep the fear from her voice.

"I didn't want to discuss this in front of Gracia. Let's sit down." He led her toward the cushioned chairs. They sat and he took her hand. "Sarita, I care very deeply for you."

"Max, I'm in love with you," she blurted. "I thought you loved me too, but ever since Miami you've been holding back. What's going on?"

Pain crossed his features. "I do love you, Sarita. Very much. But you're safer without me. Gracia is safer without me."

"No." She shook her head. "That isn't true. Ramone has nothing to do with you."

His eyes hardened. "My money caused Ramone to kidnap Gracia. He never would have asked for a million-dollar ransom if it weren't for me."

"No, he would have killed her instead." Seeing the situation clearly as if God gave her a vision, Sarita laid it out, raw and bare. "Ramone knows killing Gracia would hurt me more than anything else. I gave up everything for her, left *him* for her, and he hated her for it. He wanted her dead before she was ever born. The only reason he didn't kill her was the lure of money. Your wealth *saved* Gracia. It didn't jeopardize her."

His mouth fell open with realization and awe.

"Any hope for her survival would have been snuffed out long ago if not for the possibility of getting rich," she told Max with certainty.

"I never thought of that." He blinked as his sparkling eyes grew wet. "I thought I'd considered every angle. If I'd put all my money in a trust for Luke, Ramone would go after Harley for a ransom. I can't ask my uncle to give up everything for me. Ramone would find a way to weasel money from us no matter what scenario I thought of. The only way to protect you from his clutches was to keep you away from me."

"Rather, you are the one who protected Gracia, who hunted down the kidnappers, and who found my child."

He sat dumbfounded, staring at her.

"Protecting Gracia is no reason for us not to be together. So now what's your excuse?" Fired up, she was tired of hurting, tired of being disappointed in love. "If you don't want to be with me, just say so, and I'll be on my way." To where, she didn't know. She had no money and a daughter to support. She had a part time job here and an apartment in Ohio. What a mixed-up mess. Why didn't she stay in Puerto Rico while she had the chance?

Max stood, coming out of his stupor. "I have no excuse." He gave her a smile and she had no idea what that meant. "I...I..." He raked a hand through his hair, obviously struggling with some internal battle. "Stay right here, okay? I'll be back in a minute."

She nodded, grateful for a moment to collect her thoughts. Let him run off and come up with something. After all they'd been through together, if he still questioned her motives, so be it. She couldn't have been more genuine and didn't have the energy to keep trying in vain.

Tamping down the pain of losing Max, she needed to put him out of her mind and decide where to go from here. Uncertain and desperate for some kind of sign, she watched a storm roll over the sea.

The ocean churned beneath a gunmetal sky topped with plumes of pink cotton candy clouds that appeared lit from within. The tops of the clouds blossomed and grew, like smoke rising from a brewing volcano. Weather technology assured the east coast that a hurricane brewing in the Atlantic would not make landfall.

She let her thoughts drift, remembering tropical storms that hit Puerto Rico when she was a child. When the sky looked like that, Papa battened down the hatches and Mama sequestered her children inside.

Here in Charleston, she faced the wind and concentrated on the changing sky. Despite the possibility of hurricanes, living here seemed more tranquil than facing Ohio's oppressive gray winters and debilitating blizzards. Bundled against the frozen elements and biting wind, Sarita had yearned for her home in the tropics.

Charleston wasn't Puerto Rico, but it was a whole lot warmer than Crystal Falls.

As the ocean breeze caressed her skin, she looked out over the beach, the palm trees, and the expensive homes along the coast. Unlike Puerto Rico, this area had career possibilities for her and opportunity for her young daughter. Despite her situation, she'd already made friends.

She felt as if God brought her here.

Max sidled next to her. Her tension mounted. He'd let her down easy, or so he thought. Gritting her teeth, she determined not to care. Even so, a knife of pain gouged out her heart.

"Does the storm scare you?"

Small talk about the weather? Really? "It reminds me of home."

"Ready to head back to Crystal Falls?" With a look of concern, he caught her eyes.

Now they were getting somewhere. "Not that home. Puerto Rico."

"Ah." He nodded, quiet with his thoughts.

"Are *you* ready to head back?" She asked with reservation, unprepared for the answer. It'd be easier for her if he left.

"I was considering staying here." He watched her face.

Swallowing fear, she studied the cracks between the floorboards.

"Now that I'm older, it'd be nice to live near family - on my own terms," he said.

Imagining Max under Ruby's thumb almost made her smile. "What about your business in Crystal Falls?"

"I'd go back and forth a lot, but I do anyway." He looked out at the water and let the salty breeze wash over his face.

Sarita sensed how much he loved this place.

"It'd do me good to live here," he admitted. "Plus, it's closer to my NASCAR clients across the southeast."

Her mind spun with her own options. Interior design jobs

had to be more prevalent here than in smalltown Ohio. She had a part time job and Lily considered expanding. Could she stay here if Max did?

"Business wouldn't have suffered if I'd been keeping in touch with the customers. I can do that from here." He spoke as if thinking out loud. He was dealing with his own personal debate.

Yet she wanted to scream, 'What about us?'

"The Crystal Falls facility practically runs itself anyway." He smirked. "Not the greatest feeling in the world, but it gives me freedom."

"You trained them well. But they still couldn't do it without you."

"You're quite the ego booster." He grinned, wrapping an arm around her. "What would I do without you?"

Locking her gaze with his, she tried to read him. "You'd be miserable, that's what."

A quick shot of desire leapt into his eyes, giving her hope.

"You have no idea what you do to me, Sarita. I can't go on like this." He pulled back. "I want you so badly I can taste it. But I can't have you."

WHEN & WHERE

S arita's heart stopped. She froze.

He took his arms from her neck and stepped back.

Her hair whipped in the wind and goosebumps sprang up on her arms and legs. She feared his next words.

He didn't speak.

She stared at his feet, unable to look at him, but felt him studying her. She wasn't good enough.

He didn't want to *marry* her. No matter that she wasn't a gold digger. She was a charity case, a tainted woman who probably had some sleezy disease.

Well, she didn't. She'd gotten checked. Although she'd never turned tricks, who knew where Ramone had been?

That's why Max never slept with her. He wasn't so virtuous; he was smart enough to protect himself.

He dug in his pocket.

Déjà vu swept over her. The patrons of the strip club dug out a few spare dollars to toss at her when the show was over.

How much would he offer to send her on her way? He never wanted to be a daddy to Gracia - except a sugar daddy. The crisis was over, and he'd come to his senses. A man like Max had little use for a woman like her. Why had she let herself believe she could ever mean more than an ego boost? A trophy on his arm, eye candy – that's all she was.

A chill pervaded her inner being. She hugged herself, fighting back tears and the icy fear of certain rejection. Shoring up her resolve, she stood frozen and hard. No matter how much he offered, she wouldn't take his money. She'd make it on her own like she always had.

Her eyes flashed to his hand as he pulled it out of his pocket. His fingers held a silver band.

She gasped, gaping at the ring in disbelief.

No. It couldn't be. She hugged herself tighter. Don't even hope. She stared at the ring, refusing to let its meaning register.

Max lifted her chin and caught her gaze. The love and affection she saw in his eyes radiated within her. His burning devotion warmed her to the core.

"I can't have you without this," he said. "This time, I want to do it right."

Sarita's bones turned to jelly. She felt certain she would melt right through the decking and drip onto the patio below. She swooned and her knees buckled.

Max caught her in his arms. Never taking his loving eyes from hers, he bent on one knee in front of her.

Oh my. As sure as God sits in heaven, this was happening.

Time stood still as she memorized the loving expression on his face, the joy in his eyes, and the warmth of his hand on her knee. Surreal in the eerie light of the approaching storm, the ocean churned in the background. Its breeze ruffled his hair, caressed her flushed skin.

Breathing in the scent of sand and sea, she tasted the salty air and wanted to lick that taste from Max's juicy lips. Lightheaded, she gripped the arms of the chair.

He turned the ring to reveal an enormous diamond.

The jewel dazzled, multiplying a spark of sunlight in the

stormy sky. The giant rock set on a polished band of antique silver.

"Sarita, my beautiful Sarita, will you marry me?"

She stared into his eyes, so genuine and full of love. Disbelieving, she touched the ring.

"When did you get this?" she whispered.

"It was my mother's. Honey, this ring has been waiting for you all my life." He drew closer, smoothed the hair from her face and held the ring between his fingers, resting his hand on her lap. "Will you marry me?"

For a long moment, she searched his eyes, unable to find one ounce of guile there. No leering, 'bet-you're-hot-in-bed' undertone. No 'won't the guys be impressed with this one.' No 'come here and give it to me.'

Max looked at her like none of the men she'd ever known. He cared about *her* - not about what he could get from her. His love for her was written all over his face.

A hint of worry settled in his eyes.

Did he think she was going to say no?

"Oh, Max," she breathed. "I'm the luckiest girl alive."

His eyes lit up as joy filled his features. His evident feelings created delicious tingles throughout her body. Her insides danced. She still couldn't believe this was happening. He was waiting for her to say yes.

"Yes, Max! Oh, yes! I'll marry you and make you the happiest man on earth!"

The ring still in his hand, he flung his arms around her.

"Honey, you already have." He squeezed her tight. Then he pulled back to look into her eyes. His hand trailed a gentle caress down her left arm. He lifted her fingers and slipped on the ring.

A perfect fit. So gorgeous, so brilliant and beautiful, it took her breath away.

"Sarita, I love you."

She looked into his vulnerable eyes. He had borne his soul. And she bared hers.

"Max, I love you. Always and forever."

There was no turning back. This was it - for life. 'Til death do us part. Because right then, she knew: if Max ever left her, she'd still love him forever.

WHEN AND WHERE? Early the next morning, Sarita's mind spun with possibilities as she brewed coffee. Everyone slept upstairs, and she wasn't ready to face them. Max wanted to make the big announcement at dinner, and she would show the family her ring. The one he'd kept since childhood, the one his ex didn't want.

She tipped her hand to stare at it, as she did every five minutes or so. *Someone pinch me, I still don't believe it.*

Soon the questions would come - when and where?

"You're awfully quiet." Max padded up behind her. When he caught her eye, the smile slipped from his face. "What's wrong?"

"They're gonna ask questions. And I don't know the answers."

"What kind of questions?" His brows drew together.

"When's the wedding date? And where are we going to live? I'm not prepared for that one. No matter where we stay, someone's going to be disappointed."

"I know." He sighed and reached around her shoulders. She leaned into him, grateful for his comfort. "We talked this out last night, and we've both prayed about it. Staying in Charleston feels like the right path."

"Part of me wants a fresh start, a new life where I can forget all the terrible stuff that happened in Ohio." Sarita admitted. "But Gracia was kidnapped on the Isle of Palms." That pinnacle of horror made her feel as if she had to convince herself more than him. "I ought not want to stay here, yet I do."

"You ought not?" he teased. "I think you've been hanging with Ruby too long."

She stuck out her tongue and he chuckled.

"Gracia doesn't seem to associate the beach with the kidnapping anymore," she said. "After Ruby gave her some toys, she wanted to play in the sand. Of course, I avoided the pier."

"She's young and resilient. She doesn't seem so afraid of dark men anymore either."

"Thank the Lord. He's answered all my prayers." She touched the ring on her finger.

Max smiled and patted her hand. "Then pray about this too. He'll answer better than you expect. Doesn't He always?" He waggled his eyebrows, referring to himself.

She threw off his hand in mock disgust. "You arrogant men are all alike."

They shared a laugh. Both knew she didn't mean it - not even a little bit.

"Why don't we leave the details in God's hands?" He gave her a squeeze. "One thing I've learned is that everything gets better when God is a part of it. Not that it's perfect or painless or goes the way I planned, but when I'm open to God, His plan is so much better than mine."

"Like losing Gracia and finding you." She turned toward him. "I didn't think I'd survive it, and I wouldn't have without you. God knew that. He sent you to help me." Her voice cracked with emotion as tears welled. "Look at us now," she choked out, gazing into his eyes.

"God takes our pain and heartache and works it for our good." He waxed philosophical. "That happened when my parents died, and during the divorce - and when I thought I'd lost you." He shot her a grin. "When I crawl out of those dark corners, I appreciate the light of joy like a thirsty man appreciates water."

During her darkest days, he'd said it all before. She hadn't thought it possible, but now she understood. Now she believed.

God gave her Max and Gracia, two beautiful, precious gifts. She became overwhelmed with gratitude. All the pain she'd been through made this very moment all the more joyful. Her heart swelled with gratitude and respect for her awesome, all-knowing God.

Satan had sent her through hell, but God brought her through it and back. Tested by fire, she survived and thrived. The trial made her stronger and God blessed her more than she'd ever imagined.

MAX WATCHED the worry melt from Sarita's face. Satisfaction, gratitude, and awe replaced it - all encompassed by love. She'd come a long way. God had healed her wounded soul. Sarita's appearance attracted Max, as it did any man with a pulse, yet he had always recognized the goodness in her tarnished spirit. Now polished to a healthy shine, her inner beauty created an undeniable glow.

Like him, she'd made mistakes, learned from them, and come full circle. She'd made peace with God. Not that she talked about it, but he felt it in her attitude, her newfound joy. They'd talk when she was ready. The experience was still so fresh, the emotions too raw.

His own angst dissolved. No longer afraid of love, he reveled in the joy of it. Confident that God had blessed him with this woman's love, he looked forward to spending the rest of his life with her.

SARITA GRATEFULLY ACCEPTED Ruby's invitation for everyone to come to her house for dinner. After a wonderful day with her friends on the beach, they all gathered at the mansion South of Broad.

With the lull in conversation as everyone bit into Ruby's delicious pecan pie, Sarita caught a growing seriousness between Gracia and her eight-year-old cousin Jessica.

"Were they mean to you?" Jess asked.

Jessica's mother, Rachel, sucked in a breath.

The living room fell silent. Holding their collective breath, everyone listened in.

"Sometimes they were mean," Gracia said with a shrug. "So, I sang *Jesus Loves Me*. Then they got quiet and left me alone. I knew they wouldn't hurt me because God held me in his hands, just like Mama always said He would," she looked to her mother with all solemnity. "When I was scared, I thought about snuggling in God's big hands. I would fall asleep and dream about our happy family. My mama and daddy and my brother were there." She finished with a smile and a big hug for her mama.

All eyes stared at Max and Sarita.

They shared a meaningful look.

"Okay, our gig is up." Max set his plate on the coffee table, and Sarita followed suit. He took her hand as he addressed the group. "While Sarita and I were busy rescuing Gracia, something wonderful happened between us."

He cleared his throat and stood to make his announcement. Lightheaded and dizzy with emotion, she felt weak in the knees as he pulled her up to stand beside him in the silent room.

Ruby sucked in a breath so hard her eyes threatened to pop out. Forks hung in mid-air and plates teetered on knees.

"Last night, I asked Sarita to marry me."

"And I said yes!" she blurted.

The room exploded with cheers, whistles, and joyous laughter. Max took her in his arms and planted a huge, noisy kiss on her lips. Then he pulled her ring from his pocket where it had been hiding. Once again, he slipped it onto her finger, in front of God and everyone.

It felt good and right to get that ring back on her finger where it belonged.

"Your mama's ring?" Ruby gasped. She looked to Sarita. "I can't believe you let him hide it!"

"Uh, I - " Sarita stammered.

"I forced her." Max leaned down until his nose almost touched Ruby's. "You would have seen that ring from a mile away and ruined the surprise."

"Humph. Let me see it." She reached for Sarita's hand.

Sarita showed off the gorgeous rock. Every eye in the room zoned in on her.

The public attention brought back memories. But it felt good to exhibit an *acceptable* body part, without shame or remorse, without leering or sneers or groping.

"Someone call Myrtle!" Chad hollered.

Vanessa slapped her husband's arm. "You should hear her touting your praises, Sarita. How respectable you and Max were out on the balcony, and what heroes you were to save Gracia and put that crook back in jail. I don't know what's gotten into her."

"You're kidding." Sarita stared at her friend. "And we thought she had a hand in the newspaper reports."

"Don't think so," Vanessa said with a grin. "So, when's the big date? Inquiring minds want to know."

"We haven't set one yet." Sarita looked at Max and shrugged. "But don't worry, you'll be the first to know. If you would, I'd like you to be my matron of honor."

"I'd be *honored*," Vanessa quipped. "But I hope I have time to lose the baby fat." She patted her round belly.

"Good grief," Laura waved a hand. "You skinny girls pop 'em out and go back to skinny in two weeks." She shot a look at willowy Rachel. While Laura had to work at staying fit, her sister's natural slenderness had always been a bone of contention. "Not like some of us who have to do double work outs for six months afterwards."

"Maybe it's the chocolate éclairs," her brother Chad teased.

Laura's husband let his mouth fall open.

Laura raised one eyebrow, and her nostrils flared as if about to spew fire.

"Watch it, big brother. You're asking for trouble."

"Doesn't he always?" Vanessa gave her husband a light-hearted shove. "You have a lot of room to talk with all those pastries from the tearoom you've been eating."

"True," Chad admitted, patting his stomach. "Laura's right, I'd better watch it, or I'll be in trouble." He pushed out his belly big and round, making the children laugh.

"Your Aunt Vanessa's a good cook." With his typical drama, Chad placed both hands on his round middle and pressed it flat.

"I'd be happy to provide the pastries," Vanessa offered. "And Mama does wedding cakes now."

"Wonderful! Thank you." Pride and joy filled Sarita to see how Vanessa had blossomed.

"Rosebuds could do the flowers," Emily James suggested.

"Thank you so much," Sarita said.

"Sunflowers?" Max looked to Sarita.

"Perfect," she said, touched that he remembered.

"Will Gracia be the flower girl?" Ruby's wheels were spinning too.

"Of course!" Sarita would be grateful for Ruby's expertise.

Gracia looked over at hearing her name. She waved to her

mama but kept playing with Katie and Cameron and their father Brett on Ruby's Momeni rug.

Gracia eyed Brett's dark hair with suspicion. Although keeping a bit of distance, she responded when he spoke to her, even laughed at his silly jokes.

Her cousins Jessica and Amelia whispered a secret to her.

"Mama," Gracia piped up. "When are we going *home*?"

Sarita sucked in a breath. "You want to go back to our apartment?"

Max froze beside her, waiting for the answer.

"No, mama." Gracia giggled. "I wanna go home to the *beach*."

Max's face lit up with a knowing smile. Harley beamed and thumped him on the back. Ruby let out a tiny squeal of delight and clasped her hands together with glee. Even Emily and John appeared happy for them.

Sarita stole a glance at her mother.

Maria grinned, head held high. "If you're staying in South Carolina, I am too." She gathered her daughter and granddaughter in a warm embrace.

Max wrapped his loving arms around three generations of Santos women and planted a big kiss on Sarita's lips.

A collective 'ahhhh' reverberated through the room.

Sarita had prayed for this sign from God. His will be done!

SUNFLOWERS & JASMINE

The Honor of Your Presence
Is Requested By
Sarita Graciana Santos
&
Maxwell Luke Carter
As They Declare Their Wedding Vows
On Saturday, August 25th
At Seven O'clock in the Evening
Sunset on the Beach
53 Palm Boulevard
Isle of Palms, South Carolina
Reception to Follow
At the Beach House

Surrounded by love and beauty, Sarita's heart filled to bursting. Standing on the boardwalk in procession with her bridesmaids, she breathed in the warm salty air. With the backdrop of the ocean, everyone she loved stood before her or sat in rows of white chairs facing the tangerine sunset. Her precious grandmother sat in the front row with her mama beside her.

At the end of the white ribbon stood an arbor entwined with sunflowers and jasmine vines flanked by pots of blooming pink sweetgrass. The sheer beauty, the emotional memories, and the vision of Max brought a tear to her eye.

She and Max fell in love here. He stood near the arbor in an ivory tux. His sandy hair tousled in the ocean breeze as he joked with his friends Brett, Chad, and Elliot. His smiling blue eyes caught hers.

She needed to pinch herself.

Dabbing her eyes, she smiled up at Harley. He stood at her side with a steadying hand on her arm, ready to walk her down the sandy aisle. Strong and silent like her daddy was, he squeezed her elbow, knowing when to speak and when to be quiet. He'd become like a father to her. She blinked back fresh tears. Wishing her daddy could be here, she sent a kiss heavenward.

In front of her, Vanessa's feet shifted as they waited for the procession to begin. The matron of honor stole glances at her mother. Darla Gallagher Calvin sat close to her new husband, Wilbur Calvin. He draped a protective arm around his wife to reach their fussy grandson on her shoulder. As the new grandpa stroked the baby's cheek, little Calvin John James settled down and snuggled his head into his grandmother's neck.

Sarita leaned forward and whispered in Vanessa's ear. "We'll be starting any second."

Vanessa nodded. "Don't worry, I'm fine."

"Good." Sarita patted her shoulder. A new mother for six months now, Vanessa was the picture of health and happiness. The soft fabric of her banana yellow dress flowed around her new curves where she'd been stick-skinny before. The color flattered Vanessa's fair complexion, gave her golden tresses added glow, and made her pale blue eyes pop with color.

In front of her, Rachel's satiny dress in pale kiwi brought out her green eyes and clung in all the right places. No one would suspect Rachel recently had a baby as well. Sarita smiled at the unlikeliness of Elliot choosing the family name for Elliott III. Funny how those annoying traditions became important once you had a child.

Sarita had chosen her old-fashioned middle name, her grandmother's name, for her own daughter. At the front of the processional, Graciana jittered with anticipation.

Behind her, Laura placed a calming hand on the child's shoulder. Her dress in papaya pink and Gracia's in muted mango completed the colorful line up like Charleston's Rainbow Row. The bridesmaids carried sunflower bouquets that included soft yellow snapdragons, mango gladiolus, pink gerbera daisies, and green palm fronds.

Beside Gracia with her basket of sunflower petals, Max's son twirled his ringbearer pillow. Luke's blond hair, deep blue eyes, and lilting smile matched his father's. With Luke part of their lives, Sarita was thrilled for Max - and Ruby.

The red-headed sprite sat tall and proud; her hands clasped on her lap in anticipation. Just behind Ruby sat Myrtle Winthrop. How those two had become fast friends was beyond Sarita's imagination. What other surprises would the future bring?

Despite plenty of fodder, Myrtle hadn't spread one rumor about them. Maybe she learned a lesson after the feud with Vanessa's mom almost sent her to jail. Right in front of Myrtle, Sarita's niece Jessica seemed to be plotting the next scandal as she made faces at the son of Max's gardener across the aisle. The nervous boy kicked up sand with his once-shiny patent leather shoes. With a smile on her face, Myrtle seemed to enjoy their antics rather than issuing a stern reprimand. What had happened to her?

She'd changed as much as Sarita's mother.

In the front row, Maria twisted a tissue in her slender fingers. Since moving to Charleston, she walked every morning with

Ruby and had lost fifty pounds. Sarita couldn't be happier to see her healthy and with Abuela Gracia beside her.

All the pieces of Sarita's life had fallen into place.

The love of her life stood waiting to marry her.

Over the heads of their family and friends, they shared a look that made her weak in the knees. Moments from now, she'd be Mrs. Max Carter. And tonight, she'd have him at last.

Warmth infused her. God's love triumphed over evil. He had blessed her a million times more than she'd ever imagined.

MAX SMILED at Luke whispering with Gracia at the end of the white paper ribbon. The two bonded like brother and sister from the moment they'd met. Over the past months, Deira had relaxed her stringent visitation schedule. The weight of the world lifted from his shoulders as Max's heart swelled with gratitude.

Family surrounded them, and friends who felt like family. Beyond them all, his beautiful bride waited for him, arm-in-arm with the man he respected more than anyone in this world.

Max had been blessed and then devastated but held to his faith. God blessed him again, more than he ever dreamed possible. Sarita loved *him*. Content with his love, she never asked for anything.

Promoted to interior designer, she'd rented a condo close by. After the honeymoon, she would move into the beach house. A thrill ran through him. Tonight, she would share his bed.

The pastor stood. Max straightened and bounced on his toes, ready for the happiest moment of his life.

"READY TO DO THIS THING?" Harley whispered.

As Sarita nodded, a tear slipped out. The brawny man pulled a sweet-smelling handkerchief from his pocket and dabbed her cheek with surprising tenderness.

The wedding march began playing.

Everyone stood, turning to face them with beaming smiles.

She caught Max's gaze and their eyes locked. The link between them bonded their hearts in a union no one could break, strengthened by the love of God that wrapped around them.

Astounded by the joy of this moment, she floated up the sandy aisle, toward her soulmate, the love of her life.

God's love entwined her and Max, Gracia, and Luke - one happy family forever.

~The End~

THANK YOU FOR READING

Did you enjoy this story?

P lease share your comments through an Amazon review at
www.amazon.com. On the product page, click the star
rating. Then scroll down to 'Write a Customer Review'.

Thank you!

READER'S GUIDE

SUNFLOWERS FOR SARITA

1. When Sarita refused an abortion, her boyfriend Ramone attempted to kill her. By keeping her baby and testifying against him, Sarita lost her job and started her life over – a hefty price to save her child. Despite her career as a stripper, what does this decision say about Sarita's true character? Do you know anyone with a heart of gold who is caught in a sinful life?

2. Sarita struggles with an attraction to bad men who are good looking. Do you see her weakness for sex as any different than a tendency toward homosexuality, violence, stealing, lying, drunkenness, gluttony, greed or pride?

3. How does Sarita's weakness for men and her past as a stripper affect her relationship with Max?

4. Sarita is adamant that she doesn't want her daughter to end up like she did. How does Sarita's childhood affect her as a mother?

5. Sarita's brother Pedro not only introduced her to Ramone, he gives up her location to the man who threatened her life. Describe your reaction to this

betrayal. Have you ever been betrayed by a family member?

6. After Ramone's attack, Max offered Sarita a hideout in South Carolina. She barely knew him and had to leave her job. At the time, did you think Sarita was wise to go to South Carolina with Max?

7. Max told Sarita the beach house belonged to his aunt and uncle because he feared she would take advantage of his wealth. How do you feel about Max's lie?

8. Max's first wife turned out to be a gold digger who took away his son. In what ways do you think Max's past experience helped or hurt his relationship with Sarita?

9. Max fears Aunt Ruby will judge Sarita and fall in love with Gracia. Can you relate to his hesitance for Aunt Ruby to meet Sarita and Gracia?

10. How might Ruby and Harley's marriage have affected Max's character and his response to Sarita?

11. What impact does the beach house setting have on Sarita and Max's relationship when they first arrive? What about after Gracia is kidnapped?

12. Gracia was kidnapped from the beach while her mother was distracted. Sarita blamed herself. Do you relate to her feelings? Has something like that ever happened to you?

13. Max was determined to find Gracia even after he'd given up on his relationship with Sarita. How do you think his dedication affected Sarita's trust in God?

14. Uncle Harley expressed the need to face reality that Gracia may not be found alive. How did you feel about his "realistic" point of view?

15. Max and Sarita traced Gracia's kidnapper to a run-down trailer in the Everglades. They found a gutted alligator hanging from a tree and a puddle of

quicksand that sucked off Sarita's shoes. Did you find any humor in this scene? If not, were you too disturbed, grossed out, worried or something else? Describe your emotions during this scene.

16. When Max and Sarita ran out of gas in the Everglades, they were rescued by an angel named Chuck 'Morris with an M'. Do you believe God sends angels to earth?

17. When Max first suggested taking Sarita to her 'happy place' to see her grandmother in Puerto Rico, what result did you expect? Did you think it would help Sarita heal? Why or why not? Were you surprised when Sarita found Gracia? Describe your feelings.

18. While with the kidnapper, Gracia slept in a car, ate gas station food, relieved herself in roadside ditches, and met various unscrupulous characters. What was your reaction to Gracia's stories about her 'adventure'?

19. In retrospect, how might Max's response to Sarita's danger been different if he wasn't wealthy? Do you think wealth contributes to his character or only his ability to help in extravagant ways? How could he have helped Sarita without the means to offer a beach house hideaway, a million dollar ransom, and a trip to Puerto Rico? What about his time away from work?

20. The Bible tells us God allows difficult circumstances to bring us closer to Him. Discuss how Gracia's kidnapping strengthened Sarita's faith and helped her trust both God and Max in life-altering ways.

LILACS FOR LAURA

BOOK 1 IN THE CRYSTAL FALLS SERIES

Chapter 1 - Broken Lilacs

An eerie shadow crossed the window of Rosebuds Flower Shop. Laura James looked up from her arrangement of lilacs with a tingle of alarm.

Only May sunshine peeked in the window, filtering colorful light through the stained-glass border of pink roses and green leaves. Yet a sense of impending doom lingered.

How silly. Nothing remotely dangerous ever happened in Crystal Falls. That security was exactly why she loved her small Ohio hometown. Too bad her family heritage wasn't so secure.

Worries over finances were making her jumpy.

Breathing in the heady fragrance, she lifted a crystal vase overflowing with lilacs. Her grandfather had planted lilac bushes years ago on family land. Heaven forbid if her parents lost the farm.

She carried the vase toward a round wooden table in the center of the shop.

A shadow returned.

The door burst open, banging the wall.

Laura jolted as the antique bell jangled wildly.

In slow motion, the vase fell through the air. Shards of crystal exploded across the wooden floor.

Her eyes widened at water splashing her sandaled feet among broken lilacs and remnants of her grandmother's vase.

The antique door shut with a tinkling thud.

Her gaze jerked up to see her sister's husband.

As he sashayed toward her, lust settled in his dark eyes. Even more than the last time.

Self-conscious of her generous curves, she smoothed water droplets from her skirt. Heat crept up her neck, but she glared at Jake Santos and casually tossed her long blond hair over her shoulder.

Too handsome for his own good, Jake shot her a look that made her stomach churn. She stiffened, refusing to let him see her tremble.

"Grandma brought that vase from England," she growled. "I can never replace it." Rising panic made her breathing erratic.

"That's too bad." A strand of ebony hair fell to his forehead, Elvis Presley style. His gaze crept over her as one corner of his mouth lifted in a wicked grin.

"Jumpy today, sis?" With a bawdy laugh, he waltzed toward her like he owned the place.

At the faint smell of whiskey, Laura backed away, teetering on heels that didn't remedy her height disadvantage. Fighting hysteria, she stumbled to the closet and snatched a broom.

Willing her arms not to shake, she ran it over the edge of one sandal, where a sliver of glass threatened her lavender-polished toes. She swept glass into a dustpan and banged it on the rim of the trash can in the closet. Maybe a show of anger would mask her panic.

The wooden floor creaked with Jake's nearing footsteps. The reek of alcohol intensified.

"All alone?" His husky voice hung in the air.

Her mind raced. Her father was home recovering from knee surgery. Her mother wouldn't be back from deliveries for at least an hour. She was on her own.

With a deep breath and a silent prayer, she propped the broom in a corner.

"Can I help you?" She set her jaw, crossing her arms over her chest.

"Oh yeah, you can help me." He raised an eyebrow.

His stare made her realize, too late, that crossing her arms created more cleavage where she had too much already. She dropped her arms, digging fingernails into her palms.

Jake slowly surveyed her body. All too aware of her clingy top and fitted skirt, she wished she were wearing the shapeless apron that made her feel fat.

"Do you need some flowers or are you just here to ogle the merchandise?" She narrowed her eyes, trying to look fierce.

"Both." He cocked his head with amusement and moved closer.

Grabbing the broom, she backed up until her elbow banged a wall. Gulping air, she was cornered in the closet.

The vacuum cleaner jutted into her back. Just like the leather armrest pressed into her spine on that starless night eight months ago. Her heart pounded.

Not again. The scene flashed through her mind – a wooden steering wheel, shiny chrome gauges, and tan leather seats. Not tan. Biscuit, her then-boyfriend had indignantly corrected her. Blond hair fell across his blue eyes. His wet, greedy mouth had smelled of sickly-sweet peppermint.

She hated peppermint.

Liquor was worse.

Jake's silhouette filled the closet doorway. Grinning like *The Grinch Who Stole Christmas*, he reached for her.

"No!" Swinging the broom frantically, she whacked at his legs.

"Ow!" He stumbled backward, rubbing his shins.

She ran for the counter and skidded behind it.

"What's wrong with you, woman?"

"Get out," she hissed, brandishing the broom like a weapon. Hair stood up on the back of her neck.

Jake laughed. "But I need flowers, and you need business."

"I said get out!"

"What am I supposed to tell Rachel? That you kicked me out and wouldn't sell me any flowers? How do I explain that?"

Horror rose like bile in her throat. Her sister could never know about this. Desperate not to let Jake further diminish Rachel's fragile self-esteem, Laura glared at him.

"What do you want?" she snarled.

"Gimme the usual." He raised his eyebrow again. Leaning an elbow on the counter, he adjusted his collar to display his bronze chest. He was gorgeous and she hated him. Disgusted with her own intrigue, she looked away.

Keeping the broom handy, she half-turned to the cooler behind her. She slid open the glass door. Cool, moist air wafted over her flaming skin as she felt his eyes burn through the fabric of her dress. The invigorating floral scent clashed with Jake's alcoholic stench.

She chose eleven red roses. The twelfth one pricked her. She resisted a flinch and swiped away a drop of blood with her thumb. She laid the blooms in a long, thin box with a red bow.

"That'll be $20.00 – family rate," she stated smartly.

"Put it on account. You know the drill."

"Yeah, I know it all right. What did Rachel find this time – lipstick, a bra, maybe another pair of panties in your car?" She pushed the box across the counter. "And you think red roses make everything okay."

Hurt glinted in his eyes. "No matter what I do, it's not good enough. Doesn't mean I don't love her."

"Yeah, right."

He frowned. "Your sister doesn't understand me."

"She's not the only one."

"Come on, Laura," he pleaded. "You know I love Rachel. But I love you, too." He came around the counter.

"Get out!" She screeched, reaching for the broom.

The bell jingled and the door creaked open.

Jake stepped back. Pressed against the cold glass doors of the cooler, Laura trembled. Her gaze darted between him and the wide-eyed lady at the door.

"Later, little sister," he said under his breath. He tucked the box under his arm and smiled at the woman. Weaving between plants and flowers, he regained his swagger along the way.

"Mornin', Mrs. Hunter," he greeted the police chief's wife with an extra dose of charm. His words reverberated off the embossed tin ceiling as he waltzed out the door.

Laura shivered. He loved her too? Surely, he wouldn't have done anything more than steal a kiss, even if Mrs. Hunter hadn't walked in.

Would he?

Find the book at www.diannemiley.com

ROSES FOR RACHEL

BOOK 2 IN THE CRYSTAL FALLS SERIES

Chapter 1 - Crumb Cake

Gripping the steering wheel, Rachel Santos shivered despite the warm June weather. A chill ran up her spine as a bad feeling washed over her.

Chugging up the rural Ohio road, her rusty yellow Toyota headed for a familiar white rattletrap coming toward her. Sunlight glinted across its windshield, hiding Mr. Gallagher's shaggy white head and scraggly beard.

Yet that face plagued her mind. Ten months ago, he'd threatened revenge – slow and sweet. His daughter had died in a car accident – Rachel's husband had been the other driver. She felt horrible for his loss, but she'd had nothing to do with it. Although her husband was now dead, Mr. Gallagher's boat-sized car drove past her house frequently – slowly enough for the toothless driver to deliver an evil glare.

Watching him draw ever closer, she heard a gasp from the back seat. Screams jarred her.

"Mommy -- look out!" her girls shouted.

To her right, an old pickup barreled out of a driveway. She screeched as faded green paint filled her windshield. The driver's cue ball head gaped in terror. Tromping the brake, she braced herself.

Shrieking filled the air. Tires squealed, metal crunched, and glass shattered. The engine roared and clunked to a stop. Screams turned to frightened sobs.

Thank God her girls were alive.

Frozen in shock, she forced her eyes open. Steam poured from her Toyota's mangled yellow hood, obscuring her view. Her chewed gum lay on her lap. Bits of glass, broken china, and piles of crumbs littered the passenger seat and floor. So much for the tea cakes she'd baked for her sister's party.

Crumb cake, she thought with sick humor.

"Mommy!" Jessica cried, shaking her shoulder.

She had to move, had to make sure her daughters were all right. She pried her fingers from the steering wheel. In slow motion, she pivoted to stare into their scared little faces.

"Jessica, Amelia, are you hurt?" Fear tied a knot in her gut as she scanned their tiny, trembling bodies for blood or wounds. Relief flooded her soul when she saw none.

She leapt into the back and gathered them in her arms. Fat tears rolled down five-year-old Jessica's cheeks. Blond hair stuck to her wet face. Four-year-old Amelia's eyes overflowed. She pulled from the booster seat and clung to her mother.

"Thank God you're all right." Squeezing them tightly, Rachel rocked on her knees. "My precious girls." She kissed their cheeks and foreheads. "I love you so much."

She heard Mr. Gallagher's old rattletrap approach. Angry with the bitter old man, she scowled out the window.

Mr. Gallagher's wrinkled face pushed to the windshield for a better look at the accident. With a vengeful, toothless smile, he drove two tires through the ditch to get past without even stopping to see if they were all right.

Shuddering at the extent of his hatred, she held her daughters protectively. Turning, she faced the windshield and gasped with fresh horror.

"Baldy..." Beyond the subsiding steam of the pickup truck, Old Bald Calvin slumped over the pickup's steering wheel.

Panicked, Rachel yanked her door handle. Hinges groaned as she forced her way out of the car. Burnt rubber and leaking antifreeze stung her nostrils.

She ushered her girls from the wrecked car but struggled with leaving them in the front yard alone.

"I have to check on Mr. Calvin. Stay in the grass. Don't go near the road. I'll be right back." She kissed their cheeks.

They nodded dumbly, huddled together.

Twisted yellow and green metal crushed the driver's side of the truck. She ran to the passenger door and jerked it open.

Tremendous dread threatened to paralyze her. She forced herself to reach in, to gingerly touch his arm.

He stirred. She released a pent-up breath.

"Mr. Calvin, thank God you're alive."

He moaned, lifting his head from the steering wheel. Blood ran down his pale forehead toward bewildered, glassy eyes.

"Be still now," she soothed. With renewed purpose, she snapped into action. She climbed inside and helped him lean back. His groggy compliance overwhelmed her with guilty fear.

God, please let him be all right. She'd been distracted and could have killed this poor old man – and her daughters too.

"Rachel!" An urgent, familiar voice yelled. "Are you okay?"

In a daze, she turned to see her mother running from the cottage next door to Mr. Calvin's.

"Grandma!" The girls ran toward their grandmother.

"We're okay, but..." Rachel couldn't finish.

"Thank God." Emily James rushed to her granddaughters with breathless hugs, and then pulled back to look them over. She watched Rachel with caring concern.

"But Mr. Calvin's not," Rachel choked out.

"Laura called 911," her mother said.

"Rachel!" Her sister Laura came running from the cottage, a dishtowel still in her hand. "You okay? Jess? Amelia?" She threw her arms around Rachel.

A painful groan came from the truck.

Rachel turned to pat Mr. Calvin's bony shoulder.

"Here." Laura handed her the towel.

With a pang, Rachel recognized the blue linen that had belonged to Grandma Kate.

She dabbed Mr. Calvin's head as a wailing ambulance screeched to a halt beside them. Paramedics rushed out and shooed Rachel and Laura into the yard – just like when they'd taken Grandma Kate away last summer.

Her world had turned upside down since then.

Mr. Calvin groaned loudly as paramedics checked his vitals and carefully pulled him from the truck. Her stomach churned while they eased him onto a stretcher. As she stood in silence, the ambulance doors slammed shut.

With a howl of sirens, they whisked off to the hospital.

"What if he dies?" She searched her sister's face.

"It's not your fault," Laura said firmly.

"I never saw him coming..."

"I did." Compassion filled Laura's deep blue eyes. "I saw it all from the kitchen window. He pulled out without stopping."

"But I was distracted. Did you see Mr. Gallagher? He drove right by and didn't even stop to see if we were all right."

"He's lower than worm spit," Laura seethed. She spontaneously hugged Rachel again, even tighter this time.

Rachel knew Laura loved her. She yearned to restore their relationship yet couldn't get past feelings of betrayal.

After the accident that had killed Mr. Gallagher's daughter, Rachel's husband was missing. Since his convertible crashed into the creek, everyone assumed Jake had drowned. He'd hidden in the woods behind Laura's house, afraid of being arrested for vehicular homicide. He'd turned to Laura for help, and she'd kept his secret.

Although she was protecting Rachel, the deception still hurt. Not to mention the fact that her husband had turned to her sister in his time of need.

Rachel watched the spinning red lights of the ambulance fade into the distance. She could forgive her sister.

But could she ever forgive herself?

Find the book at www.diannemiley.com

VIOLETS FOR VANESSA

BOOK 3 IN THE CRYSTAL FALLS SERIES

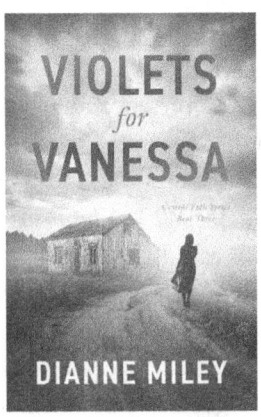

Chapter 1–Who's Your Daddy?

Dark clouds masked the hot July sun as a whining rattle descended upon Vanessa Gallagher. Picking wild violets on her walk home from work, she looked up to see a rusted white car break over the horizon.

On the wrong side of the rural Ohio road, the car wove toward her at breakneck speed. The driver's scraggly white beard tilted forward as his head leaned back, swilling a beer.

Vanessa dove for the ditch. Gravel sprayed her from the edge of the road as her father's car whizzed past. The beer can whipped from his window and bounced across the pavement.

Fear rose in her chest as clouds crashed above her. Clyde Gallagher hit the bars but saved getting drunk for fights with her mother. Ominous dread clutched Vanessa. She leapt from the ditch and broke into a run.

A piercing clap of thunder startled her. She tripped and fell to her knees on the rough asphalt. Jumping to her feet, she dashed toward home, ignoring the trickle of blood pooling in her shoes.

With an approaching rumble, a big blue beast of a pickup roared toward her. Her heart skipped a beat when she recognized the handsome driver.

He nodded.

She kept running until the truck slowed to a stop. Out of breath, she paused beside the enormous tires. Waist-high, raised white letters read Mud Luggers.

Chad James leaned his head out the window. Country music blared from inside, singing *Who's Your Daddy?*

"Need a ride?" Chad asked.

Her stomach flipped and her heart thudded.

"Yes!" she blurted, in a hurry to see her mama.

Yet she cringed at this gorgeous hunk driving up to that shack with the peeling paint and rotting steps. Everyone in Crystal Falls knew where she lived, but he didn't need the close-up view.

Chad jumped from his truck and noticed the bleeding knees beneath her black skirt.

"Did you fall?" His voice held genuine concern as he looked into her eyes. "Are you alright?"

"Yes, but I'm fine. I'm in a hurry to get home." Heat flushed her neck and face, hot to her natural platinum hairline. She had to be as red as a raspberry. There was no hiding a blush like this with skin as Scottish pale as hers. Self-conscious under his scrutiny, she wore no makeup, and her plain long hair hadn't been professionally cut in her twenty-five-year lifetime. How she wished she were prettier, more outgoing, good enough for a man like Chad James.

"Trying to beat the rain?" Chad raised a seductive eyebrow.

Like an omen, the truck reverberated into low idle, and a flash of lightning lit the sky, followed by a thunderous boom. Rain poured from the heavens, drenching them in an instant.

"Too late," she yelled over the din. At least the shower cooled her heated face.

"Come on." Laughing, he ushered her to the passenger side of his truck.

He opened the door, a courtesy that made her stare up at him in surprise.

"Hop in!"

Conflicted between her distrust of men, her attraction to Chad James, and her need to get home quickly, she scrambled to climb in the truck. Her foot slipped on the wet step. She careened but Chad caught her by the waist and hefted her up.

Unnerved by his touch, she ducked just in time to miss banging her head. He shut the door and ran to the driver's side.

In one smooth motion, he was behind the wheel. Rain dripped from the bill of his black ball cap. A lock of dark hair slipped onto his forehead as he jammed the shifter into gear. The truck growled awake and lurched forward. He turned the truck around.

"I hate to see a pretty girl all alone on the road." He winked at her before shifting into second.

Pretty? And was that a wink? Vanessa's heart floated to the sky. She'd had a crush on Chad James forever. Actually, since the day she started working in her dad's bait shop.

Chad had been her first customer. The wiggling worms kept wrangling out of the stinkin' foam cup. Her father humiliated her, as usual, but Chad showed her how to scoop them up.

Unafraid to touch her, Chad gently guided her hands. Then he looked her straight in the eye, right into her soul, without a speck of pity. She had been eight years old, and she'd never forget it.

Very few people looked her in the eye, none without pity.

In no time, her family's wooden cabin came into sight looking like a step back to the forties. A sign the length of the sagging roofline read BAIT in weathered red paint.

Chad pulled into the weedy gravel parking lot, past the

makeshift clothesline filled with dripping clothes. She cringed at the leaning outhouse, complete with a crescent moon in the door and wasps' nests in the eaves—a remnant of her childhood.

The embarrassing blush returned. Anxious to check on her mother, she offered a nervous, "Thank you for the ride." She reached for the door handle while the truck was still rolling.

"Anytime—Big Blue at your service." Chad caught her eye with a heart-stopping grin. Then his jaw dropped as he looked past her.

Her head spun to see her mother slumped in the doorway. Blood trailed from her nose and one eye swelled shut.

The big truck skidded to a stop. Vanessa bailed out in the rain and rushed to her mother's side.

"Get me... inside," Darla Gallagher choked. Her graying blonde hair stuck out in wet clumps and her rubbery limbs struggled to gain footing.

Vanessa tried to prop her up, but Darla lifted from her grasp. Tall, strapping Chad James cradled her mother in his muscular arms and carried her into the house. Back straight and strong, he gently laid her on the sofa. He inspected her arms and legs. "Is anything broken?"

"No, no, I'm fine." Darla covered her face with one hand. "I tripped and fell running in from the rain."

Vanessa recognized the lie and acutely felt her mother's shame. Chad turned to her, brows furrowed and eyes full of compassion.

"Would you like a ride to the hospital?"

"No hospital," Darla growled.

"No but thank you." Heat rose to Vanessa's cheeks. She hurried to the kitchen and grabbed a clean towel. "I'll keep an eye on her, but I'm sure she'll be all right."

"Okay." Empathy poured from Chad's voice. "How can I help?"

"You've done enough." She smiled uneasily. "I'll take care of her from here."

"If you need anything, call me." His knowing eyes were unconvinced. He dug a wallet from his back pocket and handed her a business card.

Chadwick Builders – Custom Homes Built to Your Specifications. His name and address were printed at the bottom with his office number, cell phone, and a fax line.

His warm hand squeezed her shoulder, and he caught her eyes.

"Anything, anytime—really."

Dumbfounded, she tucked the card in her pocket and nodded dismissively. At the sink, she turned on the faucet to wet the towel.

Seeming hesitant to leave, Chad looked at the muddy footprints on the cracked linoleum floor. His shoulders slumped. "Sorry about that."

"No problem." Ashamed to her core, she wanted him to leave, but he pulled out a bandana and wiped bits of mud on his way out the door.

Awed by his considerate kindness, Vanessa watched through the window as she wrung out the towel.

Long legs clad in jeans disappeared around the chrome bumper. Black work boots trudged past the front tires. The big blue truck dipped slightly as he climbed in. He looked over with a tentative half-smile.

Heart pounding with longing, uncertainty, and fear, she hurried away to tend her mother. How long before her father returned?

"You can't let him keep doing this to you, Mama. He's getting worse." She dabbed drying blood from her mother's face. Hand-shaped bruises marred Darla's arms. Vanessa lifted her mother's shorts over a purple mass on one thigh. It spread clear to her hip. Biting back angry tears, she checked her torso. Relief washed over Vanessa when she found no bruises that might suggest internal injury. "We're getting out of here. Soon. I almost have enough money saved."

Darla's moans joined the comforting rumble of Chad's truck, punctuated with eerie growls of thunder in the distance.

Big, black Mud Luggers rolled past the darkened living room window. Airbrushed white letters screamed across the tailgate: *True Blue.*

Vanessa reached in her pocket to reverently touch the embossed lettering on his card. Fragile hope tugged her heart. Would he really come back if she called?

Did she really want him to?

Long ago, she vowed never to be controlled by a man.

Unlike her mother, she'd make her own decisions and take care of herself. First, she'd get away from Clyde Gallagher as soon as she could. Once she had an apartment, her ticket to real freedom would be buying a car. No man could stop her then.

Love was a nice notion, but men stole your independence—not to mention your dignity and self-worth.

Love or independence—she couldn't have both.

Find the book at www.diannemiley.com

ALSO BY DIANNE MILEY

The Crystal Falls Series

Lilacs for Laura, Book 1

Roses for Rachel, Book 2

Violets for Vanessa, Book 3

Sunflowers for Sarita, Book 4

Nonfiction:

Time to Enjoy Your Blessings

Novella:

Velma & Clarise

Anthologies:

When You Pass Through Waters

Charleston Light - Stories Inspired by

Sullivan's Island Lighthouse

Coming Next:

The Charleston Series

Unwanted - Zinnias for Zoe

Unworthy - Jasmine for Jessica

www.DianneMiley.com

ABOUT THE AUTHOR

When she's not writing or reading, Dianne Haynes Miley enjoys walking, swimming, gardening, tea parties, cooking, decorating, traveling, and the beach. She loves spending time with her family.

Dianne also serves in women's ministry at her church and on the board of a non-profit, Sanctuary of Unborn Life in Charleston, South Carolina. She and her husband live near Charlotte, North Carolina. To learn more about Dianne and her writing, visit **www.diannemiley.com**.

Photo by Melissa Miley Photography

"'For I know the plans I have for you,' declares the Lord, 'plans to prosper you and not to harm you, plans to give you hope and a future. Then you will call on me and come and pray to me, and I will listen to you. You will seek me and find me when you seek me with all your heart.'" Jeremiah 29:11-13 NIV